Write or Wrong

XY Records Book #4

Heidi Hutchinson

www.smartypantsromance.com

Copyright

This book is a work of fiction. Names, characters, places, rants, facts, contrivances, and incidents are either the product of the author's questionable imagination or are used factitiously. Any resemblance to actual persons, living or dead or undead, events, locales is entirely coincidental if not somewhat disturbing/concerning.

Dedication

For the woman I was when I started writing stories bigger than myself.
We're going to learn a lot, you and I, but it's going to be just fine.
I got you.

Prologue

CELEBX

SORE WINNER

Zara Lorna may have won big with Album of the Year and Artist of the Year, but her night went downhill fast.

Anonymous sources say Zara got into a spat with her longtime boyfriend Logan Black.

Black, the recording artist who penned hits like "One for Me" and "When Can I Love You," wasn't nominated for any awards but attended to support his girlfriend of seven years.

The couple has been together since their teens when Black was still with the boyband "Newark Newsies" and Zara had one single on the radio. They met on the set of a music video and close friends say it was "love at first sight."

Black transitioned from music to acting and back again, while Lorna maintained her meteoric rise to fame as a pop music sensation.

Their seven-year relationship hasn't been without its hardships. Zara's intense recording and touring schedule has been the source of tension for several years, not to mention Black's alleged affairs with his co-stars, which he has always vehemently denied.

Insiders claim Zara was the one with the wandering eye in the relationship. Photos surfaced of her last year sharing an intimate moment with an unknown companion, and then again having dinner with a Hollywood hunk.

Allegedly, things between the two have been even rockier of late due to Zara's apparent refusal to take a break and make time for their relationship. Black has expressed in recent interviews his desire to get married and start a family.

After Zara's big win, the two were seen arguing backstage. The quarrel continued at the afterparty where friends of the two tried to intervene.

Zara was allegedly drunk and stormed off. Black followed her outside where witnesses captured video of them yelling at one another before Asa Young, Zara's co-producer on her latest album, put her in a car and they left together.

Neither Lorna nor Black's people have been contactable for comment.
Stay tuned to CELEBX for updates.

Chapter One
Absolution Calling

ASA

"Fuck," Asa hissed under his breath when the call went straight to voicemail. Again.

He'd called Nikki three times. She hadn't answered. She always answered.

He stared at his phone without really seeing it.

The sound of retching filled the hotel suite again. He grimaced and scrubbed a hand over his face. What the hell was he going to do?

Of all the dumbass dumbest shit he had ever done, this was by far the worst.

He raked unsteady fingers through his hair and looked at his phone again, willing it to give him a new idea.

He'd even tried to call André and he *never* called André. That was how desperate he was.

Why wasn't Nikki answering? She always answered. What could be more important…and then it clicked.

Nikki was having her baby.

Shit!

His best friend was having a baby!

And instead of being there, like a best friend should be, he was two thousand miles away in a hotel suite in Los Angeles with the most famous woman in the world puking her guts out.

It only helped drive the point home that he *shouldn't even be here!*

Nothing about this night made sense.

He knew he should have argued harder with Nikki about going in her stead.

"I won't win. You'll just have to fill a seat. Maybe shake some hands. It's no big deal."

But she should have picked someone else. It wasn't his place. This wasn't his world anymore.

But he'd gone because Nikki had asked him to. And he'd do pretty much anything for Nikki. Even when it was obvious she'd only picked him because she thought he needed to dip his toe back into the industry he had basically shunned for almost four years.

Nikki's nomination for producer of the year had left him feeling prouder than hell for his bestie. She'd worked her ass off making this album and it showed. He wasn't even a little bit surprised when her name was called and he had to walk up to the podium to accept her award.

Not surprised, no.

But overwhelmed? Yes.

His hands had started tingling the moment he'd hit the NMA red carpet. By the time Nikki's name had been called, the tingling had spread up his arms to his shoulders and settled somewhere at the base of his skull.

While he'd smiled and joked into the blinding lights and had felt a measure of satisfaction at the ripple of laughs in front of him, his insides had turned into a murder of crows. Black wings and loud caws echoed through his tired, stiff body.

The next bit had been a blur. Going backstage, short interviews, photographs, people he recognized but didn't actually know. The entire place had been like a hazy, well-dressed hallucination.

He hadn't planned it. He'd meant to go back to the hotel. He had a book waiting for him and he'd wanted to read before trying to sleep and then getting to the airport early.

But somewhere between him accepting the award and now, he'd been talked into "stopping by the afterparty."

Talked into it by the very person now hurling in his hotel bathroom.

Zara Lorna had also won big that night—Album of the Year, Artist of the Year, Single of the Year…probably others.

She'd been so hype…he'd got caught up in the energy of it all.

And he knew better. He *knew* better.

This life, this world, it wasn't for him. He didn't belong, he didn't fit. He never had and he never would.

But fuck him, right?

Because he'd gone to the stupid afterparty.

It was as if he'd forgotten every painful lesson that music had taught him.

If one thing happened—good or bad—that was out of the ordinary, then a whole avalanche of "what the fuck" was sure to follow.

He really couldn't blame Zara—well, he *could*, but he knew, he *freaking knew* it was a bad idea. And he wasn't that guy. He owned his choices. No matter how gorgeous the siren asking him to please play lemon mouth with her at the bar was.

He closed his eyes against the memory of her bright smile and amber eyes that seemed to sparkle with some otherworldly glow as she'd grabbed his hand and begged him to come to the afterparty. To do shots. To celebrate *their* win.

Her energy was contagious. He'd experienced it secondhand in the studio while watching Zara and Nikki work together months and months ago. He'd only been there to flip switches and push buttons under Nikki's direction. But Zara had been the one who'd commanded the room.

In every room.

He thought she'd had no idea who he even was until he'd nearly tripped over her backstage.

She'd grabbed hold of his lapels to catch her balance and her face had lit with recognition.

He couldn't remember the exact conversation that followed but it didn't matter. He'd been a goner the moment she'd aimed that brilliant smile at him. He'd have agreed to drive her to Mordor if she'd have asked.

It wasn't like he was a sucker for every beautiful woman that he met—he wasn't. Really.

Zara had this magnetism about her. He'd been powerless and he hadn't even cared.

Stupid, stupid, stupid, stupid, stupid.

He reached up to loosen his tie but it wasn't there; he'd already taken it off. He undid the top two buttons and made another pass across the room.

Fuck, fuck, fuck, fuck, fuck.

Was he going to get in trouble for taking Zara? Was the FBI closing in on him? Where the hell were her people? No one had even tried to stop him! Shouldn't there be bodyguards and assistants and…and…an *entourage?*

Not one person around them had tried to step in. Logan Black had yelled at the most beautiful woman in the world and everyone…took a big step back. Punk ass bitches.

"Hey," came a hoarse voice from the other side of the bathroom door.

His body locked up even as he sprinted that direction. "Do you need anything?" he asked, licking his dry lips.

"Yeah…" She cleared her throat. "Do you, uh, have anything I can wear?" she asked.

Wear?

He frowned. She was dressed when she'd gone in there. In a dark red evening gown that went to the floor. Long sleeved with a high neckline.

What had happened to that?

Oh, right. The vomiting.

"Uhh…" He rubbed the back of his head as he thought. He had his clothes he'd worn on the flight yesterday, his increasingly sweaty tux, and a clean shirt he'd been planning on wearing tomorrow. And a clean pair of boxer briefs that had holes in them.

He could let her wear the clean shirt, but he was *not* letting her see the holey boxers.

He went to his duffel, happy to have something to do for a second to maybe (hopefully) stop him from freaking out. He dug out the shirt and paced back to the bathroom door.

"I have this," he said, setting the shirt on the floor. "And I'll be back with pants." He didn't wait for her reply before he left the room.

He was down the hall and in the elevator before he'd taken his next full breath.

You know what hadn't been on his NMA bingo card? Kidnapping a pop star. The idea had never entered his mind.

And yet.

He had been trying to avoid any and all things that would result in press coverage. He knew that accepting Nikki's award would probably get him a consolatory mention in the bottom of an article or two.

But rescuing Zara Lorna from a public breakup with her *idiot* boyfriend? Leaving with her?

Those were things that brought the exact kind of attention he *loathed.*

What the hell had he been thinking? He couldn't remember. He must've blacked out or something. Nothing that involved self-preservation, that was for sure. But as all his regrets tumbled around in his head, jacking up his internal body temperature, he knew he'd do it again.

He had a distinct memory of Zara's happy face crumbling in confusion and hurt. After that, it was sort of a blur. He'd just gotten her as far away from Logan Black as he could. Moving completely on instincts he didn't even know he had.

Instincts that were probably going to get him arrested.

Or at the very least, ripped apart online.

He was going to throw up.

But no one else was going to do anything! He circled back to the fact that everyone had done nothing. They'd heard it. They'd seen it. And they'd just watched, with little smirks and calculating eyes.

So yeah, maybe rescuing her had been the worst choice for him. He was a nobody from nowhere. But no matter how many times he went over it, he knew his actions would be the same.

Taking a deep breath, he scanned the hotel gift shop. He found some gray sweatpants with *Los Angeles* written down the leg in pink.

What size did she wear? Probably small? He closed his eyes for a beat and tried to picture her.

She was five-five or so, slender, athletic. Fucking out of this world, couldn't look away gorgeous. He grabbed a medium and held it up next to the small.

Fuck, fuck, fuck, fuck, fuck.

He just needed to pick one.

She'd been throwing up for a while. Something oversized would probably be more comfortable. That's what he'd want.

Medium.

If it was too big, he'd bring it back.

He wiped at the perspiration along his hairline that he hoped no one noticed as he put his article on the counter.

"Big party tonight?" the cashier asked.

Asa stared at her, waiting for thoughts to form into words that would reach his mouth. Sweat trickled down his temple to his earlobe.

The cashier lifted an eyebrow and nodded at Asa. He glanced down. Right. He was still somewhat in his tux.

"Yeah," he finally replied, spotting a reach-in cooler nearby. "Hold on." He grabbed several bottles of water and a sports drink and added them to his purchase.

The total made his eyes bug out. Hotel markups were fucking insane.

He paid, took the bag the cashier handed him, and half-jogged back to the elevator.

The moment the doors closed on him and he was alone, he took another deep breath and brushed the back of his hand over his damp forehead.

He closed his eyes and tipped his head back.

He hadn't done anything wrong; he had nothing to worry about. The only thing he was guilty of was trying to help someone.

So what if she was the most famous person in the world?

That was beside the point. Her being a pillar of the music industry's entire existence was irrelevant.

A shiver ran through his body as the doors opened.

He stepped out and froze as his mind fought through that buzzing sound in his skull to remember which direction his room was.

He took a right and found the door.

His hands shook as he tried to get the key card out of his pocket. His hands were so sweaty that he dropped it twice.

He glanced up and down the hall, fully expecting Zara's private security to tase him at any second.

Part of him hoped for it. Just blinding, paralyzing pain, and then it would be over. He could go to jail and stop worrying.

The feeling of impending doom beat down on his shoulders making it hard to stay upright.

He fumbled the key again and shot another look down the hall.

But there was no one.

Which led him to wondering what kind of shit security lost their *one* priority? They had one job.

He got the door open and threw the deadbolt the second it closed behind him.

The bathroom door remained closed and he eyed it warily.

"I, um…" He tried to swallow but his mouth and throat were dry as a bag of cotton balls. He approached the door and knocked once. His hand shook and he squeezed it into a fist at his side. *Please don't be dead.* "I have pants and water." Even his voice was a wreck.

He set the bag on the floor by the door and took one of the waters for himself.

How was he shivering and sweating at the same time? Was he losing his mind? Was this what a psychotic break felt like? Was his internal wiring shorting out?

The room's A/C control panel was on the opposite side against the wall. He hurried over to it. He just needed to get the temperature to a respectable level. Not this sweltering, swampy, jungle biome.

Jamming the button as many times as he could until the numbers stopped moving, he stood over the vent, letting the cold air wash over his face and chest. He ripped his suit jacket off, followed shortly by his dress shirt, leaving on his thin white undershirt.

Sweat poured off his brow and dripped from the ends of his hair onto his shoulders.

He removed his belt and tossed it aside. Then he removed his shoes and socks and tried to dig his toes into the dense carpet.

He unscrewed the lid on the water and his hand shook as he raised it to his lips, splashing water up his nose and down his front.

The door to the bathroom opened a crack and his eyes darted that direction.

An arm slipped through the crack and pulled the bag inside with her.

She wasn't dead.

She wasn't unconscious.

Relief should have had his heartrate leveling out but it had done nothing.

He drained his water and tossed the empty bottle aside. Bending over he put his hands on his knees and tried to slow his breathing.

What. The. Fuck. Was. Happening?

Was he having a fucking stroke?

His focus grew dark as air rasped in his lungs.

He was either going to cry or pass out.

He hoped it was pass out. He needed a break from his bullshit brain and going unconscious seemed like a very good idea right about then.

"Are you okay?"

He jolted upright, lost his balance, fell backwards onto his ass, and hit his head against the wall between the A/C unit and the bed.

Pain radiated from the back of his skull and he blinked. Confused.

"Oh no." A blurry figure crouched beside him on the floor.

He squinted but the blurry person wouldn't come into focus.

Oh, he was definitely concussed.

"Here," came a soft, feminine voice that he would realize later was laced with barely restrained laughter.

His glasses were carefully put back on his face.

Oh.

So not a concussion.

Zara came into focus as she crouched next to him.

His gaze swept over her, taking in her ruined updo, makeup free face, puffy eyes, the whites of which were still red from crying. Her glamorous dress had been replaced with his old, black band shirt that said "Infantstructure" on it in faded hot pink, and the sweatpants he'd gotten in the gift shop.

She was alive.

And she didn't look pissed or scared or upset at him.

But still.

"I'm sorry I kidnapped you," he said, getting it out there.

Her lips tipped up on the ends. "You didn't kidnap me," she said softly.

She shifted, taking a seat on the floor right next to him, back against the wall. Their hips touched and her legs stretched out beside his but ended at least six inches sooner.

He took his first easy breath since she'd locked herself in the bathroom.

Her arm brushed his as she folded her hands in her lap and tucked them in between her thighs, crossing one ankle over the other.

He stared at their feet. Both bare.

Hers were small and pedicured, the toenails a dark red color that had matched the dress she'd been wearing earlier.

His feet were not as fancy. Much larger in size. Had his big toe always looked like that?

He flexed his feet and studied them side by side.

Huh.

Those were his feet all right.

He looked at hers again. They were really pretty. He couldn't remember ever thinking feet were pretty before in his life.

Should he be doing more with his hygiene in regard to foot care?

"You probably saved my career," Zara said thoughtfully, interrupting his thoughts.

That was too noble an accusation but he didn't argue.

Now that he was on the floor and not freaking out about the world's most beloved pop star maybe possibly dying in his bathroom, his breathing returned to normal. As did his heartrate.

A chill swept through him and he became aware of the temperature in the room.

Damp still clung to his back and underarms but he no longer felt like he was suffocating. He reached one arm over the edge of the A/C unit and reversed his previous temperature selection.

The appliance finished its cycle and shut itself off. The room grew quiet. Through the walls, he could hear the sounds of the hotel—slamming doors, children running, happy shouting.

He continued to stare at his feet that didn't match her perfect ones.

"Thanks for the clothes," she said, her voice soft and tired.

He thought he nodded. He meant to.

She was fine. He was fine. They were all fine.

Minutes passed as they sat there in silence. For as spun-out as his mind had been previously, it was now suspiciously quiet.

Nothing to question, nothing to worry about, nothing to say.

His breaths came easier the longer he sat there until he felt more like himself.

There had been a time when nothing freaked him out. When he was the one people had looked to as the levelheaded one.

He could expose his heart and thoughts to anyone interested in looking, and it didn't scare him. It had felt natural. Like that's what he was meant to do. What he'd been created for. To put into words and music the things others had a hard time expressing.

But that had been before he knew any better.

Zara stirred beside him. "This is going to make me sound like a shitty person," she said, looking straight ahead. "But I don't remember your name."

"Asa," he said, not offended at all.

Why would she know his name? She'd never used it. Even when she'd been asking him to go to the afterparty. He'd guessed she'd recognized him —he had one of those faces, or so he'd been told.

She nodded once. And then, "I'm Zara."

He almost smiled. As if he and the rest of the world didn't know who she was.

He felt rather than saw her look at him.

"You're Nikki's bestie, right?"

He let out a long, vocal sigh from bones to breath. "Yeah."

Speaking of—

He fished his phone out of his pocket to check for messages. Nothing yet. "I tried to call her, um, when you were in the bathroom. But I think she's having her baby."

"Oh, that's so great," she whispered softly.

It was great.

It was really great.

Nikki was going to be a fantastic mother. André as a dad would be… fine. Asa was having a hard time staying mad at the guy. He'd showed up a year and half ago and just kept showing up. He still wanted to hate the guy on principal—he'd made his best friend cry. But it was getting more and more difficult to do that.

"And you're stuck here with me," Zara said with a sigh that sounded more like an apology.

"I'm just glad the FBI hasn't shown up yet," he muttered his honest thoughts.

Zara snorted. But he wasn't kidding.

He looked at her deciding to ask his most pressing question. "Where are your people?"

Her amber eyes hinted at sadness even though her lips turned up on the ends.

He'd never seen her up close like this.

She was so…human.

No smoke. No sequins. No entourage. No filters. Underneath all those things she was still achingly beautiful.

Black eyelashes descended slowly over eyes that glowed to a point they were almost gold. "We used Logan's security tonight. He…" She rolled her eyes. "He doesn't like to feel crowded."

Asa narrowed his gaze. "He doesn't like to feel *crowded,*" he repeated slowly.

Something that looked like shame flickered in Zara's eyes and he immediately wanted to change how he'd said that.

She huffed a sigh. "It doesn't matter now," she said dismissively. "I texted Cas and told him where I am. He's my head of security."

The remaining weight of the unknown consequences of his actions disappeared and he felt his shoulders relax.

"You have your phone?" he verified, mostly for his own mental wellbeing.

She patted the side of her thigh. "I turned it off because Logan kept calling." She curled her lip in disgust even as fresh tears welled in her eyes. Quickly she swiped them away.

He held his hands in his lap, unsure how to respond. He'd never been great at the comforting. Women crying always made him feel helpless and therefore frustrated.

To put a finer point on it, crying was frustrating. Whether it was a stranger, someone he cared about, or himself. When he cried, he both wanted to be alone and absolutely did not want to be alone. He had no idea if anyone else felt that way. He could ask, but it seemed inappropriate to ask while someone was crying.

He was much better at shit talking. Ask Nikki. If Zara wanted to talk shit about Logan Black, Asa could do that all day every day. But if she was still in the crying stage, then she wasn't ready to hear Asa's prepared list of Logan's worst qualities. Starting with his smug fucking attitude and moving swiftly into his mediocre vocal work.

But Asa was well aware that his opinion had been born from the few moments he'd witnessed Logan and Zara's argument. And the even more superficial segments he'd witnessed as any other bystander.

The thing was, Asa wasn't usually wrong about his most scathing judgments. If he pinned someone as a dick, they were a dick.

André had been the one and only exception.

But the most irredeemable thing Logan had done as far as Asa was concerned, was be mean to Zara.

He didn't know Zara. Not personally. Not even professionally. But he knew Nikki. And his best friend of more than two decades loved the woman sitting beside him.

Nikki had once told him that Zara was basically a stressed-out angel masquerading as a human.

Those words had stuck to his insides like honey-covered fingerprints.

He'd never found evidence to contradict it either. Not that he'd looked very hard.

From his point of view, Zara had made Nikki's dreams a reality. And she'd treated her well in the process. That went a long way in Asa's book.

It went so far as to make him feel protective of that person.

"Is it okay if I don't talk about it?" Zara asked, her voice just above a whisper.

He reared back. "Of course it's okay. It's none of my business. It's nobody's business. You keep that shit locked up."

Besides, he'd heard enough. Too much really. And it wasn't like he was going to start talking about the shit that went down with him and Shelby and Gemma.

Unless you were there, you couldn't know.

Zara hummed a noise. He didn't know if it was gratitude or confusion. Maybe a bit of both.

He hated that she had to ask if she could keep her personal thoughts to herself. It really pissed him off actually. People shouldn't be forced to talk about anything, but especially not those things that exposed their hearts and souls out of context.

"Everyone is going to have so many questions," she whispered, sounding resigned.

"Do you have to answer them?" he asked against his better judgement.

She didn't answer. But maybe that was an answer of its own.

"It's no one's business," he repeated mostly to himself.

They had no rights to her. They didn't *own* her.

He needed to get off this train of thought. It wasn't helpful to her at all. And hadn't that been his entire goal in getting her out of that situation? To help?

"You think you're done hurling?" he asked, changing the subject.

She snickered. "Yeah. It wasn't what I'd had to drink so much as…" Her voice faded out and he glanced at her. She took a breath and cleared her throat. "I throw up when I get overly emotional. It's a fatal flaw," she tried to joke.

He studied her for a beat, debating what to share.

"I have panic attacks when I kidnap people," he said soberly.
Her resulting smile made most of what he'd gone through worth it.
The last lingering worries he had been clinging to, drifted away.
She was safe and she was okay.
That was enough.
"Are you hungry?" he asked.

Chapter Two
State of the Art

ZARA

Outwardly she was fine.

Quiet, but fine.

Inside, her head was a mess. A tangle of thoughts and feelings and so very many regrets.

Right now, she should be playing lemon mouth at the bar with her peers.

She should be proud of her win. Happy, celebratory, grateful. Those were the things she should be feeling. But those things were overshadowed by Logan's bullshit. Again.

Any other time, any other night, any other place, and she'd still be there. Right by his side, quietly begging him to keep his voice down and agreeing to go home early.

It had been their first public appearance in months. After a lengthy and private separation, she'd agreed to try one more time. She'd deferred to his security instead of her own. She'd worn the dress he liked best; she'd kept her red-carpet comments to a minimum so he wouldn't feel left out. Trying to prove she wasn't what he accused her of. She could compromise. It didn't have to be her way all the time.

And in return, he'd mocked her for her wins. Implied she'd performed sexual favors to get them and then laughed because that couldn't be true.

She was so bad at sex that it was comical. He had been joking. He was always joking.

He'd pointed out every woman who was more beautiful than her, every artist that *should* have won in her category. He grumbled about the entire thing being rigged.

But she'd held her head high, put on her best smile, and tried to tune out his negative remarks.

Until she couldn't.

He said the Album of the Year was partially his since he helped her write it. He'd said it in front of important people. People she respected and who she wanted to respect her.

The rest of it twisted into a blur of anger and confusion. She remembered yelling but she couldn't remember what she'd said.

And then all the swirling and confusion stopped when someone had grabbed her hand.

She knew his name now. Asa.

"I got you," he'd said. His hand warm around hers, his dark eyes sure and confident.

Her stomach had already twisted itself into knots and she needed to get somewhere to be alone until it passed. Somewhere safe.

The bestie of my bestie is my bestie in-law. Maybe not the most logical of thoughts but it had made sense in her gut.

He'd gotten her away, taken her someplace safe. And now he was coming back into the room with bags of food.

She spread out a bath towel on the King-sized bed for their late-night picnic. Catching her reflection in the mirror above the dresser, she snorted.

"Looking good, Z," she muttered to herself, getting closer to the glass. She leaned forward and dabbed at the puffiness under her eyes. Her hair looked like it had experienced a back alley mugging with no winners.

Her gaze drifted to a book sitting on the dresser. *Return of the King* by J. R. R. Tolkien. She tapped the cover lightly with her fingertips. "'*A chance for Faramir, Captain of Gondor, to show his quality,*'" she muttered.

All those times in the studio they'd never spoken. Never chatted. Just half smiles and head nods. She hadn't even tried to get to know him.

Looking back, she recalled her reasons. She tried not to make friends with many men. It made Logan suspect the worst and the tabloids to accuse it outright.

Immediately she was angry with herself.

How many times had she adjusted her life and her actions to accommodate the unreasonable demands of others?

Asa didn't have to step in. They had no connection save through Nikki. No friendship of their own for him to feel any sense of duty or obligation.

And yet, if he hadn't, she'd still be caught in the storm, with no allies in sight.

She faced Asa and watched him place the bags of food on the bed. He straightened and adjusted the glasses on his face.

"Thank you," she said, wishing she could convey the sincerity of her gratitude.

His eyebrows dipped into a soft frown.

"For stepping in tonight," she clarified. "You didn't have to do that."

He snorted. "Yes, I did."

Oh. Well.

Why did that make her head feel fuzzy?

"Thank you," she said again.

His mouth ticked up on one side and he nodded.

Maybe they hadn't been friends before but maybe they could be now.

She let her gaze flick over his shirt and it made her smile again. While they'd waited for the food to be delivered, Asa had changed out of what was left of his tux into what looked like the softest pair of jeans she'd ever seen, and a white muscle shirt that said, "tattoos are stupid."

The detailed artwork that adorned his arms from his wrists to his shoulders didn't look stupid to her. They looked deliberate and beautiful and she wanted to look at them up close because she was nosey like that.

"This look okay?" he asked, gesturing to the bags of food on the center of the towel.

She nodded and climbed onto the bed. He joined her. They sat cross-legged, facing one another with the food between them.

"So, you were a rock star once?" she asked, taking the wrapped burger Asa passed to her.

Asa snorted at her question and handed over her vanilla shake. "Nikki tell you that?"

She nodded as she bit into her burger. Her vision flickered as the flavor took over all of her senses. *Sooo*, delicious. A noise came out of her that was somewhere between a moan and a growl and Asa chuckled.

"Good?" he asked.

She swallowed and took another huge bite. How long had it been since she'd had a burger?

The beef and cheese and onion and ketchup and mustard set off a thousand and one good memories in her mind of hitting the drive-thru with her dad. Of searching through couch cushions for change so they could get something off the dollar menu. Of picking up her brother and sister from school and treating them with what her tiny paycheck from the local coffee place would allow.

Back then a cheeseburger had been a *treat.* It still felt like one now.

"Ooh!" she said, taking the lid off her shake. "Do you do this? Are you one of these?" She dipped a couple of fries in the milkshake and ate them.

So fucking good.

It tasted like home and happiness and another h-word that meant good things.

"Doesn't everyone do that?" Asa asked with a soft chuckle.

"Nope. Not everyone." Zara dipped three more fries. "Some people don't think it tastes good."

"Well, some people are idiots," he muttered.

She snickered.

This was exactly what she needed. She hadn't known that an hour ago, but there it was.

She grinned at Asa and he eyed her warily.

Part of her understood his hesitation. She'd just been crying and puking not that long ago. But cheeseburgers and milkshakes soothed all wounds. Mostly. The rest—the long-term stuff— she'd take care of her other favorite way; by writing about it.

"What did you play?" But because her mouth was full it sounded like, "Whada oog progh?"

Some burger escaped and dropped into her lap.

Whoops. That was embarrassing.

Asa's mouth curved into a full smile and he shook his head with a sigh. "You are a straight up menace right now. Act like you've been somewhere, Artist of the Year." He handed her a napkin.

She swallowed despite her urge to laugh out loud.

"Sorry," she said, wiping her face. "I asked what you played? In your rock band?"

He eyed her, amusement flickering in his dark brown eyes. "When you say that it doesn't sound like you're making fun of me at all," he said with a touch of sarcasm.

"I'm not!" she protested. "I swear."

"Sure," he said, like he didn't know if he believed her. But he answered her question anyway. "Bass guitar." His cheek twitched. "And I wrote the songs and music."

"Do you still play?" she asked.

He rubbed a napkin across his lips before answering. "Not really. I play piano a couple nights a week at this piano bar downtown."

Interesting.

So he'd gone from bass guitar in a rock band to nearly nothing.

She tried to remember if Nikki had given her details about any of this but she didn't think she had.

"What was the name of your band?" she asked.

"You've never heard of us," he said, dipping his chin and shaking his head.

"Why do you think that?" She could guess but she didn't want to. She wanted him to say it out loud that he thought she didn't listen to his style of music. It's what everybody thought.

It was strange to have so much of herself out there for public consumption and yet have people get so many things wrong about her. They had all the pieces but they'd chosen to put them together in a way that fit their own idea of who they thought she should be.

"Because we weren't popular," he said and added with a shrug, "And you weren't our target audience."

She put a hand to her chest. "Now I'm offended."

He met her eyes and smiled slightly. "Wasn't trying to offend." He rubbed a hand along his jaw and the dark whiskers there. They weren't long enough to call a beard, but they looked fuller than just a day's shave away. It matched the dark hair on his head which was thick and black with a hint of a wave on top.

"What was the name of the band?" she asked again. Hoping, hoping, hoping she knew it so that she could rub it in his face. In a nice way, of course.

"Our band was called Winking Pete," he replied, crumbling up his cheeseburger wrapper and tossing it in the bin nearby.

Her shoulders fell. "I haven't heard of you," she admitted grumpily.

He barked a laugh and something lit up inside Zara's mind at the sound.

"Don't feel bad," he reassured her. "We weren't worth hearing about."

Somehow, she doubted that.

She was somewhat upset with herself for not knowing the band anyway, simply because she adored Nikki. And it had been Nikki's band too. Even though Nikki hadn't ever wanted to talk about it. Zara could have still investigated on her own for more information. Then she could've impressed Asa with all her intimate knowledge of his once upon a time rock stardom.

Rookie mistake.

"Do you still write?" she asked.

"Nah." His eyes slid off to the side and she wondered about that.

She wrote all the time. Couldn't seem to stop. She'd never met another songwriter who had just…stopped.

Weird.

She wanted to ask more about that specifically.

"What comes next for you? Another album of the year?" he asked, deliberately changing the subject.

Fine. She'd allow it. But she'd be coming back to this subject eventually. Maybe not tonight, maybe not soon, but she'd get to it.

She hummed, distracted by his assertion. "Maybe. I already have one finished—"

"Do you live in a recording studio?" he asked, amused.

"It feels that way sometimes," she admitted.

He shook his head, a flicker of something, maybe sorrow, hitting his eyes before he blinked it away.

Thunder rumbled ominously and they both glanced at the window, covered by heavy hotel curtains.

"Sounds like a storm." He set down his fries and started toward the window. He was almost there when the lights dimmed and then came back. "Uh oh."

He slowly turned toward her, an eyebrow lifted.

The lights dimmed again, and the room buzzed with labored electricity. They brightened once more.

She jerked her chin up. "Take a look," she said, referring to the window.

He drew back the curtains just as a huge bolt of lightning seared across the sky. The lights in the room blinked one, two, three times, then stayed dark as thunder rumbled through the building.

Excitement flared in her chest along with a little squeal. Maybe she should have been embarrassed by that, but she just wasn't. At least it wasn't a full-on cackle like that one night in Barcelona. Her backup dancers said she'd sounded like a witch.

Oh well.

She lived in the moment.

"Was that a happy noise or a scared noise?" Asa asked climbing back onto the bed.

He'd left the curtains open and the strobe effect of the lightning against the dark backdrop felt… cozy.

Was that weird?

Probably.

It wasn't a full blackout; she could see lights further off in the distance. But their little section of the grid remained dark.

Both of them shifted where they'd been sitting on the bed so their backs were to the headboard and they could watch the storm out the window.

Zara loved, loved, *loved* thunderstorms.

"When I was a kid," she started, not knowing why she was revealing this part of herself to Asa. Maybe because it felt safe there in that hotel room. Maybe because he'd already told her she didn't have to share anything if she didn't want to. Maybe because he was connected to Nikki and as a consequence, she naturally trusted him. "Eating in the car with my dad while it rained was one of my favorite things."

He grunted softly.

The rain pelted the window, running in thick watery lines down the glass. Thunder rumbled through the ground and into her chest. The combination echoed in her mind as an under riff and she hummed it to herself.

Asa chuckled beside her. "Are you writing right now?"

Yes.

She was always writing.

But she didn't want to turn her phone on and risk being interrupted by the outside world.

"Can I use your phone?" she asked softly. He could say no and she'd be fine with that. She'd probably be able to remember what she was thinking for later.

But he didn't say no.

She heard the quiet rustling of his jeans as he took it out of his pocket and the faint click of him unlocking it.

He slid the warm rectangle into her outstretched palm. They had the same phone. His didn't have a case or a crack running through the screen though.

She opened the voice memo app and hummed the under riff. A melody started to form and her voice wandered into that area for a while. No words, just feelings. She tried to capture the atmosphere of the moment as best she could. When she'd exhausted her ideas for the time being, she set the phone aside.

"You're the real deal, aren't you?" Asa asked, voice deep and soft at the same time.

She glanced his way and tried to read his face in the dark.

"I don't know what you mean," she replied hesitantly.

He chuckled, the sound rich and warm, as he rubbed a black eyebrow with a knuckle. "I just mean to say…" He sighed and rested his hands in his lap. You're what, twenty-five?"

"Twenty-three," she corrected him softly. "Until February."

"Holy shit. Sorry. I didn't mean to say that, but holy shit." Asa covered his mouth with a hand.

Her cheeks heated. It wasn't the first time someone had remarked on her age in combination with her career. She never knew how she was supposed to feel. Was she supposed to feel bad about it? Or embarrassed?

So, she was twenty-three. Did that make her talent illegitimate?

"I'm sorry," he said again, trying to catch her eyes in the lightning. "I was just surprised is all."

She shrugged, trying to push the discomfort off her shoulders. "People assume because of my age that I don't know what's going on. Or that I don't understand people or the world or business or what have you."

"That's not what I thought at all."

She lifted her eyes to his, trying to measure the intentions of this person she knew but didn't know. A moment ago, she'd been ready to trust him without question. But the remark about her age knifed into a constant sore point in her ribs.

She grew tired of having to *prove* herself as a valid artist on the industry's stage. Like she'd gotten everything because of luck or happenstance. Or worse, her success wasn't hers but the result of someone else's work on her behalf.

Was Asa one of those people who thought she hadn't earned her spot? Who thought she was just a pretty face working someone else's agenda?

He shifted so he was facing her more fully. His eyes met hers head on, dark and sincere and endless.

"When I was twenty-three, I was a little punk," he admitted, voice rough like it was pulled over gravel and into the conversation against its will. "I was just a baby. Ask Nikki. I was stupid and impulsive. And I certainly wasn't capable of running an empire."

Some of her apprehension faded. He wasn't misjudging her, he was comparing where he'd been at the same age. That made more sense. The knot that had started to coil in her stomach eased.

"How old are you now?" she asked.

"Almost thirty." He blinked and a slow breath went in and out, his chest rising and falling. "In February."

They shared a smile. She wondered how close their birthdays were.

"All grown up?" she asked.

His lips tipped up on the sides and his Adam's apple bobbed with his swallow. Somehow the pause he gave said more than words could. He'd grown but not because he'd wanted to. Because he'd had to.

Her gaze dropped to the tattoos on his arms blurred by the darkness. His admission that he no longer wrote came back to her and she bit her tongue before asking about it again.

They weren't good friends.

They didn't have shared history.

But she couldn't deny that there was something there. An elusive connection that underpinned everything that had happened that night.

He'd had no reason to step in between her and Logan. He hadn't been involved.

But when she thought back to that moment, when Logan had once again said something cruel and unwarranted in front of her peers, her shame and anger had been eclipsed by Asa's hand taking hers.

"I got you."

She'd met his eyes and it was as if her heart *knew* his.

And there in the dark, the thunder sending trembles through the ground and through her doubt, she felt it again. Clearly.

A knowing she couldn't define.

"What happened to Winking Pete?" she asked.

Nikki had never said. But she knew Nikki was talented as hell, so it was safe to assume Asa was as well.

He didn't speak for several minutes. His dark eyes focused on the window, his lower lip sucked in his mouth like he was scanning the contents of the memory. Trying to decide if he really wanted to share it or not.

"We were on our first overseas tour and our lead singer was…unhinged. She always had been. We just assumed she'd eventually get her shit sorted. Anyway, one night she showed up to the show drunk, high, late, and pissed off. I tried to get her to calm down, tighten it up. Most of the time I could convince her to get it together. But not that night." He shook his head. "She shoved Nikki off the stage and Nik broke her arm. That was the end." He made a ppfft noise with his mouth. "Done."

"Oh," Zara replied, a sick feeling twisting her stomach at the violence involved. "Was Nikki okay?" she asked.

He nodded, but his gaze drifted lower. "Yeah."

Something heavy and sad filled the space around him. It pressed on her mind and heart.

"Were you okay?" she asked quietly.

He took a slow breath, like he was coming back from a memory he didn't visit often. When he glanced at her, the self-recrimination made her lungs hurt.

"Yeah," he lied.

They held eye contact.

She could call him on his lie, but what good would it do? He obviously blamed himself. And she knew from experience that when someone had decided who was at fault for something, it was difficult to convince them otherwise. Especially if you weren't there. You couldn't know.

But a deep ache opened in her chest for the man across the bed from her.

She wanted to help in some way but no words came to mind.

So she gave him what she always wanted when she was breaking inside. The same thing he'd given her just that night.

Presence.

She gathered their garbage and dropped it in the bin before returning to the bed. Instead of resuming her seated position, she laid down on top of the covers and put a hand behind her head. The other she rested at her side, nearest to Asa.

Rain filled the silence between them.

After a while he spoke. His voice a whispered rumble that reached into her ribs. "You ever just stay somewhere, even when you know you shouldn't?"

"Yeah," she answered. Because did she ever? Not just Logan but friends, business partners. "Staying too long happens to be my favorite bad decision," she said, voice soft. "Is that what happened?"

She didn't think she needed to be specific with her question. He hadn't come back from whatever memory he'd gotten stuck in.

The bed dipped and moved as Asa adjusted to lay down beside her. Not close, not far. She could reach out and touch him if she wanted.

"I wanted it so much. I tried to hold it together with good intentions and duct tape." His voice was soft but dipped in layers of cynicism and anger. "I didn't leave until people I cared about got hurt."

Light danced along the ceiling, making shapes in the shadows. The rain soothed the quiet conversation, insulating them from everything and everyone that might interfere.

"I should have left Logan years ago," she admitted. She'd never said it out loud. Never confessed it to anyone, not her friends or her sister, no one. It was her own secret shame that she carried on her own.

Asa didn't say anything for a long time but she could practically hear him holding back his thoughts.

"You can say something," she said with a soft laugh.

He let out a hiss of a sigh. "I don't get it. He was wearing *sweatpants* tonight."

Zara groaned with the reminder. "He said because he wasn't nominated he didn't have to be uncomfortable."

"There's a reason he wasn't nominated," Asa growled back. "Sorry," he muttered.

"You're not wrong," she replied. She'd never admit that to anyone else. No matter how many times Logan had embarrassed her in public or in front of her people, she defended him, excused it. Reasoned it away. Because it felt like they weren't just judging him, they were judging *her*. But shouldn't they? She was the one who never left.

But it was more than that. Logan had been there in the beginning. They'd grown up in the industry together. She cheered for him as much as anyone else. Even if he'd stopped cheering for her a long time ago.

It hurt to think about. But talking about it in the dark with this handsome pseudo stranger felt better. Like coming up for air after being underwater for too long.

"He was mad that I won so many times," she said, anger and shame stirring in her belly. "He called it excessive."

"He's a jealous little bitch," Asa muttered.

She snorted a surprised laugh. No one around her talked like that. Especially about Logan. They were all afraid it would damage them professionally.

"It's the fucking job," he said, disgusted.

"What do you mean?" she asked, swiveling her head his direction.

"Job is probably the wrong word for it. But if someone wants to be in a relationship with you, they're gonna have to check their ego at the door. They have to be secure enough to step back and let you shine. They should be your biggest fan. I feel like that goes without saying."

She didn't know if the warmth that spread through her was embarrassment or validation, but either way, she was flustered. He spoke boldly, as if being wrong wasn't an option he considered.

And his boldness bolstered her own.

"Right? Like…somehow, it's my fault that I'm successful? For something I've worked my whole life to do? I should apologize or be ashamed of those things? Oh, but he wouldn't want to give up all the perks that come with my job. The houses and the parties and the invites and the people," she rattled off, not realizing how much she'd been wanting to express these frustrations. "It feels like there's this expectation that I should be successful, but not more than him. That I should leave 'Zara Lorna' at the door and be his doting girlfriend. Encourage him and baby him and tolerate his fuckups for the sake of his happiness. But you know what? I'm pretty sure he still wouldn't be happy."

"Yeah, he's not the one for you," Asa agreed.

"Maybe I can't have both," she said thoughtfully. "Maybe love and my job can't coexist. Maybe I have to choose one or the other."

"Nah," he dismissed her words easily and it made her smile in the dark. "I would have probably agreed with you a few years ago but not now. You just need the right person. You know Sunshine and Sabine, right?"

He was talking about Sunshine Capone, the hip hop artist and his wife. They'd met at an awards show a while back and became instant friends. It was through Sunshine she'd met Nikki.

"Of course."

"Take them for example. They are both very much individuals but committed to each other in a way that's inspiring. You know damn good and well that if Sabine asked Sunshine to quit the biz so she could pursue her lifelong dream of being the world's greatest teacher—"

Zara snorted a laugh.

"I don't know. Probably not that, but you know what I mean. He would do it. He'd drop it all and fall at her feet and be fucking *elated* to do it."

She nodded, seeing what he meant. "But she'd never ask."

"Of course not," he agreed with her. "But we *allll* know she could. She knows she could. And it's *that* kind of security that I'm talking about. Where you need to be with someone you would do anything for, but also know they'd never ask you to do something that would hurt you."

Her heart pinched at the idea of someone loving her like that.

"That's rare," she said, her voice suddenly rough.

"Fuck, yeah, it is." His voice equally rough.

"Feels impossible," she whispered, her nose stinging.

"I can imagine."

Her thoughts drifted with the thunder. She was okay. She'd always be okay. She had the love of her family and the gift of being able to do what she loved for a living. And while, yes, it could be lonely, she was sometimes gifted with moments like this one. With being able to share a moment, a personal connection, with another human. That's why she wrote and sang in the first place. Because it was her way of connecting her heart to others. So maybe she didn't need a life partner or soulmate or whatever. Maybe it was enough to have these moments that felt bigger on the inside.

"Maybe I'll start a wildlife refuge for rabbits," she said softly. Unable to keep herself serious, she snorted. "Not fancy rabbits. But like, regular ones. I could lean in and get real weird with it. Make them hats. And a reality show. Like *The Bachelor*. Imagine the drama."

The silence lasted for maybe four seconds before Asa busted up laughing.

"Oh, my God," he said around a chuckle. "Fuckin' rabbits," he muttered.

She joined in his laughter, the bed vibrating with their mutual amusement.

"It's a solid plan b," she concluded.

"It's a million-dollar idea for sure," he agreed.

She grinned up at the ceiling, pleased with herself for getting such a great laugh out of him. And what a laugh. She liked it more than most laughs. It felt like someone hugging her brain.

In that moment she decided she was going to be spending more time in Chicago. She missed Nikki anyway.

"Can I ask you something?" His deep voice turned soft, curious.

"Sure," she replied.

"How are you still so happy?" he asked.

She glanced his way and realized he wasn't looking at the ceiling but was on his side, facing her, one arm tucked beneath the pillow under his head.

"What do you mean?" she asked, rolling onto her side to face him.

His black eyebrows dipped and his mouth pulled into a frustrated line. "How has this world not ruined you?"

She wasn't sure how to answer that. "It's nice that you think I'm not ruined," she said.

"Are you joking?" he asked. "You're joking. Have you met you, Zara?"

She laughed and tucked her hands under her cheek.

"Look at you, still smiling away," Asa said like he was disappointed in her, and she laughed some more. "Like you didn't just have a messy fight with your boyfriend—"

"*Ex*-boyfriend," she corrected quickly.

His lips tilted to the side. "Right. Like you didn't just have a messy fight with your ex-boyfriend in front of literally everyone in the industry." He stopped speaking for a beat like he was withholding additional commentary. "You ruined your dress," he went on, voice pitched lower. His eyes drifted over her face and her chest got tight under his slow examination. "This could not have been how you pictured spending tonight. You should be celebrating."

She swallowed as heat crept into her eyes. Hadn't she just been thinking those exact thoughts?

"How do you put it all aside and not lose yourself?" he asked.

He wasn't asking for pity's sake. No, this question came from a place deep inside him that needed an answer she couldn't provide.

But she'd still try.

"They're always going to get it wrong," she said. "By tomorrow there'll be a dozen stories about tonight. But no one really knows, do they? My whole life I've had to hear about all the shameful things I've been a part of. I could go out there and defend myself, try to explain things that don't require explanation. But that would be it. That would become my new occupation. I'd never be able to stop because they never stop."

She chewed on her bottom lip as she thought about all the times she'd compromised on who she was and what she wanted for the sake of Logan, or a record's release, or the threat of bad press.

No, she hadn't always made the right call.

But even in those times, a part of her had known better.

"Maybe being happy is my own type of denial," she admitted. "Maybe I use it as a way to ignore what I actually need to change. I don't know."

"I don't see that about you."

Her gaze flicked back to his.

"Maybe you're so adept at growth that you give others around you the opportunity to do the same."

"You make me sound like the kind of person I want to be," she said softly, the thunder rumbling through the building and her bones.

These were the kind of conversations she never had. So often she was surrounded by cameras and microphones and people looking for an angle. She'd learned to guard her words and her mind from being *too* honest.

But there, in the dark, across from Asa, she felt her soul relax its cautious nature. She wasn't the Artist of the Year there in that hotel room.

She was just Zara.

"Logan Black is beneath you," Asa said into the quiet.

She held his gaze without flinching.

"It's not my place to say, but I hope you know you're too valuable to be in that kind of a situation. No one should ever speak to you the way he did."

Her heart stung with the truth in his words. "Are you still trying to rescue me?"

"Maybe." His eyes narrowed briefly. "You can write a song in a thunderstorm and find meaning in a ruined dress and give too many chances to someone who doesn't deserve it. It's reckless and amazing and distressing to someone like me. What makes you live life like all of it is a gift?"

"Because it is," she replied simply.

It's not like she ignored her feelings. Or pretended like it didn't hurt. Sometimes it hurt beyond the telling of it. But she also wasn't afraid to feel it. Every emotion had a purpose. She'd learned long ago that the purpose wasn't to harm her, but to teach her. It's what made it possible for her to write music that touched others, that spoke for them when they couldn't speak for themselves.

Taking a breath, her heart caught in her throat, knowing she was about to admit more than she usually did. "Life is a frustrating, terrifying, beautiful act of defiance," she said. "My dad always says that I was born already in love with life."

His frown deepened and his eyes moved over her face like he was trying to read something beyond what he saw.

But there wasn't anything more there. It was just her. It was always just her. She lived her life fully exposed and fully alive because she didn't know any other way to be.

"I get to live for a moment. I'm a flash of pain and joy and breath. I've known that my whole life. Tell me why that isn't the most terribly wonderful gift someone can be given?"

Chapter Three
Ultraviolet

ASA

Her driver picked her up in the morning, shortly after sunrise.

She put her number in his phone and stole his copy of *Return of the King* with a promise to return it with his shirt.

And then she was gone.

He hoped he hid his surprise well when the sun had started to come up.

Somewhere between his panic attack and her leaving, he'd become a huge fan of Zara Lorna. Not just the musician—though that too—but the woman.

They'd talked all night long about art and music and life.

They talked about their families and how they'd grown up. She was from Jersey, raised by a single father and had much younger siblings that she adored. She didn't push for him to talk about his own family but for the first time, he'd kind of wanted to.

They talked about how they'd first gotten into music and what parts of writing were their favorite. About touring and what places had surprised them.

They talked about *Lord of the Rings* and he found out what an incredible dork she was.

And when a text from André had come through at 3:30am of a picture with Nikki holding her brand new baby girl, Zara had asked if she could hug him.

So they'd hugged and cried over the new human, Amber Nicole Debois.

It was easily in the top five of the greatest hugs of all time. Probably top three.

Normally staying up all night long would have made him grumpy for the day ahead. He abhorred missing sleep.

But for some reason he didn't care at all. Something about the scratchiness in his eyes and the fog in his thoughts made him feel…lighter. If that were even possible.

Maybe that was because he had developed a massive, unrealistic, and unexpected crush on her.

But who wouldn't, he reasoned. Spending that kind of uninterrupted, unfiltered time with one of the greatest artists of their generation, anyone would be helpless to resist her magnetism.

She was…

She was incredible. He could honestly say he'd never known anyone like her. So full of life and fire. It was almost enough to make him think he had a little bit of those things left burning inside him as well.

He sat down at a charging station, plugged in his phone and put in his earbuds.

Had it really been that long since he'd stayed up all night talking about music with someone?

Not just anyone either. But someone who knew music as well as he did.

Maybe even better.

It was a wild realization he'd had around four in the morning when Zara took his phone and made another voice memo of her humming a melody and a chord progression that blew his mind.

He'd promised to play with it and send her something.

Which—okay, yeah, pump the brakes. But it had just fallen out of him. The offer to write music with her seemed like harmless fun. And he hadn't had fun in a while.

He opened his messages and stared at her number as he listened to the voice memo again and again. Lost in her clear voice and the small laugh he'd coaxed from her.

Her mind was always on. Nikki had talked about Zara's focus and intensity. But that wasn't it at all. She lived in an active creative state at all times.

Her emotions close to the surface. Limitless in the full exploration of the human experience.

How was she still so bright and beautiful living in this world?

It didn't make sense to him.

His phone chimed and he jolted.

It was a text from Nikki.

NIKKI: what the hell happened last night?

He frowned, his mind playing through last night's greatest hits and wondering what Nikki was referencing. He didn't have to wait long. She sent a link to an article from an online entertainment news magazine.

The headline read, "Is Zara Lorna having an affair with her co-producer?"

He clicked on the link and the page opened to photos of him and Zara leaving the party the night before.

Had that really been less than twenty-four hours ago?

His eyes scanned the article but he couldn't focus to read it.

He took a deep breath, rubbed his tired eyes, and tried again.

After winning big last night at the NMAs, Zara Lorna left the afterparty early with her co-producer, Asa Young.

The two reportedly grew closer during the production of her latest award-winning album. Sources say that Zara's longtime boyfriend Logan Black had suspected something more was happening with the producer.

Asa Young is the former bassist for the failed rock band, Winking Pete. Notably, he's older than Lorna by ten years.

Friends have voiced their concerns about her seeing the older man but say she wouldn't listen to anyone. They fear he only wants to use her fame for his own benefit.

Witnesses at the afterparty say Black and Lorna argued, and she left with Young.

Click here to see the relationship timeline for Logan and Zara who have been together since they were teenagers.

Sources close to both of them said that Black had been talking about marriage but the songstress kept putting it off.

Maybe now we know why.

Stay tuned to CELEBX for updates.

. . .

Whoa.

They'd manufactured an entire relationship in the span of a few hours.

That was some fast gossip.

So much of it was wrong, he was surprised they had his name right. But there it was in black and white. They had his age wrong. Mostly. He wasn't ten years older. It was six, but whatever.

Fuck.

He wasn't the co-producer either. He'd helped mix like, two songs. That was barely anything. And using her for what? He produced jingles for cat food commercials for fuck's sake! Also, Logan was the one being the shithead last night.

Damn. His people must work fast.

Zara had been hiding out with him eating burgers while her ex had been trying to dismantle her character.

He glanced up, suddenly feeling overexposed in the crowded airport. He pulled his hat down lower over his eyes like that would somehow disguise him and tried to ignore his increased heart rate.

He'd never, not once, worried about being recognized in public. Not even when he'd been in Winking Pete.

He'd been the *bass player* for fuck's sake.

But being attached to Zara romantically could put him on the radar of strangers all over the world.

Fuck.

Poor Zara.

They did this to her all the time, didn't they?

Make something up for the clicks and the public ate it up.

He knew he shouldn't but he scrolled through the comments on the article.

"She's always been a whore."

"She'll just use him too."

"LOGAN! Call me! I would never cheat on you!"

"'Failed rock band' LOL I've never heard of them."

His stomach churned and his throat tightened.

This fucking sucked. It was all lies!

He opened his texts to say something to Zara and stopped.

What could he even say? Sorry for existing? He imagined her people were already in her ear about what to do next, the steps to take, the words to say.

She didn't need any tips from him.

No, the best thing he could do was nothing. Better not to be another voice in the shitstorm surrounding her.

He rubbed the back of his neck and closed his eyes, trying to focus. But his mind was a whirlwind.

He'd just been trying to do the right thing. And instead, he'd possibly made things worse for her. Not only that, but now his name was back out there. They'd start digging and repeating all the same shit they'd said years ago.

Fuck.

They'd call Shelby.

Of course they'd call Shelby.

And his mom.

All the carefully constructed walls surrounding him started to chip and crumble.

This was what happened when he let music back into his life. Life took it away again immediately.

How Zara managed to stay afloat in a world that felt like a constant tsunami, he would never know. But he couldn't do it.

He wasn't that guy.

That guy had left the building years ago.

His flight started to board.

He texted Nikki instead.

ASA: none of that happened. I'll explain when I get there. ttys

Then he shut off his phone.

* * *

When Asa finally found Nikki's hospital room, it was full.

Nikki's parents, Bob and Mary, were cooing over the little bundle in André's arms. Nikki spotted Asa hovering in the doorway and gave a little wave with her tired smile.

Mary glanced up at him and did a double-take.

"Asa." She moved his way and grabbed him in a tight hug. The moment she released him, Bob was there to hug him as well.

"It's good to see you," Bob said, slapping him on the back before releasing him.

"We saw you on the television last night accepting Nikki's award," Mary said, pride shining from her eyes. "Didn't think you'd make it back so soon."

"I couldn't miss meeting my new niece," Asa said with a smile.

Growing up, Bob and Mary had been more supportive of him than his own parents. Too many times he'd wished that he and Nikki were actually related so he could claim them as his own.

"She's perfect," Mary sighed, turning back to the baby now fussing in André's arms. "Eight pounds of stardust wrapped in a blanket."

The baby's grunts and protests grew louder and André moved closer to Nikki.

"I should probably try to feed her again," Nikki said, holding out her arms.

"Do you want me to get the nurse?" André asked, setting the bundle carefully in Nikki's hold.

"No, I think we've about got this thing figured out," Nikki said, voice soft.

André arranged the blanket around the mother and child so Nikki could nurse in privacy.

"Mom, Dad, would you please make sure André eats something?" Nikki asked her parents. "He's being stubborn."

"I just want to be here in case you need me," André said.

"I'm fine," Nikki reassured him. "I'm well taken care of."

"Come along, son," Bob said, patting André's back. "Let us buy you lunch."

André sputtered a bit, his gaze bouncing from Nikki to her parents to Asa.

"Go," Asa encouraged.

"Call me if something happens?" André asked.

Asa nodded. "Of course."

André let out a heavy sigh. "Okay," he muttered to himself.

Mary looped an arm through André's and he allowed her to lead him out the door.

Once they were gone, Asa brought the only chair in the room closer to Nikki's beside.

"You're such an overachiever," he said, voice quiet. "Winning Producer of the Year and giving birth in the same night. Who does that?"

Nikki smiled, blue eyes shining. "It was kind of a big night, huh?"

Asa nodded. She didn't know the half of it.

He still hadn't turned his phone back on, afraid of what might happen next. Not that keeping his phone off prevented any more pandemonium, but he could pretend.

Nikki winced. "Breast feeding fucking hurts. They keep telling me that it gets better and my nipples will get used to it but, damn." She shook her head.

Asa chuckled at his best friend. "How was labor? Did you go natural like you had planned?"

"Fuck no," she said, making a face that had him cracking up. "I chickened out of that almost immediately. Nothing went according to plan. Homegirl was lodged in my pelvis and I wasn't dilating. It was a whole drama. Then when they did the epidural, they nicked an artery and blood sprayed everywhere."

"Oh shit."

Nikki rolled her eyes and nodded. "André held it together. I was pretty out of it. And then they were telling me to push and here we are."

"You're a fucking legend," Asa said, meaning it.

Nikki hummed as she peaked under the blanket at the baby. Her deep blue eyes tracked back to Asa and he felt the question before she asked it.

"What happened with *you* last night?"

He recounted the events of the night before, playing up his panic attack because it made her laugh. He left out some of the more personal things he and Zara had shared because they didn't seem relevant anymore.

"She's pretty cool, isn't she?" Nikki said.

"She really is," Asa agreed.

"How are you feeling about…?" Nikki didn't finish the question. She didn't have to. He knew what she was asking.

Was he freaking out about being back in the media's crosshairs?

He shrugged and forced a swallow. "I accidentally read the comments—"

"Asa!" Nikki scolded keeping her voice low.

"I know. I know." He rubbed his tired eyes with his palms.

Never read the comments. He'd violated one of the basic rules of internet protocol.

He dropped his hands away from his face and sighed.

"I don't want to turn my phone back on," he confessed.

Nikki nodded. If anyone understood why, it would be her.

"Maybe they won't notice," Nikki suggested. "Maybe it'll blow over quick and they'll never even see your name." She maneuvered the small baby in her arms and started patting and rubbing her back.

"Yeah, maybe."

But they both knew the likelihood of that. Once Shelby saw it, she'd call their mom.

That horrible, trapped feeling lurked at the edges of his mind. He didn't know what he hated more, the anticipation leading up to the fight, or the fight itself.

Because it was always a fight.

And his sacrifices had never been enough to get them to leave him alone.

"Would you like to hold your niece?" Nikki asked, breaking into his dark thoughts.

Asa immediately stood and went to the sink, washing his hands. He returned to Nikki's side and took the tiny bundle she offered him.

Amber grunted and blinked at him sleepily. The warmth of the newborn soaked into him and eased his residual tension. He slowly sat back down in the chair.

"She's perfect, Nik," he whispered.

She really was. With her scrunched up face and her tiny, tiny eyelashes. She was the most perfect thing Asa had ever held.

He started humming one of his and Nikki's favorite songs before he began singing the words out loud.

"Best of Friends" from the movie *The Fox and the Hound.*

They'd watched the movie so many times when they were younger that they'd worn out the VHS copy and had to wait until it came out on DVD. They had the entire thing memorized.

Every time Asa saw a copy of it for sale, he bought it. Just in case.

It was still a comfort watch for him on those really tough days.

"Damn you, Asa Young."

He looked up at Nikki, who was wiping her eyes, and he grinned.

"Have to start her young," he explained. "It's imperative that she know her family history."

Nikki snorted and reached for the tissues on the tray table beside her.

"When do you get to go home?" he asked, taking Amber's tiny fist and rubbing the soft skin with the pad of his thumb. She even had tiny fingernails.

"Uh, tomorrow I think."

"Is the apartment ready or do I need to go over and finish things for you?"

"You're the best," she said. "No, I think it's ready."

He glanced up at the tone in her voice. She was looking off to the side in thought.

"What's going on?" he asked.

She lifted her eyebrows and slid her gaze back in his direction. "I was just thinking about all the stuff we have to finish at the house."

"Don't get ahead of yourself, mama. You have time. And you know I'll help wherever I can."

She smiled and blinked slowly. "I know. That's because you're the best." She yawned. "I think I might take a short nap," she said.

"Go for it," he said. "I'm not going anywhere."

Nikki nodded and closed her eyes, sinking back into the pillow.

Asa adjusted his hold on the sleeping baby and got comfortable himself.

Maybe the rest of his life was in the process of burning to the ground. But right there, in that moment, all was well.

His best friend and her baby were happy, healthy, and alive. And he honestly couldn't ask for more than that. So he set aside all his outside worries and let himself soak in the peace of the moment.

Love existed here.

Here he was happy.

Chapter Four
Bastards

ZARA

At least she'd slept a bit on the jet. From the looks of her living room in her NoHo penthouse, she wasn't going to rest again for a while.

Cas had warned her on the drive over from the airport that an "all hands" meeting had been called.

She expected nothing less after last night.

And sure enough, Sonja, Kenna, and Gregor—manager, publicist, assistant, in that order—were chilling in the main living room.

This was going to suck. She just knew it.

Zara sighed and dropped her tired body into an overstuffed chair. "Let me have it."

It was a little weird that Sonja was there in person. She usually called in through Zoom or FaceTime since her main office was in Boston. So either Zara was in deep shit or Sonja had already been in the city for other reasons.

Zara's publicist had been with her since her second album. Which was about the same time Zara stopped going on the internet. She didn't even run her socials anymore. Kenna's team took care of most of that for her.

Gregor, her assistant for only the past year, handed out waters to everyone.

She liked Gregor. He was soft spoken but firm. He didn't let anyone push him around, not even her. Which was exactly what she needed. He also had a pretty dark sense of humor which she loved. They got along very well.

Sonja nodded at Kenna.

Kenna sat forward and cleared her throat.

"Who is Asa Young?" Kenna asked.

Zara blinked and sat up straighter. "Damn. The devil works hard," she muttered. "He's a friend. He's actually more Nikki's friend than mine but…" She chewed on her lower lip. "Okay, so last night…"

And she launched into everything that had happened the night before. All of it. From winning, to Logan being a dick, to Asa getting her out of there, to burgers, milkshakes, and music. She let them know everything. It would save time in the long run.

Kenna nodded along, taking notes on her tablet.

When Zara finished, Kenna folded her hands on top of her tablet and leaned forward. Her ruby lips were striking on her pale skin. Her short blonde hair slicked back in a way that seemed effortlessly cool. More than once Zara wished she had the natural style and poise as Kenna who seemed way too sophisticated to be working for Zara.

"Logan's people are working fast. It's being reported that you've been having an affair with Asa for some time now and that's why you haven't gotten married yet. Also, Asa is older, so they're trying to make that work somehow with you being manipulated and used."

Zara scrunched up her face in disgust. "Right. Because they still see me as a child."

Kenna gave her a look and Zara shrugged, rubbing her eyes.

"Most publications are focused on Logan being jilted. He's playing the wounded puppy. He was photographed outside a café in Malibu this morning looking sad and alone, checking his phone repeatedly, looking distressed. You know the drill."

Yes, she did.

Logan had done this before. Every time she'd tried to break up with him, he would use the public to get sympathy. Meanwhile, Zara stayed off the streets and everyone accused her of being cold and distant.

Fun times.

"I have some ideas for things we can release to downplay this entire thing. Put suspicion on Logan's version of the story. But those photos of you and Asa are already everywhere. And one popped up this morning of you in that shirt."

Zara frowned and looked down at the shirt she'd borrowed from Asa she was still wearing. She needed to get it back to him eventually. "From where?"

She hadn't stopped anywhere after leaving Asa's room.

Cas had snuck her out the back stairs and into a vehicle with blackout windows.

"Getting on the plane."

At the private airfield?

"Fucking vultures," Zara grumbled. She had no privacy.

"Can they connect that to Asa?" Kenna asked a very valid question.

Zara's cheek twitched. "I don't think so. He said it was a band he had with Nikki in high school."

Kenna nodded and added to her notes. "I'll do a deep dive on him and see what we can find."

"Eh," Zara said with a wave of her hand.

Kenna glanced up, fingers paused in mid-type. "No?"

Zara's gaze bounced from Kenna to Sonja's watchful gaze. So far, Sonja hadn't said a word but Zara could tell she was absorbing every last detail.

"He's just a guy who tried to do the right thing. I don't want his life turned upside down by all of this."

"So you're not seeing him again?" Kenna asked.

It wasn't an accusation or fishing for information. Kenna had always made it clear that her job was never to judge Zara, just to handle the press. And she did a wonderful job at it.

Zara thought about how much fun she'd had with Asa. She wanted to talk to him again, she knew that much. But with her life being what it was, there was no way to know when that would ever happen.

"If it's not on the schedule, I'm not sure how that's possible," Zara admitted with a yawn. "I'll keep my distance for a while and let things cool down."

Kenna nodded and typed some more.

"I'll push for more coverage of your win last night. Would you like me to leak anything about Logan?" Kenna asked hopefully.

Zara narrowed one eye at Kenna. "Do I sense *glee* in there somewhere, Kenna Summerfeld?"

Kenna straightened her shoulders and smoothed her expression. "It's a possibility."

Zara chuckled. "Yeah." She sighed. "I'll leave it up to you what you want to say."

Kenna's eyebrows lifted. "So it's over-over?"

Zara nodded, her blinks getting heavier. "It was over-over months ago. But now it's no longer amicable. I'm not interested in helping him look good moving forward. You have free rein. Do what you feel is best."

Kenna sucked in a quiet breath and typed furiously on her tablet.

Zara almost felt sorry for Logan.

Almost.

She wondered if Asa had made it home yet. If he'd been able to meet Nikki's baby.

If he'd seen the articles.

"Are they being mean to him?" Zara asked.

"Logan? Not yet. But give me an espresso and an hour, and that'll change."

Gregor snorted.

Zara blinked at her publicist. Kenna glanced up, realizing what she'd said out loud.

"I meant, Asa," Zara said, deciding not to address Kenna's vengeful streak.

Kenna's lips twisted to the side.

That was a yes.

Dammit.

This was all her fault.

No. *No.* It was some of her fault and some of it was Logan's fault. She wasn't going to take responsibility for him anymore. He was a grown ass man.

Which reminded her.

"We need to change the codes and locks at the house in LA," Zara said.

"Cas has already made arrangements for that," Sonja spoke for the first time. She leaned forward and folded her hands on her lap. "Let's talk about what comes next. I think, in light of the aggressive way Logan's team is handling what happened last night, we need to consider they will be a problem for the next album's release."

Zara opened her mouth to protest but then she realized Sonja was right.

Logan *would* try to pull some shit just to mess with her life and make sure he had her full attention.

Ugh.

Zara sat up fully. "I'm gonna need some coffee." She searched for Gregor and found him already headed into the kitchen. "What are your ideas?" she asked Sonja.

* * *

Eight hours later she was finally alone.

Cas and Devan had gone through and changed the security codes and locks in her place. Gregor had packed up any and all things that belonged to Logan. Boxes would start shipping one at a time to his mama's place in Jersey.

Part of her felt bad for dumping Logan's things on his mom. But she'd raised him; she could deal with him now.

Zara had a shower and ate the orange chicken bowl Gregor had made for her before he'd left.

She washed her one dish and single fork and put them away.

And looked around her beautiful, clean, enormous penthouse.

Wandering down the hall to her bedroom, she shut the lights off on the way. Her Cal-King called to her and she dove face first into the pillows.

She rolled over with a groan and stared up at the dark ceiling. It was painted navy blue and covered in gold and silver flecks patterned in constellations that sparkled when the light was just right.

They weren't sparkling at the moment.

Her phone made a noise and she reached for it with an unladylike grumble.

It was just Cas letting her know that the locks had been changed in LA.

Fucking Logan.

Why? You know? Why did he have to be such a selfish asshole?

Last night hadn't really been that different than any of the other times he'd dicked out in public. It was her who was different. She was tired. Tired of forgiving him and him not actually being sorry. Tired of letting the public's perception tell her who she should be with.

Especially when they had no idea who Logan really was.

She did though. She'd known him since they were both teenagers. Their relationship had been a fortuitous meeting for the Powers That Be. Arranged, produced, executed to perfection.

But she'd really fallen for him.

Of course, she'd been a child. So falling in love at the drop of a hat was kind of what she did.

She wasn't sure when she'd stopped loving him. Sometime after the second time he cheated on her and before the third. After that her heart had disconnected from him, followed shortly by her mind. And then one day she just saw him as another part of the performance. Nothing to take personally.

Until last night.

When he'd said her win was partially his because he'd basically helped her write it. Which, no, he didn't.

She'd just… lost it.

It made her so *angry* that he would try to take credit for something he had no part in. The love songs weren't *his*. Was he crazy? Those were moments she had cried and labored over. Alone. He hadn't been there.

She'd been about *this* close to showing the world how much of his hair was actually a weave. And then Asa had waded in.

Without regard for his own reputation and what might come next. Though finding him mid-nervous breakdown in the hotel room *had* been kind of funny.

He was very odd, wasn't he?

Rock star yet slightly neurotic.

Caring and kind, yet standoffish.

Musically gifted, but he didn't use it anymore.

And he didn't talk like other people. She couldn't really put her finger on it, but she could hear it still. The cadence of his voice, the choice in his words.

She searched her music app for Winking Pete.

One album. Ten songs.

She hit play and made sure her phone was connected to the speakers in her room.

Oh.

Ohh.

A deep base line joined shortly by a heavy drum had her heart climbing into her throat.

Okay, crunchy guitar, I hear you.

Was that Nikki?

She followed along with the lyrics on her phone and scrolled to the bottom.

Written by Asa Young.

He said he'd written the music. For some reason she'd assumed he meant he'd written it *with* others. Like Nikki. She already knew from experience how talented a songwriter Nikki was. Album of the Year, hello?

But this didn't sound like Nikki's writing.

It was rich and deep with metaphor. Complicated and driven.

It was brave and real and not at all like the cagey man she'd hung out with last night.

She stared at the constellations on her ceiling and willed them to sparkle. Just a little. To reflect a partial glow of the stars she knew were way above the city somewhere.

Song after song after song played through her room and her soul.

On one hand she wanted to turn it up as loud as it would go and rock out. On the other, she didn't want to miss a single word or chord progression. She wanted to memorize every bridge that gave her goosebumps and figure out how to get the sound *inside* of her.

The lead singer was okay. Zara had some notes she could give her, but the band was fucking mint.

She knew she'd decided earlier that day to give space between her and Asa. But her fingers itched to send him a text. Her brain yearned to create music with him.

He should be on a stage somewhere.

He shouldn't be locked in a dark studio mixing jingles for an all you can eat shrimp feast.

He should be writing songs for the biggest names in the industry. He should be winning awards.

He should be a star.

So even though she shouldn't, even though it might cause more trouble for both of them, she texted him anyway.

Chapter Five
Landmine

It had been a week since he'd started getting texts from Zara.

The first one had come in less than a day since they'd said goodbye.

Z: I hate myself for not knowing anything by Winking Pete. You are amazing.

He hadn't replied.

One, he didn't know what to say. Her text had been hugely unexpected and made him feel a certain way.

Two, after reading fifty articles that basically all said the same thing, *"Look at this loser taking advantage of Zara. He's going to ruin her life,"* he didn't think he should say anything to her at all.

She'd mentioned that she already had a finished album which meant that she was going to need to start promoting soon. The last thing she needed—the last thing he wanted—was to corrupt that plan.

It didn't matter that what was being published was a lie. The public believed it and the public's opinion made and destroyed careers. Sometimes within hours.

Zara's people had gone on the offense right away and there were now competing stories that painted Logan in a less than favorable light.

But all of that was so far from Asa's world, he had no idea what to make of it.

Also, he didn't *want* those things to be part of his world.

Fame, notoriety, attention? Fuck. No.

Sure, he'd gone to LA at Nikki's urging to "make connections." But he'd never been sure that was something he wanted to pursue again.

Now he was certain he didn't want that life.

He wanted no part of it.

Which was why, when she'd started texting him, he decided not to reply. He wasn't going to make either of their lives harder than they already were.

After a minute, with her busy schedule, she'd forget about him.

And if she came to visit Nikki, he'd be busy in a different part of town.

Excellent plan, Asa.

Thank you, I thought of it myself.

But the pull to respond to Zara never fully went away.

Especially when she started messaging him two to three times a day. Sending jokes and random thoughts. His lack of response didn't seem to faze her. She never addressed it.

He reread her last two texts that come in back-to-back a few minutes ago.

Z: remember that voice memo I made for you? I want to hear it with a crunchy guitar.

Z: let me clarify. I want to hear YOU play it on a crunchy guitar.

So, funny story. He *had* recorded it on a crunchy guitar. Just that morning in fact.

Because even though he had no intention of contacting her, he'd still been playing with the idea she'd handed over to him. Like he'd won the Showcase Showdown on *The Price is Right* on his birthday.

He played the voice memo of her humming again and felt that now familiar buzzing in his mind.

He hadn't been excited about writing in longer than he could remember.

Music, the music that he used to live to make, hadn't been a safe place for him for a long time. After everything with Shelby, he hadn't been able to return to it. Not without the ache of knowing all that was gone and all that had been wasted.

It *hurt* to make music.

Like he was forging weapons that would be used against him in the future.

So he avoided it.

Except for the very rare times Nikki had talked him into small things. The mixing of commercials, listening to what she was working on and giving his opinion. The piano bar.

But that stupid fucking voice memo in his phone had had him in a chokehold for seven days.

He thought about it constantly. He'd written lyrics, finished the melody, wrote a bridge and a chorus and an outro. He dreamed about it. He woke up in the middle of the night humming it.

It was fucking terrifying.

He hadn't felt like this about music in so very long that he had honestly thought that part of his soul was dead.

Not in a melodramatic way, but in an actual, literal, not alive anymore, no hope of resuscitation way.

And then Zara Lorna had given him a shot of adrenaline straight to the heart and he was gasping and flailing and *alive.*

And that was terrifying in a different way.

He reread her texts way too often for someone who wasn't going to be texting her back. But it was better than reading the ones that had come in from his mom.

Those had started immediately with a benign, "How's it going?" And had escalated to unfounded accusations and weird demands. He'd muted the conversation immediately and hadn't gone back to it. But every few hours it would be at the top of the inbox with new messages.

And texts from an unknown number started the day after that. He knew without looking that it was Shelby. He blocked the number. It was only a matter of time before she used a different one.

She was a human shaped hemorrhoid and there was not enough witch hazel in the world to stop that inflammation once it started.

"What's that?"

Asa clicked the lock button on his phone before turning around.

Shawn Torres lifted his chin in greeting as he took a seat on the leather couch in the control room of Studio X.

Asa tugged at his left earlobe. "How much did you hear?" he asked the younger musician.

A crooked smile slowly spread across the twenty-one-year old's face. "Why? Is it a secret?"

This cocky son of a bitch. Asa couldn't help the chuckle that rumbled out of him.

Shawn had basically grown up in the studio his brother owned. It hadn't been a secret that he wanted to be a recording artist on the same level as Sunshine Capone and Zara Lorna. But Johnny had been reluctant in letting him chase that wild dream.

For good reason, in Asa's opinion.

But Shawn had been persistent (and smart) and he was well on his way to making a name for himself.

In fact…

"When did you get back?" Asa asked.

Last he'd checked, Shawn was opening for Sunshine Capone on tour. Talk about opportunity. He was getting out there and being heard and seen in a way that didn't make Johnny want to rip out all his hair.

Opening for a huge name like Sunshine was a dream gig for new artists. As far as Asa knew, it had been going very well indeed.

"A couple days ago," Shawn answered his question stretching his long arms up and folding his hands behind his head. "Don't change the subject. What were you working on?"

Pesky, pesky.

Even though he was irritated that Shawn had overheard the voice memo, he wasn't that upset. The kid had an ear and a passion that rivaled… Zara's, actually. Huh.

That thought led to a mad scramble of ideas involving getting Shawn and Zara to work together.

Which, mysteriously and shockingly, sent a spike of jealousy shooting through the center of him.

Weird.

"I wasn't working on anything." Lie. His brain immediately rebelled. "Nothing important," he clarified.

"Uh-huh," Shawn replied. "All I was gonna say is if you *were* working on something, I want to hear it because it's been a long time. Hasn't it?"

Asa shrugged. Shawn's brown eyes narrowed just slightly before he pumped his eyebrows and changed the subject. Sort of. "Do you ever sit in on writing sessions with anyone here?" he asked a little too casually.

Asa hummed and crossed his arms over his chest. "That's not really my thing. Nikki does, but she's out for a few weeks. You looking for a writing partner?"

Shawn shook his head as his gaze lost focus.

It wasn't often that Shawn came to him for advice, a pep talk, whatever. He had Johnny and Hannah Lee and Nikki. The few times he'd come to Asa were because he had things he wanted to work through that he didn't feel he could with the others. They knew him differently. In a familial way. And they couldn't look at him without that filter in place.

But Asa talked to him like he would any other artist. Not like he was a kid.

Shawn's eyes focused on him again. "Can I ask you something?"

Asa was pretty sure that was a given but okay. "Go for it."

"Have you ever had a muse?" Shawn asked.

Asa kept from smiling when he really wanted to. "Why? You got one?"

"Sometimes," Shawn muttered, a frown clouding his features.

Zara's face flashed through Asa's mind and he blinked it away. He leaned forward and rested his elbows on his knees. "A muse is great. As long as it lasts. And as long as you understand it's a temporary gift. It's not permanent."

Shawn stared at him, his thoughts working behind his eyes. He took a slow breath. "Keep them at arm's length."

"Something like that." A muse was a dangerous thing. It could be the greatest thing to happen to an artist, or their absolute ruin. The key was to know what you were getting into before you started. But it was difficult because the inspiration that came from it was like a drug. The best drug you've ever had.

And you'd do just about anything to keep from coming down.

But the high eventually faded, no matter how tight you held on.

And then you had to figure out how to be a creative without your brain soaking in all the happy chemicals. It was sobering and sad. And the loneliness could drain every creative idea from a body.

Not that he knew from experience or anything.

Shawn rubbed his jaw in silent contemplation.

He'd brought up something Asa hadn't considered though. Maybe this thing he was feeling about the voice memo and writing was just that. His brain's attempt to jumpstart itself with a muse. Something that had worked for him in the past.

And maybe having Zara live so far away made it a safe option. He could live off the hours they'd spent together for weeks. Months even, if he just opened himself up to the reality of it. If he saw her as his muse, and didn't think they were friends, and embraced the inspiration that would undoubtedly flood his thoughts.

Arm's length.

She'd never know.

And he could start writing again. For himself.

"I'm supposed to be working on something," Shawn said haltingly. He followed that with a slow blink and humorless laugh. "But I am distracted."

"By anyone in particular?" Asa asked, his lips tugging up on the ends.

Shawn's gaze cut to his. "No one I want to talk about just yet."

Asa lifted his chin in understanding.

Because there was the muse and then there was the *muse*.

"How was opening for Sunshine?" Asa asked.

Shawn's face brightened and a broad grin spread across his face. "Oh my God, Asa. It was amazing."

Asa crossed his arms and sat back in his chair as he let Shawn regale him with stories from the road. He missed that youthful exuberance. The untarnished version of himself that loved music because he didn't know how not to.

He hoped Shawn never lost it.

* * *

ASA: I'm just headed up now

He slid his phone back into his pocket as he hit the button for the elevator.

Nikki had asked him to stop by after work to hang out. She'd been out of the studio for a couple months and he was pretty sure she was going crazy not knowing if it had burned down or not.

He was happy to report that everything was progressing just fine without her. Though he didn't phrase it quite like that. He didn't want her to think they didn't need her because they absolutely did. But she'd set them up so well before she'd gone on maternity leave that there hadn't been any issues.

56

Plus, Hannah Lee's sixteen-year-old little sister Piper was working there as a runner and part time office manager until Nikki got back.

If Asa thought Hannah Lee was intimidating, she had nothing on Piper. That girl *ran* the studio. No one missed an appointment. No one was late. No one crossed her.

She was like this really adorable tyrant who used her powers for good. Which, thank God for that. Otherwise, she'd be a monster.

Nikki liked Asa to stop by so she could quiz him on whatever worries had plagued her that day. Truthfully, he thought she just missed living with him and needed an excuse to make him come over. But she didn't need an excuse. He'd always show up for her no matter the reason. She only had to ask.

He stepped off the elevator.

And stopped.

Just outside André and Nikki's door stood a huge man, with a military style haircut, dressed all in black, his eyes already on Asa.

Asa recognized him from the morning he'd picked Zara up from the hotel room. He swallowed, his throat suddenly tight.

"Cas, right?" Asa guessed, approaching the bodyguard slowly.

Cas lifted his chin a fraction, grunted, and stepped away from the door so Asa could enter.

If Cas was here that meant…

Fuck.

No really.

Fuck.

He hadn't texted Zara back at all and now he was going to have to look her in the eye and lie. Because no *way* was he going to tell her the truth.

"Uh, yeah. I haven't texted you back because I like you too much and I'm afraid I could destroy your entire career. Because even though I'm aware that I'm a nobody with no hope of ever being anybody, I still think I can make things worse."

Maybe he could leave and come back later. He could tell Nikki he'd lost track of time and just wait outside for Zara to leave…*like a fucking stalker.*

That was somehow a worse idea than telling Zara the truth. Which he still wasn't going to do.

Besides, Cas might be monosyllabic with him, but he might be chattier with Zara (she brought that out in people), and he might tell her.

"Are you here a long time?" Asa asked, not really expecting an answer but shooting his shot.

Cas's steel gray eyes slid him a look. "No."

Cool. Coolcoolcoolcoolcoolcoolcool.

Asa pressed his lips together and nodded. He knocked on the door.

"Have you eaten anything?" Asa asked. "Can I get you some water or a protein shake or something?"

Cas remained unblinking and unamused.

"Okay, well just give a holler if you change your mind," Asa said, widening his eyes at the door.

The door opened and Asa had never been so relieved to see André.

Even though Asa had forgiven him, he still gave André a hard time whenever he saw an opportunity.

André smiled like he knew he'd just been having the world's most awkward conversation with Cas the Bodyguard.

"Asa's here," André announced, stepping aside and letting him through the door.

Cool.

No hiding in the pantry then.

Asa walked the short distance to the living area and all the air left his lungs in a woosh when he saw Zara standing in the sunlight.

The last time he'd seen her she was in his shirt and sweatpants, her face makeup free and hair messy.

Today was different.

Today she was full-blown popstar gorgeous.

In high waisted black dress pants with a dark teal fitted V-neck t-shirt that dipped just a fraction too low. Her black hair was swept up into a twist in the back, showing off the slope of her neck. Her amber gold eyes were lined in black, making them glow. Three silver necklaces adorned her in varying lengths. Two had pendants he couldn't see in detail, and one was a plain thick chain.

He bet that if he were a more devoted fan he'd know more about the necklaces. He made a mental note to look it up later.

What he did know about the woman standing before him was that her eyes got soft when she talked about her family. And that she threw up when her emotions got the better of her.

And he knew that she was funny and intelligent and kind. Probably the most gifted artist of their time. Definitely the most gifted he'd ever met.

And she was twenty-three with an entire life ahead of her that didn't include him—the nearly thirty-year-old washed up wannabe who never got to be.

Wow. Was he feeling sorry enough for himself?

He swallowed and finally met her eyes. It was like looking into the sun.

"Ace of Spades," she said with a half-smile. Her eyes flicked up and down his person and his skin prickled with awareness. "It's good to see you again."

He nodded and tucked his hands in his pockets, changed his mind and crossed his arms over his chest. No, that seemed too defensive. Back in the pockets.

"What's up?" he said going for aloof and casual, but it came out high and squeaky.

Her lips trembled with her withheld laugh.

"Are you okay?" Nikki asked from her seat on the couch.

He lifted his eyebrows and turned to his bestie. "I'm great. How are *you* feeling?" he asked.

Nikki eyed him suspiciously. If anyone in the world was going to be able to read his mind, it would be her.

The question was, would she betray him?

And then baby Amber let out a howl that could break windows.

Thank God for the baby.

Nikki moved to get up, but Asa was already around the front of the bassinet.

And every single ounce of nervous energy left his body as he gazed down at the loudest, most beautiful girl in the world.

He picked up the burp cloth on the edge of the bassinet and then scooped the tiny screaming bundle into his arms.

"Oh, listen to those healthy lungs," he said softly. "So loud. You're gonna change the world with a voice like that."

Amber's cries lessened and lessened, her red face staring up at Asa's. Her little bottom lip jutted out and tears leaked from the sides of her eyes.

He'd never thought about having children. Babies hadn't been on his radar in any capacity. But babies were amazing.

"I don't know how you do that," Nikki muttered. "It's like the moment you two laid eyes on one another, you became besties. I think she prefers you over me."

Asa snorted. "Shut up with that nonsense. Our souls are just very old friends, aren't they?" he cooed to Amber. Her eyes zeroed in on him for a brief second and he could swear she understood him.

Within a week he realized he'd march into battle for this child. He'd die for this child. She had wiggled her way into his soul and he was an absolute goner.

He placed Amber on his chest, her little head resting just below his chin. He discarded the burp cloth knowing she'd more than likely spit up on his Motörhead t-shirt, but he didn't care. It wasn't anything he hadn't done himself. He hummed a tune deep in his chest and started a hip sway that would make his nonna proud. "Does she need to be changed?" he asked softly.

"No, I just changed her," André said coming to look over his shoulder. "She's supposed to be napping. Looks like you're taking care of that."

Asa darted a look to André but the man only had eyes for his baby girl.

"She's so warm," Asa said around a low chuckle.

"I know," André agreed, keeping his voice just as soft. "It's like cuddling a tea kettle."

"The cutest tea kettle ever."

They both chuckled at their shared joke.

Asa glanced at Nikki who was curled into the corner of the couch with Zara leaning into her side. "What?"

Nikki held up her hands, palms out. "Don't mind us. We're just watching the bromance bloom."

"Finally," Zara added with a small smirk.

Asa made a strangled noise, but he didn't argue. His gaze slid to Zara and then away again. For all of his apprehension when he'd first arrived, it felt normal to have her there. Beside Nikki. In their circle of friends and family.

And for all intents and purposes, she seemed completely at ease in that role as well.

Which meant it was only him who had felt weird. And that was only because she'd tried to be his friend and he couldn't handle it.

That was really the problem, wasn't it? His inability to let anyone in.

Even in a small way. And especially if they were involved in music in any capacity.

It was too much of a risk.

It hurt too much when it was over.

His conversation with Shawn earlier came back to him and he wondered if maybe he should shelve the idea of a muse. At least in his case. Arm's length was all well and good but what about times like this? When she was right there, in his life. He'd be inclined to shorten those arms pretty quick.

But maybe even the idea of writing again was the real problem. Maybe he needed to let that part of him stay dead in the grave.

No resurrections.

Zara's phone went off and she silenced it immediately.

"Time to go?" Nikki asked.

Zara pouted. "Yeah. Unfortunately. I'm headed to LA. Logan hasn't moved out of the house yet and says he 'wants to talk.'" She gagged.

Nikki made a face. "Gross. Logan sucks."

Zara nodded but didn't vocally agree.

"You're still with him?" Asa blurted. He shouldn't have said anything. The words had fallen out because he was so surprised.

Zara's golden eyes landed on him and she shook her head. "No. Definitely not. I haven't been taking his calls. Which is why he's playing squatter like a little bitch in the house I paid for." She rolled her eyes. "He said he'll move out if I just talk to him."

"That sounds like a trap," Asa remarked.

"I'm sure it's intended to be one," she agreed. She stood and gathered her purse from the coffee table. "Don't worry about me. I'm sly like a fox." She winked at him.

He felt a smile tug on his mouth. "I'm sure you are," he said around a low chuckle.

She hugged Nikki and fist bumped André. Then she circled around to Asa and the baby. When she placed her hand on Amber's back, it overlapped Asa's.

"I'll see you again soon, baby girl," she whispered to Amber.

Her eyes moved over the sleeping face and then up to Asa. They were standing so close he could feel the heat of her body against his side. Her golden gaze drifted over his features and the back of his neck got hot. Her pink lips were stained red in the center from biting them and he wanted to ask why. What had been causing her to worry so much that she'd made herself bleed? Because they hadn't been that way a week ago.

The smile she'd used on Amber softened into something else and she opened her mouth to say something but stopped. Then she hummed and took a deep breath.

"See you, Asa," she said it like a statement but her eyes made it sound like a question.

"For sure," he muttered.

Her gaze flicked between him and the baby and she took a step back, letting her hand drop.

Nikki walked her to the door and they laughed about something Asa couldn't hear above the roaring in his ears. Once again, being near her had opened up a cavern of possibility and ideas.

The door closed behind her and he took a deep breath.

Arm's length.

* * *

ZARA

"Was everything fine with Nikki and the baby?" Gregor asked.

Zara turned toward her assistant. "Hmm? Oh, yeah. They were great. Why?"

"You're very quiet," Gregor pointed out gently.

"I just have a lot on my mind," she said, flicking her gaze up to see Cas eyeing her from the rearview mirror and then back to G.

The things on her mind couldn't really be put into words yet. If ever. Mostly she was feeling a pang of longing and loneliness that she usually didn't. Watching Asa and Nikki's friendship had unexpectedly plucked at a tender wound in her heart.

When was the last time she'd had that easy a connection? That sweet a friendship?

She liked to think of herself as being a decent friend. But when had she felt someone care about her in the same measure?

These were questions she had no one to ask. And even if she did, she didn't want to know the answer.

But she'd gotten to see Asa and that had been…

She let out a deep breath.

It had been right there, on the tip of her tongue, to ask him why he hadn't replied to her texts.

But as she'd stood there, taking in his tattooed arms, shaggy black hair, short beard, and Motörhead shirt while he held Nikki's baby, she realized how incredibly hot he was.

It was a lot.

He was a lot hot.

Which shouldn't have been a revelation. Rock stars were usually hot. It was in their DNA. But it had taken her by complete surprise.

And you know what hot rockstars usually had?

Girlfriends.

She was so short sighted sometimes.

Of course the hot rock star with the wounded heart had a girlfriend. What woman wouldn't take one look at him and go, "Yeah. That one."

And she'd been texting him nonstop for a week. Like a completely selfish and unaware idiot.

No more texts then. Not until she met the girlfriend and they were on the same page with what was and wasn't okay.

That just made her want to meet the girlfriend now.

She had to be awesome to be with someone like Asa. Besides, Zara had a hundred percent track record with the ladies of XY Records. She was positive she'd be able to win over Asa's lady love too.

Her stomach gurgled and she grimaced.

"Antacid?" Gregor asked.

"Yeah," she agreed, holding out her hand for the tablet he was already dispensing.

"Not looking forward to seeing Logan?" Gregor guessed.

Zara nodded and looked out the window.

Sure. Logan. That's what was bothering her.

Chapter Six
Nice to Know You

ZARA

Her house in Calabasas had been her second in the Los Angeles area. She'd had high hopes when choosing the magnificent mansion with double height ceilings, the wine cave cellar, and enough gorgeous landscaping to offer better than average privacy.

This was the home she'd chosen with Logan and their future in mind. A place for them to be *them*. A place to hide away from the chaos that had been their lives since they were sixteen.

It was also the place he'd brought his first side chick.

Ugh.

She hated that expression.

At the time, she'd been so furious at the other woman. Everyone knew Logan and Zara were together. *Everyone.* They'd been the It couple. Both their camps had made sure of it.

But while Logan had been filming a TV series in LA and Zara had been overseas on tour, he'd convinced his costar they had an open relationship.

And they hadn't been discreet.

Zara had found out five minutes before it had hit the public.

That had been their first breakup.

She'd tried to move past it but she couldn't stop wondering where they'd done it and how many times and if it had been only the one woman or had there been others? She hadn't been able to stay in the house since. Instead, she would stay at a hotel when she was in town.

A few months later, they'd reconciled and but she still couldn't sleep in the Calabasas mansion. Logan didn't have the same issue. He'd basically moved in even though he had his own place in Studio City.

She crossed her arms over her middle and wandered over to the floor-to-ceiling windows near the kitchen that looked into the backyard.

It really was a beautiful place. Peaceful, airy, and bright. It just didn't bring her any peace at all.

"G," she said softly, not wanting Logan to overhear. He'd had to take a call and had stepped away just as they'd arrived.

Gregor stepped closer.

"Let's sell this place, yeah?"

Gregor made a noise in his throat and nodded.

"Sorry about that," Logan rejoined them. "That was Rachelle." His publicist. "She wanted to go over a few things."

Zara took one more breath before turning around to face him. They hadn't spoken since the afterparty and apart from the glimpse she'd caught of him when they'd arrived, they hadn't seen each other either.

Logan Black, former teen heartthrob and three-time winner of the Youth's Pick Award for "best hair." Her first friend in the game, first kiss, first everything. Her gaze drifted over his charcoal button-down, designer jeans, and luxury house shoes. Six feet of white boy, styled dark blonde hair with natural looking professional highlights threaded throughout, and a day's worth of scruff. She'd helped him pick that look years ago.

Her heart pinched with the memory of that young man who had once been so eager and wide-eyed. They'd had so much in common. Raised in Jersey by single parents, had to fight for every opportunity. Both faced with fame at too young an age, they'd clung to one another. Because no one knew what it felt like to be in the middle of it. All they'd had was each other.

Which was probably why she came back again and again.

But not today.

While she still held affection for the person she used to know, she felt nothing for the man standing before her.

Logan slid his hands into his pockets, his eyebrows pitched up. It was his "please believe me, I'm about to lie my ass off" face. She knew it well. His eyes flicked between Zara and Gregor. "I was hoping we could talk in private."

Zara stopped herself from rolling her eyes. "Fine," she said, with a nod in Gregor's direction.

Logan watched her assistant walk towards the front of the house and then waited until they both heard the heavy door close behind him.

He turned those cool gray eyes back on her. "I missed you."

"What do you want to talk about?" she asked, ignoring his statement.

He took a few steps in her direction. "I know this week has been crazy," he said, voice soft. Controlled. "But I really have missed you."

Oh, so he was going to push the issue. Missed her how exactly? She wanted to ask. Because it was very clear Rachelle had made all the shots she'd taken in the press.

"Look, Logan," Zara started, trying to keep her voice neutral. "Let's not make this take longer than it needs to."

His eyes narrowed a fraction. "You have somewhere to be?"

She nodded. Of course she had places to be. She *always* had places to be.

His mouth grew tight and a muscle jumped in his jaw. "So are you with that guy then?"

"What guy?" she asked with a frown.

"The one you left with. Your producer."

Zara blinked, her eyebrows raising slowly into her hairline. "Are you serious?" she asked, being completely genuine.

"I don't get it." Logan shook his head. "He's so old and not even your type. What the hell is that all about? Is this to get back at me for sleeping with Mandy?"

Zara held up a hand, palm facing him as if that would stop the words from reaching her. She licked her lips, blinking several times as she tried to decide what horrible declaration she wanted to address first. "Hold on. Just a second."

The one thing she'd wanted to avoid that day was fighting with him. She didn't want to yell or get so upset it made her sick.

"You know his 'band' never even broke the top one hundred, right?" Logan did the air quotes and everything. "He's a nobody."

"Please, shut the hell up," Zara said, pinching the bridge of her nose. She took a breath and tried to talk herself out of screaming at him.

What was it about knowing someone for so long that patience went right out the window when they acted like an ass? At one time, Logan had been her entire world. She'd never wanted to hurt him or tell him to shut up. But he'd said less than fifteen sentences and she was ready to drown him in the pool out back.

What was she supposed to even say to all that?

Her stomach churned and she pressed a hand to her belly. "You actually slept with Mandy?" she asked.

He shifted uncomfortably on his feet as it dawned on him that she hadn't known about that one.

Truth be told, she wasn't entirely surprised. She and Mandy hadn't been as close after Zara had become friends with Mandy's ex, Sunshine Capone and his wife Sabine.

But damn. It still hurt.

Zara put her hands on her hips and stared sightlessly at the floor, slowly shaking her head. "You know," she started, swinging her gaze up to meet Logan's. "I never cheated on you. Not once. It never occurred to me to be that kind of person." She'd never even slept with anyone besides Logan. Not even the times they were broken up. But she wasn't going to tell him that. She had a feeling his ego would shoot through the roof. He'd assume it had something to do with his sexual ability. It didn't.

"As far as Asa?" She let out a disappointed sigh. "He's none of your business. I don't know why I stay and stay and stay. So many chances. And for what? So you can fuck my friends and live in my house?" She rubbed the fingertips of one hand over her forehead.

"Zara—" Logan started to walk toward her, desperation in his tone.

She stepped back and held up her hand. "No. We're done. There's nothing to talk about. Get your stuff and get out."

"I know you're mad, but if you'd just let me ex—"

"I'm selling the house," she continued over him, staying calm. "Don't call me. Don't do anything really. Not if it involves me."

"Please, Zara," Logan pleaded.

She met his eyes and felt that last small piece of her heart that held onto him with nostalgia and teenage naivety shatter. It didn't hurt. It didn't feel like anything.

"Goodbye, Logan." Her voice came out flat. Dead. Disappointed. He'd been someone else a long time ago. Pretending like he could ever be that person again was foolish.

She glanced around the beautiful house that had never felt like home. Her purse was in the car with Cas. She had nothing to get before she left.

Her footsteps echoed on the marble floor as she headed for the door. Sorrow flashed through her for a brief moment as she realized this was it. She wasn't coming back. Not to this house, not to Logan.

She reached the door, her hand on the solid, bronze handle, thumb on the latch.

"Wait. Please. Just…don't go. Let's talk about this."

She glanced at him over her shoulder. A hundred times she'd been here. A hundred times she'd given it one more conversation, one more try. But she just didn't have it in her to do it again. "No," she said. Then she opened the door and walked away for good.

* * *

She'd gone straight from Calabasas back to NoHo. No stops in Chicago. She was too grumpy and didn't want to inflict that on people she cared about. It was bad enough that Gregor and Cas had to deal with her.

They didn't seem to mind, but she did. She minded. Her ill feelings were her own to deal with. They had hard enough jobs without her being a drama queen. Even though she knew that if she said that to them, they'd roll their eyes and tell her to knock it off.

They were the best.

By the time she'd returned to her penthouse in New York, Logan had already lashed out in a truly epic way.

Just as Sonja had predicted.

Dissatisfied with just using the media as his weapon, he'd turned on her art. He'd filed a claim that he'd written her next album. The one they were getting ready to release.

Zara's lawyer and Sonja had video called her before she'd even set her bag down.

Logan wanted writing credit added to the album which would set him up forever in residuals. They could try paying him off in one large payment. But Zara knew he really wanted her to come back to him.

His life was easier with her. He was trying to force the issue. In one phone call and one fake promise, he'd stop doing this.

But that wasn't going to happen.

About twenty-five percent of her was furious with him for using this tactic. The other seventy-five was dangerously quiet on the subject.

So, her options came down to either adding him in a writing credit on each track, or shelving the album entirely, or fighting him on it. The last one was the least appealing. Logan would make it as public as possible. And even when she won (because that asshat didn't write shit), the damage to her public persona could be catastrophic.

Her label wanted her to choose the first option rather than not release an already produced and paid for album. They'd want to recoup their costs and also make mad cash as they always did with her. She didn't think it was arrogant to recognize how beneficial she was to their entire operation. Sure, they had other artists. But she knew she was the one who kept the lights on.

Seeing as they had planned on releasing the first single in two weeks, she needed to decide what to do soon.

What was one more crisis on her plate, right?

She also needed to deal with the Mandy issue.

"G, how would you handle it if one of your friends had slept with your boyfriend?"

Gregor's look was glacial. "Obviously they were never my friend if they'd done that."

"Fair point."

"So, they'd be relegated to their proper place in my life. Back behind the velvet rope, boo." He blinked his pale blue eyes at her. "Why? Who was it? One of the models?"

He and Kenna always referred to Zara's rotating entourage as "the models" even though only a handful of them were actual models. But in this case, yes. Mandy was one of "the models" and also an actual model.

"Mandy," she said.

Gregor twisted his mouth to the side and squinted. She recognized it as his way of holding back his true opinion on the matter. Which she could about guess.

But he couldn't hold it very long.

"Biiiiitch," he let out in a low hiss.

Zara snickered unexpectedly.

Gregor huffed and pulled out his tablet. "I assume she's out, yes?"

And by "out," she knew he meant more than out of her inner circle. Though, now that she thought about it, Mandy had never been in Zara's *real* inner circle. None of the models were. Her inner circle was really just her dad and sibs. And Nash Ellis but only because he was sort of her mentor in the industry. And Nikki.

Huh.

But Mandy was currently living in Zara's London house. Had been for the past six months.

God, was she really such a doormat? Mandy in the London house, Logan in Calabasas. All of her friends knew they could stay at any of her places for as long as they wanted. Mandy had her own room in the penthouse where Zara currently stood.

"I think I need to make some changes to my open-door policy," she said followed by a tired sigh, flopping down onto her couch.

Part of her wanted to run away.

To just pack a bag and go stay with her dad for a while to get away from all of it. But someone would find out where she was and she'd have to dip out again. Knowing that, she wouldn't even be able to relax while there. She'd just be waiting for the other shoe to drop.

If she wasn't careful, she could easily start to freak out.

And that wouldn't help her at all.

"I'll text Mandy tomorrow and tell her to move out. Wait three days and send her lawyer something official."

"How long do you want to give her?" Gregor asked, making notes on his tablet.

Zara squinted one eye his direction. "I don't know, like a month?"

She didn't miss his tiny eyebrow lift and the jaw tick.

"Is that too much or not enough?"

He raised his eyes to her. "You want my opinion?"

"Always," she answered easily.

He let out a vocal sigh. "I think a month is way too long. If it were me, I'd send Devan" (one of Zara's security detail), "to see her freeloading ass to the curb tonight. But since this is you, maybe a week." He shrugged, a small glint in his eye. "Or I can fly out tonight and do it myself."

And he would.

Gregor had only been with her a year after her former assistant burned out. Not that Zara could blame her; her life was hectic. Cas had brought up Gregor as an option and Zara trusted Cas's judgment. He knew Gregor through work, they'd both served as security for an ambassador many years ago. Gregor was a former army medic with combat experience. Transitioning to civilian life had been hard because he didn't exactly qualify for the jobs he was most proficient in. Private security was one of the only jobs he could get.

Zara had worried that being a popstar's assistant wouldn't be an interesting enough job to make him want to stick around. Gregor had not only excelled but thrived in the position.

Logan had pitched a fit. He didn't like the idea of a smart, attractive, muscly army vet being at her beck and call. It didn't matter that Gregor was gay or that Zara never cheated or even considered cheating.

It hadn't taken very long for Zara to decide Gregor was the world's greatest assistant and she didn't give a shit what Logan thought.

"All right. A week then," Zara said.

Gregor nodded, adding to his notes. "Anything else before I go?

"No, thanks, G. I'm good." She planned on a chill night in with some white wine, a bath in her hammock bathtub, and lots of quiet contemplation.

Gregor nodded and left.

See? She had good people on her team.

The best.

Zara got up and moved to the wine fridge in her kitchen, continuing her plans for the evening. She opened a new bottle of Riesling and poured the appropriate amount into a glass she'd gotten in a set as a gift from Paige and Nash.

She capped the bottle and put it back.

Taking her glass, she went down the hall to the wet room. She didn't use the bath often, because some things still seemed like an indulgence. And a hammock shaped carbon fiber tub that looked like it was floating in the middle of the room was definitely an indulgence.

She added bubbles to the water as it filled the tub and gazed out at the bright city lighting up the night.

The wall that faced the city was made up entirely of mirrored glass so no one could see inside.

She loved New York. Ever since she was little and her dad had taken her into the city to see a Broadway show for her birthday, she'd wanted to live here.

She smiled to herself. The world had seemed so big and exciting back then.

It still was. She was just too damn busy to enjoy it.

Maybe she should shelve the album.

Yeah, it would make her sad and break her heart a little. But she'd rather that, than give Logan anything else that was hers.

But that would mean pissing off her label and probably fans too. They expected a new album soon. She'd have to make something entirely new and that took time.

It was a lot to think about.

Chapter Seven
Stop Making This Hurt

ZARA

Two days later she sat down at a small table in a coffee house in SoHo across from Nash Ellis. Devan and Gregor sat at the table closest to them, Cas at another table nearby.

She'd asked Nash for a meeting, because she still hadn't decided what to do.

Nash Ellis was a rock star.

That was an oversimplification but it painted an accurate picture. He was only a couple years older than Zara and had been in the industry about the same amount of time. His experience had been vastly different from hers. They'd met through mutual friends a couple years ago and since then had struck up an easy friendship. She got along well with his girlfriend Paige and would often run her ideas by Nash if something felt weird. He had the survival instincts of a snow leopard and she trusted his intuition.

She'd woken up that morning, after another terrible night of sleep, with one resounding thought pounding against her temples: she was done playing the game.

She'd been fine with certain tactics and schemes throughout her career. As long as it didn't hurt anyone, she usually signed off on it. But bit by bit, it had taken little chunks out of her. *She* was the one it had hurt.

And she was done.

Two full days of a media onslaught orchestrated by Logan and his people had her feeling overly exposed and misjudged by everyone. From radio DJs, to her fans, to strangers on the internet, suddenly they all had an opinion.

One of the national morning shows had even had a segment devoted to dissecting her. They'd called it "Zara Lorna: Diva Behavior?" People Zara had never met weighed in on her character and her integrity.

"I don't think that she even sings her own songs. I heard she has one of her friends do it. Let's give credit to the real artists and stop popularizing phonies."

"She's incredibly calculated. She knows exactly what she's doing."

"I've never bought the sweet Jersey girl next door persona. I've always thought she was annoying."

"She's just another diva."

"It was apparent after her tirade at the NMAs that her ego has gone unchecked for too long. Remember when Ashton James lost it? Not everyone is mentally equipped to handle the pressure of being famous. She just cracked."

And she was suddenly very over it.

It was a startling thought. She was the kind of person who thought things through, was often accused of scheming when she was just being thorough. She could count on one hand how many times her brain had just decided, with very little to no deliberation. Just a very definitive decision.

It had happened when she was sixteen and had her first single on the radio and her mom had reached out. Because "suddenly" she wanted a relationship with her daughter.

Zara knew at once that she wasn't going to entertain that heartache.

It had happened again when she'd met Nikki. They shared a moment in the studio and Zara's heart went, "This is the human who will tell your story the way you want it told." It was immediate and she didn't doubt it. Those impulses had never, not once, steered her wrong.

It had happened that night at the afterparty when Asa had taken her hand and said, "I got you." She hadn't even had to think about it. She'd just known.

So, when she'd woken up with the very loud and repeating thought of, "I'm done with the game," she was alarmed.

She needed to talk to someone who had done both.

Hannah Lee, aka Ashton James, came to mind.

She'd managed to be at the top, leave, and quietly come back to their industry on her own terms.

But they weren't close. Had only met in passing.

Then there was her friend Nash Ellis.

He'd been up and down and in between. He'd also experienced the worst the internet and industry had to offer.

He hadn't said much since they'd sat down.

His brilliant blue eyes watched her and he listened to every one of her fears and ideas spill out. And spill she did. Like an oil tanker on the highway—messy, messy, not enough Dawn dish soap in the world to help kind of mess.

Finally, she took a breath and sat back. "What would you do?" she asked.

He arched one, pierced eyebrow. "I think you know what I would do." He leaned forward on his elbows and pinned her with a look. "The question is what would *you* do?"

She frowned. If she knew what she should do, she wouldn't be asking him.

But he wasn't done.

"Who do you want to be? At your core? If the people who love your music could see into your heart, what message do you want them to take away?"

She sucked in a breath as his words hit her.

Oh shit.

She hadn't thought about it like that.

"I want them to know they're worthy of love and they don't have to be what other people tell them to be."

"And how are they gonna know that?" he asked.

She touched her lips and her gaze drifted away. "By living it," she whispered.

He sat back and took a sip of his coffee.

She shook her head at his knowing smirk. "You're an ass."

"Yes. But a brilliant ass."

"You are kind of brilliant," she admitted.

"So," he folded his arms on the table. "What would you do if you had no one telling you what to do? No schedules, no albums ready to drop, no paparazzi following you." He waved to the photographer taking a picture of them in the window.

"I'd spend time with my friends. Learn something new. Sleep. Eat." Her voice turned wistful as she indulged the daydream. "I want to bake cookies and learn how to make an omelet. I want to take my dad to Florence because he hasn't been back since he was a kid."

She refocused on Nash and sighed. "But all of that is impossible."

He squinted an eye at her. "Is it?"

She squinted right back. "It could be career suicide."

He nodded. "Maybe." He shrugged. "Or it could be the best thing you've ever done."

"I came to you because I needed advice, not because I was looking for a cryptic puzzle to solve."

"Zara," he said, black eyebrows lifted and all amusement gone. "I can't tell you what to do. That's the exact thing you're upset about. You have to be the captain of your own destiny. If you're happy with the status quo, then don't change anything. Release the single, do the interviews, play the game. You'll win. Guaranteed. You're too good *not* to win. It's not even a risk anymore." He tilted his head to the side. "But maybe risk is what you're missing."

* * *

Hours later she was back at home, staring up at the stars on her ceiling as her mind spun with everything she was supposed to decide.

Her phone rang and she looked at the screen.

Kenna. This would probably be awesome. Not.

"Yeah?" she asked, wondering what she'd done now.

"Pictures of you and Nash Ellis are everywhere. Business or pleasure?" Kenna asked.

"Business," Zara ground out.

"I will alert the masses," Kenna said and hung up.

Zara threw her phone across the room, rolled over and screamed into her pillow.

Her phone rang again from the corner and she growled.

What now? She got off the bed and stomped over to answer it kind of surprised it hadn't broken when she'd thrown it. She really wished she'd taken the time to look at the call screen.

"Who am I dating now?" she asked.

"Hey, babe."

Fucking. Logan.

She went to hang up but he was still speaking and her mind snagged on his words.

"Wait," she stopped him. "What did you just say?"

"I was asking if you wanted to record the remix together or just use your vocals as they are and I'll do mine separate."

The room tilted and her stomach cramped.

"What remix? What are you talking about?" she asked, voice hollow, because she knew. She fucking *knew*.

"'The Under/Over', the single dropping in ten days. The label said they wanted to release a response remix with me for the second version a week after the single releases." He drew out the words like she was a child who needed something simple explained to them. Irritation ran down her spine and she ground her teeth together. "I already have it written. Do you want to hear it?"

"What?" she clipped, trying to understand what he was saying.

He repeated his words but that's not what she was having trouble with. They had gone ahead and made the decision without her?

Why would they do that?

Also, no. She wasn't going to share writing credits with this twatwaffle on a song she'd written for herself and *not him*.

"Disrespectfully, Logan, go fuck yourself," she said and hung up the phone.

She immediately dialed Gregor.

"They sent it through five minutes ago," Gregor said tightly. "I was just calling you."

"So, they told everyone else and me last?" Zara asked even though the answer was obvious.

"What would you like me to do?" Gregor asked, voice low and controlled.

"Team meeting. Everyone. Here. In the morning." She could hardly get the words out without wanting to shout them. Her stomach churned and she took a deep breath.

Gregor promised he'd take care of it and she hung up.

She stared sightlessly at the bedspread as she waited for her stomach to calm down.

Realizing it wasn't going to be that easy, she went to the kitchen and made ginger tea.

* * *

ASA

He really needed to stop reading the news bites. They all said the same thing and he knew none of it was true.

But he clicked the link in his text that had come through from his step-mom. His fucking *stepmom* was sending him this shit.

What happened to Winking Pete?

Asa Young, the former rock star who's been spotted with Zara Lorna multiple times in recent weeks, was once the bass player for a band with a shiny future. They canceled a tour in the middle of it without explanation. But rumors surfaced of drug use, jealousy, and backbiting amongst the members.

CELEBX reached out to Shelby Mallory, the band's former lead singer and she had a lot to say about her former bass player.

"Asa has always been drawn to the most talented person in the room. He gets off on taking credit for other people's ideas. He's definitely using Zara to make himself relevant again."

An interesting take, considering what's being said about Zara Lorna this past week. Perhaps the old saying about "birds of a feather" is true in this case.

Zara Lorna's camp declined to comment.

But the story wasn't real. They had a sliver of a piece of something and had run in the completely wrong direction.

And now Shelby was back in the spotlight again. She had to be loving that.

After he'd seen Zara a few days before at Nikki's, he'd considered sending her the music he'd made. He had almost talked himself into it.

And then additional shit had surfaced.

Now he was more worried about losing his job than what Zara thought of his shitty writing.

"Sorry, that took so long," Johnny said, closing the door to Nikki's office.

Asa closed the article and shoved the phone back in his pocket.

Johnny came around the desk and sat down. "It's been crazy around here," he said.

Asa clenched his jaw and nodded.

It had been crazy because of him.

One of the stipulations for working at XY Records was the utmost secrecy regarding one of the studio's owners who was also Johnny's fiancée.

Hannah Lee James, also known as Ashton James, had been one of the most paparazzi stalked celebrities in the world before she disappeared from the public eye.

She'd been living in Chicago for over a year in anonymity before Johnny's little brother recognized her and opened a whole can of worms. Now three years later, she was part owner and production partner of the small studio.

But to keep the media out of her life, strict rules had been applied. She used aliases when she produced albums. Her security routinely went through the backgrounds of employees and anyone who came into the studio. Asa had had his entire life sifted through and dissected before he even filled out his W-2s.

But that was the gig.

Working for XY Records meant you were probably going to be exposed to the biggest names in the industry and no one would ever know.

Which Asa was perfectly fine with.

He was done chasing that fame monster.

But now that he'd been spotted with Zara and the press that had followed, he couldn't help but think this meeting with Johnny was going to be his walking papers.

He ignored the tightness in his chest. Or tried to. But a slight buzz had begun in the back of his mind.

He hadn't even wanted this job! He'd been doing just fine being a no-one. Not making music, not creating anything for anyone. Just playing someone else's songs three times a week at the Blue Iguana. He had been. Just. Fine.

And then Nikki had asked him for a favor, saying it would be "good for him to get back into it."

He should have said no.

"Look," Asa started, clenching his sweaty hands into fists in his lap. "I know—"

He was interrupted by a light knock on the door. It opened and Hannah stepped inside, closing it behind her.

Asa temporarily forgot what he had been about to say.

Hannah Lee James was quite possibly the most terrifyingly beautiful woman he had ever seen. Maybe in all of existence.

Her long dark hair cascaded over her shoulders and down her back. She wore black jeans and a soft blue sweater that made her icy blue eyes even brighter.

She smiled at Asa and came around the desk as Johnny stood. She took his seat and he stood behind her, brushing her hair with his fingertips.

Shit.

He'd been worried about being fired?

Hannah was probably going to murder him.

She had a reputation for being able to verbally eviscerate a person.

He'd never experienced it, but he'd heard stories.

And the part that really sucked about his impending unemployment was that he actually *loved* his job. Sure, maybe all he did was write and mix jingles, but he got to work with people who loved the same things he did. Whose entire lives existed in a creative space. Even if he hadn't been brave enough to flex his creative muscles beyond commercial jingles, he still enjoyed seeing others excel at it.

"Asa," Hannah said, gentler than he expected.

He wiped his palms on the top of his jean clad thighs.

"You're in a bit of a pickle," she said.

"I'm really sorry," he said.

Her striking blue eyes narrowed slightly. "Why? Have you been moon-lighting as a writer for CELEBX?"

"No?" He cleared his throat. "No, of course not."

A ghost of a smile graced her lips. "I have this…associate. He makes sure I stay invisible. I've asked him to look into what we can do for you."

Asa struggled to swallow. "Okay…?

"You don't own any property," Johnny joined the conversation. "Your cell phone plan is routed through Nikki's name which disappears in the XY Records business account. You still live at Nikki's house, so you're not on any leases. You had a Mazda you sold last year but it was registered at an address in southern Illinois. Nikki told me you ride a motorcycle now…?"

"It's in my dad's name," he croaked. It was kind of creepy how much they knew about him. But those would all be public records; anyone could find them.

Ohhh. Anyone could find them.

"It's common knowledge that you work for us. Except last year, Hannah's *associate* created a satellite studio that doesn't really exist in Miami. Last week we put your name on the employee roster there."

Asa frowned. "So I'm being transferred to Miami?"

"No. Miami doesn't exist. But that's where they'll look for you," Johnny said.

"Al—er, my associate thought it would be a good idea to put your name on a condo lease down there as well."

"I don't understand," Asa said.

"We hid you. From anyone looking, really. Now, unless you tell anyone, no one knows you live and work here in Chicago."

"But what happens when they get to Miami and I'm not really there?" Asa asked, a vibration starting in his hands.

Hannah blinked at him. "Do you trust me?" she asked.

He opened his mouth and then closed it.

He barely knew her. She didn't know him.

"Why are you doing this?" he asked.

"You're a part of our team," Johnny said like the answer was obvious. "And something like this was bound to happen to one of us anyway. It was easy to put this together because the provisions had been made long ago."

"I'm a paranoid, high maintenance woman," Hannah said matter of factly. "My backup plans have backup plans."

"You're not gonna fire me?" Asa asked, hearing the strain in his voice.

Hannah's face softened. "No, Asa. We want you to stay."

He exhaled with his entire body.

"We do need to know if there's something…" Johnny searched for the right word. "Significant about your relationship with Zara Lorna."

Asa's stomach tightened again. So much for relaxing. His mind raced with all the ways he could answer that question.

Significant?

Maybe. But it was only on his side. And it was more like a professional crush than anything else. Still, he didn't want to lie and then get caught. Though he had no idea how he'd get caught.

Being hyperaware of truth tended to make him overshare and over explain.

After a beat of silence, Hannah pursed her lips. "There's no wrong answer, Asa. Zara attracts a certain amount of attention. So, if say, she starts making trips to Chicago to visit someone, we could prepare for that ahead of time. Get in front of it. Also, I can talk to her myself and make sure we're all on the same page."

This was just getting better and better, wasn't it?

Asa's head swam with possibilities. The last thing he wanted was to put even more on Zara's plate.

"No. There's nothing significant there," he finally said. It was the truth, but his gut reacted like it was a lie.

He was way too into her.

He could see that clearly now.

"She's good friends with Nikki. I was just in the right place at the right time and it got spun into something else. We don't have contact otherwise."

"Okay." Hannah nodded. She sounded like she believed him, but there was a subtle shrewdness in her gaze that made him squirm.

He needed to make what he said the absolute truth.

Not just to save his own ass, but Zara's as well.

* * *

Z: I hope you're okay. I keep thinking about you. I know that probably doesn't make sense. My publicist told me what's been happening. I'm so sorry. Let me know if there's anything I can do.

He had been staring at the text for an hour.

She was too sweet for her own good.

This was why people kept taking advantage of her. Because she honestly cared about others.

Thinking back to his first assumptions of her, he wanted to kick his own ass. She wasn't spoiled or entitled. She was a very talented artist who worked hard and deserved to have that hard work recognized.

He wasn't going to be one more person taking advantage of her goodness.

But it was easier said than done.

Which was why he'd spent an hour sitting on the back porch, in the growing cold, listening to the sounds of the city, and avoiding what he knew he needed to do.

His thumb hovered over the delete button on her text thread. He bit the inside of his cheek. He *knew* it was the right call, to sever all connections with her. He was only hesitating for selfish reasons.

He hit the button and watched the thread disappear from his phone.

He took a deep breath of cold air and found her contact information.

The night they hung out, sharing secrets and ideas and space flashed through his mind once more. Just because he deleted her contact information didn't mean he deleted that moment. He'd be able to call it up whenever he needed something to make him smile.

Because no matter what the media reported or what rumors were shared, that was a moment that was all theirs. It had been real and he had been there.

He deleted her contact.

There.

It was done.

He dropped his phone in his lap and crossed his arms over his chest.

It was too cold. He should go back inside.

Chapter Eight
Gold Rush

SIX MONTHS LATER

ASA

Routine was one of things he was always going to loathe needing.

He wished he could be fine with no schedule, no plan, no system. But every time he tried to live wild and free, he ended up depressed.

And not a little depressed but a lot depressed.

Routine kept him—well, not exactly *happy* but not unhappy.

Routine kept him. End of sentence.

It had taken him years to understand that about himself. And just because he understood it didn't mean he liked it.

So maybe it was good that his band and all of his hopes and dreams had imploded years ago. Because getting everything he wanted probably would have killed him.

How's that for irony?

Six months ago, after the Zara Lorna, NMAs, CELEBX incident, he'd realized he needed just a little more in his routine to occupy his mind. Otherwise he found himself scrolling the internet endlessly reading everything about her that he could.

So, he'd muted her name and Black's name on all his socials. Then, when he still couldn't seem to stop checking, he'd deleted his socials.

He'd started rock climbing and bouldering with his friend Steinhoff. They used to do that when they were younger and he'd gotten away from it. Coming back to it at thirty was a harsh reminder that his body was aging and if he didn't start using it, it was going to waste away.

He'd stopped playing at the Iggy. It was just too hard to go back to music even after the gossip sites had cooled down. Creating music, existing in that space had only ever led him to pain and chaos.

Hannah and Johnny had given him more managerial duties at the studio. They tried to gently nudge him into working with indie artists that needed some guidance but he kept dodging it.

He was the last person who should be giving advice.

But the jingles kept him busy. Sometimes he'd get a bonus if a client liked his work.

It wasn't what he thought he'd be doing with his life. But he liked it enough to keep going.

He was currently on the shave part of his day.

Which was why he was having existential thoughts about routine. Looking at himself in the mirror often prompted an internal conversation.

Especially since he still wasn't used to seeing himself with a beard.

It wasn't a mountain man beard. It was short and thick; he had to trim it every day or it got out of control quickly.

But sometimes he'd see himself and think he looked way more grown-up than he felt.

Hopefully how he appeared would eventually take over how he felt.

The sounds of power tools and boots scraping on bare wooden floors in another part of the house had also been a prompt for his pragmatic conversation.

The routine was about to be interrupted.

And he wasn't sure how he felt about that.

Actually, that wasn't true. His life was about to be upended and he knew exactly how he felt about it.

He hated it.

But he'd told Nikki he was fine with it.

And so now he was trying to turn his lie into the truth. He *wanted* to be fine with it.

Nikki and André were getting close to finishing the renovations on the house. And that meant Asa needed to move out. He had known this was coming. But he hadn't even started looking for a place because he was in denial.

But at least he *knew* he was in denial.

That was better than denying he was in denial. Right?

At least that's what he told himself.

He had a couple more months and then it was so long, farewell, goodbye to ol' Asa Young and his time at the Lil Snug House.

Al had left first, followed by Steiny.

Nikki had been living at André's apartment since they'd gotten married (the audacity). Leaving Asa in the huge old Victorian all alone.

So far he hadn't been able to find anyone else he wanted to be roommates with, so he was going to have to look for a small apartment for just him.

He rinsed his face, patted it dry, and put his glasses back on.

Loud laughter and voices rang through the house followed by the sound of a drill. Or maybe a power saw. He had no idea. He was a musician, not a carpenter.

Or at least he used to be a musician. Now he was just a button pusher.

He went into his room and removed the towel from around his waist, tossing it on the bed.

This room was new for him; his old room had been upstairs. Most of his stuff was still up there. But when Steiny had moved out, Asa had moved down to the larger bedroom because it was connected to a bathroom.

And also, he really wanted the "big" room before he had to move out.

He was such a child sometimes.

He was still sleeping in a twin sized bed for example. Though that made it easier to move around. Maybe someday he'd get himself a "big boy bed."

It did make for awkward moments in dating.

He reached for his boxers and paused.

Was the wall moving?

Nah.

He squinted at the far wall. The one he shared with the dining room.

For a second, he thought he saw it sway. That couldn't be right.

He held his breath and waited.

Okay. That had definitely moved. Like a banner in a light breeze, the wall to his room moved ever so slightly back and forth.

A loud thud caused him to jolt. Dust and plaster puffed out of places in the wall. Another thud. Followed by another.

Someone was knocking down his wall.

His mouth opened to shout—something, he didn't know what—but it was too late.

Plaster and sound exploded inward and knocked him on his ass.

He didn't move for at least a minute as his mind tried to process what had just happened. He coughed and waved futilely at the white cloud covering his vision.

What. The. Fuck?

"Nikki!" he yelled.

"Oh my God! Asa?"

He could hear her, but he couldn't see her.

He couldn't see anything.

He coughed again, harder.

Plaster dust settled slowly around him like miniscule snowflakes in a snow globe.

"Asa, are you okay?"

Was he okay?

He continued to cough and pushed his glasses to the top of his head.

It didn't help much. He was still surrounded by a cloud of white dust. Like a wizard's house party in his bedroom.

"Asa?" Nikki's voice came closer.

"I'm not—" He stopped and growled, looking around at the remains of the bedroom. "I'm not wearing…anything."

He struggled to his feet. Chunks of plaster and splintered wood rolled off him. He brushed away some of the debris but it made no difference. He was covered.

Bleck. It was in his mouth.

He coughed more.

What the fuck had Nikki done now?

"Asa! I thought you were at work!" Nikki hollered through the fog.

Right. If he'd been at work what? He'd *not* notice an entire wall of his bedroom was gone?

He found his damp towel among the rubble and quickly covered himself.

"What the fuck happened?" he asked, stepping through the mess and ignoring the way it cut at his bare feet.

"Are you mad? You sound mad."

That wasn't Nikki.

He cleared his room and stepped into the sunlit workspace that used to be a formal dining room.

Nikki, in safety goggles and a hot pink work helmet, and gray workman's overalls, held an electric saw in one hand.

"So the thing is—" she started to say.

"You took a fucking wall out of my room?" he said—more like yelled. "You didn't think I'd notice? I'd come home from work and think, 'Oh, right. This is normal. Don't see anything wrong here.'"

Nikki made a face. "It wasn't supposed to disintegrate like that."

"What the fuck was it supposed to do?"

He was swearing a lot. Even for him.

But the adrenaline of nearly dying had kicked in and he didn't have anywhere else to put it.

"I was *naked*," he yelled. "I could have lost my dick and balls! The only real friends I have left!"

"That's not even your room! Steiny moved out! How was I supposed to know you'd be in there *naked!*" Nikki yelled right back.

"It was my fault."

Asa swallowed and finally looked at the other person standing in the room. He had assumed it was André, Nikki's husband.

He had assumed wrong.

The figure held up a hand and wiggled their fingers. His glasses were still on his head so his vision was too impaired to know for sure who it was.

But there were literally only three people in the world he didn't want to see standing in his home. Two of them, Nikki would never let through the door. The other though?

"Zara." He heaved a sigh, ignoring the way his fingers tingled and his skin heated. "You're the last person I expected to try to castrate me."

"Okay, let's all calm down," Nikki said, suppressing a laugh. "We need to find you some pants, bud."

"Castrate you?" Zara replied, her voice that low, husky timber that drove him crazy. Somewhere between seductive and bored. A trademark of her brand and one of the reasons she was the most famous and successful singer in the industry. And also why even though he'd been avoiding her and any mention of her, she still showed up in his dreams every once in a while. "I would never."

Asa shook his head and turned around to go back into his room, knowing full well that both Nikki and Zara were going to get an unobstructed view of his ass since he hadn't wrapped the towel fully around himself. They could kiss it for all he cared.

"Whoa. Asa. Pants," Nikki sputtered.

He stomped as best he could in bare feet over crumbling plaster and the remnants of the wall back into his room. Or what used to be his room.

"I have to shower again. I'm going to be late."

"Wait." Nikki followed him. "Please don't shower. All that plaster in these old pipes?"

He dropped his glasses back onto his face but that was worse, so he shoved them back up again. He turned to scowl at her. "And what do you suggest?" he asked.

"You look like Santa," she said, really testing the limits of their friendship.

She snorted and he glared harder.

"I'll call Johnny and let him know you'll be late while you go out back and have Zara hose you off."

"You've got to be kidding me," Asa replied.

"I think that's a great idea," Zara contributed. "I am an excellent hose wielder."

His lip curled in her general direction, annoyed that she was there. Annoyed that he was happy to see her. Annoyed that she was adorable no matter what the circumstances.

"I'm really sorry," Nikki said, dropping her voice. "I really didn't know you were using this room. Also, the wall wasn't supposed to come down like that. I had a whole plan. It was—never mind. That's not important now."

Asa closed his eyes and dropped his head.

"Just go get hosed off and I'll have this cleaned up before you get home tonight. I promise."

He didn't reply. Not with words. He sighed and adjusted his towel so it was wrapped more securely around his waist. What did Nikki expect? For him to get fully nude in front of Zara Lorna in the backyard while she hosed him down?

If you'd asked him yesterday what his worst nightmare was, he would never have come up with that scenario. And yet there it was.

He picked his way carefully through the construction of the old house and headed towards the back door.

Nikki had always worked on it, trying to fix it up. But after she got married last year and then immediately got pregnant, her motivation seemed to go into hyperdrive. She wanted to finish the house. Either for herself or to sell it, she hadn't decided.

He knew him having to move out was fast approaching. He hadn't realized it was happening today.

Not that she would make him leave. But he couldn't take it anymore.

The stress of living in a place that was chaotic and unpredictable? No. He needed his home to be his. He needed quiet and peace and not walls collapsing and nearly killing him.

"Where is good?" he asked, stopping in the soft green grass of the backyard.

At least their fence was tall enough that no neighbors could see.

At least it was a warm spring and not a frigid Chicago winter.

At least he had very little shame left to his name.

"Right there is fine," Zara said from somewhere behind him. "I'm just getting…the thing." She grunted and puffed as she labored to get the hose where she wanted it.

He was not going to help.

He was never helping her again.

Once.

He'd helped her once and even that had been too much.

* * *

ZARA

"Brace yourself."

It was the only warning she gave before she sprayed his face with cold water.

She did not enjoy how he gasped and shivered and growled.

She took no pleasure in his discomfort. Nor did she think it was funny to see him covered in plaster, including his glasses.

That would be rude.

If she'd have known he was naked on the other side of the wall, she would *not* have hit it even harder with the sledgehammer.

Nope. No way.

Because she didn't wish horrible things on anyone.

Not on people she disliked such as her ex, or the press that seemed to judge her (incorrectly) for every little decision she made. But especially not on people she liked.

Even if they had ghosted her and never once returned a text.

As comical as it was to see a grown man looking like a powdered donut, she really hadn't meant to do any harm.

She'd just been trying to get some feelings out with a sledgehammer at the suggestion of one of her best friends.

The plaster rinsed free of his skin, revealing unexpected muscles and a deep tan on his olive skin.

Huh.

She hadn't seen that coming.

Asa had never struck her as the muscular type. Glasses, thick black hair, usually in jeans and a band tee of some kind. Or a flannel. Sure, he had that hot rockstar persona but… Had she just *forgotten* how hot he was?

The last thing she thought lurked under his clothes was a very defined six-pack, rock hard pecs, thick thighs, defined biceps, and round shoulders. She could now see the tattoos on his arms. He had two full sleeves that stopped at the curve of his shoulder. No tattoos anywhere else on his sun-darkened olive skin.

Dark hair sprinkled his chest and trailed down to the towel he still held around his junk. The towel that *had* been wrapped around his waist but she'd managed to spray free.

"Turn around so I can get your back," she said, hearing the amusement in her voice and wondering if he'd comply.

He did. After a glare in her general direction, he slowly turned to reveal a tight, round booty and back muscles that said he worked out. Or something. Also, his hamstrings were like rugby hamstrings.

She stopped spraying him for a moment.

"Do you play rugby?" she asked.

He frowned at her over his shoulder. "No. Are you done?"

She rolled her eyes and turned the water back on. His shoulders flinched with the cold water's return.

"I have some clothes for you," Nikki said, appearing next to Zara. "Oh," she said, seeing Asa's glorious butt. "That's not—" She shook her head and glanced at Zara.

Zara shrugged, a smirk creeping along her lips.

Asa had a beautiful booty.

"I think you got it all," Nikki said.

Zara reluctantly shut off the sprayer. Asa turned around as Nikki handed him a fresh towel.

Nikki set the pile of clothes on a nearby lawn chair and motioned for Zara to turn around.

Fine. Zara dropped the hose, crossed her arms and faced the house.

After a few minutes, Asa walked past them into the house. Fully dressed.

Nikki grimaced and raced after him.

"Asa, I'm so sorry."

Zara trailed after them.

Asa stopped at the front door to put on his shoes.

He still had plaster in his beard.

Which was new.

She'd never seen him with that much facial hair. It probably looked good without all the extra stuff in it.

"It is what is, Nik," he said. "I'll make some calls and see if I can find a couch to crash on." He straightened and ran his hand through his wet hair. It was longer than the last time she'd seen him six months ago. "Maybe I can sleep at the studio while I look for a place to live."

"Asa," Nikki whispered, worry and pleading in her voice.

He lifted his eyebrows. "I don't get it. What was even the plan?" He waved a hand back towards the remnants of the wall. "And why are you even here?" he addressed Zara. "Aren't you supposed to be getting ready for a huge album release?"

Zara opened her mouth. Closed it.

Nikki looked between them, struggling with whether or not to reveal Zara's secrets. "She needed to vent. I needed to take down a wall. I thought it would help."

That was essentially the truth.

Asa narrowed his brown eyes at Zara. "Forget I asked." An exasperated sound rumbled from his chest.

Was he mad at her for the wall? Or was there more there?

They hadn't even spoken in six months. And the last time they'd seen each other she thought they were maybe becoming friends. She had told him things. Things she didn't talk about because of the way she was afraid people would look at her. And he'd listened without judgment. Or so she'd thought. But then when she'd tried texting him over the next few weeks, he'd never replied.

She could take a hint.

But mad at her? That seemed excessive.

It had to be because of the powdering of his donuts.

She'd figure out a way to make it up to him.

Asa's eyes flicked to Nikki and back to Zara. He swallowed, shook his head, and left without so much as a wave.

Nikki sighed and dropped her head back to look at the ceiling.

"So does he play on a sports team or something?" Zara asked, her mind lingering on Asa's *assets*.

Nikki rolled her head to look at her. "What?"

"His muscles." Zara shrugged. "Just trying to figure out where they come from."

Nikki's frown deepened. She righted her head and faced Zara. "His muscles?"

Zara shrugged. "Asa's hot. I had no idea."

Nikki screwed her face up like Zara had just said that pizza was over-rated. "He is not."

"Okay," Zara said, though her tone said she did not agree.

"You know," Nikki said, tapping her chin, eyes narrowed suspiciously. "I still haven't heard the full story of what happened that night in LA."

Zara blinked slowly, keeping her expression neutral.

If Asa hadn't told his best friend about that night, she wasn't going to do it.

Besides, she believed that night had been for her and him and no one else. She couldn't speak for Asa, but she knew what it had meant to her.

And it wasn't up for interpretation.

"How about we clean up Asa's room before he kills both of us? And then

I can come over tonight and snuggle that baby," Zara suggested with a crooked smile.

Nikki's suspicion melted away with the mention of her baby.

Easy as pie.

Unfortunately that's where easy ended.

Asa's bed was coated in plaster and debris. And the room itself was not suitable for sleeping. Zara and Nikki had to wear masks so they could breathe.

They cleaned the room out as best they could though.

Zara gathered the bag they'd filled with rubble and hauled it outside. Nikki and André had gotten a dumpster for their renovation rubbish and Zara hurled the bag in. It landed with a thud.

She dusted off her hands and removed the face mask and safety glasses. She tipped her head back, closed her eyes, and stood in the warm, late morning sunshine.

It was weird to not have her security with her. Scary. But also, freeing.

It wouldn't last.

She was too famous and people were too predictable for her to be without an escort for any length of time.

But for that moment, she was just Zara.

Not the award-winning pop star, nor the focal point of every media publication for the past six months.

For one small breath she was neither amazing nor villainous. She just was.

Her team knew. Sonja, Gregor, Kenna, her dad, Cas. But no one else. Not really.

After what had happened in LA and everything that followed, she'd decided to pivot. And not in a small way. She needed space. And time. And to be around people who didn't rely on her for their paycheck or clout.

One night on the phone, lamenting to Nikki about how suffocated she felt, Nikki had invited her to Chicago. To come see the baby and just chill for a bit.

No agenda, no album, no interviews.

And for the first time in months, Zara had felt the pressure in her chest ease.

She'd already shelved her unreleased album. But getting out of New York seemed like the next best step.

Gregor had worked with Cas to find her a place in East Lincoln Park. They leased it under an alias hidden under an alias, buried in an LLC that didn't have her name attached to it.

As long as she didn't go out into busy public spaces, she could pretend for a minute she wasn't the most watched woman on the planet. At least for a while.

A black SUV pulled up alongside the curb at the end of the block. Zara shielded her eyes from the sun as she watched her longtime bodyguard Cas step out. Bodyguard number two, Devan, exited the passenger side and pushed her aviator shades to the top of her head.

Zara waved once. Cas nodded.

They didn't approach. Devan, dressed in jeans and a loose casual tee that hid whatever superhero contraptions she carried on her person, started walking away from Zara. Scouting the area, checking for threats, seen and unseen.

It was the best Zara could have hoped for.

They were trying to give her the space she'd asked for, sobbed for.

But they also needed to keep her safe.

And after the stalker that was found sleeping in her bed in LA a couple weeks ago, they wouldn't let her be alone for too long.

All the negative attention in the media had emboldened the already unhinged. Threats increased; stalking incidents went up. And she'd started to feel like she couldn't go anywhere without someone trying to scream at her because they felt entitled to.

There were a lot of people who truly believed she deserved to be hurt for the things Logan had accused her of.

She understood on some level that it wasn't really about her. Those types of people were loose cannons in all areas of their lives. But they'd fixated on her and that made it very dangerous.

Taking another deep breath of fresh air, Zara went back inside.

"I really don't think Asa is going to be okay with this," Nikki said, surveying the work they'd done.

Zara concurred.

What self-respecting human would?

"I thought he was still living upstairs," Nikki repeated for the twenty-fifth time.

"I'm sure he doesn't think you did this on purpose," Zara pointed out. "It was obviously an accident."

"Yeah," Nikki said, not sounding as convinced. "It's just," she turned to face Zara. "I worry about him, you know. We've been friends forever and now that I'm married, and Steiny and Al are gone, he's all alone. And it feels like my fault."

"I'm the one that knocked the wall down," Zara pointed out.

"But I handed you the sledgehammer and said, 'let 'er rip.'"

They both chuckled.

"Oh man," Nikki pressed her palm to her forehead. "What am I gonna do? He can't sleep on the couch at work!"

Zara opened her mouth but closed it because she couldn't just make an offer. She had to check with Cas first. And she was trying to get away from being the type of person who gave and gave and gave to those who really didn't care about her at all.

But she had an enormous house that was well-furnished. It had several unused rooms and the girl that grew up in Jersey saw that as a waste.

Instead, she said, "I'll help you think of something."

"This has been his home for *years* Nikki said softly. "I am the *worst* friend."

"Oh, my goodness," Zara said. She grabbed Nikki by her shoulders and looked her in the eye. "You are not the worst friend. This is a terrible set of events and we can solve this, yeah?"

Nikki nodded sadly. "Yeah, okay."

"Maybe he can rent a room from me," Zara said despite her earlier reservations on sharing that idea. "I have the space."

Nikki's blue eyes turned wary.

"I'll have to run it by Cas before I mention it to him, obviously."

Her security would have a fit.

They'd crawl so far up Asa's ass that when he brushed his teeth, he'd be brushing Cas's too.

Zara crossed one arm and rubbed her chin with the opposite hand. "I am the one who swung the hammer that destroyed his bed," she pointed out. "It's the least I can do. It's not like you can invite him to stay with you and André."

"No," Nikki agreed.

André and Nikki lived in a loft apartment. It was the perfect size for two people. But then they'd added baby Amber. Which was why they were pushing to finish the house. So, it could be a home for them.

Nikki's gaze sharpened on her. "He'll want to know why you're sticking around."

"Probably."

Nikki sniffed a laugh and shook her head.

"I'm surprised you haven't told him yet," Zara teased. Nikki was known for talking too much. But Zara liked to think of it as "chaotic sharing." She loved the freedom with which Nikki lived. Flat out and full of heart.

Zara needed more of that in her life.

"Oh, I probably would have by now if he'd asked." Nikki shrugged.

Meaning Asa didn't care enough to ask.

Why did that make Zara a little bit sad?

Chapter Nine
Paper Fish

ASA

"People are the worst," Asa announced as he entered the upstairs lounge a week later.

"Uh-oh," Nikki replied, moving aside so he could get to the coffee maker.

"Uh-oh is right." Asa took off his jacket and tossed it over the back of a chair. "I am so screwed."

He nodded good mornings to Johnny and Justin who sat on the couch with coffee already in hand.

The morning meeting at the studio was mostly routine. Sometimes they discussed what was on the docket for the day, but usually it was coffee and shooting the shit.

Asa had almost been late because he'd been busy finding out he'd been scammed out of his first and last month's rent plus deposit on the only place he'd been able to afford.

The worst part was how stupid he felt. How had he fallen for such an obvious con? He was smarter than that!

Wasn't he?

His brain had been a mess for seven days. Every other thought was about Zara. Why had she been in Chicago? What was going on with her album?

Why did she look so sad?

"Is this because of the apartment?" Nikki asked.

Asa grabbed the half and half from the fridge before answering her.

"There is no apartment. Well, the apartment exists. But the person who I gave all my money to doesn't have the authority to rent it." He got a cup off the shelf and added the cream.

"Oh no!" Nikki covered her mouth with a hand.

"Yep." He let the word end in a pop.

"You can stay at the house for longer," she said quickly.

Asa rubbed his fingers over his forehead. "No, Nik," he said softly. "You have to finish your house. You have plans."

"You can stay there until you have enough money to move out," Nikki pressed.

"Nikki," he said, pain radiating through his brain as he thought about the amount of money he'd lost that day. And it wasn't even nine in the morning yet. "It was fifteen grand. It cleaned out my savings. That'll take me months to recoup. Not to mention I have to buy a new bed." He made a face as he poured coffee into the cup. It would take longer than Nikki realized because he hadn't told her he quit the Iggy and he'd been turning down extra jobs from Johnny. "Did you know how much mattresses go for these days? Because I didn't."

He squeezed his eyes shut and tried not to let the overwhelming feeling of dread take over.

"I'm gonna have to move back in with my dad and stepmom," he croaked. "In the *burbs*."

"No, that's crazy," Nikki argued. "You're too punk rock for the suburbs. You'll never survive. We'll think of something."

God, she was so optimistic.

Fuck he missed living with her.

But living with your friends forever wasn't realistic.

Nikki married her soulmate and now they had a baby and she was the happiest he'd ever seen her.

Shit. Now he felt like crap for even thinking about how it used to be.

He really didn't want to move in with his dad for two enormous reasons. First, he got along better with his retired police detective father when they didn't see each other often. Second, Dad still had somewhat of a relationship with Shelby. Asa didn't need to make it easier for Shelby to find him. Christmas Day had proved that. Again.

"What's going on?"

Asa turned at the sound of her voice, knowing it was her, and yet still shocked when she was indeed standing in the doorway of the lounge.

He nearly swallowed his tongue. What was she doing there?

His eyes connected with Johnny's and he could read the man's question that echoed his own.

"What are you still doing here?" he asked with *way* more force than was necessary.

Zara's eyebrows lifted and she made a face. "Still mad about your powdered donuts I see."

Nikki snorted and Johnny and Justin pretended to study something interesting on the ceiling.

"Cool. So, everyone's heard about that," Asa said. He closed his eyes and focused on getting the coffee into his mouth and therefore caffeine into his bloodstream.

When he opened his eyes again, she was still there.

In black skinny jeans that had rips along her thighs. Her shirt was a black graphic tee with the words "chaotic good" on it. She'd tied it into a knot off center, showing the barest hint of golden skin at her midriff.

Her black hair was in a loose bun at the nape of her neck and she wore big silver hoops in her ears. Along with three silver necklaces of different lengths. One with a wolf's cross pendant that nestled at the notch in her throat. One was a plain, thick chain, and one was a silver oval pendant with a rose on the front and a Z engraved on the back that hung lower than the rest.

He knew way more about those necklaces than he should because even though he hadn't been texting her, he'd watched every single fucking interview he could find before he'd muted her on everything.

He knew the wolf's head made her feel brave. And the pendant was from her grandmother to remind her of where she came from.

"Asa got scammed on his new apartment," Nikki ever so helpfully informed her. "He needs a place to live."

Zara gave Asa a look.

He should have braced.

"You can move in with me."

Asa smelled burning rubber as his brain short-circuited.

Wait.

Hold up.

Stop.

Seriously stop.

"Asa?"

He glanced up to see her dipping her head to try and meet his eyes, a concerned expression on her face.

"What?"

The grin she flashed him did something funny to his chest.

Asa swallowed and his gaze bounced from person to person, looking for an ally.

"I can't just move in with you," he finally sputtered.

"Why not?" Nikki asked.

"Yeah. Why not?" Zara repeated, crossing her arms over her chest.

"Because it would be…weird," he replied haltingly.

"How?" Nikki and Zara asked at the same time.

Johnny snorted.

Asa pointed between Nikki and Zara. "Not loving this dynamic."

Zara's lips quirked and her eyes sparkled.

She looked less sad than she had the other day, which eased something in his chest. But there was still a tightness around her eyes he didn't like. And he absolutely could not ask about.

"You've been sleeping on the sofa in control room X, haven't you?" Johnny asked, entering the conversation.

Asa slowly slid his eyes over to his boss. Johnny was trying to hide his smile behind his coffee cup.

"You have not," Nikki said, whacking Asa in the bicep.

He glared at Johnny before turning the glare on his best friend.

"First, *ow.* Second, it's fine." Even if it was causing a pinch in his neck that probably added to his dour mood. "It's just sleep. I still shower and everything at the house. For now."

Zara moved further into the lounge and opened the fridge. The ease with which she moved around his place of employment was unnerving. She moved like she belonged there.

He didn't like that he liked it so much.

She got out the half and half and poured herself a cup of coffee, using the last of it. Without saying anything, she rinsed the carafe, tossed the used filter, and made a fresh pot. Perfect coffee etiquette.

"I have a place in East Lincoln Park. It's enormous. Already furnished. Which gives you time to save money and buy a new bed without having to sleep on a couch." She faced him and leaned a hip against the counter.

It took him a second to process what she'd said.

"I have so many questions." He ran a hand through his hair and stared at the floor.

What about her release? Wasn't she supposed to be announcing a single any day now? *Why was she still here?*

"Let me see if I can guess what those questions are." Zara squinted one eye and looked upward. "What about the album that's supposed to be dropping soon? Don't you have obligations? Aren't you supposed to be planning a tour to support the new album? What about the three-year schedule? Are you crazy? What does your manager think? What did your dad say? Are you sure you're feeling all right?"

She took a drink of her coffee and flattened her mouth. "Did that cover it?"

Asa grimaced. Because those were a lot of the questions he had. But not all of them.

"Well," Zara went on. "I can tell all of you because you're my inner circle at this point."

Asa and Johnny exchanged a look.

"The album is…" Zara made a slicing motion with her hand near her neck accompanied with a clicking sound. "Done. I pulled the plug months ago. I've canceled everything. All of it. The release, the tour, any and all appearances. I wiped the calendar clean. Actually, I threw away the calendar. No more anything for a while."

"You put so much into it though," Nikki said gently.

Zara's expression flickered with sadness but she blinked it away. "It had to be done. Sometimes we have to kill our darlings."

She said it with such certainty that Asa found himself leaning in. To ask her to expound. They had spent one night talking to each other and he had spent six months wanting more. Missing her voice and ideas and energy.

Six months had done nothing to curb his curiosity.

But maybe it was okay for a moment. As long as he didn't get carried away and stay too long, he could enjoy her presence.

"How do you do that?" he asked, turning his body and sinking into the pull of her gravity.

She flicked her warm eyes to him and a soft smile touched her lips. "Just because I shelve something doesn't take away its value to me. The value was always in the creation in the first place. And making it settled the itch I had at the time. Sharing it lives in a different space in my heart. Not everything I make needs to be shared."

"But you wanted to share it once," he pointed out.

She nodded. "And then I changed my mind."

"That easy, huh?" he asked, his mouth relaxing into a crooked smile.

Zara's own mouth stretched into a knowing smile. "Speaking of changing your mind…"

Asa chuckled. He'd walked right into that one.

But he couldn't live with Zara Lorna. The offer was too good. Not just because of the timing and the location but because it was *Zara*. He couldn't separate that from the offer.

If one person saw them together one time, lives would be turned upside down. Again.

His gaze flicked to Johnny.

He'd told Johnny there wasn't anything significant between him and Zara. Roommates would absolutely register on the "significant" spectrum.

See? And this was the danger of returning to Zara's orbit. It was warm and cozy and wonderful. But he needed to remember why he'd cut off contact with her in the first place.

Because it would start all over again. Shelby talking to the press, people calling the studio asking for him, lies about him using her, Zara's reputation smeared and scandalized on every website. And his middle of the night anxiety attacks that he hadn't told anyone about.

Johnny and Hannah had already gone to so much effort to hide him so he could keep working there.

He took a deep breath and glanced at his watch.

Speaking of work.

He finished his coffee, rinsed his cup, and headed for the door.

"Bye?" Nikki called.

He flicked two fingers her direction but otherwise didn't look back.

Distance.

Distance from Zara Lorna was the only way to make sure nothing exploded.

* * *

ZARA

"If I smelled like b.o. you'd tell me, right?" Zara asked the room.

Nikki snickered. Johnny and Justin smiled.

But no one answered her question.

She lifted her arm and sniffed her armpit. Then she checked the other one.

Nikki barked a laugh.

"I don't get it," Zara said honestly. "That is the second time he's left so fast, I'm surprised there's not flames shooting out his backside."

Nikki shrugged. "I don't know. Asa's been a little on edge since…" She stopped speaking and cleared her throat.

Hmm.

Since what had happened after the NMAs?

He'd been put through it. For someone who didn't like the limelight, that had probably been very uncomfortable.

Had he attached her to that discomfort?

Damn, that sucked. Zara really liked Asa.

When she'd made plans to move to Chicago, she'd secretly planned to hang out with Asa again. She liked how his brain worked.

Logan was still taking things away from her.

This next part of her life was supposed to be about reclaiming what was hers. Even if she didn't know what it was anymore. She was determined to figure it out.

And she wanted to be friends with Asa.

If he wanted that.

* * *

ASA

. . .

It had taken a couple hours but he mostly forgot that Zara Lorna was upstairs drinking coffee.

Commercial jingles were distracting that way.

They hooked into your brain and didn't let go. In fact, that was their entire reason for existing. So that you sang stupid little songs all day long and subconsciously bought the product you were singing about.

Was it the way he'd wanted to spend his career in music? No. But it was safe enough.

Also, sometimes Nikki had him mix things for important artists like Ashton James, or Sunshine Capone…or Zara Lorna.

Fuck.

Now he was thinking about her again.

Avoiding her had been incredibly easy over the past six months.

Well, avoiding her in person that is.

She was on every magazine, pop news banner, and gossip site in existence. She and her ex fighting through their publicists.

Hopefully she would go back to New York or London or wherever she lived these days.

And he could resume his life that didn't involve thought-provoking conversations with beautiful women.

He played the jingle again and his forehead hit the control panel with a soft thud as he slowly died inside.

It was finished. It was better than it needed to be.

He wouldn't call himself a perfectionist. Unless it was something he had a hand in. Something he created or was responsible for. And then he had to keep tweaking it until someone finally took it away from him.

Which Johnny usually did.

The hairs on the back of his neck prickled and he froze.

His hand hovered over the control board as he waited for a sign that he was in the clear. He held his breath, the damn cat food jingle playing on a loop through his headphones.

A soft touch on his shoulder told him his gut had been right.

She was here.

She'd come downstairs to torture him in his dungeon—he meant workspace.

He swiveled in his chair, bracing, frowning, putting every ounce of effort into looking as unapproachable as he could.

It was difficult with the meowing melody ricocheting through his ears.

He reached over and shut it off. Then he removed his headphones.

His eyes caught on the silver hoops in her ears. And the slope of her neck. And the soft smile she was offering him that hit him in all the places it shouldn't.

"Can I talk to you for a minute?" she asked.

He waved a hand at the leather couch.

She sat down and took a breath. Her eyes skated over the control panels and along the walls of switches and equipment.

Asa didn't want to have to ask. He wished she would just tell him what she wanted so he could get back to work.

Even though his work was done. She didn't know that.

"What are you working on?" she asked, not starting where she wanted to start.

"A cat food commercial," he said with a sigh. He flicked a switch and the jingle played through the speaker.

Zara's light laugh tickled his eardrums and he turned away from her pretty smile.

"I like it," she said. "It's cute."

He rolled his head to the side, stretching his tight neck.

"Are you mad at me?" she asked quietly.

He swiveled around to face her.

Should he lie and say yes? It might be easier to let her believe that his anger is why they couldn't be friends. Why they couldn't even be acquaintances. Why they couldn't even share a cab.

But he had that overzealous need to be honest.

Thank you, trauma.

She leaned forward and rested her elbows on her knees, folding her hands together. "I get it. What happened after..." She looked away and shook her head. "You didn't deserve *any* of that. I'm sure it didn't make life very easy for a while. So I get it, why you'd want to stay away from me."

His eye twitched.

She thought he was mad about what they'd said about *him?*

Like he was some whiny little Logan Black crybaby?

Fuck that noise.

"I wasn't mad about what they said about me," he said. "I was mad about what they said about *you.* You didn't deserve that." He snorted in disgust and crossed his arms. "You never deserve that. It's bullshit."

"You don't deserve it either," she said.

He had no reply to that because he disagreed but didn't want to argue about it.

Her pink tongue slid along her lower lip as she studied him. "So, you're *not* mad at me?"

He opened his mouth and then shut it.

They stared at one another in silence for a minute.

"I'm sorry about your bed and room getting destroyed," she said, guessing again as to why he was being an ass.

He shrugged. Because every time he spoke, he revealed way more than he was comfortable revealing.

"Okay, cards on the table, I already had my security go through your background to get you clearance."

His eyes went wide and he blinked at her.

"That's why I didn't offer right away last week. I had to make sure they would approve. They've been really strict after the stalker thing a couple weeks ago."

"What stalker thing?" Asa asked, his chest churning with alarm and anger.

She waved a hand. "Oh, some guy broke into my house in LA and security found him in my bed." She made a face. "It was all over the news, I'm surprised you didn't see it."

He scratched the side of his neck. He hadn't seen it because he had her muted everywhere.

"Anyway, you've been approved! Yay." She waved her hands in a lowkey celebration. "I have the place for six months. It'll give you time to rebuild your savings without having to sleep here." She looked down at the couch beneath her.

It probably looked pretty sad from her perspective.

He licked his lips, trying to get moisture back into his mouth. "You're really staying in town a while?" he asked, realizing that avoiding her wasn't a plan he could keep.

And also realizing he didn't really want to.

She blew raspberries. "Yeah. I'm—" She shook her head like she didn't know what to say. "I'm taking some time off. From all of it."

"But what about your album?" he asked. She'd been so excited about it just a few months ago. "You really shelved it?"

A pained look crossed her face. "Indefinitely."

"Why?" he asked, his voice quiet.

"Asa," she said, like he knew better. "You know why."

He rubbed the back of his neck as heat gathered in his chest. This conversation was barreling right toward the place he wanted to avoid.

Right back to that night where they'd talked and talked and *talked*.

Fuck.

She was so easy to connect with.

She was too damn likable.

He knew he should be rude and end the conversation. Tell her to leave. Risk Nikki's wrath.

But he couldn't.

When it came to Zara, he was just too damn weak to commit to the asshole bit anymore.

And just like that, he let go of the edges of emotional distance he'd been clinging to by his fingernails. He fell, fell, fell, into the warm, cotton-soft rapport he had only found with her.

"It got worse?" he asked.

"So much worse," she confirmed with an eye roll. "And I could release it. I could. It would be a legal battle with Logan because he wants credit. But even then, you know everyone will read into it. Everyone will pull apart the lyrics and dissect them looking for clues as to why I'm the villain. Looking for the proof of all that I've been accused. They're determined to paint me as a gimmick or a fad or worse, a fake."

He gave her a look. "You are *not* the villain."

Her lips curved into a sad smile like she didn't quite believe him. And he should have stopped, but something took over and he couldn't.

"You're not a gimmick or a fad. You're not the product of a boardroom trying to sell an image. You're… remarkable. Gifted even. Fuck, I'd bet that if the entire industry reversed course tomorrow you'd still come out on top. You're the realest fucking thing this industry has ever known. You shouldn't have to apologize for any of it." He swallowed, realizing he'd said way more than he'd intended but he wasn't going to take it back. It was all true.

Her eyes flickered with something, a spark of something he hadn't seen since October and he had really fucking missed it.

"Maybe I just don't know if I have the guts for it right now." Her eyes tracked to the floor. "Or if I even want to."

He pushed aside the queasiness that accompanied her confession. Ignored how much he wanted to ask more questions. To listen to her low, husky voice explain what was happening in her life that had brought her here.

She forced a smile. "Anyway, all that to say, I'm here for a while. I have a place. It's quiet. No one is doing construction." They shared a smile. "You can have a room for however long you need it."

She really meant that too.

It was part of her nature—to give without expectation. To help where she saw need. To show up when no one else would be able to find the time and do it all with a smile.

"Please," she said, something new in her tone. "I'd really like it if you'd let me help you. Consider it repayment for everything you had to go through on my account."

Fuck.

If he declined, she'd keep believing she owed him when she didn't.

Her amber eyes pleaded with him. She chewed on her bottom lip as she waited for his answer.

"Okay," he said, surprising himself as the words left his mouth.

She smiled a tentative smile. "Really?"

He shrugged. "Sure."

This was probably going to end badly. But the way her entire face lit up and how she pressed her hands to her heart like he'd just given her a gift, made him feel like he could handle whatever came next.

"Oh, I'm so glad." Her head dropped back and closed her eyes. "I thought you were going to harbor a lifelong grudge against me."

He sniffed a laugh. She stood to leave.

"I'm going to get you a key. Let's move your stuff tonight if we can," she said, clapping her hands once.

He flicked two fingers her direction as a goodbye.

Yeah, it wasn't a lifelong grudge he was harboring.

But she didn't need to know that.

Chapter Ten
Overdrive

If someone asked her to describe how she felt when Asa had finally agreed to move in, she only had one word.

Yay!

Cas had gotten her an extra key and Johnny had given Asa the rest of the day off to get his things moved.

And yes, Zara had been trying to keep from being overly generous. But this was *Asa.* The guy who had waded in and saved her from a public drama. The same guy who didn't ask for anything from her. Who held babies and loved his friends.

He wasn't going to take advantage of her.

"You have a lot of guitars." She put her hands on her hips and surveyed the upstairs room.

"Yeah," Asa agreed, rubbing the back of his neck.

"It's a really good thing you hadn't moved all your stuff downstairs," she stated the obvious. "Or you'd have had more to deal with than powdered donuts."

He shot her a look and she made a face. "Sorry. Too soon?"

He turned away, shaking his head. But not before she saw the lopsided smile.

She looked around the room again, trying to decide where she would be the most helpful. Outside of the guitars and amps, he didn't have much. A couple milkcrates of vinyl, a tall dresser, two floor lamps, a couple framed posters, and a large stereo set up.

And whatever she couldn't see in the closet.

"Is this it?" she asked.

"To get out of the house, yeah," he said around a grunt as he took a box off the shelf in the closet. He set it down. "I have a couple boxes of stuff at my dad's, but they can stay there."

For some reason she'd expected way more. All of his stuff could fit into two trips in Cas's SUV. Granted, he didn't have a bed. But still.

"I live light," Asa said by way of explanation. "When I was twelve, the basement flooded at my dad's. I had just moved down there and had everything set up so cool." He put his hands on his hips and smiled at the memory. "I had this enormous collection of Pokémon cards. I'd spent years building it and organizing it." He took a breath and shook his head. "But then the water main broke. All ruined."

Her heart pinched. The idea of Asa as a boy and losing something he cared about hit her in a place that felt familiar.

"That sucks," she said, frowning hard to keep from having a different reaction.

He shrugged. "It's just stuff."

Well, sure. It was just stuff. But she remembered being that age, and sometimes your stuff felt like part of your identity.

"I still have more than I need." He brought down another box and put it on top of the first. "Like, records. And guitars." He chuckled to himself.

"You've always been a collector then, huh?" she asked, filling in a little more of what she knew about Asa.

"Yep." He struggled to reach the last box on the top shelf. "I hold onto things others consider a waste of time." He reached the box and pulled it down.

Something new washed over his face and she stepped closer.

He sighed and put the box on top of the others.

"What's in that one?" she couldn't help but ask.

His eyes flicked up to hers and back down.

For a minute, she thought he wasn't going to tell her. But then he lifted the lid and she peered into the opening. It was packed full of notebooks and loose paper. All of it looked like it had been written in.

He put the lid back on. "Like I said, I hold onto things others consider a waste of time."

"Are those…songs?" she asked, her eyes still on the closed lid.

He turned his back to her to reach inside the closet. His broad shoulders shrugged in answer to her question.

The box of notebooks was one of those banker boxes—white carboard with oval holes punched out for handles. But it was absolutely packed full.

Winking Pete had only released one album. An album she'd listened to so much in the past six months that she had it memorized. For some reason she'd thought there wasn't more. The way he spoke about it in LA made it seem like there wasn't anything else. Which was ridiculous. As a writer herself she knew there was always way more than what anyone else saw.

Her eyes darted between Asa's still turned back and the box as she made an internal vow. She was going to get into that box eventually. Someday. She'd earn it. She'd convince him or bribe him or threaten him into letting her into that box of music.

"Can I start taking these out to the truck?" she asked, turning back to the guitars.

"Yeah," he called over his shoulder.

"Cool," she muttered to herself. A thought occurred to her and she spun back around. "Hey, Asa?" she called, shoving her fingers into her hair and stopping when it reached the knot on the crown of her head.

"Yeah?"

"Um…" Shit. How should she ask this question?

Asa set down another box and straightened, putting his hands on his hips. "What's up?"

"Do you…uh…" Oof, this was weird. Even though it shouldn't be weird. Which made it weirder. "Did you tell your girlfriend you were moving?" There. Her voice hadn't been squeaky at all. Shut up.

His eyelids dropped low over those dark brown almost black eyes. The pause between them stretched so long that she wondered if maybe she hadn't asked the question out loud.

"Don't have a girlfriend," he said, voice neutral.

"Oh." She swallowed and tried to run her hand through her hair again. And again was stopped by her topknot. His eyes flicked from her face to the top of her head and his lips twitched. "I'm going to start taking the guitars down."

He nodded once, glancing behind her, and then disappeared inside the closet again.

All right, Zara. No big deal.

If she wasn't such a chicken shit, she would have asked why he hadn't ever texted her back. Having a girlfriend made the most sense. But he didn't have one. He just didn't want to text her back.

That was fine.

This was all. Fine.

She double checked the latches on the guitar cases before starting the trek to the truck. Counting as she went, and ogling the instruments a bit as well, she found that Asa had an amazing collection. Of the electrics she counted; two very used Fender Stratocasters, three Les Pauls, an ancient but well cared for Rickenbacker 360, two Ibeniz RGs. Of the acoustics were, two Martins; one more used than the other. He only had two bass guitars: a Fender jazz and a Rickenbacker 4001.

"For a self-proclaimed bass player, you sure don't have very many bass guitars," she remarked, flipping the locks closed on the last case in the room.

A ghost of a smile graced his lips and his eyes crinkled at the sides. "I don't know what to tell you. I guess I just know what I like in a bass. I don't need other options."

She snickered and stood up, bringing the last bass with her. "Well, don't be surprised when I come knocking on your door begging to play with your collection." She didn't stick around to see his reaction as she hoofed it out the door and down the stairs.

Cas took the last bass from her when she reached the street.

"I'll take these over to the house and be right back," he said.

"Do you want me to come with you to unload them?" she asked.

He gave her a look like he thought she was ridiculous.

Okay then.

Devan pulled to a stop at the curb in an identical SUV with blacked out windows. Wait. They had two vehicles? How had she not noticed that before?

Devan opened the back and one of the side doors, revealing she'd removed the middle and back seat for more room.

"You guys are the best, you know that?" Zara remarked.

Devan winked at her and then headed into the house to start loading boxes.

It didn't take more than thirty minutes for the three of them to finish loading Asa's possessions.

"Is that it?" Zara asked, walking through the house that really didn't look comfortable. Poor Asa had been living in a construction site for months. No wonder he was grumpy.

"Of my meager belongings? Yep."

Devan finished typing something out on her phone and snapped her fingers at Asa. "You have vehicle?" she asked in her thick Russian accent.

Asa's chin jerked slightly and Zara figured it was because it was the first time he'd heard Devan speak.

"Yeah. A motorcycle," Asa replied, jerking his thumb over his shoulder, indicating the alley behind the house.

A motorcycle? That was kind of awesome. Zara hadn't been on a motorcycle since she was a kid and her uncle Leo had gotten one after getting really into Steve McQueen.

Devan nodded and then gestured for Zara to get in the SUV with her.

Zara flashed Asa a smile. "I think that means you have to follow us."

"What's the address?" he asked, flicking his eyes to Devan. "Just in case we get separated in traffic."

"Oh. Of course." Zara pulled out her phone and texted him the address. Just as she hit send, she wondered if maybe she didn't have the right number and that was why he had never replied. But the thought had barely finished forming in her head when his phone dinged with the received text.

Ouch.

Okay.

Their eyes met and she almost asked him. But she didn't know if she was ready to hear the answer yet so she kept her mouth shut.

"See you in a minute," she said and got into the SUV with Devan.

* * *

ASA

. . .

The house was easy enough to find. For some reason he expected a fortress of sorts but it was just a really nice four-story home tucked into East Lincoln Park surrounded by houses very similar to it. No yard, obviously. Chicago was too crammed for those sorts of amenities.

Cas was waiting for him in the alley behind the house. He waved him down the short ramp into the underground garage that opened as he approached.

Was this really fucking happening? Was he really moving in with Zara Lorna?

His stomach threatened to be very upset about the entire situation but he ignored it.

The garage was a lot larger than he expected. It held both SUVs and his motorcycle easily. A large workbench sat empty against the back wall next to a door with a security panel.

He killed the engine and took off his helmet.

Cas gave him a look and motioned for him to follow him into the house.

Asa knew his eyes had to be nearly bugged out as he went through the door that led into the house. Zara and Devan were sitting on a low bench opposite the door. It had a shelf below it meant for shoes.

Zara gave him that smile again. The one that made his limbs tingle and want to make bad decisions.

"Cas is going to make you go through orientation," she said. "It's pretty great. Not to ruin anything for you but he rhymes verified with terrified and I laughed until I choked."

Asa chuckled and nodded.

Cas started his tour/orientation immediately after that.

Asa followed along as the large man walked him through the house and talked about what was and was not allowed. He taught him how to use the security panel and gave him his own code. More than once he mentioned his background and specific skillset. Asa felt adequately threatened.

Everything Cas went over was a strange echo of things his father had taught him growing up. Double check locks on doors and windows, extra sensors hidden inconspicuously in addition to the obvious cameras, blackout curtains that were to be closed at night.

When he'd been younger, he'd taken for granted the overabundance of caution his father had forced him to practice. But it sure was coming in handy now.

They visited three of the four floors. The house had a personal elevator that had a regular door with a handle on it instead of the sliding doors like in hotels. The fourth floor was Zara's room and Cas made it clear that it was off limits to Asa.

Meanwhile, Zara followed along with the tour making silly faces every time Cas made a new threat.

"If you don't stop doing that, he won't take me seriously," Cas finally said, exasperated.

Asa withheld a smile as Zara rolled her eyes playfully. "I'm sure he takes you seriously," she said. "Besides, you're making it seem like this place houses the Mona Lisa or something. It's really not that big of a deal. It's just me."

Cas inhaled sharply through his nose and flattened his mouth. Asa could see the conflict in the man's gray eyes. Zara trying to diminish her importance aggravated him. He was also left with the impression this wasn't the first time this had come up.

"I'm taking you seriously," Asa said after a beat of silence. "I'm well aware of her significance. I will respect your rules."

Cas studied him for a breath before moving on.

Asa darted a glance to Zara whose cheeks had reddened. She chewed on her lower lip and stared at the floor.

Maybe he shouldn't have said anything? Except she must know that Cas cared for her more than as a client. She wasn't just anyone to the world. And she wasn't just anyone to the people who knew her.

The tour ended back in the kitchen which was probably the coolest room in the house in Asa's opinion. All white with antique glass and quartzite counters, mirrored ceiling, and stainless-steel appliances.

"So, which room do you want?" Zara asked, having recovered from whatever had made her quiet a minute ago. "You can choose any of them."

"Uh, probably the bottom one. By the garage. That way I can go to work without disturbing you."

"You're not going to disturb me," she scoffed.

Cas nodded like he agreed with Asa's choice.

Zara's brow scrunched like she was frustrated with his decision. But even though he'd agreed to live there *temporarily*, he still needed to keep some space.

He didn't want to.

He *wanted* to start asking her about the album she'd shelved. If he could hear it, even though he had no business asking that kind of a thing.

It was like, when he got around her, he forgot every hard learned lesson that life had taught him. He felt young and new and curious. And it was the curiosity he needed to really be careful with. A question here and there was probably fine. But he couldn't exactly pepper her with inquiries like he was a child and she was the most amazing, brilliant, gorgeous, extraordinary human in all of existence.

They went out to the garage to start unloading his things and his pulse amped up, making his hands shake. What the hell was he doing? He couldn't live with her. He looked over the sum of his belongings stuffed into the back of an SUV that probably had reinforced windows.

He had nowhere else to go.

"I could so easily freak out right now," he muttered.

"Can I watch?"

He jumped and turned to find Zara by his side.

She smiled up at him. "I didn't get to see the whole freakout last October, only how it ended."

He shook his head slowly. She was teasing him.

A soft chuckle escaped him and her eyes may or may not have sparkled. The tension and anxiety faded from his limbs and he forgot again why this was a bad idea.

"So that room off the kitchen," he said. "The one with the piano?"

She nodded.

"Would it be okay if I put the guitars in there?"

Her eyes widened and she nodded more emphatically. "Of course!"

"You can use them whenever." He turned back to the SUV, unable to hold her excited gaze for too long. You'd think he'd given her another Artist of the Year award with the way she lit up at the idea of using his worn-out guitars.

"Wait." Zara stopped. "What are those?" She pointed to a box.

He grabbed the edge and pulled it over. "These," he said, picking up one bejeweled croc and holding it up. "Are my house shoes."

"You wear those?" she asked, her lips trembling with humor.

"Absolutely," he confirmed with a somber nod, returning the croc to its place.

Zara snickered and took the box, backing away from him. "You're so fun," she said around a laugh. "I hope I don't disappoint you."

Asa took a breath and watched her go. "Impossible," he murmured to himself.

It didn't take much more than an hour to unload his things and get his room set up. They put all but one of his guitars in the piano room. He decided at the last minute to keep his favorite Martin in his bedroom.

It wasn't like he had plans to use it. But he wanted it within reach.

Just in case.

Chapter Eleven
February Stars

ZARA

Zara's gaze wandered around the lounge area of XY Records. The lounge that André had built for Nikki. It was gorgeous with its dark ceiling, exposed rafters, and gleaming copper ducts. Framed album covers that they'd produced hung on the wall, including the one they'd done together, along with vintage band posters and political art from the 80's.

Their love had been one of her favorites to witness. Sabine and Sunshine too. Just a beautiful and honest acceptance of another soul. She wanted that someday.

If the small neighborhood that housed XY Records knew the number of celebrities working in their midst, they'd shit themselves. A collective shitting. Everyone at once.

But as it was, the people who worked there were able to do so quietly and under the radar. Making it one of the most incredible workspaces she'd ever experienced. The freedom of anonymity making it possible for the art to take shape in an authentic way.

She'd come down to the studio because she was hoping she'd be able to run into Asa and ask him…something. She hadn't figured out the right question. Was he avoiding her? Had she pissed him off?

Asa had been living with her for almost two weeks and she had seen him exactly once.

And that had been just barely.

She'd come back from hanging out with Nikki and she caught sight of his back and shoulders disappearing behind his closed door.

She never heard him or saw any evidence that he lived there.

Sometimes food in the fridge would be missing but it was replaced by the next day. She still didn't know if Asa had been doing that, or Cas and Devan.

Last night she'd crept down the stairs in her fluffiest socks and sat in the bend of the stairwell. Just listening.

But still, no noise came from beyond the closed door.

Maybe the insulation was just that good.

Or maybe he was a ninja.

She had finally given up and gone back to bed, deciding he was either sleeping or not home.

It felt like the kind of thing she should ask him about. But, as history had taught her, he didn't answer her texts. It would have to be face to face. If only she saw him.

Hadn't they had fun on moving day? Goofing around and joking with each other?

So what was the deal?

Or was she putting way too much on the small connection that they had shared?

Maybe it had only been significant to her. Maybe he connected like that with people all the time.

She'd gotten up that morning determined to speak with him, but he'd already left. He wasn't at the studio either. Apparently it was his day off.

Hannah and Nikki's laughter broke through her thoughts. She focused her gaze back on them only to find them looking at her.

She smiled anyway, knowing she'd missed whatever joke that had cracked them both up.

"You look like you have a lot on your mind," Nikki said.

Zara didn't argue.

"You sleeping okay?" Hannah asked.

Zara thought about her sleep the night before. "Sometimes," she answered with a soft frown. "Last night was okay."

Hannah nodded, her expression thoughtful. "It was difficult for my mind to adapt to a new rhythm when I first quit. Not that you've quit," she added quickly. "But your ingrained habits probably aren't consistent with your current lifestyle."

"That's true," Zara agreed quietly. "I'm so used to being overly booked and overly busy that having time to myself feels…" She shook her head because she didn't know the word. She didn't know the feeling. It was new to her.

"Guilty," supplied Hannah.

Zara's head came up. "Yeah."

Hannah's eyebrows tilted with compassion. "I think that's normal. Or at least expected. We can get so used to being busy that we think we're doing something wrong when we stop."

Truth rang through Hannah's words. Zara didn't like that. She remembered a time when being busy hadn't been her entire personality. She used to play and have fun and create. Where was that girl now?

"Maybe I should try some new hobbies," Zara said.

"You could try knitting," Hannah suggested.

Nikki snorted.

"I mean, you can't be any worse at it than I am," Hannah said with a crooked smile.

"How's the new roommate?" Nikki asked.

Zara took a breath to answer but had no idea what to say. She shrugged.

Nikki's eyes narrowed suspiciously. "Is he being a good houseguest?"

"Yeah," Zara said quickly. "He's such a good houseguest that you can't tell he's even there. I never see him or hear him. I'm not even sure he eats. There's never a dirty dish or towel or anything. He might, in fact, be a ghost."

"Hmm," Nikki hummed thoughtfully.

"Is that normal for Asa?" Zara asked. "Or is that special for me?" She tried to sound like she was joking but she heard the harsh edge in her tone.

"These days? Nikki shrugged. "Asa used to be a lot like you, actually," she remarked ruefully. "We fed off each other's ridiculousness. He loved being happy. If he wasn't happy, he'd make it a mission and chase it down like a hunter." Her gaze lost focus like she was accessing a memory. "We'd amp each other up and drive Shelby absolutely nuts. She'd get so mad at us…" Nikki's expression turned sad and then shuttered. "I suppose she won in the end." She shook herself out of the memory and pasted a tight smile on her face. "Asa is who he is now. I've given up on trying to get him to be something he's just not anymore. He's a grumpy old man now and I'll love him in this form just as much."

Who the fuck was Shelby and why had she stolen Asa's joy?

Hannah and Nikki left to do something in studio X, leaving Zara to her thoughts in the lounge.

Nikki's information helped in one aspect—it alleviated Zara's guilt about Asa's standoffishness. But it also signaled to her that sometimes life circumstances left deep scars. He'd hinted at that, hadn't he? By confessing he didn't write anymore; by the way he changed the subject when his music came up.

If that was the case, if he was being haunted by ghosts, she really couldn't do much about it.

She couldn't imagine how many ghosts would still be haunting her if she had stopped writing. It was how she processed everything; the world, her emotions, things she didn't fully understand.

He should be writing.

The bossy thought made her roll her eyes.

Right. Because the guy who avoided her on the regular was going to be open to her unsolicited advice.

Her phone rang in her hand, interrupting her thoughts. She grinned at the picture of her little sister Bianca on the screen.

"Hello?"

She tried to call home at least once a week but it had been more than that since she'd called Bianca directly. Between everything with her label and Logan and moving to Chicago, she'd been more distracted than she wanted to admit. And she knew she wouldn't be able to hide the stress in her voice from her family members. They would worry. She didn't want them to worry.

"Did you know that I thought you were dead?" Bianca said by way of greeting.

Zara laughed. God, she missed her brother and sister so much. "Well, then why didn't you call me sooner?"

"Because you kept sending me memes so I knew you weren't dead dead," came the sixteen-year-old's quick reply. "And Oscar told me you called him a few days ago."

Oscar was a year younger than Bianca and if Zara didn't call him regularly he would start to send her pictures of sad animals. It was one of her favorite forms of guilt tripping.

Zara asked B about school and if she was dating anyone and how everyone was.

They laughed and joked and the longer they spoke, the easier Zara breathed. She really would have loved to go home and spend time with her family. But it would eventually turn into a circus and she couldn't do that to them. Not again.

But maybe she could fly them all out to see her for a weekend soon. Which she suggested before she overthought it.

"Hey, remember the girl who bullied me in first grade?" Bianca asked.

"Yeah! She stole your Barbie and cut all her hair off. I thought you would never stop crying."

"Yeah, good times," Bianca replied flatly making Zara chuckle.

"Why? Did you run into her or something?" Zara asked.

"No. But I was thinking about when you made cookies with me to make me feel better."

"That's right," Zara said. She'd forgotten that part. Geez. Had she even made cookies since then?

"Cookies make everything better," Bianca said. "When I come visit, I want to make cookies with you again."

"I love that idea."

They said their goodbyes and Zara returned to her thoughtful state of mind.

Cookies, huh?

Maybe baking could be a new hobby. Cas wouldn't even be weird about it because it was an indoor activity.

She tapped her chin with her forefinger. If Bianca wanted to bake when she came to visit, Zara should know what she was doing. She *was* the older sister after all.

* * *

She was reading in bed late, not really focusing on the words because she couldn't stop the "what ifs" and "maybes" from interrupting. Another night she found it impossible to relax.

It was way past two when she heard the garage door open, signaling Asa's return.

She put the book down and stared at the ceiling.

Was she just not good at living alone?

Was she really so insecure that a few days without talking to someone had her believing they hated her?

Maybe.

But when she specifically thought about it being *Asa* that wasn't speaking to her, she felt… queasy? Was that it? It was subtle and sort of in the pit of her stomach. And if she focused on it, she could accidentally hurt her own feelings.

It was just…

He was so easy to talk to. Sort of like Nash Ellis that way. He had knowledge and experience she didn't. He saw the world differently, but he spoke in a way that she understood.

She knew, rationally, she couldn't *make* someone be her friend.

And she didn't need Asa's acceptance or approval to validate her existence. She was a valid human being with or without anyone else saying it.

Right?

She realized she was chewing on her lower lip again and purposefully stopped, flopping her arms down by her sides in frustration.

Maybe she should just confront him and ask him what it was he didn't like about her.

She opened the security camera app on her phone and watched him come in the door.

He was in dark pants and a button-up shirt. He had a large shoulder bag slung across his body.

He carefully closed the garage door, input the alarm code, and reset it for the night. He glanced at the stairwell and paused several seconds before going to his room.

She waited for him to close his bedroom door before she slipped from her bed, silent as a cat in her fluffiest socks.

Sliding past the elevator, she padded down the four flights of stairs to the lower level.

She crouched close to the wall and peered around the corner.

The door to his room was still closed. He was definitely still in there.

And probably still awake. If she knocked on the door, she wouldn't be waking him.

But he would definitely think she was spying on him. Which she kind of was.

Okay, Z. You've gone full stalker.

What was she doing? Spying on him like a little kid?

Stupid, stupid, stupid.

If she wanted to talk to him, she should just walk right up to him and talk to him.

Or maybe she could get Cas or Devan to hold him down first.

As she crouched on the stairs in the dark, ruminating on all her poor life choices that had brought her here, soft guitar strumming filtered through the solid door and reached her ears.

She sat down on the step and just listened.

He started and stopped and started over, finding the melody.

Goosebumps raised along her arms and the back of her neck.

His deep voice joined the guitar, too soft for her to make out the words.

She rested her head against the wall and just listened.

The music and his voice soothed that anxious feeling deep in her chest that she'd never lived without. The one she kept hidden because she had long believed it was just part of who she was.

Soon after that, her limbs grew heavy and her eyes got harder to keep open.

Silently, she retreated back up the stairs, turned off the light in her room, and crawled into her bed.

She was asleep before she hit the pillow.

* * *

ASA

It was the curiosity.

Overwhelming and obtrusive, it pounded through his body like a pulse.

He hadn't seen her or talked to her since the day she'd helped him move in.

And that had been deliberate. He had to make sure her generosity wouldn't backfire on her. Just the thought of Shelby finding out how close he was to everything she thought she deserved…it was enough to keep him in hiding when the coolest person he had ever met was in the same house.

But almost two weeks later, not one media publication had found out he was living in her basement. He knew because he'd checked.

He'd gone from having mentions of her muted, to turning on alerts for his own name.

All had been quiet on the internet.

It felt too good to be true. And that had made his pause longer. Just to make sure. He thought he hadn't been conspicuous but then he'd received a string of aggressive texts from Nikki yesterday.

NIKKI: What the hell are you doing?

ASA: I'm out with Steiny, why?

NIKKI: Pull your head outta your ass. We both know you're not stupid. Stop avoiding Zara. She already thinks you hate her.

ASA: What?? I don't hate her!

NIKKI: *I* know that. But you're acting like a bad friend. You're a lot of things, Ace, but a shitty friend isn't one.

NIKKI: I know you're going through shit and you don't want to talk about it blah, blah, freaking blah. But you're not the only one going through shit. She needs someone who gets it. And. You. Get. It. Be the friend I know is in there somewhere.

Obviously he hadn't been as lowkey as he'd hoped.

And truthfully, he didn't want to avoid her. He wanted to hang out with her all the time. Hear her thoughts, get her opinions, her laughs, and her sincerity. Every time he was in the same room with her, he wanted to soak up every drop of goodness he could get.

And it freaked him out.

Last night he'd stayed at Steiny's as long as he could before going back to Lincoln Park. He had every intention of going straight to bed but his eyes landed on his guitar as he shut the door and something happened.

Something that he hadn't let happen in a while.

He wasn't ready to talk about it, or even define it. It was just a moment, like a long held deep breath releasing all at once. A relaxation of all his strict borders and limits. Something that was just his.

When he'd woken up that morning, he'd felt…different. Something inside had shifted imperceptibly.

And it had made room for the curiosity that now pulsed through his veins.

What was she doing? Did she really think he hated her? Why was she here? In Chicago? Why was she so good to everyone around her?

He paused—one hand on the railing, one foot on the first step.

Her clear voice spilled down the stairs and cuddled his eardrums. She was singing "Mona Lisas and Mad Hatters" unaccompanied and it was… amazing. Her vocals were always strong, but there was a freedom to them now that was full of power and soul.

He rubbed his hand over his chest and let out a deep breath.

His legs carried him up the stairs, no longer checking with his head. He reached the doorway to the large, open kitchen, and leaned a shoulder against the wall, sliding his hands into the pockets of his jeans.

Zara was in light blue short shorts, a beautiful contrast against her tan legs. Her oversized cropped white t-shirt showed a tan midriff that was hard to look away from. Her black hair was in a thick braid so haphazardly entwined that several tendrils had escaped.

Ingredients lined one countertop while a half dozen mixing bowls took up another.

Sensing his presence, she lifted her head. Instead of being startled or embarrassed, she flashed him a bright smile that was like a shot of pure sunshine to his soul. She immediately dialed it back like she didn't want to frighten him.

He knew that was his fault.

He'd caused her to question herself.

Oh, Asa, you really are a dipshit.

"Hi," she said, sounding cautious and careful. "I'm making cookies."

"Yeah?" he asked.

"Well, I'm gonna try," she amended, glancing at all of her supplies. "I haven't made cookies since I was fifteen." She tapped on the tablet on the island in front of her. "I'm looking for a recipe that looks vaguely familiar."

He'd been a dick. She had every right to call him on his shit and shame him back into the basement. But there she was, making cookies. Talking to him like he was still her friend.

He was going to be a better friend.

He pushed off the wall and came forward, craning his neck to see the screen. "What kind of cookies?"

"Chocolate chip."

He nodded. "Classic."

Stopping by her side, he eyed the recipe she had been studying. Looked about right. His eyes drifted to her and he realized she was gazing up at him, questions in those amber gold cosmic swirls she dared to call eyes.

"What?" he asked.

"Nothing." A soft smile spread across her face and she shrugged. "I just haven't seen you in a while."

He swallowed. "I'm sorry about that. I've since pulled my head out of my ass."

"Good."

That was it. No guilt trip, no hesitation. Just acceptance and grace.

Something in his ribcage took its first easy breath in too long of a time. It was too complex for him to call his lungs. But it was something.

His eyes couldn't decide which part of her to focus on. Her smile, her insane braid, or the fact that she was only wearing one earring. He touched her empty earlobe and her eyebrows dipped. "You're missing an earring."

She grabbed the earlobe and her gaze lost focus. "Ha." Her lips quirked to the side. "Maybe I'm making a style choice."

He rolled his lips inward and took a step back. "Okay, killer. Do you want help with these cookies?" He glanced around the kitchen, rubbing his palms together.

"Really?" she asked, sounding surprised.

Guilt rolled through him and he shook it off. He could be better. He *would* be better.

He washed his hands in the sink and dried them on a paper towel. "You know that story about the Little Red Hen?" he asked.

She narrowed those otherworldly eyes.

"I know how it goes." He tossed the paper towel in the trash. "I don't get cookies unless I help make the cookies." He held his hands out. "And I definitely want cookies."

She grinned and spun around on her toes, making a little squeaking noise that sounded like, "Yay!"

He shook his head and came up beside her again, looking at the recipe.

"Do you have experience making cookies?" she asked.

"I do," he confirmed.

"Does this look like a good recipe?"

He scrolled through it. "The ingredients are right. But I have a technique I like to use that enhances that cookie experience."

"Enhances, huh?" She snickered and the sound filled his chest with something like joy.

He could do this. He could be better. He could be the friend she needed without making it about himself.

"We brown the butter," he explained, backing away. "Where's the…?" He spotted the butter on the counter. "Get a saucepan and a whisk."

* * *

She closed the cookies in the oven and hopped up on the counter, bare legs swinging back and forth.

His gaze caught on her tan, smooth skin for longer than he'd intended and he shook himself out of it.

Gorgeous pop star is gorgeous, he reminded himself.

"Why the sudden urge to start baking?" he asked, hopping onto the counter across from her while they waited for the first tray of cookies to bake.

She tucked her hands under her thighs and chuckled. "My sister called me and said she wanted to make cookies when they come to visit. And I thought I better have some idea of what to do."

"When will they be here?"

She shrugged and looked away. "I don't know yet. We have to make sure everything aligns. I miss them," she ended softly. She took a deep breath and forced a small smile. "Hopefully soon."

He hoped so too. He remembered how she'd spoken about them six months ago. How much affection and love had shone through then and now.

"When did you see them last?"

"Last February. They came up to New York for my birthday." Her eyes sharpened on him. "Your birthday is in February too, isn't it?"

He nodded once.

"What did you do?" she asked. "Big party for turning thirty?"

He swallowed. Two things happened inside him he didn't expect. One, her remembering his birthday caused his chest to compress with what could only be described as *longing*. And two, she remembered how old he was,

133

which sent a surge of dopamine through his brain. Which didn't make any sense and yet he wasn't surprised.

"No big party," he replied, keeping his voice even. He frowned, trying to decide how much to reveal. "My mom…" He sighed. "She has a tendency of making my birthday about her and causing a whole drama. So, I don't celebrate on the day anymore. Nikki and I do something stupid the week before. This year she gave me a makeover."

Zara bit her lower lip even as she smiled. "I'd love to see that."

He chuckled, remembering how much fun they'd had. "I'm sure she has a picture she'd be more than happy to show you."

She stretched her leg out and tapped his knee with her toes. "Sorry about your mom," she said, softness stretching through her gaze in his direction.

He shrugged like it was no big deal. But the truth was stuff with his mom always stung. She was his *mom*. Even though she hadn't always acted like it.

"What did you guys do for yours?" he asked instead of dwelling on his sad musings.

Zara's expression turned reflective and she hummed. "Promise not to make fun of me?" she asked.

He scoffed. "I feel like that's a given."

She rolled her eyes. "They stayed for the weekend and we watched Lord of the Rings in the theater room in my place in NoHo."

He grinned. "Nerd. Which one?"

A hint of pink touched her cheeks and she looked away. "Return of the King, which, by the way, I still have your copy of and I still plan on returning to you."

"Sure," he teased, like he didn't believe her.

"And your shirt," she added. "I still have that too." She made a face. "Though I *might* not give it back."

He barked a laugh. "Why not?"

"It's really soft!" she defended with round eyes. "I've never had a shirt that soft and cozy. I wear it…often."

His throat tightened at the idea of Zara wearing his shirt on the regular. Heat rushed through him and he took a slow breath. "You can keep it. I guess," he said, sounding appropriately reluctant.

"Yeah?" she asked.

He nodded. Of course she could keep it. But he needed to change the subject before he said or did something *very* stupid. He stretched his leg out and tapped her shin with his toes. "Can I meet your family when they visit?"

"You want to?" she asked, surprised again.

Asa, you're the dumbest boy in school.

He dipped his chin in affirmation.

"Okay," she said, voice light. "I think they'd like to meet you too."

The timer on the oven went off and she jumped down from the counter.

"These look perfect to me. What do you think?" she asked, holding out the sheet pan toward him. "You're the cookie expert."

He chuckled. "Those look great," he said.

She turned and grabbed the spatula. He watched her carefully move them one at a time from the pan to the cooling rack.

"Where do you get your shirts?" she asked, her back turned to him. She set the pan down on the stove top to cool and took off the oven mitt.

Which shirt was he wearing? He glanced down.

Nice one, Ace.

It was pink and said "this is your mom's shirt" in iridescent sequins.

Deciding to own it (because he did, in fact, literally own it), he shot her a wink. "I know a guy. Why? You want one?"

The laugh that rippled out of her hit him squarely in the chest. His smile grew large and he bit his lower lip. That laugh, her laugh, best sound ever.

"I love shirts like that," she admitted. "But I don't wear things with writing on them." She blew raspberries and rolled her eyes. "I was told it would be bad for my image."

"Right," he said. "Because you alone have been the one holding up society."

"If it crumbles, it'll be my fault."

They were smiling, but they weren't joking. Because that's how the world treated her.

Who she talked to, what she did, where she frequented, all of it was up for public discussion and dissection.

He read once that she had more power than the President of the United States. How fucked up was that?

No wonder she needed a break.

He was definitely getting her a shirt of her own. He had the perfect one in mind.

Chapter Twelve
Wake Me

ASA

He glanced at the clock on the wall.

It was after 3am. He'd completely lost track of time.

After making cookies, he'd gone to have dinner with his dad. Out to the burbs for gnocchi. He'd thought about inviting her but didn't think Cas would approve.

Maybe next time. Maybe not. The whole idea of it made him nervous. One thing at a time. Inviting friends over to meet his dad was often an event. Not because anyone planned it that way, it was just how his dad was.

He'd made it back to Lincoln Park around midnight but instead of going to bed, he reached for the guitar again.

And after three hours of jotting down notes and playing with a melody, he was hungry. For cookies.

He set the guitar back in its stand and stared at the sheet of paper he'd been scribbling on. He couldn't remember the last time he'd written something just for himself. It had been a while.

He definitely deserved a cookie, he decided.

He should be able to sneak upstairs and not disturb anyone.

And by anyone, he meant Zara.

Her bedroom was two floors above the kitchen but he still tried to be as quiet as possible. Not because he thought she'd get upset if he was loud—she wouldn't. But because it would be rude. He was a guest and he was not going to take advantage of her goodness.

He left his bedroom and didn't close the door behind him. The downstairs was mostly dark except for the track lighting in the stair well.

Skipping the first three steps, he took two long strides to the first landing, turned—

And stopped.

He almost yelled but he recognized Zara immediately and his brain processed the information quickly enough that his surprise died and turned to confusion.

She was sleeping on a step, her head resting on her folded hands on the step above, an open book fallen at her feet.

What in the world was she doing here?

He looked around, for what he didn't know. Looking for someone to tell him what to do because he had no idea.

Should he wake her up? Leave her there?

Right away, he dismissed the idea of leaving her there.

But wake her? She was so tired that she'd fallen asleep on the stairs?

Nothing about this situation made any sense. He looked back the way he'd come. Was she... No. That would be ridiculous.

He picked up the book. *The Hobbit*. He shook his head. Nerd.

He set the book aside and rubbed the back of his head, having already made his decision but not knowing how to act on it.

Guess he could just...pick her up.

He practiced the motion with his arms. He would just...put one arm under her bent legs, the other kind of under her lower back, and lift.

Okay.

That didn't seem too bad.

He looked up the stairs and back down. The elevator would make sense. What did he have to prove by passing out before making it up the four flights?

He took a breath, preparing himself.

Dropping into an uneven squat on the stairs, he slid his arms under her and pulled her close.

Slowly, he straightened.

Her warm body pressed against him in various places that he tried to ignore. She was softness and curves and she smelled incredible. It was familiar but he couldn't place it. Or maybe he just didn't know what it was called.

Carefully, he descended the stairs and carefully turned the knob to the elevator.

The door opened and he grimaced at the bright light inside.

She didn't seem to notice though.

It was smaller than he expected.

Rich people were weird.

He angled his arms and tilted her towards his body. Her arms cradled close to her chest and she turned into him.

He hit the button for the top floor. It lurched upwards and still, she didn't wake up.

He stared down at her peaceful face. Her hair was in a messy knot on top of her head, her pink lips slightly open, her thick black lashes resting against her tan skin.

Her pajamas were fucking adorable. Pants and a matching top, pale pink with little white buttons.

The elevator came to a halt, he opened the door and stepped out.

And stopped.

He'd never been up here before.

The elevator opened to a short hallway that became the main bedroom. He carried Zara to the bed and carefully laid her down on the open covers.

She must've been in bed to start.

What was she doing sleeping in the stairwell?

He pulled the covers over her, his eyes flicking to the balcony on the other side of the bed.

It looked like simple glass doors. And her roof was connected to the roof next door.

No wonder Cas was so intense about the security. How the man slept at night knowing the only thing in between his client and any crazy stalker out there was a couple inches of glass, Asa didn't know.

In fact, now that he knew that, he might have to have a conversation with Cas himself.

Zara stirred and his attention returned to her.

Her eyes fluttered and she squinted at him.

"You fell asleep on the stairs," he said.

He couldn't tell if she was awake enough to really hear him.

She blinked at him sleepily.

"I'm sorry I'm a mess," she said.

His lips tugged up on one side and he brushed a strand of hair off her forehead.

"You're not a mess," he reassured her.

"But I am," she said. "When I am most myself, I am a chaos."

She rolled onto her side and hugged a pillow before returning to whatever dreamland she'd briefly stepped out of.

He hoped it was peaceful and beautiful there. She deserved at least that.

* * *

ZARA

Consciousness claimed her slowly. Images from her sleep flickered behind her eyelids and she sat up.

She glanced around the room but it was empty.

The space in the bed beside her had not been slept in.

But she had a distinct image of Asa standing in her bedroom.

She rubbed her eyes and tried to run her fingers through her hair but they got stuck immediately. So much for the bun on top of her head keeping her hair nice.

Her fingers searched through her hair until they found the stretchy band.

She got out of bed and went to the bathroom, still tugging and pulling on the elastic. After using the facilities, she washed her hands and took a look at what was going on with her hair.

It was as if it had a whole life outside of her. Like when she went to bed, her hair went out to party and had come home with a hangover to be proud of.

It was large and in charge.

Dee Snyder *wished* he could get the kind of volume she happened to acquire in her sleep.

She left the bathroom and stopped in her bedroom again.

Why did she think Asa had been in here?

Had she dreamt it?

She went down to the kitchen and opened the refrigerator to get her half and half.

And closed it.

Asa sat at the island, eating a bowl of cereal and reading a book.

Her book.

He glanced up and lifted his chin in greeting.

His dark hair was still wet from a recent shower, his beard freshly trimmed. He was dressed in jeans and a white, Black Flag t-shirt, his tattoos spilling out of the sleeves.

Asa, so far whilst living with her, had yet to grace her with his presence in the morning. If she'd known he was going to be there, she may have tried a little harder to tame her hair.

He looked so casual sitting at the bar, eating breakfast. Like he did it every day.

How did he get her book?

She blinked in the direction of the stairs, trying to remember if she'd brought it with her last night… She'd been reading in bed…took her book to read in the stairwell…Asa had been playing…

She frowned harder, like the force of the frown would fill in the rest of the missing information.

Did she leave the book on the stairs and he'd picked it up?

Also, why was he in the kitchen? Not that she wasn't happy to see him. But they'd just spent some quality time together the day before. And going by his previous behavior, Asa usually avoided her right after that.

So many questions.

"What…?" She didn't know which one she wanted to ask first.

His eyes drifted to her hair and his lips twitched.

"It's a little early to be electrocuting yourself, isn't it?" he asked.

"Hilarious," she deadpanned. She touched her hair, still staring at him, then let her hand drop to her side. "What are you doing?"

"Having breakfast," he answered.

"Right." Taking a deep breath that she hoped would shove more oxygen into her foggy brain, she shuffled over to the coffee maker. "Do you work today?" she asked, popping in a coffee pod and closing the lid.

"Nope," he replied.

She glanced over her shoulder. His head was dipped to read from the aged book on the counter in front of him. He flipped a page, his eyes tracking up to the top. He was really reading.

Reaching for a mug out of the cupboard above the coffee maker, she wondered what his plans were. Maybe he wanted to hang out again? Was that why he was in the kitchen? Had he been waiting for her?

She shoved aside the little bit of delight that slid through her at the idea.

Yesterday had been awesome. A little awkward for her, internally anyway, but she could tell he was trying and that meant... Well, it meant more than she could really say at the moment.

"Can I ask you a really weird personal question?"

She darted him a look but he seemed to be speaking directly to his cereal.

"Go for it."

"Why did you pick this place to live?"

She frowned, watching the coffee sputter from its spout and fill the cup below. "Like, why Chicago?" she asked, taking the full cup and turning around to face him.

He shook his head and finished chewing. "No. I mean this house. Why here and not like a penthouse downtown or, I don't know, something with more security? Like where Hannah and Sunshine live?"

She narrowed one eye at him. "Have you been talking to Cas?"

He chuckled.

Where was the half and half? She'd gotten it out of the fridge, right?

"Um," she blinked against the heavy feeling in her eyelids and opened the fridge again. There it was. "I didn't want to draw a lot of attention. But I also didn't want to feel so..." She wagged her head back and forth, pouring the cream into her coffee. "*Away* from everyone. I love Chicago, you know? The energy and the people and even the light is different here. Being hidden away in a fortress or a tower?" She shook her head and screwed the lid back on and returned the carton to the fridge. "I feel like that would defeat the purpose of coming here."

He didn't say anything for a long time as he frowned in thought. His spoon held aloft but the cereal forgotten.

"You have an opinion about that," she said. It wasn't a question.

"You're trying to live like a regular person," he said but it sounded like an accusation.

Irritation ran down her spine and her left eye twitched. "I am a regular person."

He tipped his head to the side and made a noise in his throat. "You're not though."

Acid churned in her empty stomach and heat rushed up her neck. "I am," she said, but even she didn't sound like she was convinced.

She put her cup down so hard the coffee sloshed up the side. "I'm a regular person, Ace. I'm not better or worse than anyone else. I breathe and eat and have trouble sleeping and fight with my boss and love my family and want better for the world." She closed her eyes and took a breath as she tried to sound less defensive. "I'm a person. I'm just a person. Just like anyone else."

His expression shifted as she spoke—going from thoughtful to watchful and then something else she wasn't familiar with. He left his seat and came around the island, stopping in front of her, stern and focused.

"Zara," he said softly. "You're a person. Absolutely. But you know…" He dipped his head and caught her eyes. "You *know*… nothing about your life is regular."

Her sinuses burned and she blinked away the moisture. "I know." But she hated that it was true. She didn't want it anymore.

Which immediately made her feel guilty and ungrateful. She had so much more than so many and she was crying about it?

He put a finger under her chin and lifted. His dark eyes scanned her face, soft and serious. "You are a person. Of that I have no doubt. But you're not regular folks. Even without all the albums and the awards and the fame. You're top tier folks."

He was being funny again and it was almost working. Maybe because he was still saying real things, just in a funny way.

She smiled and his eyes dropped to her mouth and held. His hand fell away and he took a step back.

"Can I ask *you* a weird personal question?" she asked, picking her coffee up again and changing the subject.

His lips pursed and he nodded once.

"Why are you reading my book? Did you take that from my room?"

His mouth pulled up on the side in that lopsided smirky hot way and then he rubbed his thumb over his lower lip.

She should have known by his reaction that his answer wasn't going to be the distraction she was seeking.

"You, uh, you fell asleep on the stairs last night. I carried you upstairs."

What?

She blinked and shook her head, positive she hadn't heard him right.

"You don't remember?" he asked, watching her carefully.

"I fell asleep on the stairs," she repeated.

He nodded.

"You carried me. Upstairs." Her mind raced through everything she could remember from the day before.

She felt queasy. Heat rushed up her neck to her cheeks.

"Well, not up the stairs. I took the elevator," he clarified.

"That makes sense," she whispered, chewing on her bottom lip.

"Hey." He stepped forward and grabbed her chin in a gentle pinch. "Stop."

Her eyes darted to his.

"Stop chewing on that lip. It's fucking raw." He sniffed a laugh and let her go. The heat from his touch lingered on her skin. "What were you doing sleeping on the stairs?" he asked, completely unaware that her brain had stopped working entirely.

When was the last time someone had called her out on her lip biting? Her dad, maybe? It had been years since she'd struggled with the habit but it had come back over the last month without her really noticing until she saw the evidence when she looked in the mirror.

She measured the distance between them. Took in his relaxed posture and open body language.

"Are we friends?" she asked.

He shifted, expression turning guarded but he didn't turn away.

"Because I want to be super upfront with you," she hurried on. "But I have no idea if we're friends."

He looked at her like he thought she was being weird but he wasn't going to stop her. "Yes, we're friends."

She nodded and crossed her arms. Okay, she could do this. They were friends. New friends, but still friends. She could tell him the truth and he wouldn't disappear on her again.

"Since leaving New York, I've been having a hard time sleeping. My mind just…goes. Like it's on a loop of all my greatest worst mistakes."

He made a face.

"A couple nights ago…" She swallowed. She could do this. She wasn't a crazy stalker. She *had* crazy stalkers. She was just insecure and weird. Not. A. Stalker. "I was awake and I heard you come home and I went downstairs because I wanted to ask you why you hate me."

Shock and concern rippled across his face but she pushed on.

"And I heard you playing," she said softly. Big swallow. "And singing." Another slow breath. Was it hot in here? "And I…liked it." she shrugged. "It was very soothing… And I know that makes me sound weird and creepy but whatever," she rushed out as fast as she could. "It was nice. And I was able to sleep."

There.

She'd told him.

He narrowed his eyes and she shifted uncomfortably.

"You've been sleeping in the stairwell?" he asked.

"No!" She huffed. "That's the first time I've actually fallen asleep before getting back to my room."

His gaze dropped to the floor and he tugged at his ear. "I had no idea," he muttered.

"I know. I was afraid to tell you because I was afraid you'd…stop." She scrubbed a hand over her face like it would wipe away all of her discomfort.

He arched an eyebrow at her. "It's a little weird."

She glared at him. "Whatever."

"I didn't know you weren't sleeping." His teasing tone faded to one of concern.

"It's fine," she said, waving it away. "I think my body clock is all screwed up."

He eyed her skeptically but didn't argue. She heard it anyway. She'd been on a new schedule for a while now. It wasn't her body clock.

She also noticed he completely bypassed her listening to him play and sing. If that was good or bad, she didn't know.

He hummed, a thoughtful frown creasing his brow. "What do you have planned for today?" he asked.

She shook her head once. "Nothing," she replied definitively. That had been the point in coming to Chicago, hadn't it? She'd wanted a break?

But not being able to go places and do things was starting to make her feel trapped in a different way.

Asa hit her with those deep brown eyes as he poked at the inside of his cheek with his tongue. And then he said the last thing she expected.

"Do you think Cas would let me take you out on the motorcycle?"

Chapter Thirteen
Drive All Night

ASA

Asa had had a lot of bad ideas in his life. More than he could count. His guardian angel probably had a spreadsheet somewhere.

But this idea?

This was a very bad idea.

Take the world's most beloved woman on the back of a motorcycle? Was he deranged?

Except the moment he'd suggested it, her amber gold eyes lit up in a way he wasn't sure if he'd seen yet. And he really, *really* hoped Cas would say yes.

Because Nikki had been right, he was a better friend—a better person—than how he'd been behaving. So what if people saw them together? Fuck Shelby and Gemma and everyone who thought they knew his business.

They didn't know anything.

They never had.

Something had happened last night when he'd found her in the stairwell.

It hadn't been some huge revelation or lightning striking epiphany. No, it had been subtle. Unassuming. A gentle shift in his mind that he didn't notice until he'd lifted his eyes and saw her sleepy, confused face in the kitchen.

All the reasons he'd had for keeping her at arm's length seemed so very insignificant.

She'd texted Cas to come over and then had breakfast. They chatted about the book she (and now he) was reading, and she went upstairs to shower and get ready… for whatever the day might bring.

He went back to his room and found the shirt he'd decided to give her. It was new; he'd never worn it.

He held it up and immediately smiled at the ridiculous graphic. She'd love it.

The garage door started to open and Asa froze.

He held perfectly still and tried to ignore the slight tremble in his hands as he listened to Cas and Devan enter the house and go upstairs.

He wasn't *scared* of Cas. Okay, maybe a little. But it was a healthy fear, not an irrational one.

What the fuck was he doing?

She found comfort in my music.

He shook his head, trying to rid his mind of the thought that kept floating through it like a whimsical bubble in a rain shower.

He could do this. He could talk to Cas about taking Zara on the bike.

She was an adult, not a child. She'd been living this life longer than most popstars had successful careers.

But if Cas said no, that would be it. Idea dead. No more ideas.

But he had a sneaking suspicion Cas would say yes.

Asa climbed the stairs, long sleeve shirt tucked under his arm.

Cas was waiting for him in the kitchen. He had a cup of coffee in front of him and Asa was pretty sure it was the first time he'd seen the Terminator have a human function.

Actually, he hadn't seen Cas drink from the cup yet. It could be a prop.

Asa took a casual stance, leaning against the counter, ankles crossed, facing the bodyguard.

Cas arched a single eyebrow.

"Mornin'," Asa said.

Cas nodded once.

Asa took in a slow breath. Cas wouldn't murder him right there in the kitchen. He'd wait until 4am when Asa was sleeping and he'd throw a hood over his head, haul him out of the house, and toss his body into the Chicago River.

"I could be wrong," Asa started. "And if this is a terrible idea, I trust your judgement. I don't want her to get hurt."

Something flickered in Cas's eyes but he otherwise didn't move.

"I want to take her for a ride on the bike. South. Toward Peoria and back. It's an easy loop. Couple hundred miles. There's a state park where we can stop for a minute if she wants. Nothing crazy." His voice got softer. "You and Devan can follow us. You *should* follow us." *Aaannnd* he was sweating. Had he remembered to put deodorant on? He swallowed, trying to work moisture back into his suddenly dry mouth. "I think, and again, I could be wrong, but I think she needs to get out."

Cas didn't say anything for a long time.

Ultimately, Asa knew that Zara would make her own decision. But it would help a lot if her head of security was on board. He cared about her probably as much as her own father. If he expressed concern, it should be heard.

Asa looked at the larger man and decided to reveal something Zara probably never would.

"She's not sleeping," he said.

The lines between Cas's eyebrows deepened slightly. He had to be wondering how Asa knew Zara wasn't sleeping since they lived on separate floors. Asa wasn't going to go into the details of how he knew.

The corner of Cas's mouth may have twitched. It was hard to tell.

"Where's the state park?" Cas asked.

Asa pulled out his phone and typed it into the search. He handed it over to the big man; the phone disappeared in Cas's enormous grip.

Devan materialized out of the woodwork and Asa nearly jumped. That woman was a fucking ghost.

He rubbed his chest with a hand, trying to act like his soul *hadn't* just been snatched from his body.

Cas handed the phone over to Devan and they communicated telepathically. Or at least, that's what Asa assumed since no words or gestures were exchanged. Didn't bodyguards have to graduate from a special mindreading school? He thought he'd read that somewhere but it may have been a dream.

Zara stepped into the kitchen, fresh and ready for whatever came next. Her hair had been tamed into a braid. She was in jeans that looked thicker than average, a long sleeve tee, and Docs. A black leather jacket hung over one arm.

Something about her showing up ready to go without knowing how Cas would respond to Asa's idea seemed very ballsy on her part. It was that kind of confidence that let her step out onto the stage in front of seventy thousand people and sing about the things that made her hurt.

It was really fucking hot.

Cas cleared his throat and handed the phone back to Asa. He gave a subtle nod.

For whatever reason, Cas's approval was even more nerve-wracking than waiting for it. Asa's stomach took a dive. He took his phone and slid it in his pocket before he looked at Zara again.

Could he take one of the most photographed women in the world out into public and not have anyone recognize her?

Or was he going to throw up first?

His mind flashed back to the night he rescued her from the afterparty. He'd been a wreck about that too. And then it had somehow turned into one of the best nights of his life.

He could do this.

"You wanna go for a ride?" he asked.

A slow smile spread across her face.

"There's not a lot of space in town." Asa dipped his chin. Because duh. "But we can head south and just ride. Or stop at the state park and walk around a bit. If you want."

She laced her hands together and held them under her chin.

"I don't want you to get too excited," he warned, thinking about the very mediocre landscape that was Illinois. "It's not life changing."

"I don't care. Please, let's do that. Oh please." She grabbed his arm and he was pretty sure she wasn't aware she was even doing it. "Please don't change your mind. I know I'm acting like a psycho but I'll behave."

This was not the first time she'd apologized for her excitement and Asa decided if he ever met Logan Black again, he was probably going to jail.

He couldn't be sure it was Logan who'd made Zara feel like she needed to be "less." But he didn't doubt it.

Fucker.

Instead of saying any of that though, he held out the shirt he'd brought upstairs.

She took it, giving him a curious look.

His stomach felt weird.

Good weird.

She unfolded the shirt and held it up.

If his stomach felt weird before, it was nothing compared to how his entire body felt when she laughed out loud.

Like he'd touched a shorted-out cord. Tingles raced over his skin and scalp and left him with a buzzing sensation in his fingertips.

Zara, completely oblivious to what was happening to Asa, held the shirt up against her body and showed Devan and Cas.

Devan cracked a smile and Cas's eyes crinkled at the sides. That was the equivalent of a belly laugh from that guy.

The long sleeve tee was baby blue and too big for her; extra-large. Screen printed on the front in white was a very recognizable face and the words "Rick Astley is my emergency contact."

"This is getting worn *today*," Zara declared. "I'll be right back." She ran upstairs.

Asa looked at Cas and Devan to find them both watching him. He forced a smile.

"This is a good idea, right?"

He didn't expect an answer.

He didn't get one.

* * *

ZARA

Zara met Cas's eyes as Devan lowered the helmet onto her head.

"We'll be right behind you," Cas said, handing her an Air Tag which she slipped into her back pocket.

He didn't look worried. Or even annoyed. Cas seemed…fine. Whatever that was about.

She knew her life wasn't exactly normal. And yeah, sometimes she felt like a child when Cas and Devan had to check the house before she went inside. Or like right then when Cas handed her a pair of leather gloves.

Except she was also very aware that without them she probably wouldn't be alive anymore. More than once, her profession had put her life in danger. And Cas and Devan had been there to keep her safe.

But this was regular life stuff. Not part of her profession. Going for a ride with a friend shouldn't require her security detail going with her. She wasn't the president.

Logan always hated it when they would go out and Cas and Devan would be nearby. He said it made him feel like he couldn't be himself.

Asa hadn't expressed any sort of feeling about Cas and Devan coming along. In fact, she was pretty sure Asa expected them to be there.

Huh.

She thought about the time they'd spent together when they were *alone* alone and the times when Cas had been around. Asa's behavior was relatively the same on both counts.

Maybe that was something to think about. Or maybe it wasn't anything at all and Logan was just an asshole. Maybe both things could be true.

In the alley behind the house, Asa started the bike and Zara had to keep herself from skipping over to his side.

She had promised him she'd be cool about it, but the kaleidoscope of butterflies in her belly had other ideas.

The seat behind him was small but she swung her leg over the bike like she knew what she was doing and settled in behind him. Her thighs aligned with his hips and she gingerly placed her hands on his back.

He reached back and grabbed her hands, pulling them around to his stomach where he held them for a beat. Her chest was right up against his back, her groin completely flush to his lower half.

Her pulse picked up and she almost chickened out, but then Asa patted her hands around his middle and said, "I got you," over the rumble of the motor.

And with the same words he'd used on her six months ago, she tightened her hold and believed him. He lifted his legs and the bike took off down the alley.

She clutched tightly to his body and tried to control her breathing.

The next several minutes as he navigated their way out of the busy Chicago traffic, she had to remind herself that she'd wanted this. No one was forcing her. If she wanted to stop and get off, she knew Asa would let her.

The rumble of the Harley was unfamiliar and she tried not to freak out over ever new sensation. She had to trust that Asa knew what he was doing.

That's when it hit her, she couldn't remember the last time she'd handed over her life to someone else. Sure, she relied on Cas and Devan in a life-or-death way. But every decision Zara made was made *by her*. Even the record execs and the media and everyone who had tried to *make* her do something ultimately failed in the end. She hadn't been a passenger in so long, she almost didn't know what to do with it.

These were the thoughts that occupied her mind as they wound through traffic and headed southeast.

And then the road opened up before them and Asa let out the throttle.

The wind whipped through their clothes and whistled through the visor on the helmet.

Zara's heart continued to thunder and she knew she was gripping Asa tighter than was probably necessary with everything she had. But how else could she respond when it felt like she was about to start flying at any moment?

* * *

ASA

He would not tell her that the first part of their journey had felt like a twenty-five-mile Heimlich. But that's something he'd laugh about to himself for probably the rest of his life.

She eventually relaxed her grip enough that he knew she wasn't as freaked out as when she'd started.

And then he just enjoyed it.

Her so close he could almost feel her heartbeat through his back, the sun, the wind, the open space.

More than once he'd been given a hard time for owning a motorcycle as his only vehicle when he lived in a city that didn't allow for comfortable riding. But it was always worth it when he got out of the city.

Never had U.S. Route 6 been as beautiful as it was that day.

They drove along the winding road until he spotted the sign for the state park. He pointed at it and felt her nod behind him.

It would be a nice, relatively private area for her to stretch her legs and rest.

Cas and Devan pulled up about five minutes after them. They got out of the black SUV but kept their distance.

Again, Asa thought about the night he'd taken Zara away from the after-party. It seemed like those events were never fading in his mind. He had a feeling that if Cas had been there, Logan wouldn't have acted the way he had.

But who knows? Maybe Logan didn't give a shit who heard him.

Zara unzipped her jacket and took it off. She took out the elastic in her hair and redid her braid as she looked around at their surroundings.

Only a couple of cars were parked nearby and he could hear voices from the picnic area.

He darted frequent glances at Zara, trying to read her expression to see if she was uncomfortable or worried about anything. But she was just quiet. Relaxed. Peaceful.

Silently they moseyed around the nearby canyon and then over to the river.

At one point he caught her watching the water, a serene smile ghosting her lips.

They used the bathrooms nearby and then Asa went into the nearby lodge and got everyone lunch.

Cas looked surprised when Asa brought them a couple of sandwiches. But it would be incredibly rude to eat in front of them. His dad would kill him if he did something like that.

He and Zara sat at a picnic table facing each other to eat their lunch.

"Thank you," she said around a mouthful. "I can pay you back when we get home."

He snorted. "It's a couple sandwiches. I think I can afford it."

She narrowed one eye at him but didn't argue. "Do you do this drive often?" she asked.

Was it his imagination or was she trying to sound casual?

He shook his head. "Not often. I should though. I always forget how pretty it is out here." He looked around at the spring foliage.

"You really undersold the Illinois countryside."

He canted his head to the side. "You get to see some of the most beautiful places in the world." He shrugged, figuring that explained it.

The smile on her face went a little funny and she snickered. "Oh, Asa." Her tone was light. "Everything is beautiful."

She looked around at their surroundings, truly enjoying whatever it was she saw. He felt that tingle in his limbs that he usually did when he was with her. Like a low-level buzz of awareness coursing through his entire body.

The sun brightened the gold in her eyes turning them almost citrine. He used to think they brightened them artificially for events or music videos. But that just wasn't the case. At first glance, one would assume her eyes were a light brown; maybe even hazel. But different light, her mood, the presence of tears, could alter the color in significant ways.

"Where did you get your eyes?" he asked. "I've never seen that color before."

She turned those eyes on him with a look that almost made him laugh. "Are you about to tell me they're beautiful?"

He chuckled. "You don't like to hear that?"

She rolled her eyes. "Telling someone they have beautiful eyes seems like the most obvious compliment." She dusted the crumbs from her fingers.

"What do you mean?" His lips quirked up on the side, amused at her irritation.

She flattened a look his direction. "Because all eyes are beautiful."

"No, they're not," he disagreed.

"Yes, they are." She leaned forward and lifted her eyebrows. "Name one person with ugly eyes. Just one."

He opened his mouth and then closed it.

"Go on. I'll wait."

He sighed and shook his head because she was right. He couldn't think of an example.

She sat back and crossed her arms. "See? Eyes are beautiful. All of them. They're like little swirling galaxies rolling around in people's heads."

He barked a laugh. "Didn't exactly stick the landing with your metaphor."

She shrugged one shoulder, unworried. "You know what I mean. Eyes are amazing. But it always feels so disingenuous when someone points it out. What am I supposed to say?" She fluttered her lashes and pitched her voice higher. "Why, thank you," she cooed. "I grew them myself."

He tipped his head back and laughed long and loud. He tried to sober himself but for some reason what she'd done hit him in a spot in his gut that hadn't been punched with humor in a long time. It was hard to stop laughing.

When he finally did, it was with his forehead on the table and both hands holding his stomach.

He righted himself, still smiling and just stared at her.

"You okay?" she asked, looking just as pleased as she should with herself.

He nodded. He was very okay.

"My dad says I got my eyes from his mom's side. She was from Brazil," she said, answering his original question.

"Your dad doesn't have the gold eyes?"

"Nope." She thought about it for a moment. "I think I have a second cousin with eyes like mine. It's hard to remember."

"Did your dad grow up in Brazil?"

"No." She propped her chin on her hand and her elbow on the table. "He was born in Italy. That's where his dad is from. They moved to New Jersey when he was twelve or thirteen. After he graduated from high school, his dad passed away and his mom moved back to Brazil. I don't know anything about my grandparents on my mom's side."

Asa arched his eyebrows.

"You're a little Italian too, right?" she guessed.

"A bit. My dad is Italian and my mom is…" He snorted because he almost said, "crazy." Instead he just shook his head. "What about your mom?" he asked.

Zara hummed and dropped her hands into her lap. "My mom is white. I don't know much else. We don't have any contact."

Ah. So they had the mom thing in common.

"The only contact I have with my mom is through text," he said. "And that's just because it's easier to ignore her that way." It wasn't until the words had finished exiting his mouth that he actually heard them.

His gaze darted to hers, hoping she didn't assume that's what he'd done to her. Even though that was exactly what he'd done to her. But for a completely different reason.

Her lips parted and her head tilted in question.

He waited for her to ask about the unanswered text messages. If she did, he would tell her; he wouldn't lie. Even though it wasn't a conversation he ever wanted to have.

After a beat she rubbed her palms on her thighs. "Are you still working at the piano bar you told me about?" she asked.

Guess she wasn't going to ask about the one-sided texts. He should have felt relief but it only twisted the guilt deeper into his gut. Especially since he'd already decided not to lie to her and then she asked about the one thing he'd been keeping a secret from everyone else.

"No," he answered slowly, gaze drifting to the table. "I quit there a couple months ago."

"Oh," she said, sounding sad if he wasn't mistaken. "Can I ask why?"

He took a deep breath and thought about how to answer. His quitting was very closely related to why he'd never texted her back. And how was he supposed to give his reasons without sounding like he was blaming her?

Because it wasn't her fault. It was just the circumstances that came along with being near her.

And *that* had him feeling even worse about his reasons.

How was he supposed to say that he shut himself off from music because it just *hurt* too much at the time? It sounded as cowardly as it felt.

"Ask me again later," he said.

She held his gaze for a beat before nodding once.

He stood and gathered their trash. "It's probably a good time for us to head back."

She stood as well and put her jacket back on. "Asa?" she asked, stopping near him after he'd thrown the garbage away.

"I'm sorry if I asked about something that wasn't my business," she said softly.

And now he felt even worse. Which was the only explanation for why he did what he did next.

He took her hand and rubbed his thumb over the back of her knuckles. "You did absolutely nothing wrong. I'm having the best day with you." Then he tugged her forward and wrapped his arms high up around her shoulders. Her arms went around his middle and he pressed his cheek to the top of her head. "Ask me about it later," he repeated. She nodded in his arms and he released her.

She put her gloves back on and he helped her with her helmet before they both got back on the bike.

And for the next two hours, the only thing he let his mind think about was how amazing it felt to have her limbs wrapped around his body. And how he wanted it for a lot longer than he should.

Chapter Fourteen
Broken Songs

ZARA

She couldn't stop thinking about Bruce Springsteen.

Being born and raised in Jersey and having a dad with a blue-collar job meant that The Boss was never far away. She knew his songs almost as well as she knew her own.

And a motorcycle ride through middle America had triggered a specific desire.

The house was quiet. Cas and Devan had left. Asa had dropped her off and gone somewhere else. He didn't say where and she didn't ask.

She took a shower, put on a pair of black sweatpants and a thin white tank top, and poured herself a glass of white wine.

On the second floor of the house, just off the dining room, was a room with a grand piano. It was also where Asa had set up the guitars he'd brought when he'd moved in. The sun had been down for a while and she turned on one side lamp on the far side of the room.

She walked slowly around the room, looking at all the instruments Asa owned in the various stages of wear. It was obvious which ones were favorites. Or had been.

Her heart pinched when she thought about how he didn't seem to do that anymore. Aside from the couple of times she'd heard him play through his bedroom door, she didn't think he spent time with music at all. Not the way he used to. Not the way this collection said he once had.

She finished her wine and set the glass down on the table by the light she'd turned on. Then she went to the piano and took a seat. She'd lived there for over a month but hadn't messed with the piano yet.

Growing up, they'd had a small upright piano in the living room where her dad had taught her to play. He'd taught her every Springsteen song he knew. She'd always believed it's where her love of songwriting had come from. The way the story unfolded with the music, how it pulled at her soul and gave sound to the undefinable things in her heart.

Music had been and always would be magic to her. How could it be anything else?

Her fingers found their place on the ivory keys. It had been a while but after a couple false starts, she felt it come back.

She let herself get lost in "Thunder Road," remembering the ride in the sun that day with Asa, the times she'd played this song for her dad while he'd pretended not to cry, the constant and dependable friend that music had always been to her. No matter what she was going through, how clouded her emotions, she could find *rightness* in the music. Belonging.

That's all she wanted to do for everyone else. She shared her music with the world because she didn't want anyone to ever feel alone.

Coming to the end of the song, she opened her eyes, not realizing they had closed.

The first thing they saw was Asa, standing with a shoulder to the doorway, hands in his pockets. A gentle look at his face.

He'd changed his clothes since their ride. He must've showered again because his hair was wet. He had on a pair of navy-blue sweats and a gray muscle tank that showed off his heavily tattooed arms.

Drool. Worthy.

Not that she was a drooling type of individual. But if she had been, *whoo buddy!*

Taking her hands off the keys, she tucked them between her knees and gave him a small smile.

"I didn't know you were back," she said.

"I don't think I've ever heard 'Thunder Road' sound quite like that," he said, voice rough. He took a deep breath. "You are..." He rolled his lips inward and shook his head once. "Something else."

She snickered, her gaze drifting back to the keys before her. "I used to play for my dad. He actually taught me how."

"And he taught you using Bruce Springsteen?"

She nodded. "Jersey, remember? So it was a lot of Springsteen and quite a bit of Bon Jovi," she added with a chuckle.

"Yeah?" He took a step into the room, coming straight toward her. He slid onto the piano bench with her, his hip and thigh aligning with hers. "Let me hear some Jovi."

She puffed a soft laugh, feeling abnormally self-conscious. But she rested her hands on the ivory again anyway.

He bumped her shoulder with his. "What you got in there, Baby Boss?"

She snorted but started to play "Thank You For Loving Me" anyway. "I played this at my dad's wedding to my stepmom."

She'd always loved this song. Though at the time she'd first learned it, she hadn't understood it. Not in the way it was meant to be understood. She'd been a child and had no concept of romantic love. But again, the magic of the music was undeniable. Just because she hadn't understood it, didn't mean she couldn't feel its weighty significance.

And now, as an adult, as someone who had loved and lost and loved again, she understood the gratitude that would come along with someone loving her as she was.

As she pounded through the chorus of the song, she wondered if that was even a real possibility anymore. Maybe she was simply meant to be the catalyst for other people finding love.

That was a noble accomplishment too, she supposed.

Her fingers flew over the keys, seemingly on their own. She barely had to think about the song, she'd played it so many times.

When it was over, she rested her hands in her lap again and let the silence have a moment.

"Wow," Asa murmured by her side.

She bumped his shoulder with hers. "Your turn."

"Uh, what?" He tried to play stupid.

"Just play something for me, Ace. Don't overthink it."

He hummed and his fingers tested the keys. He shifted on the bench and she moved down so he had more room. He slid right up beside her again, their bodies touching.

"How about something *I* grew up on?" he asked, starting a song that sounded vaguely familiar. "This is Chicago's 'Hard to Say I'm Sorry.' Though I'm not sure I can do it without singing. It's a force of habit. So if my voice offends, just pretend like you can't hear it."

Goosebumps raced across her shoulder blades.

Asa's voice was smooth and warm and soft. It grew in confidence as the song progressed and she couldn't help but think he was singing this song to music itself. Making promises to make it up, to fix it, to come back because he wasn't complete without it.

She swiped at the tear that had dropped onto her cheek and swallowed.

The hurt and pleading in his voice pierced her sternum and settled in a space between her breasts.

I knew it.

She knew that his avoiding music went deeper than the surface. For some reason he no longer felt deserving of the love and acceptance she'd always found in music.

More tears joined the first and she didn't swipe them away for fear he'd notice her movement and stop. She let them run freely, feeling every chord, every note, every desperate plea he poured out into the piano and into the night.

All the times she'd sat in a room with Logan helping him work on a single or an album and she'd never been moved to tears. Which said a lot because she cried easily. She was a person who kept her emotions close to the surface where they were effortless to access and get overwhelmed by.

The song ended, and they sat in the silence for a beat. Asa took a deep breath and let it out.

She rested her head against his shoulder, lending her warmth to whatever brittleness he was battling inside.

"Why did you quit the piano bar?" she whispered.

His body tensed. He cleared his throat and for a moment she thought he wasn't going to answer.

"Because it made me happy and I didn't deserve it."

A wave of sorrow washed through her but she didn't move from where she was. Even though everything in her wanted to wrap her arms around him and cover him in peace.

"I thought if I played small it wouldn't matter. No one would get offended. But then..." He swallowed. "No one knows I quit the piano bar. Not Nikki. Not my dad. No one. If I try to explain it, it's going to sound bad.

And Nikki especially will try to fix it and she has way too much going on in her life. She doesn't need that kind of pointless drama."

"What happened?" she asked softly.

Beneath her head, his shoulder sagged. Not with relaxation or relief, but with fatigue. Like he was tired of holding onto whatever it was he wasn't saying.

"It's so stupid," he muttered. "Almost immediately after those pictures of you and I together hit the internet, Shelby started harassing me."

"Shelby the singer from Winking Pete?" she asked to make sure she knew exactly who he was talking about.

He hesitated but then said, "Yeah."

From the little Zara knew of Shelby she already hated her. Maybe it wasn't fair. But maybe it was only natural to be protective of her circle.

"How was she harassing you?"

"Texts, emails, phone calls. I had to private all of my socials. I was afraid she'd show up at the bar next. Shelby has a way of making a spectacle. I panicked and quit. Because I knew if she found out I worked there, she'd try to get me fired at the very least."

Shelby sounded like she needed a cooter punch.

"Have you thought about getting a restraining order?" Zara asked carefully.

He made a noise that was part groan part growl. "That's where it gets tricky." He rubbed his palms on his thighs. "Taking out a restraining order on my sister would absolutely cause family drama. And there's already enough of that to go around."

Zara stopped breathing. "Your *sister?*"

He glanced down at her with a frown. "I thought you knew that."

She sat up slowly, her pulse thundering in her ears. She shook her head.

He studied her face for a beat. "I guess I assumed Nikki told you."

All of it made sense. It hadn't exactly been a secret; she'd just never put all the floating pieces together. He had told her he didn't speak to his sister. All the times he'd talked about Shelby made so much more sense. Why he was still hurt by her actions. It had seemed too much to be an ex or even a friend but what did she know? She was still navigating life after Logan. Maybe it took longer to heal for some people.

"Your *sister?*" she repeated, thinking of all the things that had been said about Shelby. "She broke Nikki's arm?"

Asa licked his lips and nodded, wariness entering his expression.

"Why?" she finally asked because it was the loudest word echoing in her head.

"Why what?"

Had he shifted away from her or was she imagining it?

"Why…?" Zara blinked, her mouth opening and closing again and again because no words would form. All she had was anger and confusion and what she thought might be vengeance all pinging around in her brain like a hyperactive pinball machine.

Since the NMAs she'd had the distinct impression that he was hiding. Hiding his gifts, his talent, his obvious passion for music. She'd stupidly thought he was just bitter about the band breaking up. But bands broke up all the time. Most successful bands had gone through several facelifts over the years as they fought for their place in the industry. Being a musician was a hard life. It meant having to risk your heart again and again with zero guarantee that you'd ever find your audience.

And he'd had a taste of what could be and his *sister* had been the one to fuck it up?

"She's not even that good!" Zara blurted.

Asa's head cocked to the side in question.

"Sorry," she said, realizing she wasn't making sense. "I'm just so *mad.*"

Oh, she was going to text Gregor as soon as possible and send Shelby a basket full of dildos. Ugly ones.

Asa slid to the end of the piano bench and stood up. "I shouldn't have said anything." He paced across the room. "Can we not talk about it?"

Whoa. What just happened?

Zara turned her body so she could see him better. Clearly agitated, he took off his glasses and rubbed his eyes with the side of his hand.

"I don't understand," she confessed, her mind still a whirling mess of inexplicable outrage and details all trying to connect.

"Listen, I know…" He closed his eyes and tipped his head back. His Adam's apple bobbed with a hard swallow. "I know it shouldn't get to me and I know I should be able to move past it. I get it. I really do. I just don't want to talk about it, okay?"

But he really should talk about it. And he should talk about it with her.

Because if anyone understood, it was her.

"Asa," she said softly. His dark eyes cut to hers, wary and tired. "There's not a statute of limitation on betrayal."

His eyes narrowed and he put his glasses back on. He hadn't left the room or cut her off. So far so good.

"Shelby sucks," she said.

His lips twitched.

"No, really. I was just mentally making a list of all the horrible things I want Gregor to send her. I'm so…" She closed her eyes and clenched her hands into fists in her lap. "*Enraged.* I had thought Shelby was an ex or something—" His eyes widened in horror and she held up a hand. "But sister makes it so much worse. I'm so sorry that happened to you."

No wonder he'd shut down and cut off contact with everyone.

She'd essentially done the same thing, hadn't she? She'd shelved an album, canceled all appearances, and hidden away in a city where no one would look for her. The one big difference was that she had run to music for comfort and Asa hadn't felt like he could do that.

It broke her heart.

"Is that why you never texted me back?" she asked.

His mouth pulled to the side.

She puffed a humorless laugh. "I thought it was because you had a girlfriend."

Honestly, she would have preferred he had a girlfriend over the reality. Somehow this was so much worse.

"Shelby hurts people I care about," he said, voice rough.

It felt like he was telling her something important. Something she really shouldn't miss, but it was moving too fast and she couldn't quite pin it down.

All she could think about was the injustice of it all. Asa had so much talent, and he felt he had to hide it to keep that pesky little cockroach from contaminating every area of his life.

Bet the holidays are awesome, she thought bitterly.

But she'd already gotten him to share more than he'd planned. Follow up questions would be held until later. Or pitched to Nikki.

"What if…" She flexed her hands, open and closed, changing tactics. "What if we just do this every once in a while." She touched the piano keys. "Just mess around with music. It…it helps me."

He eyed the piano suspiciously and his gaze drifted to the unmoved guitars sitting around like gravestones.

"I won't tell anyone you touched an instrument," she said, testing a small smile.

His gaze cut to hers, but there was a hint of good humor lurking in there that hadn't been a moment before. His lips twitched, which she took as a good sign.

"Promise?" he asked.

She pretended to zip her lips and throw away the key. His lip twitch turned into a tiny smile and somehow that made her feel like she'd just won a massive victory.

One she wouldn't take for granted.

Chapter Fifteen
Crack the Code

ZARA

"You have your mama's eyes. Did you know that?" Zara asked.

Amber kicked her legs and squealed.

"Yep. Which is a good thing because blue eyes are the most beautiful in my opinion. Of course, that's probably because I don't have them." She secured the diaper and straightened out the onesie.

Amber's full tummy called to her and she bent down and blew raspberries. Amber squealed, giving her a happy toothless grin.

Zara buttoned up the yellow onesie covered with little giraffes. Baby clothes were so cute. She wrestled a pair of white socks on the kicking feet.

She was at the point in her life where her friends were having families. It was both exciting and terrifying. She'd never stopped working long enough to wonder if she wanted kids someday. Sometimes she thought she did. But then maybe she only wanted to be a kickass aunt. It was too hard to know for sure.

"But that's why we're here, isn't it?" she said in a soft, sing-song voice. She tossed a burp rag over her shoulder before gathering the baby in her arms. Amber straightened her spine and looked right at Zara. "Right? We're here to ask ourselves the hard questions and finally get some answers."

Amber yelled and a pudgy hand slapped Zara in the mouth. She caught the little fingers with her lips and pretended to munch on them. "Mmm, nom, nom, nom. Baby fingers are my favorite."

Movement in the corner of her eye caught her attention. She turned, wrapping her arms more securely around the baby with the failing arms.

Asa leaned casually against the doorjamb, his hands in his pockets. It was one of his go-to postures and it was so familiar to her now she probably wouldn't recognize him if he stood any different. Today's shirt was light blue and said, "I am a fucking delight" in fancy black script.

Since their road trip two weeks ago, they'd settled into a comfortable routine. They shared at least one meal a day together. He didn't always have breakfast with her, but if he wasn't there for breakfast, he was there for dinner.

She'd begun playing the piano daily. Sometimes he joined her, most times he didn't. But that was okay. He was trying and she wasn't going to push.

Her writing had picked up in a way she hadn't expected. Writing for her had always been something she did alone. So, the days when Asa was out of the house tended to be her most productive. She hadn't told anyone she was writing. Mostly because it was just for her at the moment. She still hadn't decided what she wanted to do with any of it.

And every night, when it was late and she couldn't sleep, she'd sneak back into the stairwell. Because even though he didn't play with her often—and even then, it wasn't anything of his own—he still played in his room when he was alone.

And she loved it.

She hadn't made the mistake of falling asleep on the stairs again. She had no idea if he knew she was listening, they never spoke of it. She didn't ask and he didn't volunteer.

But those hours she spent listening to him play were the best parts of her day.

Unless she was invited over for dinner at Nikki and André's and she could snuggle the baby. Baby snuggles were superior to all else.

"Look," she said, squishing her cheek next to Amber's. "It's Uncle Asa."

"Ah!" Amber hollered, reaching a flailing arm in Asa's general direction.

He immediately came closer, reaching for the baby.

"It's pretty obvious that you're the favorite." Zara reluctantly handed over the baby. But the reluctance was short lived when Amber grabbed Asa's short beard with both hands. His mouth split into a wide grin and Amber yelled right in his face.

"She just likes my beard," Asa said.

"Duh," Zara said with an eye roll. "Who wouldn't mind holding onto that beard with both hands?"

His eyes cut to hers and her face and neck flamed hot.

Shit.

Had she really just said that out loud?

Her mind scrambled to come up with something funny to say to deflect from her previous comment. But she was caught in his heated gaze and she was no longer breathing.

"Dinner's ready." Nikki stepped into the room.

"Ma!" Amber yelled, reaching for her mother.

Zara took full advantage of the distraction and hurried around Nikki and Asa to the kitchen. "Great! I'm starving."

Oh boy, oh boy, oh boy. That…that wasn't anything to think about. Who didn't accidentally flirt with their friends sometimes? She made a face. She didn't. She never flirted with friends because she knew how easily something could be assumed or misconstrued.

And it wasn't like she hadn't meant it.

Wait. No. She didn't mean it.

Holy crap.

She opened André and Nikki's freezer and stuck her head inside. Cold air rushed over her heated face.

It wasn't like she thought about his beard all the time or something. She'd noticed it, sure. It was a nice beard. Short and dark and thick. Sometimes she wondered if it would feel soft or rough on her…hands.

Stop it! Stop it immediately! No sexy thoughts about Asa! What is wrong with you?

"What are you doing?"

She yanked her head out of the freezer to find Nikki giving her a weird look. "Nothing."

Nikki's eyebrows lifted. "Nothing?"

"I was looking for something?"

Good job, Z. That's waaay better.

A knowing smile spread across Nikki's face. "Well, while you're in there, could you grab Amber's teething ring?"

Zara grabbed the teething ring and headed out to the cement balcony where Nikki had a table set for the five of them.

A cool breeze lifted the heat of the day and Zara was glad they were eating outside.

Dinner at André and Nikki's had become one of her favorite parts of the week for a lot of reasons. But the small apartment had trouble accommodating several people. The cement balcony was large enough for a grill and a set of table and chairs and it sat in the shade during early evening.

One of her favorite restaurants in New York had seating on a rooftop terrace and she missed the open-air dining.

She handed Amber her teething ring and then realized that the only available seat was next to Asa.

When they ate inside, the chairs were arranged with one on each side and Amber's highchair at the corner between her parents.

The size and shape of the balcony didn't allow for that though.

She squeezed between the chair and the table to sit down. Pulling herself closer to the table, her leg bumped into Asa's.

"Sorry," she muttered, trying to adjust so as to give his long body more room. But her other leg was pressed up against the table leg. She couldn't move over any further.

"It's fine," he replied casually, knocking his knee against hers.

"I know it's cramped," Nikki apologized, handing a plate of grilled pineapple across the table to Zara. "I just really wanted to eat outside."

"I love eating outside," Zara said, using the tongs to place a slice of pineapple on her plate.

"Yeah?" Asa asked.

She glanced to her right. Oh boy. He was very close.

"You don't eat outside at home," he pointed out.

She cleared her throat and passed him the pineapple. "Ah. Well the best place would be on the terrace, and Cas has asked I don't go up there alone. He said it's 'too exposed.'"

"That makes sense," Nikki agreed.

"I'll go with you," Asa offered, bumping her with his elbow. "I'm not as big and scary as Cas, but I can act as a human shield in a pinch."

She lifted her eyes to Nikki's. But Nikki was looking at Asa with an amused expression.

"Remember that time we were playing at the VFW and someone threw a rotisserie chicken at us?"

Asa chuckled.

"Are you serious?" Zara asked.

He glanced at her, those dark brown eyes warm and smiling. "Local shows are…" His lips twisted to the side. "Exciting."

Nikki snorted. "I saw it coming and ducked behind Asa. He absorbed the blow."

"I never got all the grease out of that shirt. I finally had to throw it away."

Zara shook her head, trying to wrap her head around the idea of an audience that threw food. Nope. She couldn't. Brain wouldn't stretch that far.

The meal progressed with pleasant chatter about work and Amber's milestones. André told a couple stories about some of his students from last year. Then talk turned to the home renovations at Nikki's Victorian.

"The attic dormer is pretty much done," Nikki said. "I just need to get in there and paint it."

"I can paint it," Zara offered.

Nikki lifted her eyes.

Zara shrugged. "I'm not doing anything anyway. And helping you with house stuff was one of the reasons I came here in the first place."

"Do you know how to paint?" Nikki asked, her tone curious instead of skeptical. Which Zara appreciated.

"I mean, it's paint," Zara said. "It can't be that hard. I can look up some tutorials online or something."

"That's true," Nikki agreed.

"I can help." Asa refilled his glass of ice water with the pitcher on the table. "I have tomorrow off." He grabbed Zara's glass and refilled it as well. "And I already know how to paint so I'll teach you."

"Thanks," she said, taking the glass.

Nikki's head tilted to the side as she thought. "If both of you did it, it would go faster and André and I could keep working on the kitchen."

Asa's knee bumped into Zara's and held there. "So breakfast on the terrace and then painting at Nik's?" he asked her. "Sound like a plan?"

"Where will the baby be?" Zara asked, trying to ignore the heat from his leg against her own.

"My parents are driving down tomorrow to stay for a couple days so we can knock out a bunch of work on the house. Johnny said he'd call if they needed me. Which reminds me." Nikki pointed her fork at Zara and then to Asa and back again. "Shawn is in the studio this week. Would one of you mind stopping by and checking on him?"

"Check on him?" "What's wrong?" Asa and Zara asked at the same time.

Nikki made a face. "I don't know. He's…in his head maybe? He's avoiding me and Johnny but he might talk to one of you."

Asa nodded like he understood. He probably did. He was way more intuitive than Zara had known in the beginning.

"Sometimes it's hard to be honest with people who know you best," Asa said, his focus on his food.

Zara and Nikki exchanged a look and she could swear they were both thinking the same thing.

André caught them having their silent conversation and he hid his smirk behind his glass.

Amber hollered and threw her teething ring across the table. It landed in the potato salad.

Something warm and welcome flooded through Zara's veins. It was new and soft and felt an awful lot like home.

She knew her life would always come with a very obvious caveat. But these people, here, in that moment? They accepted her and spoke to her like a friend. Like she was part of their family. Part of something peaceful and solid.

She hoped she never made any of them ever regret it.

* * *

Zara had never felt so stupid.

Painting was not easy. At least not for her.

Bless everyone at that table who'd heard her say, "how hard could it be?" and had not immediately started laughing at her.

First, Asa had had to show her how to tape everything. That in and of itself was a major task. How was the tape not sticky enough to stay where she wanted it to go and yet so sticky that if it came within inches of her body it stuck to her clothes? It felt like imaginary physics.

And then there were the drop cloths and the different brushes and rollers and pans. She nodded along to all of his patient instructions but she had no idea what he'd said. She recognized most of the words he'd spoken but the order they were in made no sense to her.

And then he'd left her to start on her own—giving her the simple task of rolling paint onto the wall—while he'd gone to do the trim on the other side of the room.

She'd started out so innocently eager. Thrilled to be out of the house, to be doing something helpful, to be with *people*.

But there was something wrong with her roller. It wasn't putting paint on the wall like it was supposed to. And why was it so streaky? And runny? Was the paint broken? Could that be a thing?

Maybe she wasn't strong enough.

She pressed harder on the roller as it moved over the wall. That looked even worse.

Was she *too* strong?

"How's it going over here?" Asa's voice came up behind her.

Zara swallowed and stepped back from her work. She didn't look at Asa as he silently observed the streaky, runny mess she'd created.

He didn't speak for so long she assumed he was trying to find a nice way of telling her she should just go home and stop making things harder.

Asa hummed softly, deep in his throat. His warm hand closed around hers as he carefully took the roller from her.

Using thorough and controlled movements he covered her streaks and patches, making the wall look completely different.

"I'm sorry," she said, feeling like shit.

He squatted to add more paint to the roller and glanced at her over his shoulder. "What for?"

She made a face and gestured to the wall. It seemed pretty obvious to her. "For sucking."

His mouth flattened and he stood back up. "Don't be sorry for not knowing how to do something you've never done." He handed the roller back to her.

She took it, their hands connecting briefly.

"Try again. Like you saw me do it."

She took a breath and stepped forward, feeling like an even bigger idiot. Now she had to do it while he watched?

Asa's stifled chuckle had her side-eyeing him.

"You look like I asked you to butcher your first chicken. It's just paint and it's just me."

She nodded with his reminder because he was right. The only other person here was Asa and if he was going to make fun of her, he'd already had plenty of opportunity.

He coached her through the next several minutes. Showing her how much pressure to use and to go in different angles for a more thorough coverage.

Sweat trickled down her temple and she blew a loose strand of hair out of her face. Asa's eyes tracked the hair's journey up and back down. She grinned at him. "Thank you."

"Of course," he replied, his mouth tugging up on one side. He turned to go back to his side of the room.

She watched him go before turning back to her task. A task that she now felt more equipped to tackle. She wanted to express her gratitude in more than just saying "thank you," but nothing came to mind. How do you tell someone thank you for not making you feel stupid?

She thought about it as she continued painting.

Someone had set up a small radio in the corner and it had been playing oldies and classic rock all day. Not loud, just enough to keep the attic space from feeling too quiet.

Chicago's "If You Leave Me Now" started to play through the tiny speakers and she sang along.

"Are you—?" Asa started to ask and stopped.

She squatted to refill her roller. This was going way better now.

"Are you singing along to Chicago?" Asa asked, sounding confused.

She glanced his direction and flashed a smile. "Guilty. I've been listening to them. You know what I love about this song?" she asked. "It reminds me of the theme song from *The Man From Snowy River*."

He didn't respond but that was okay. She returned to her wall—she was making good headway now—and kept singing.

Goosebumps broke out along her shoulders as Asa's rich voice joined hers.

God, that man could sing.

The next song was Bill Withers' "Ain't No Sunshine" and they kept singing. Together.

Same with the next song and the one after that. Soon, she lost count of how many classic songs they had sang together, drowning out the small radio speakers.

Through it all, the walls got painted a beautiful pale yellow. The lid of the paint can called the color "Moonglow" and Zara decided it was the perfect choice.

"Wow."

Zara had just set the paint roller back in the tray, having finished her last little section. Nikki stood at the entrance to their little space. She crossed her arms and surveyed their work.

Zara hoped she had done an alright job for her friend. It wasn't until she was more than halfway done that she thought maybe she should have just paid professionals to do it. But there was something *joyful* about doing the work herself. She was contributing to Nikki and André's future with effort and time. Things she couldn't often do for her loved ones. She didn't know if it meant anything to them, but she knew what it meant to her.

"You guys did a great job," Nikki said, sounding pleased.

Asa cleared his throat and stepped back. He looked around the room and then flashed Zara a smile. "We make a good team."

"In more ways than one," Nikki added. "We could hear you from downstairs. That was next level."

Zara snickered but she agreed. She just didn't want to point it out in front of Asa since he was still so shy about the music thing.

"You're not wrong," Asa said, surprising Zara.

He was scraping his brush against the side of the paint can.

Zara and Nikki exchanged a look that was more like a conversation. It went something like this.

Did he say what I think he said?

He sure did.

What does that mean?

I have no idea.

Why not? You're his best friend.

You're the one living with him.

"Stop doing that."

They both snapped their gazes to Asa's narrowed eyes. He gave them a calculated look and shook his head. "It's weird. Don't talk about me like I'm not here."

"We didn't say anything," Nikki pointed out.

Asa's lips flattened and he snorted.

Nikki and Zara looked at each other and cracked up.

* * *

That night, after Zara had scrubbed yellow paint off her face but failed at getting it all out of her hair, she snuck downstairs to her favorite spot.

The light under his door was on and she didn't have to wait long for him to start playing.

But it was different somehow. His voice seemed stronger. Freer. The guitar clear and precise.

She sighed and rested her head against the wall.

That's it, babe, she thought. *You've got this.*

Chapter Sixteen
Finally // beautiful stranger

ASA

He found Shawn in Studio Y.

Since dinner the other night, he'd been thinking about what Nikki had said. The last time he and Shawn had spoken in depth it had been about whether or not it was a good idea to have a muse.

But that had been…shit, October? Eight months ago? Had it really been that long since the NMAs?

Time was weird. Some days lasted forever; some days were a blur.

And all the days with Zara were in vivid color.

He had nothing to compare it to. He couldn't remember a time in his life when he'd felt so dangerously, haphazardly, completely *alive*. Not in his youth, not when Winking Pete had gotten signed, not their first international tour. All of those moments had been amazing but they'd also been underlined by constant stress and anxiety. Worrying about Shelby's mental state, wondering if she'd be sober enough to do the show, waiting for her to sabotage all their hard work.

Not to mention the emotional toll it had taken on the band, on their family, on his relationships. He'd gotten so used to carrying the weight of it that he had no idea what it felt like to put it down.

The night he'd opened up to Zara about Shelby had been confusing. Her reaction triggered an unpleasant memory. Of trying to communicate to Gemma what he was feeling and how fucked up Shelby was being and having her turn it around on him.

For some reason he thought Zara was going to think the same things. Was going to take Shelby's side or question his perspective.

She hadn't though.

And it was still confusing him.

But the confusion had slowly melted into comfort and now... Now he was always waiting to see her again. Waiting for her to let him know what she needed.

Because without knowing how, without being asked, she'd given him more than he knew he wanted. Space to feel, without telling him he was wrong. The ability to connect with music in a way that didn't feel like a risk.

He was feeling things for her he had no business feeling. But he didn't want to fight it. It was softer and more sincere than those spikes of electricity he'd experienced months and months ago.

It was all those things she'd given to him—given back to him—that gave him the confidence to seek out Shawn and see if he could help the kid out.

The young musician was sitting behind the drum kit in the dark. Not playing. Not moving. Just staring off into space, too much on his mind.

Nikki was right, he was too in his head. Asa could read it clearly from across the room.

"Are we jammin'?" Asa asked, picking up a nearby bass and plugging it in. He looped the strap over his shoulder.

"Huh?" Shawn shook himself out of his thoughts. "Oh, hey," he said, finally seeing Asa.

Asa started tuning the bass. "What are we messing with today?"

Shawn huffed a laugh and tapped the drumsticks on the top of the snare. "I don't know."

The kid sounded so glum Asa wanted to hug him. But he knew from experience that wouldn't help anything. Unless it was a hug from Zara, but that was beside the point.

Getting the bass sound where he liked it, he gave a few experimental thrums.

Shawn lifted the sticks and he poked at the inside of his cheek with his tongue. Asa waited. After a minute, Shawn started a beat, simple and easy.

There was a reason Asa enjoyed playing the rhythm section in a band. It was the heart of the song. Without it, the music was lifeless.

Shawn set the tempo and Asa provided the low-end sound of a tune they found along the way. Together they created a groove they got lost in.

How long had it been since Asa had just jammed with someone? Sure, he played the piano with Zara occasionally. But those weren't his songs. Those were sounds well established by others and easy to fit into.

The rush of creating and collaborating came over him like a wild wave and pulled him out to the untamed ocean of possibility.

He wasn't sure when he closed his eyes, but all he could see in his mind's eye was miles and miles of open space. Unowned and undefined.

And words began to float through his brain. Snippets of ideas, words that conjured images of golden skin and bright eyes, delicate twists of lyrics that were just there, at the edge of where he'd been hiding.

He could almost touch them.

He had no idea how long they played. Sweat trickled along his hairline and his shirt stuck to his back. He glanced over at Shawn to see the kid wiping perspiration out of his eyes while maintaining the beat, his face flushed with exertion as he shot a lopsided grin to Asa.

Movement in the corner of his eye drew his attention.

Zara stood in the doorway.

He hadn't seen her since breakfast on the terrace that morning. At the time she been in pajamas—sky blue with little white clouds on them. Her hair had been epically messy. She'd laughed at a joke he'd told about wishing he had dip for the chip on his shoulder.

Every time he saw her, he was stunned by her beauty. Whether it was in pajamas or in jeans or evening wear. She could wear anything or nothing and… fuck. His fingers slipped at the idea of her in nothing. He regained his rhythm and shook his head at himself.

He should probably look away from her. But he didn't want to.

Her long black hair was down, the layers framing her face. She wore those three silver necklaces that seemed to be her daily staple. He couldn't tell if she was wearing earrings because of her hair. Black leggings, a cropped Bon Jovi t-shirt, Doc Martins.

Effortlessly, casually cool.

And those eyes that seemed to shift and change with her mood and time of day. Sometimes amber gold like they were now. And sometimes when she was tired and introspective, they were dark and deep, making it difficult to distinguish where her pupil ended and the iris began.

When those eyes were on him, he felt like he could do anything.

It wasn't until a few minutes later he even noticed Nikki standing right beside her.

Shawn acknowledged their audience and stopped playing. Naturally Asa did too.

Shawn stood up and shoved his sweaty hair out of his face. He came out from around the drum kit and Asa, having returned the bass to its stand, met him in a hand clasp and back slap.

"That was…" Shawn shook his head and folded his hands on top of his head. He didn't need to expound because Asa got it.

"Same, dude," Asa returned.

"I'd like to track that," Shawn said, sounding almost shy. "Would you mind?"

"Doing a drum track for you?" Asa repeated. "You got it." He backed toward the stairs that led up to Studio Y's control room. "How long do you need?"

"I'll be ready in… fifteen?" Shawn was moving toward the door and Nikki and Zara. "I just wanna check in with Z."

Asa nodded, his gaze lingering briefly on Zara's smile as she greeted Shawn.

Huh.

Something uncomfortable curled in his stomach and he pushed it down. Taking the steps two at a time, he entered the control room and started flipping switches. His gaze drifted out the glass window to where Shawn and Zara were talking below.

They were about the same age, weren't they? Or close.

"Hey."

He flinched at Nikki's unexpected presence. "What's up?" he greeted casually, taking a seat on the stool where he couldn't see Shawn and Zara anymore.

"How's it going?" Nikki asked, sidling up to him.

He puffed a laugh at her pretend casualness. "Fine. How's it going for you?"

"Fine."

He finished turning on what he'd need to use and swiveled to face his longtime friend.

She regarded him quietly, her cool blue gaze narrowing as a small smile tugged at her mouth.

"What?" he asked.

"Nothing," she said. But her expression said it was something. And whatever that something was made her happy.

He suspected the reason but he didn't want to give her false hope. So instead of addressing it, he picked up a nearby rubber band and flicked it at her. She swatted at it too late and it hit her on the shoulder.

"Be careful," she said in a teasing tone.

"About what?" Asa asked, picking the rubber band up off the floor.

Nikki didn't answer and he glanced back up at her.

She had a look on her face he wasn't sure he'd ever seen before. Which said a lot because he'd been with her the first time she'd bought tampons.

In other words, they knew each other. Well.

But he didn't know that particular look.

She studied him for a beat and that soft smile grew a little. "You're still relatively new here. But those of us who've been around for a while know this studio isn't ordinary. It has magical powers."

"Magic, huh?" he asked with a chuckle. "Magic isn't real, Nik. Pretty sure I'm safe in that department." He spun back around to see if Shawn was ready yet.

Nikki was a goof. Though he couldn't really argue with her belief system. After all, she'd made an award-winning album within these walls and André had miraculously gotten his shit together too. To her, that had probably felt a lot like magic.

"It's okay, Ace," she said, a not so small edge of smugness in her tone. "You don't have to believe in magic for it to still knock you on your ass."

He spun around to say something snarky in return, but she was gone.

"Fuckin' nut," he muttered.

Shawn returned to the drum kit and shot him a thumbs up through the window.

And Asa completely forgot about Nikki's warning.

* * *

He made it home in time for dinner that night. It had been a very productive day for both him and Shawn.

Shawn had moved around some music.

And Asa had moved around some internal baggage.

It felt…good. Really good.

He and Zara made linguini together and split a bottle of wine. They ate on the roof terrace, talking about anything and everything as the sun sank low in the sky. They did the dishes together and she asked if he wanted to open another bottle of wine.

He really did.

Grabbing a new bottle of Riesling from the wine fridge (he's learned it was Zara's favorite), he poured them each a glass that would be considered way too full and joined her in the music room. Which was how he'd been referring to where the piano was.

She was still in black leggings and the cropped Bon Jovi tee but she was barefoot. He walked in as she was putting her hair into a sloppy bun on top of her head. She sat crossed legged on an ottoman with an electric guitar in her lap. It was plugged into a small amp he didn't remember seeing in there before.

"Can I show you something?" she asked as he handed her the glass.

"Absolutely," he replied, taking a seat at her feet.

She smiled, taking a drink of wine. "You're so great," she said. She set the glass aside and adjusted the guitar on her lap. "Now this is still very, very rough so bear with me," she warned.

And then she proceeded to blow him away.

It wasn't her typical sound. It was moody and rich, the chords pulled from somewhere deep in her soul. She was finger picking on a Fender Stratocaster (because of course she was) like she'd invented the concept. The sound reverberated through the air and into his soul.

This fucking woman.

The song didn't have words. But he heard the story in it. The way it rose and fell, the chorus, the bridge. The sound took hold of something in his chest and he wondered if every song she wrote would have this effect on him.

She finished and reached for her glass of wine. "What do you think?" she asked, taking a long drink.

What did he think? How was he supposed to put what he'd just experienced into words that wouldn't sound trite or cliché?

How was he supposed to tell her that she wasn't like any musician he had ever known? That she was unlike *anyone* he'd ever known?

She walked around this world with her heart held up in front of her, sharing it with a world that didn't deserve it. Daring it to be better, do better, *feel* better.

"I know it needs, you know, all the things. But…" She shrugged.

"It's amazing," he said softly. She flashed a quick smile. He took a deep breath. "Is this what you've been working on?" he asked, hearing the jagged edges in his voice. Because it had hit him that deep.

She nodded.

"Why are you sharing it with me, *tesoro*?"

Her chin lifted slightly and she blinked like she didn't understand the question. "Because I trust you to tell me the truth," she said simply.

He bit down on his lower lip and shook his head slowly. "It's incredible," he said honestly. "I can feel the story taking shape in the sound."

Her eyes brightened and she beamed at him. "Yeah?" Like she was surprised.

"Yeah," he confirmed, his smile spreading across his face. "You got anything else you want to blow my mind with?" he asked.

She swallowed down the last of her wine and set the empty glass aside. "If I have your attention, I will use it," she confessed unashamedly. She didn't wait for a response before launching into a completely new song. This one a little slower, a little brighter. Still extraordinary.

He finished his wine and laid down on the floor, letting her music wash over him. She played three or four more things, each one a gift. Maybe it was the buzz from the wine, maybe he was just intoxicated by her absolute breathless talent. Maybe it was just the nearness of her, the joy and peace that she gave so freely. He didn't know the cause, he didn't want to know. But a thought drifted through his mind, unencumbered and subtle.

Slow like progress and wanted like a kiss,
Your eyes are a gift,
that hurt as much as heal…

His mind swam with words and phrases. Some in order, most not. Apprehension and joy curled in his chest as he realized what was happening.

Without asking, without pushing, without even knowing, Zara had unlocked that sacred door in him that he'd forgotten about. Behind which he'd boxed up all of his hope, trust, and words.

What was the opposite of an existential crisis?

"Are you okay?"

He opened his eyes, not realizing he'd even closed them, to find dark gold ones staring back at him.

Zara had put down the guitar and joined him on the floor. She was up on her knees with a concerned frown dipping her black eyebrows.

"Are you drunk?" she asked, narrowing one eye. "Do you need a designated driver back downstairs?" She blinked. "Or I guess you could just take the elevator. That would make more sense." She sat back on her heels. "You gotta watch out for the wine. It sneaks up on you."

He chuckled, lacing his hands together and putting them behind his head. "Not drunk. Just enjoying the moment." He watched her eyes flick over his body and back to his face. She blinked at him and he knew he wasn't supposed to have seen her do that.

"Can I ask you a question?"

"Anything you want," he replied easily. He'd learned that Zara's questions could range from silly and innocent to deeply personal. He'd also learned that he could trust her with whatever answer he gave. Even if it was a non-answer. She just accepted it at face value.

"Can I touch your beard?" she asked seriously, her lips twisted to the side.

He barked a laugh, surprised by her yet again.

"Why?" he asked, still chuckling.

She huffed. "Because I want to know what it feels like. I've never touched a beard before."

He narrowed his eyes at her very open and honest expression and thought about the men she'd dated.

"None of the men you've been with ever had a beard?" he asked, trying to remember if he'd ever seen Logan with facial hair.

She rolled her eyes. "C'mon, Ace. You're smarter than that. Just because I've been photographed with someone doesn't mean we dated. The only guy I've ever been with is Logan." She stuck out her tongue and gagged. "And he never even tried to grow facial hair."

She'd only ever been with Logan? He felt two things in that moment. One, jealousy like he couldn't fucking believe that Logan had ever touched her. And two, shame for even questioning her in the first place. She didn't lie to him. She'd never even stretched the truth.

"Go ahead," he said wiggling his shoulders like he was bracing himself. He closed his eyes and tipped his chin a little higher. "Touch away."

She made a little excited noise in her throat that made him smile.

He could so easily fall in love with this girl. He was halfway there already.

And not the popstar, not the woman who sold out stadiums and had countless number one hits. But the beautiful weirdo who squeaked when she was delighted and couldn't cook an egg to save her life.

Tentative fingers touched the hair on his face along his jaw line, down to his chin, and back up again.

"Oh, it's soft," she whispered.

He cracked one eye open. She was so close to him, the heat of her body washed against his side.

"You didn't think it'd be soft?" he asked, trying not to move his mouth too much.

"I hoped," she said, her fingers gained confidence and she used both hands on each cheek. "I thought it might be scratchy."

"I condition it," he said.

Her thumb brushed over his lower lip and heat swept through his body and he swallowed.

"Do you have to trim it every day?" she asked, still stroking him in a way that somehow felt more intimate than he'd expected.

"Mm-hm."

Her eyes snapped to his. This close he could see her dilated pupils and the pink tinge on her cheeks.

"Sorry," she whispered.

But her thumb brushed his lip again and he held himself as still as he could when everything in him wanted to catch her by the back of her neck and pull her to him.

"I think I want to kiss you," she said, sounding slightly confused and a lot breathless.

His pulse thundered below his skin and he knew he should end this. Push her hands away and blame it on too much wine.

But he didn't.

He reached out a hand and curved it around her jaw, his fingers reaching back to the nape of her neck, his thumb resting on her cheek. He did an ab curl, bracing himself up on his other forearm.

She didn't move back and they met in the middle, their lips separated by millimeters.

He took a deep breath, inhaling her sweet scent that had started to haunt his dreams. Her warm breath washed over his mouth and he closed his eyes.

"Ace," she whispered. "Is this a good idea?" Her lips brushed over his as she spoke, sending spikes of awareness to his lower extremities.

He wet his lips with his tongue and it grazed hers in the process. Electricity shot through him, making it difficult to concentrate on anything other than her mouth and its proximity to his.

"I don't know," he answered honestly, trying to keep his head clear before he did something they both regretted.

If she wanted this, she would have to make the final move. She'd have to close the gap because he didn't want her to feel pressured in any way. People were always expecting so many things from her.

He wasn't going to be another voice pulling her in a direction she wasn't even sure she wanted to go.

Their mouths hovered too close to be considered innocent though. A line had been blurred. They could still go back. If she pulled away, he wouldn't stop her and he would never bring it up.

But this moment, her heat, her breath, her mouth, he would dream about this moment for the rest of his life. Because he'd been *this* close to everything he never knew he wanted.

A soft whimper washed over his mouth just before she kissed him. He let out a groan of relief as the warmth of her mouth crashed into his. His fingers flexed against the back of her head and he pulled her closer.

Her lips opened over his and his tongue answered the invitation, tasting wine and honey. The softness of her mouth, coupled with the heat of her breath, went to his head, making him dizzy with desire.

Slow, slow, so fucking slow, he moved his mouth against hers. Paying attention to every pressure, every tremble, every breath.

It was just a kiss. Kisses happened every day. But not like this. And not to him. Electricity and warmth spread through his body, setting his fingertips on fire. He used those fingertips to delve deeper into her thick hair.

Her tongue slipped past his lips and he groaned. Fuck.

Her hands slid from his face to his neck, the back of his head, nails

lightly scratching his scalp. Her touch filled him with heart-pounding awareness. He was flying, he was falling, he was so fucking *alive* in that moment
he knew he'd never be the same. Her kiss had changed him. Was still
changing him. It burned through every doubt and hesitation in his mind and
all he wanted was to be lost in her forever.

Since he'd met her, he'd done his best to keep himself carefully
distanced. As if something in him knew that the second he found out how
her lips felt on his, how her hair felt in his fingers, he'd never want to go
back. Life before was nothing compared to the violent awakening of his soul
in her arms.

The house alarm started going off and both of their phones started
ringing simultaneously.

They broke apart wearing matching frowns and breathing heavily. She
blinked, disoriented, and realized what was happening a second before
he did.

"The alarm," she said, scrambling to her feet and out of his arms.

"Wait," he said as she started for the nearest alarm panel on the wall. Asa
pulled his phone out of his pocket, his heart still hammering, his body still
on fire. She glanced at him over her shoulder.

"Cas," Asa answered, his eyes on Zara.

"Are you both there?" Cas asked earnestly.

"Yeah, she's checking the cameras." Asa got to his feet, willing his body
to calm down. His heart began to pound for a different reason as his mind
sluggishly processed the change of focus.

Why was the house alarm going off?

Zara barely glanced at the camera view before she snorted and waved a
hand at him. "Oh. It's fine." She went to the front door they never used and
Asa had basically forgotten was there.

"Wait," Asa said, worry rippling through him. He started in that direction, intent on stopping her, but she opened the door.

"What?" Cas asked in his ear. "What's going on?"

Asa backed up, chuckled, and scrubbed a hand over his face. "It's her
family."

Cas said something that Asa wouldn't repeat and then, "Be there in
five."

Asa hung up and forced a smile as Zara introduced him to her family.

And any hope he had of finishing that kiss died a sad quiet death.

Chapter Seventeen
Glitch

ASA

The first thing he noticed about Zara's family was how excited they were to see her.

He may as well have not even been there.

Her dad, a happy man with thick black hair, brown eyes, and a bright smile, hugged his daughter and then held her face in both his hands. He said something to her that Asa couldn't hear and then hugged her again.

A woman who had to be her stepmom did exactly the same. And then a younger version of Zara except with brown eyes shoved her way to the front and threw her arms around Zara. Zara stepped back at the force and belted out a laugh he wasn't sure he'd ever heard from her before. The brother rolled his eyes and when it was his turn for a hug, Zara grabbed his cheeks and squished them before hugging him tight to her.

Then Cas came barreling through the door and Asa wished he had it on video.

The family turned as a unit towards Cas and all of them reached their arms his direction calling, "Cas!"

The bodyguard's face flushed a deep red as he was hugged and patted with affection.

A whisper at his side had him glancing over. Devan stood at his shoulder with a smirk on her face, enjoying Cas's discomfort as well. No one tried to hug Devan Asa noticed.

"Who are you?" Zara's sister asked, stopping in front of Asa with narrowed eyes.

He opened his mouth to answer but Zara beat him to it.

"This is Asa. He's my friend who's staying here for a little while," she introduced quickly. "Asa, this is Bianca, Oscar, my dad, and my stepmom Renata."

Her dad stepped forward to shake his hand.

"Nice to meet you Zara's dad," Asa greeted. What? He couldn't call him Mr. Lorna. There was no way that was her last name let alone his.

"Call me Tony," her dad replied with a smile. The handshake lasted all of two seconds before her dad was ooing and ahhing over the house.

Devan tugged on Asa's sleeve and they backed toward the stairs. "This will be awhile," she said.

Ah. That made sense. He nodded and glanced back at the crowd of people in their once quiet home. Everyone was speaking all at once and Zara's overjoyed expression let him know she was more than happy with the surprise. He headed for the stairs and turned around for one more look.

Zara's eyes met his through the bodies and she lifted her eyebrows like she just remembered he was there. He smiled and flicked two fingers at her. He didn't want to interfere with the reunion.

They'd be able to talk about what had just happened later. Not in front of her entire family and Cas and Devan.

He made it to his room and closed the door.

What a day.

From beginning to end, none of it had gone like he'd expected. It was a break in the routine. And he wasn't freaking out.

And for a moment there, Zara's lips had been connected to his and it felt so damn *right*.

* * *

Sleep that night had not been restful. His dreams were filled with honeyed kisses and soft skin. His alarm went off and he practically skipped to the shower.

190

Once again, unconcerned that he'd lost sleep over Zara.

He showered, shaved, and put on his Illuminati Hotties t-shirt with jeans.

Climbing the steps to the kitchen, he listened for any sounds that might indicate anyone else was awake.

Cas came into view as he entered the kitchen. The big bodyguard sat at the island with his prop coffee in front of him. He tipped his chin up at Asa and Asa considered that an absolute win.

He wondered if Cas and Devan had stayed the night after Zara's family had arrived but didn't ask. He wouldn't get an answer anyway.

Asa went about making his own coffee.

"You've got to be kidding me," came a disgruntled teenage voice behind him.

He turned around. He tried, he really did, but he couldn't stop the automatic smile at seeing that Bianca's hair did the same thing that Zara's did in the morning.

She was in an oversized black t-shirt and gray sweatpants. Her eye makeup was smeared across one side of her face.

"Coffee?" he asked, taking another cup out of the cupboard.

"Yes," she said, but she made it sound like he'd just asked her the stupidest question in existence. She slid onto a stool next to Cas and eyed the big man. "Did he make you coffee too?"

Cas patted the top of her head, eyeing the epic hairstyle. "No."

She huffed.

Asa hid his smile as he started another cup. He retrieved the half and half from the fridge, grabbed the sugar bowl and a spoon, and placed them in front of Bianca along with the steaming cup.

"Thanks," she muttered, eyeing him suspiciously. She spooned several scoops of sugar into the cup. "So, *Asa*," she said his name like she didn't believe it was his real name. "Are you mad that we're here?"

He grabbed the half and half with a frown. "No. Why would I be mad?" He flicked his gaze to Cas who lifted an eyebrow and almost shrugged one shoulder.

Bianca took her time answering as she watched him stir the half and half into his coffee.

"Because we weren't allowed to stay with Zara when Logan was around," Oscar said, entering the kitchen.

Asa turned his body to the side. "Seriously?" he asked. He knew Logan was a dick, but come on.

Oscar slid onto the stool on the other side of Bianca. Asa hesitated for exactly one second before making another cup of coffee for the fifteen-year-old.

Oscar's hair was jet black and sort of long on top, a rooster tail of some significance stood straight up on the left side of his head. Already tall, he was close to if not six feet. But he still had that gangly, loose-limbed body that young men had.

Asa put the full cup down before Oscar, and Bianca pushed the sugar his direction.

"Logan didn't like us," Oscar said. "He always stayed up in his room when we came over. He never wanted anything to do with us."

"That's because we could see through his bullshit," Bianca said, aiming a pointed look at Asa.

Asa curled a lip before taking a sip of his coffee. He probably shouldn't voice his opinion *buuuuut*... "That's so stupid." He shook his head and sniffed. "Every time I hear something about that guy I'm surprised no one has kicked his ass yet."

"Oh, he better hope he never runs into me," Bianca said, lifting her cup. "Because it's on sight."

Asa chuckled. Despite Bianca's obvious distrust of him, he really liked her. "Hey, you guys want breakfast?" he asked, getting back in the fridge for eggs.

"I could eat." Oscar shrugged.

Bianca rolled her eyes.

"I'll take that as a yes," Asa said.

* * *

Thirty minutes later he placed a huge bowl of scrambled eggs on the island, along with a stack of plates, sliced peppers, shredded cheese, blueberries, and some chicken sausage he'd found in the freezer. He stuck a spoon in the eggs.

"Serve yourself," he said, backing away.

Oscar dug in immediately. Bianca took a small amount of everything.

Asa took what he needed and ate quietly, standing in the corner, facing the island. Cas even took a few blueberries and sausage.

Zara stepped into the kitchen, rubbing her eyes. "What's going on?" she asked around a yawn.

He took in her pink pajamas and huge hair and smiled. It didn't matter which version he got of her—pajamas and bedhead, full glam red carpet, jeans and tee—he was into it in a big way.

"Just having breakfast," he said. He pulled his phone out of his pocket to check the time. "I have to go to work soon. You want a cup of coffee?" He reached into the cupboard for another cup.

"You have to work today?" Zara asked. The disappointed lilt in her voice hit a spot in between his ribs.

He started the coffee. She came to stand right by him, resting her lower back against the counter. Her hip bumped against his thigh and stayed. He didn't move away.

"I will be home later. What are you guys doing today?" he asked, trying to keep his eyes on hers and not let them drift to her mouth.

Zara shrugged. "We can't really go anywhere so we'll probably just hang out here."

"Not a bad day," he replied.

She nodded in agreement, her expression still sleepy and unfocused. He poured half and half into her coffee, stirred it, and handed it over.

"There's food. I'm not sure it's enough for everyone." He shot a look at Oscar who was going back for seconds. "But I can bring home more groceries tonight if you just text me what you need."

"Thanks," she said. Their eye contact held for longer than a few seconds and he licked his lips. Her gaze dropped to his mouth *aaaaaand* it was time for him to go.

* * *

ASA: do you have stuff to make cookies with your sister?

    ZARA: Let me check

    ZARA: No. We're out of eggs. I wonder how that happened.

    ASA: *angel emoji*

    ASA: I'll bring home cookie supplies tonight. Do you need anything else?

ZARA: No, my dad and Renata are going to the store later. They want to have a tamalada and I know they're going to make too many because my dad is always worried about me not eating enough *eye roll emoji*

ASA: ... what's a tamalada?

ZARA: it's a tamale making party. They'll make like 100 and fill the freezer and leave town. They've done it before. And then Dad will call every other day to make sure I eat them and don't let them go to waste.

ASA: I have tomorrow off

ZARA: you're making tamales

ASA: yes I am

* * *

ZARA

She loved her family. Like, really loved, down to the depths of her being, adored them.

But their timing could not have been worse.

Or maybe they'd showed up just in time, saving her from whatever was about to happen with Asa.

Because holy shit *that kiss.*

How were his lips so soft? His mouth so warm and intoxicating?

She wanted more. She wanted to kiss him and kiss him and kiss him and then kiss him some more.

Kissing was her favorite. She'd forgotten that somewhere along the way. And she had *missed* kissing. She couldn't even remember the last time she'd been good and kissed. It could have been years. How sad was that?

What if he didn't want the same? What if it had been wine and mixed signals and she had read into something that wasn't there? Those were all the thoughts that had been racing through her mind the moment her lips had touched his and electricity had shot through her.

She had questions she didn't want to ask with her family present. They would have to wait.

But for what it was worth, Asa wasn't acting like he regretted it. She was going to take that as a good sign and try to be patient.

Their text exchange earlier solidified her belief that no matter how the conversation went about The Kiss, they were okay. He wasn't freaking out and hiding.

She tried not to read into that either. But it was weird, right? He used to freak out all the time. The night of the NMAs he'd had a panic attack.

But kissing her hadn't registered the same way?

No. Nope. Nu-uh. She wasn't thinking about it. She wasn't going to analyze any of it until she could talk to him.

Besides, every time she got lost in the memory of the kiss her sister threw something at her. The items had started soft: a sock, a scrunchie, a pillow. And were now getting more dangerous: the remote, an empty water bottle, a shoe.

She'd have plenty of time to relive it later. Or she assumed so. Her fam was only going to be there for two days. And who knew when they'd get uninterrupted time like this again? Between her schedule, her dad's job, Renata's job, and the media frenzy that could pop up at any time, they usually snuck in as many tiny visits a year as they could.

And she loved every single one of them.

Though she did find herself checking the time as it got closer to when Asa normally got home.

Was it weird that she wanted him to hang out with her family? For them to hang out with him?

"Have you been writing?" her father asked when they all ended up in the music room after dinner.

"A little," she confessed.

Renata sat on the floor with a glass of wine in her hand. "Are you excited to make tamales tomorrow?" she asked with a glint in her dark eyes.

Zara couldn't help smiling.

Her dad and Renata had met at a tamalada thrown by Renata's mom. They had lived in the same neighborhood and the single father with the overly talkative little girl drew a lot of attention.

Renata's mom—or Abuela as all the kids in the hood referred to her, because she treated them all like her own—had decided to make sure Tony and Renata were stationed next to each other for three tamaladas in a row. By the fourth one, Tony had asked Renata on a date, Abuela offered to babysit Zara who had been only seven at the time.

Zara had thought Renata was the most beautiful woman she had ever seen. She still did. With her dark, dark eyes, bronze skin, constant smile, and thick black hair. Her dad never had a chance.

Bianca came along a year later. They were married a few months after that. Oscar was born on their one-year anniversary.

Renata was the closest Zara had ever had to a mom. She had never treated her any differently than her other children. It never mattered that Zara wasn't hers by blood, she'd always felt loved and cared for. Which would forever be something she strived to do for others.

Sometimes Zara wondered about her other half siblings. The ones she'd never met. Maybe someday she would try to reach out to them. But not now when she'd have to go through the woman who had abandoned her and her dad when she was less than a year old.

Maybe she would invite them over for a tamalada. It was tradition after all.

"Zara, my love," her dad said in a tone she recognized immediately. He took Renata's wine glass and set it on the nearby table. "Would you do me a huge favor?" he asked, reaching for Renata's hand. He tugged her gently to her feet.

Zara slid onto the piano bench, snickering at the twin eye rolls from her siblings.

Their dad did this. He loved to be mushy with Renata and the more it annoyed the younger kids, the more he did it.

"Would you play our song?" he asked, pulling Renata into his arms.

Maybe this was why Zara had such hope for long term love. Because this was the standard that had been set.

"I'll sing."

Her head swung over in time to see Asa enter the room. She had no idea how long he'd been there. Obviously long enough to know what was going on. He shot her a wink (yes, a fucking wink) and crossed to the chair she'd sat in last night. He picked up the Fender Stratocaster and plugged it in.

Renata and her dad barely noticed as they were already dancing without the music anyway.

But Bianca's eyebrows were in her hairline as her gaze bounced from Asa to Zara and back again.

Zara was still stuck on the wink to be honest. But also, did he look different?

Hmm. He almost seemed…happy?

He quickly fiddled with the settings on the guitar that he probably knew better than anyone and then looked to her to start.

Which she did.

He came in at the exact right time (*how?* They hadn't rehearsed or even talked about playing this one together) and then his voice…

Electricity buzzed along her skin, across her shoulders and down her arms. When the chorus started, she automatically sang the harmony.

Again. Full. Body. Chills.

Like the day they had sung while painting Nikki's upstairs, their voices joined effortlessly.

He even did the Richie Sambora guitar solo!

It was a good thing Zara was a fucking professional otherwise her jaw would be resting on the keys and hindering her participation. But since she *was* a fucking professional, she not only held it together, but she gave it her fucking all.

Was she swearing too much?

Also, she should mention the eye contact. The *heavy* eye contact between her and Asa. On one hand, it did things to her little heart that would make another person order an EKG. But on another, more mentally stable hand, it anchored her.

The song ended and still she sat, staring at Asa. He, being a fully functioning adult without all of her heart hiccups, behaved like they did this shit all the time. He spoke to her parents, showed Oscar the guitar, laughed at something someone said.

A throat clearing near her shoulder turned her head.

Bianca had slid onto the piano bench with her.

She met her sister's eyes and hoped like hell Bianca wouldn't say anything embarrassing. The girl had been a wild card since conception.

"We gonna make cookies or what?" Bianca asked in the most flat, bored way possible.

"The eggs are in the fridge," Asa said, having stood up and come closer.

"Thanks," Zara mumbled, now finding it difficult to look him in the eye. So she looked at Bianca. "It's kinda late…"

"Nonsense," Bianca said, slipping off the bench. She stood before Asa and looked him up and down, unimpressed. "You wanna make cookies, Tall, Dark, and Handsome?"

Asa's chin jerked back as a smile tugged at his lips. He shot a look to Zara.

"I heard you really know how to, ah, brown the butter," Bianca said in a way that made it seem like she meant something overly scandalous.

Asa pressed his lips together and Zara sighed.

Maybe she would smother her sister in her sleep later.

* * *

ASA

He knew Bianca asking him to join them for cookie making wasn't because the teenager wanted to bond with him. It didn't even mean she liked him. It was a test.

One he didn't know if he could pass. Mostly because he didn't understand the rules but he knew that *not* participating was a guaranteed failure.

Tony and Renata passed on making cookies and went to bed early. It was only nine locally but ten their time.

Oscar slid onto a stool at the island and declared he would be the official taste tester.

And Asa decided his best bet would be honesty. Whatever Bianca threw at him, he wouldn't hide from it. Even if it made him look bad. Which was a very real possibility.

Everything had been going fine. They'd gotten out the ingredients, the measuring cups and spoons, all the bowls they'd need.

Bianca played it all very lowkey. The only hint that something was coming was the underlying tension in the kitchen.

She waited until they were scooping balls of dough onto the cookie sheet before finally going for it.

"Do you have a girlfriend?"

Asa glanced up to find Bianca's shrewd gaze on him.

"*Bianca,*" Zara whispered, sounding embarrassed.

"What? I'm nosey. Sue me," Bianca replied, unapologetic.

Asa chuckled. "No." His eyes flicked to Zara for a beat. Bianca noticed.

"How recent was your last relationship? I want months and years."

"Bianca Riley Rossi," Zara said, no longer messing around.

Bianca, unfazed by her sister's ire kept her serious gaze on Asa.

He didn't mind the third degree. Honestly it was nice to know her sister was looking out for her; he had nothing to hide. Not anymore. This was all information Zara should have anyway. Assuming of course that that kiss wasn't just a kiss but was a starting place for something new for both of them.

"I had one serious girlfriend. Gemma. We met in high school, broke up when she went to college—"

"You didn't go to college?" Bianca asked.

"I did." He frowned, scooping into the dough again. He placed it on the tray. "I stayed local. I never finished my degree because I thought I was gonna be a rock star."

"And then what happened?"

"She came back and we reconnected." His mind drifted over the hazy memories. He didn't think about Gemma much anymore. It was sad in a way, at one time he thought she'd been his endgame. And now he barely thought about her. "We were together three years?"

And that was it.

He'd dated but nothing long term or serious.

"Do you miss her?"

"Nope." Which was also sad. He probably wouldn't even recognize her if he saw her.

"Why did you break up?" Bianca asked.

Zara growled and he suppressed a smile.

"Hmm, well." He thought about how to answer that. "It didn't work for a lot of reasons. I think I was more invested than she was after a certain point." Did he need to mention how she'd taken Shelby's side every time something happened? How she and Shelby were still besties? Probably not.

"Were you in love?" Bianca asked, her voice sounding funny.

"I was," he said, not looking up. "I was all in and she…" He snorted, thinking of how gone he'd been for Gemma. The shock he'd felt when he realized she didn't feel even a fraction of what he felt. "It was real for me."

What else was there to say?

"Let's get these in the oven," he said, picking up the full cookie sheet.

It must've been enough to satisfy Bianca for the moment because the next question was directed at Zara.

"What happened with you and Mandy?"

Zara snorted. "Why?"

"Because it's all over social media that you two had a falling out."

Asa honestly didn't care who Zara's famous friends were. It wasn't a world he would ever want to spend any extended time in, so the less he knew the better. Mandy wasn't a name he was familiar with.

Zara arched an unconcerned eyebrow and nodded. "I mean, I kicked her out of the house. So there's that."

Bianca cackled and hopped onto the counter.

"Not a fan of Mandy's, I take it?" Asa asked, leaning his back against the counter opposite Bianca and crossing his arms.

"God, no," Bianca exhaled.

"You never like my friends," Zara said with one eye narrowed at Bianca.

"Not true," Bianca replied matter of fact. "I like Nikki and Sabine and Sunshine." Bianca's eyes flicked to Asa and back. "I don't like liars is all."

But she liked Nikki, Sabine, and Sunshine. Good. They were good people.

"Mandy and Logan slept together," Zara said.

The silence that followed was deafening.

Asa's gaze bounced from Zara to Bianca to Oscar, trying to figure out who he should be paying attention to.

"I'm gonna kill her," Bianca said so quietly that it sounded like it was a promise meant only for her own benefit.

Zara shrugged one shoulder, pretending like it didn't still hurt when he knew her well enough to know that it did.

"How has Logan made it this far without completely imploding his career?" he asked into the stillness.

"His team is really good at their job," Zara replied.

"How do you…?" he started asking without thinking about who was around. "*Cope* with all that shit? I had one bad experience and it completely wrecked me."

She lifted those amber gold eyes to his and gave a slow blink with her dark lashes. "I use music to process the world. It keeps me sane. It keeps me happy."

Asa's eyebrows dipped at her words. Something about them sounded like a trumpet through the caverns of his soul.

From the moment they'd met she'd been showing him the way out of his own self-imposed prison.

He thought about the song he'd written while he'd been living there. The words that had started to float through his mind again like they used to. No. Not like they used to. It was different this time. The words were changed now. Stronger, more sincere, better.

He owed her.

He owed her everything.

Chapter Eighteen
Chinatown

ZARA

As always, time with her family went by too fast. They spent the day making tamales. And just like she'd suspected, it was to stuff her freezer.

She would never be hungry again.

She would also be taking a bunch of tamales to the studio.

Asa impressed her by staying the entire day with her family. He didn't try to escape or find something else more important to do.

Instead, he'd shown up and manned his station with ease. He'd laughed at her dad's jokes, listened to Renata talk about how they'd met, heard way too many stories about her when she was little, showed Oscar some stuff on guitar that she didn't even know how to do, and he hadn't murdered Bianca. That last one was the most impressive.

Bianca hadn't let up on him the entire visit. Not once.

If he was fatigued by her endless interrogation, he didn't show it.

They left the next afternoon. Asa had gone to work that morning so she was alone when they departed.

She cried.

She always cried right after they left. She'd be fine, it was just hard to always be so far apart.

She was sitting at the kitchen island eating cookies and feeling pretty sorry for herself when Asa came home.

"Hey, killer," he said, sliding onto the stool next to her.

She wiped the tears off her face and bit into her cookie. "Hey," she said, mouth full.

"Everybody gone?" he asked.

She nodded, tears slipping down her cheeks.

He rubbed his big, warm palm on her back. Up and down her spine, circle in the middle.

"It's just hard, you know?" she said, knowing she was starting a conversation in the middle but not caring. "My job bought them their dream home and makes sure they never have to worry about medical expenses. But that same job means I never get to see them either. Because if I'm spotted *once* in New Jersey, it's a fucking circus." She swiveled his direction to find him already sitting sideways, facing her. "Did you know the media reports that I'm *estranged* from them? And we don't correct it because it's safer for them if the entire world thinks I'm just some megalomaniac popstar who doesn't know how to love.

"It's just…so fucking lonely sometimes."

His dark eyes watched her so, so carefully. Calm and warm and patient. She could fall into those eyes and never come out.

Grabbing a cookie off the counter, she held it out to him. "Cookie?"

He took it, a small smile tipping his lips briefly. He set it aside and took her hand into both of his warm ones.

"Your family knows you love them," he said. "And they love you just as much."

"Yeah," she replied, glumly. "I'm just being a baby." She dropped her head, knowing she had so much to be grateful for and no right to complain.

He caught her chin with one of his hands and lifted, bringing her eyes back to his earnest stare.

"You miss your family. Don't feel bad about that."

She tried to force a smile but it just didn't take.

"Fuck." He let go of her only to wrap both arms around her shoulders and pull her off the stool and into his chest.

She smashed her face against the soft cotton of his shirt and inhaled his scent. He was all clean man smell, like soap and laundry detergent and a hint of whatever he used in his beard.

Somewhere along the way she'd associated his scent with familiarity and *home.* She snaked her arms around his middle and stepped into the space his open legs provided.

He didn't tell her not to cry or that it would be all right. He just held her and let her get her tears all over his shirt. It was a nice shirt.

"I feel like if I just had one person, you know? Just the one." She was speaking nonsense of course. Because there would never be anybody. Even if she found someone she could trust like that, trust to have her back and not betray her, who would want that kind of life? It wouldn't be anything close to normal. She'd never be able to provide for them what she was asking them to provide for her. It wasn't fair and no one ever said it would be.

"You wanna go for a ride?" Asa's deep voice spoke low, right in her ear.

She tipped her head back and he leaned back to see her. "What?"

He cupped her shoulders and ran his hands down her arms to her elbows and back up again. "Do you think Cas would be okay with it? If we took a ride?"

She blinked at his soft, careful tone.

He really was the best kind of person.

She nodded. "Yeah." She wiped at her face. "I'll text him."

"You want to do that?" he asked, trying to catch her eyes.

She kept nodding. "I do. I want that."

He cracked a smile. "Okay."

Twenty minutes later they were both changed and in the garage.

She'd texted Cas her plans. His reply had been short and carefully worded. He told her to be careful and to wear the Air Tag. She slipped it into her back pocket like last time.

It said something that Cas didn't immediately call her and tell her to at least wait for him. Apparently, Asa had won Cas's trust. Something Logan had never been able to do. Not that he'd tried.

Asa got on the bike and gave her a nod. She couldn't see his face through the visor but she could picture his serious frown.

She climbed on behind him, forgetting for a second how close their bodies had to be for this to work. She had no sooner settled behind him than he grabbed her hands and pulled them around his middle. He said those words that affected her in a way no others ever had, "I got you."

The bike came alive with a rumble that destabilized all of her fears and sorrows.

He took off down the alley and she held on.

* * *

Like last time, it took a while to get out of the city traffic. He took a different route this time and headed northwest.

Unlike last time, she got to experience the sunset.

How had it gotten this far?

Her life that is.

How had doing the one thing she happened to be good at left her hopelessly reaching for things she would never grasp? Things like love, companionship, and peace. It's what everyone wanted, right?

She got to sing about it. Be the soundtrack to countless first loves and romance and promises of forever. But she was always watching through a glass wall.

Or maybe she was just feeling sorry for herself and she needed to knock it off.

Asa pulled over at a fast-food place while she was contemplating all of her life choices. He cut the engine and took off his helmet.

Looking at her over his shoulder he said, "If I get you an ice cream cone, will you eat it?"

She nodded. He grinned and helped her off the bike. He pointed to an outside set of table and chairs as he walked to the door. She took off her helmet and sat down.

The restaurant was moderately busy. Mostly teenagers and one dad with a handful of children in baseball uniforms. She could see Asa through the window, standing in line. He kept glancing in her direction, keeping her in view.

The sound of the nearby interstate was more soothing than she would have thought. Though how many people spent most of their teens and twenties on a tour bus?

She rested her chin in her palm, elbow to the tabletop as she gazed out into the dark nothing beyond the streetlights.

She could quit.

She almost had when her label had tried to play that trickery with Logan and her single release. Sonja had talked her into taking a break and really giving it the thought it deserved.

And that was the bullshit of it all. Here she was, bemoaning her life and all of its "hardships" when she couldn't actually picture herself stopping. She loved what she did. She loved 99.99% of it. The recording, writing, touring, fans, meeting people like Sunshine and Nikki, winning awards. Her job had brought so much joy to herself and to others.

So what if she died alone?

Yikes.

She really needed to come up with a better retirement plan. Maybe she could get one of those birds that lived a long time and talked. That was sort of the same as a life partner, right?

Ugh.

And here she was, back to not knowing what the fuck she was doing. She'd been in Chicago for months and was no closer to knowing what to do about any of it. But the brand had kept right on going without her. That's why Gregor hadn't come along to Chicago. Someone had to stay behind and run the business.

The door of the restaurant opened and Asa came toward her with an ice cream cone in each hand.

How long until he resented her too?

She would have to leave before it got that far. Before he grew tired of the cloak and dagger and all the hoops. Because if he looked at her with that special fatigue that wore through a person's best intentions, she wasn't sure she'd get through it intact.

Chicago had never been a permanent plan. It was just a side quest and she couldn't forget that.

Asa took a seat beside her while handing over a cone.

So," he said, his leg bumping into hers. "Should we talk about the kiss?"

She almost choked on her ice cream.

Wow. That was the very last thing she'd expected him to say.

Swallowing it down she looked around their surroundings. "Here?"

"I figure here is better," he replied, his dark eyes connecting with hers.

"Why?"

He gave her a look and she got it. Here was better because if they were alone they might be tempted to…do things.

See?

He was a really good guy.

Also, it was really fucking refreshing to have him casually bring it up. Like an adult.

"All right," she said, taking a deep breath. "Let's talk about it."

He licked his cone thoughtfully and she deliberately kept her eyes on his hand instead of his mouth.

"Honesty?" he asked.

She nodded once in agreement. "Honesty."

He shifted in his seat, facing her more fully and resting an elbow on the table. "I liked it," he said, his eyebrows and lips twitching with good humor. "I wouldn't mind doing it again. Maybe for longer."

Heat rushed up her neck and tingles shot through her lower belly. Or maybe it was lower than that.

"I haven't kissed anyone in a very long time," she confessed. "And kissing has always been my favorite."

He narrowed his eyes playfully. "Pretty sure you could get anyone you wanted to kiss you if that was something you needed done, babe."

She ignored the babe word and lifted her chin. "Yes, but I was in a relationship with a walking crash test dummy—" he barked a surprised laugh and she smiled, pleased with herself. "And I might be stupid, but I'm at least loyal."

"You're not stupid," he said, his eyes shining as he looked at her.

She licked her ice cream and noticed he watched her mouth for a second before clearing his throat and looking away.

"Do you want to kiss me again?" she asked, just going for it.

He held her gaze for a long time before he finally answered. "I do. Badly."

Those tingles tingled some more. Definitely lower than her stomach.

"However," he said, straightening his posture. "You are becoming..." His eyes drifted to the side and then back. "Have already become, one of my closest friends." He licked his lips, his expression serious, the playfulness gone. "And I'd really like to not mess that up."

His words hit something soft inside of her and buried deep. She got it. Oh boy, did she get it. As someone who had so few close friends, she understood the rarity of finding someone you could be yourself with.

And kissing often led to other things that led to broken hearts and unanswered phone calls. And then nothing.

She considered what it would be like, knowing Asa how she knew him now, and then not knowing him anymore.

Not having his voice and his teasing and his hugs in her life.

The very idea hurt in places she didn't know could hurt.

"But," he said after she hadn't spoken for a few minutes. "I also don't want you to go without your favorite thing."

Her eyes shot to his and she knew she looked overly eager but she didn't even care.

"Or worse, kiss a bunch of losers who might be mean to you," he added.

She was already nodding. "That's a very good point. What if…what if it doesn't have to mean anything more than just kissing?"

His mouth tugged up on one side. "Just kissing for kissing sake?"

"Yeah," she said hopefully. "And we can have very strict boundaries so it never gets weird."

His good humor was back. "What kind of boundaries?"

"Like…" She thought quickly, incentivized like no other. "We don't kiss in front of other people."

"Okay," he agreed easily.

"And we don't kiss in any bedrooms."

"Bedrooms off limits, okay." He nodded.

"And no kissing anyone else because then it gets complicated." He narrowed his eyes and she hurried to add, "If we meet someone else we want to date or whatever then the kissing stops."

But just the idea of Asa kissing someone else filled her with intense jealousy. She pushed that aside to think about later. Or never.

"Do you have any?" she asked him.

He thought about it while finishing his ice cream cone.

"We don't tell anyone," he said. He meant Nikki and she totally agreed. "And if either one of us starts having a problem with it, we have to tell the other. No hiding it."

He gave her a look and she was pretty sure she read his mind. He meant if she caught feelings, which could lead to expectations.

"Agreed," she said, her throat tight.

He looked at her like he wasn't sure she was really all right with it. But she wasn't going to tell him that it was too late for the feelings part. She already had some pretty significant feelings for him.

But it was because of those feelings she knew she'd be able to keep to the boundaries set down and not risk losing his friendship.

Because now that she had him in her life, she was going to do what she could to keep him. Even if that meant pretending her feelings for him were less than they actually were.

Maybe he could love her. Maybe he could fall for the idea of her. But all the stuff that came with her? No one could love that. Not for long anyway.

But for the moment, they had this.

And if she was smart about it, she could keep him in her life while also keeping him removed from all the shit that surrounded her. And she would be the only one who knew the significance of what he'd given her with his friendship.

Chapter Nineteen
Echo

ASA

One week after their night-time motorcycle ride and they hadn't kissed again.

He'd had plenty of chances. More than he could count. Opportunity wasn't the problem. The problem was the boundaries. Specifically the one where he said that if one of them had a problem with it, they would tell the other.

He had a problem with it.

And he didn't want to tell her.

Which he knew didn't make sense. It had been his idea after all. He was more frustrated with himself than anything. He'd spent the week, not *avoiding* her, but not really *not* avoiding her.

They still had breakfast on the terrace in the mornings and played music together most nights of the week. But he'd successfully dodged any more heartfelt conversations and lingering looks.

Which really just made him feel *awful*.

He was all twisted up inside and kept waking up in a cold sweat, worried she'd gone back to New York before he'd had a chance to…

To what?

That was where his mind stopped and he'd start the spiral at the top again. It was disorienting, like getting off a carnival ride right before it got fun.

Kissing the most beautiful woman in the world with zero obligation or strings sounded like a literal dream come true.

So what the hell was his problem?

Did he want the strings?

He froze and his vision lost focus as that final question echoed in his mind.

Did he want the strings?

"What's wrong?"

He lifted his eyes to Zara sitting across from him on the terrace. The early morning sun lighting up her bronze skin exposed by her pale blue tank top and black sleep shorts. Her hair down and tangled and everywhere.

"Is it bad?" she asked, her amber gold eyes wide and worried.

"Huh?" he asked, sounding like the idiot he was.

"The omelet." She nodded at his plate. "Is it that bad?"

He glanced down, trying to reorient himself in time and space. "No. What? No, the omelet is great." He took a huge bite of the French omelet she'd made that morning.

She sat back, her dark eyebrows knit into a frown. "Then why did you look like you'd just swallowed a pinecone."

He cracked a smile. "I was just thinking about something." He cut into the omelet and raised another bite to his lips. "What have you got going on today?" he asked.

She cradled her coffee cup in both hands and gazed towards the city horizon. A soft hum came from deep in her chest and she clicked her nails on the ceramic mug. "I'm working on something."

"Anything you want to talk about?" he asked.

Her eyes came back to him and he sensed her hesitation. Something soft settled in his bones as he realized he knew her. Knew her expressions and tone and intention. He only had that with a handful of people in his life. Some of them were due to survival instinct—being able to anticipate a mood in someone could make or break a day.

Learning Zara had happened much the same way he'd returned to writing music—reluctantly at first, unsure and untrusting; followed by gentle steps that eventually led to a place that felt familiar and golden.

Both ways left him feeling thankful and undeserving.

His mind circled back around to wondering if he wanted the strings. And why he wasn't kissing her breathless at every opportunity.

When he considered what it would mean to pursue her, to admit his feelings and everything that came with it, he paused.

Because she was the kind of woman who deserved full consideration.

He wasn't stupid. He knew what they had was limited. They existed in a bubble of peace and uneventfulness. It was the elephant in the room they never talked about and always talked around.

What they were doing wasn't permanent. Eventually she would go back to the tours and the promos and the fully booked schedule.

Could he live in her world? Could he learn to handle his media induced anxiety? Could he suspend every single one of his insecurities and fears? For her? For them? For what could be?

Those were the things he needed to figure out before he'd risk both their hearts.

And none of that included all the things she might be feeling or trying to figure out. Because she also hadn't leaned in for another kiss.

They were in a holding pattern of sorts. Circling around each other, waiting for the other to make a move.

"I do," she said, answering his question. "But not right now."

He nodded a small smile twitching at his lips.

"What are *you* doing today?" she asked.

"Work. And then I meet Steiny after that. Probably be home late." He reached for his coffee and noticed a slight shift in her expression.

"What do you guys do?" she asked.

"Climb." His eyebrows dipped. "I guess I thought you knew that."

She shook her head once and averted her gaze. "Nope."

Were her feelings were hurt? That surprised him. But it probably shouldn't. If he thought she was out hanging with other people and having fun and he was being kept out of it that would feel shitty.

"I would have invited you a long time ago but it's really public. And Steinhoff doesn't know about you being here, so that would be a whole thing. Not sure he'd pass Cas's background check," he ended with a chuckle.

Her gaze sharpened on him. "He doesn't know I'm here?" she repeated like she wasn't sure she'd heard him right.

He shrugged. "I haven't told anyone. Why would I put you at risk like that?"

Her lips parted and her brow furrowed as if she wanted to say something but she had no idea where to begin. "No one?"

He rolled his lips inward and shook his head. Not even his dad, even though he was certain his dad had no idea who Zara Lorna even was.

His phone beeped and he checked the time. "I have to get going." He stood and started gathering their plates. "I'll help you with the dishes first."

They went back inside, downstairs to the kitchen.

She rinsed and he loaded the dishwasher. When they were finished, he turned to her and took in a long look, knowing he was going to miss her all day. It was an odd sensation. A few months ago he wouldn't have thought that his day needed to include absorbing as much of her joyful energy as possible. But now he didn't know how he would ever go without it.

"Have fun today," he said.

"You too."

The small smile she gave him said so much. Her belief in him was all he needed in life. It made him feel like he could do anything.

He caught her face with a hand and brushed his thumb over the apple of her cheek. Her lips parted and she gazed up at him with those amber gold eyes he got lost in more than once a day. His gaze drifted to her mouth and he felt her body lean toward him.

He dipped close to her face and captured her upper lip in between both of his, tender and warm, he lingered there for a beat. When he lifted his mouth she was still leaning into his touch, eyes closed, lips patiently waiting for more.

How he wanted to give her more.

Instead, he folded her into a hug and pressed his mouth to her temple. "I'll see you later," he said, voice rough. He released her and didn't dare look back as he headed downstairs. He was seconds away from falling at her feet and pledging his heart and fealty to her in any way she would take him.

But that would be insane.

Or would it?

Because when he thought about it again later that day as he was messing around with the song they had started that night in LA in the middle of a thunderstorm, he couldn't imagine going back to a life that didn't involve Zara in an essential way.

* * *

ZARA

Her day had been mostly uneventful. She wrote and wrote and wrote. She didn't finish any songs but had several pieces that seemed to just pour out of her. It wouldn't take much to turn them into fully formed songs. She had more than enough for an album. Several in fact.

Writing had always come easy for her. None of it should have been a surprise. But it felt different somehow.

More honest.

Urgent.

Like if she didn't get it out it might consume her.

And she knew, without fully acknowledging it, that it was whatever was happening between her and Asa that was the fuel for all of her productive creativity.

Because whatever was happening between them was two things at once. It was both powerful and intentional. Like both of their hearts were taking their time with every next step. No rushing. It wasn't hesitation so much as careful consideration.

And she wasn't going to stop it.

Maybe she liked the ache of the unknown. Maybe she took too much pleasure in the mystery of it all.

That small kiss that morning had left her twisted and needy and *happy*. Because it had felt like one of the most honest kisses of her life. No expectation and no demand.

Just his lips on hers.

Twice he'd kissed her. The first kiss had been the best kiss of her life, topped only by the second. Her lips had tingled all day.

And she used that tingle to fuel her writing. She was getting to a point where she needed to show it to someone. Like her producer best friend. Or the man who'd been starring in all of her dreams lately.

She heard the garage door open later that night and took her customary seat on the stairs in the bend outside his bedroom. Where she waited for his gentle voice to fill her head and heart with its comforting sound.

The guitar started and stopped. That wasn't unusual. It often took a few false starts to get going.

The bedroom door opened and she froze.

Shit.

He was going to catch her!

Maybe not. Maybe he needed to use the bathroom or something. As long as she didn't make a sound, he wouldn't have a reason to check the stairs.

She held her breath and waited.

"Zara."

It wasn't a question.

She leaned forward and peeked around the corner.

Asa stood in the doorway of his bedroom, a small smirk on his lips. He twitched two fingers, motioning her to join him.

Heat crawled up her neck and she crept the rest of the way down the stairs, stopping at the bottom. She twisted her fingers together in front of her. "I…" How was she supposed to tell him that she wasn't trying to be creepy; she just couldn't sleep.

"Get in here," he said, jerking his head toward the interior of his room.

Her heart gave a little surprised hiccup and she pushed onto her toes with a bounce. "Really?"

He rolled his eyes but couldn't hide his crooked smile. "Stop being cute and get in here before I change my mind."

She made a noise that was something between a squeak and a squeal and hurried into his room. And froze.

He closed the door behind them and came around to her side.

The box of notebooks that he'd shown her on moving day sat on his bed with various pages opened and scattered on the comforter.

This wasn't just a casual invitation to mess with music together. This was so much bigger. He was inviting her *in*.

That little hiccup her heart did sometimes turned into a staccato rhythm. Her throat tightened as she tried to swallow down the huge lump of emotion suddenly clogging it. She turned toward him and tried to keep her voice as even as possible. "Are you sure about this?"

His lids dropped slowly over his dark eyes as his gaze went from each of her eyes to her mouth and back again. No hint of hesitation or anxiety. His hands hung loose at his sides and his mouth tugged up on the corners. "Yeah."

It was a word. Just one. But coming from Asa—a man who thought things through, considered multiple viewpoints and endings—it was all she needed.

Chapter Twenty
India Ink

Nikki had been his best friend since he could cogitate. It was hard to remember when they had become friends because in his mind she was always there. He didn't remember a time without Nikki. Even his oldest memories that didn't include her, his mind put her somewhere in the background. He had more memories with her than his own family.

Or maybe Nikki was his family and always had been. They often joked about how they'd gotten separated at birth by some horrible accident and good thing they'd found their way back to one another.

Nikki had this amazing way of encouraging people to be themselves. She didn't judge and she didn't shame. She reveled in people's uniqueness. The weirder the better. She was the only person he'd ever felt comfortable being himself around.

Until now.

He lay on his back on his bedroom floor staring up at the ceiling, his ankles crossed, his hands folded behind his head, listening to Zara hum and strum and scribble on the bed beside him.

"My goodness," Zara murmured. "Your mind... You didn't even use your best stuff for Winking Pete."

"I wanted to save some of it back. Just in case."

She peeked over the edge of the bed. "In case of what?"

"I don't know," he replied honestly then chuckled. "Something."

She narrowed her eyes at him and then went back to whatever she had been working on.

For several hours every night for the past three nights, they'd been in his room going through his shit.

And he wasn't freaking out about it.

If anything, he was completely at peace.

"Okay, what if this actually goes with this..." She wasn't really talking to him. Mostly she was just thinking out loud while he enjoyed it.

She began to play the old acoustic and he closed his eyes. It was the song he'd been working on every night, the one she'd been listening to through the door. But she had a lighter touch than he did and it changed the sound of those steel strings.

He did an ab curl and sat up. Her eyes flicked to him but she didn't stop playing. He grabbed the paper in front of her and scanned the words until he found what he was looking for.

Zara grinned. "And then you can shift it here." Her fingers moved expertly over the frets, changing the key.

She hummed where words would be and he grabbed the pencil off the bed and started scribbling.

"Play that part again," he said. She did and the words kept coming. He stopped writing and she went back to playing the original part of the melody.

"Please tell me you have that memorized," he said, sitting back on his heels.

She snorted and nodded at her phone. "Dude. When I'm writing I record everything."

He shook his head, admiring her. It was never a question why she was at the top of everything she did. But every once in a while, he was reminded that she wasn't just anyone. She outworked everyone in every room, stayed locked-in to her creativity, and never wasted a single drop.

"You're remarkable. You know that, right?" he asked knowing that his words and respect were nothing compared to the accolades she received all the time. He was a nobody with a nothing career. But sometimes, like right then, he was able to be a part of something magnificent. And it took his breath away.

She beamed at him, sticking her tongue between her teeth in a cheesy smile. Then she patted the paper on the bed. "Write me a bridge, rock star."

He watched her for a beat as she returned her fingers to their starting position and began to play again.

And then he wrote her a bridge.

* * *

"Are you sure this is okay?" Zara made a face like she was worried she was breaking eight laws at once and the cops were around the corner. "I don't want you to get into trouble."

Asa snorted and grabbed her hand, tugging her down the hall of XY Records to the control room of studio Y. "Killer, you're Zara Lorna. No one is going to be mad at you for being in a *recording studio*."

She snickered behind him and he shot her a grin over his shoulder. She looked up at him through her dark lashes with a flirty smile and he almost stumbled.

Living with her, spending time with her, seeing her every day had not desensitized him to her beauty. If anything, she was more potent than she'd ever been.

He tore his gaze away as they entered the large recording space of Studio Y. It wasn't a space he got to spend a lot of time in, but it was his favorite.

The thirty-foot ceilings, high windows, open space. The first time he saw it, he knew he wanted to make music there.

Not music for someone else. But something of his own.

And now he was going to do exactly that.

They'd gotten to a certain point in their writing where both of them voiced their desire to start putting it together. Which was why he was sneaking the world's most famous woman into a neighborhood recording studio in the middle of the night.

Johnny wouldn't mind.

Probably.

Hopefully.

The really cool part about writing with Zara (okay, all of it was awesome) was that they both had talents in different areas. In a way that complimented one another.

And then there was the flow.

The mystical space where creatives connected on an almost spiritual level while constructing something. It bordered on insane, looked a lot like telepathy, and felt like intoxication. A hazy fog of ideas, emotions, words, and music.

He could honestly say he'd never experienced it at this intensity though.

Zara had spent enough time in recording studios that she knew what to do. They switched off and on, taking turns with instruments, the soundboard, the vocals. Just messing around and playing the way he had in his youth. With zero hesitation or thought of an outcome other than making *something*.

The flow they found themselves in was so powerful that he was honestly shocked when he looked up to find Nikki standing in the doorway.

"Nik. Hey," he said, surprised. Had the neighbors complained? Or…?

"Hey…" Nikki's curious frown shifted from where Asa sat on the couch to Zara who was lying beside him, her bare feet in his lap. "What's going on, guys?"

He flicked a glance out the control window and saw sunlight peeking through the high windows. "Oh shit."

Zara chuckled, deep and low, and he grinned at her. They'd been playing in the studio for hours. She hadn't slept and she still looked as gorgeous as ever. Wearing black leggings and a dark green hoodie of his she'd swiped from his closet before they'd left. It was enormous on her but seeing her in his shirt stirred something in him he wasn't sure he'd ever felt before. It was almost possessive but mixed with adoration and attraction.

He was so fucking gone for her. In a way that he never wanted to come back.

Tearing his eyes away from Zara and back to Nikki, he cleared his throat. "We've been writing."

Nikki's gaze sharpened at him. "You've been writing?" She tried to make it sound casual but he heard the barely stifled surprise.

He nodded once, holding eye contact.

Nikki swallowed hard and blinked too fast.

"For fuck's sake, Nik," he muttered. "Don't cry."

She shook her head in denial even as her blue eyes got glassy.

Zara sat up and dropped her feet to the floor. "Why are you crying?" she asked, concerned.

Nikki wiped under her eyes and blinked up at the ceiling. "It's uh…" she cleared her throat. "It's allergies."

Asa rolled his eyes, but his chest compressed with something that felt like guilt. She'd been worried about him, he'd known that. But he had no idea she would have this kind of a reaction.

Nikki took a deep breath and looked at Asa seriously. "It's good. I'm glad is all."

"Do you want to hear what we have so far?" he asked, already knowing the answer.

"Are you joking?" Nikki asked like he was crazy.

He got up from the couch and went over to the control board. Zara sat on the stool by his side and keyed up the track they had roughly finished putting together earlier.

A low hum filled the room, the echo he'd had stuck in his head and body since that night in LA. He'd managed to find it in a particular keyboard at the studio. He'd plugged it in and it had lit up every neuron in his brain. The sound was how it felt to be near her, to create with her, to know her.

The hum was joined by an under riff she'd written and then played on that same keyboard. It was heavily synthed and reverberated throughout the control room. A sound that wasn't all her and wasn't all him but was something new. Something that didn't exist until they'd met.

The drums they'd added had a tight popping snare that sounded like a slow heartbeat that he could feel in the center of his chest. It was welded to the rest of the sound with his characteristic bass notes and her talent for melody.

It still needed a lot of work. It was *rough*. Backing vocals and echoes and mixing, just to start. But he could hear it. The song that had started in the middle of a thunderstorm months ago. It was alive and starting to breathe on its own.

The song ended and he shared a smile with Zara. She could hear it too. He turned to get Nikki's reaction.

His bestie was staring at him with wide eyes, her arms crossed over her middle.

"Holy shit, Ace," she said just above a whisper.

He tipped his chin down. "You think you could polish this up? Maybe make it into something?"

Nikki's eyes darted from him to Zara like she wasn't sure she heard him right.

"I mean, unless you're busy," Zara added when Nikki hadn't responded after a minute.

Nikki's expression turned annoyed before she barked a laugh. "You two are going to kill me, aren't you? With all this—" she wiggled her fingers to encompass both Zara and Asa— "extreme talent working together. What's the plan? Is this a Zara record or something new?" She arched an eyebrow with her question.

Asa shrugged. He hadn't really thought that far ahead.

That was a lie.

He'd thought about it. He wanted it to be hers. For all of it to be hers. He just wanted to be around to help make it.

"We're still discussing that," Zara said, spinning back around on the stool.

Nikki shot a curious frown to Asa but he didn't have an answer.

"Hey, Nik, have you talked to—oh." Johnny came into the room and stopped when he saw who was there. He scratched the back of his head. "Hey."

Nikki took a deep breath and blinked at their boss. "No. I just found them in here. Johnny, you gotta hear what they've made."

Johnny nodded and took a seat on the leather couch, elbows on his knees.

Zara played it again and Asa made a note on the page they'd been passing back and forth. She leaned over and read what he'd written and then took the pencil from his hand, her fingers warm and soft against his, and added her own idea.

"You keep making music like that here in this little place and I'm going to have to rename it to XYZ Records," Johnny said when it was finished.

Asa curled his hand around the back of Zara's neck and gave it a soft squeeze. She tipped her head back and smiled up at him sleepily.

"We should go home and sleep. Or you should at least. I have to work," he amended.

She pouted and he almost laughed.

Too bad they'd agreed not to kiss in front of anyone, because he really wanted to kiss her in that moment.

"I can nap in Nikki's office," Zara offered hopefully.

She was in the same state he was; she didn't want to risk leaving the flow. It was hard to know if it would fade when you unplugged. FOMO to extreme detriment.

"Whatever is happening here, let's not mess with it," Nikki said. "I'll get you food and you can both nap in my office. I have blankets and everything. Does anyone need to tell Cas where you are?"

Zara stood up. "I texted him earlier. He knows I'm here. Where are my shoes?" she asked, looking around.

Asa spotted them on the far side of the couch. He handed her sneakers to her.

After she slipped them on, he followed her down the stairs and out of the studio, down the hall to Nikki's office.

Andre had redone the space in year the year before and it was clean and cozy. The couch against the far wall was covered in fluffy pillows and dark shades were drawn over the windows.

Nikki grabbed a blanket out of the pull-out cabinet and handed it to Zara.

"I'll get food when you guys wake up," Nikki said as she left the room.

Asa watched her go over his shoulder and turned back to Zara and stifled a yawn. "I can nap in one of the lounges—" he stopped speaking as Zara's gave him an impossibly cute frown. "What?" he chuckled.

She shook her head and approached him but didn't say anything. Taking one of his hands in hers, she tugged him away from the door, then she shut it. Still holding his hand, she led him over to the couch and pointed at it.

He should really nap in one of the lounges.

But instead he laid down on the couch on his back. She shook out the blanket and wrapped it around her shoulders. Then she crawled into the space between him and the back of the couch, snuggling her small body in the gap. She draped one leg over his hips and pulled the blanket over the both of them, resting an arm over his middle. He wrapped his arms around her and they both let out a long exhale, their bodies melting against one another.

How did this feel more intimate than kissing?

Maybe some friends could snuggle with each other and not have it mean anything. He was just now realizing he wasn't that type of friend.

She let out a soft sigh that went straight to his gut and various other locations. Her scent floated around him, filling his lungs and stirring his thoughts to ideas he had no business having in Nikki's office.

They weren't at home and he needed to remember that.

He closed his eyes and the heat of her body lulled him to sleep in seconds.

* * *

ZARA

A few hours later she woke up to the smell of tacos. She rolled over on the couch where she'd crashed earlier.

Asa was on the floor with a bag of food between them and a couple canned drinks. It wasn't where he'd been when she'd fallen asleep. Which was probably for the best she reluctantly decided.

She sat up and pushed her hair out of her face.

Asa's lips twitched as his eyes scanned her. "So, your hair just does that even when you haven't slept that long."

"My Medusa hair is my superpower," she croaked, her throat dry.

She lowered herself to the floor and he pushed a bag her direction.

"I got you a variety since you like pretty much everything." He set two cans of different kinds of carbonated water in front of her. "And Hannah keeps the lounge stocked with seltzer water. So you can go to town on those."

"Thanks," she said, starting with the water to help her dry throat.

They ate silently for a few minutes. Neither one speaking, the writing fog still heavy around them. Something occurred to her and so she asked, "Am I going to get you in trouble?"

He snorted. "What for? Coming into the studio?"

"No. You're supposed to be working and I've been monopolizing all of your time."

Asa finished chewing and his eyes wandered to the ceiling. "I'm still getting all my other stuff done."

"You are?" That surprised her. He'd been coming home early and going in late and then last night's all-nighter.

He shrugged one shoulder. "My job's not that hard." He rolled his lips inward like he was thinking about how much he wanted to share. "They've been trying to get me to take a bigger role with some of our other artists. I've been…reluctant."

She understood a little of what he was saying. When they'd met, he'd been very closed off to even the idea of making music again.

"Then why work at a recording studio?"

His mouth tugged up on one side. "Nikki asked me for a favor."

He said it so simply. Like it was obvious.

"You're a good friend," she said.

"So are you," he replied. He took a breath and the exhale seemed to release a lot of the tension he usually carried around with him. "You gave me the space I needed."

"What do you mean?" she asked, a funny feeling sliding through her insides.

"Living with you, spending time with you. I've never felt as free as when I'm with you. And that's made all the difference."

Her heart hiccupped like an inebriated sailor having the best night of their life. Warmth spread through her body, blooming from her heart. Tears tingled at the back of her throat and she swallowed them down.

Don't cry, don't cry, don't cry.

No one had ever given her such an enormous compliment. He was giving her too much credit for work he'd done himself. She was thankful that anything she had done had helped. To be a part of anyone's journey back to where they belong was an honor. But especially when it was Asa.

"You okay?" he asked, his eyes scanning her features and posture.

She glanced down at her hand pressed to her chest like her heart was trying to escape. "Yeah," she said, voice rougher than she expected. "Asa." She took a breath and met his dark brown gaze. Eyes that had become so much of a home to her over these past months.

Words that she never expected to say to anyone again held still in her throat. Her pulse roared, thundering through her veins like she was possessed by another force entirely.

A knock on the door stopped her from having to make a huge decision she wasn't sure she was ready to make. The door opened and Nikki poked her head in.

"I'm ready for you in Y when you're done here. Ooh, La Morenas?" she asked.

Asa chuckled and held out a paper bag. "I gotchu."

Nikki swiped the bag of tacos. "You've always been my favorite," she said.

"Yeah, yeah, yeah." Asa waved her away and got to his feet, their moment over.

Zara crumbled up her garbage and tossed it in the can Asa held out to her.

"You ready to make something awesome?" he asked.

She got to her feet nodding. "I really am."

She was ready for a lot more than she realized.

* * *

She folded her legs up, wrapped her arms around them, and rested her chin on her knees. "Play it again."

Nikki hit the playback and they listened to the track for probably the fiftieth time.

The sun had gone down long ago and fatigue pulled at her. She was too tired to make any decisions but she didn't want to walk away yet.

A warm hand slid up her spine and she recognized Asa's close presence before he spoke.

"I think we need to get home and sleep for a bit."

She knew he was right. She needed a shower and to sleep for at least ten hours.

"We can come back tomorrow," Asa promised, his voice low and so close to her that she felt his breath on the side of her face.

"Johnny and I made arrangements so no one will be in for the rest of the week," Nikki added around a yawn.

That's what finally did it. Seeing her friend exhausted and knowing she had a family at home waiting for her. No one was waiting for Zara. Sometimes she forgot about that small fact.

"Okay," she agreed, unfolding her body and standing.

Asa put a hand on her lower back and guided her out of the studio. Cas waited by the door to drive them home.

In the back of the SUV, she sat in the middle beside Asa, their sides pressed together. Her mind swam with everything they'd worked on that day and everything she wanted to do next. She was drowning in ideas.

Part of her was amazed at the intense height her creativity had risen to. But most of her wasn't surprised at all. She'd been writing and making music the entire time she'd been in Chicago, but the moment Asa had let her in, had given her that trust, everything shifted. She'd been catapulted into the stratosphere.

It was almost as if everything in her life had been leading to this.

To him.

They got home and Cas and Devan searched the house before taking off. She said goodnight to Asa and then went to go shower.

As the water cascaded down her hair and back, a soft chorus began in the back of her mind.

"Endings are sad, so they say,
And I've known my share of pain,
But yours was a special kind of blame,
Did you even miss me?
Did I cross your mind once?
Did you know I thought it was my doing?
Your reason for moving
On"

She finished in the shower, humming the melody over and over. She wrapped a towel around her hair and one around her body before picking up her phone and taking a voice note.

The song wouldn't leave her alone as she brushed her teeth and moisturized. She put on a short, black, satin nightie with lace detailing on the bodice and neckline and matching satin panties. She'd have to change before heading down for breakfast in the morning but that was later. Right now all she wanted was to sleep for three days.

She crawled under her covers and passed out the moment her head hit the pillow.

* * *

A crack of thunder woke her up some time later. She swam to the surface of consciousness and rolled over. The words that had snuck up on her in the shower came back just as strong.

She rubbed her eyes and blinked at the dark ceiling. Lightning flashed across the room and she swung her legs out of bed. She checked her phone. She'd only been asleep for a couple hours. Not nearly enough time.

Did you even miss me?
Did I cross your mind once?

227

Not even once?

Well shit. It wasn't going to leave her alone, was it?

She took a deep breath and then headed for the stairs. She detoured to the kitchen for a glass of water before moving on to the music room.

Rain pelted against the windows, adding a rhythm to her thoughts that hadn't been there before. She slid onto the piano bench, the wood cool on the backs of her bare thighs and flipped to a new page in the notebook she'd left there. Taking the pen out of the spiral binding, she quickly jotted down the words that hadn't let her go.

Putting the pen down, she rested her hands on the keys before her. Carefully, she tested the notes and chords until she found what matched the sound in her soul.

The words came almost too quickly for her to catch them. They poured out of someplace she'd kept locked for too long a time.

Back and forth, her hands moved from the keys to the notebook, her lips constantly moving and repeating. She tried not to play too loud, not wanting to disturb Asa downstairs. But she must have because after a while she felt his presence hit the room.

She lifted her eyes to find him watching her from the doorway in dark blue lounge pants and no shirt. Momentarily distracted, she let her eyes linger on the hard packed muscles of his chest and abs. She hadn't seen them since that day she'd hosed him off in Nikki's backyard.

"Sorry," she muttered. "I didn't mean to wake you."

"You didn't," he said, his voice impossibly deep.

"I had to get it down. It wouldn't leave me alone," she explained with a small shrug.

He nodded once, his dark eyes never leaving her face. "It's about your mom?"

Her smile was soft and sad. "How'd you know?"

"I could hear it."

And didn't that say everything about Asa? That she didn't have to explain something complicated because he just *knew* what she meant.

"How have I lived my life up to this point without you?" she whispered, not really intending him to hear her.

But he did.

His beautiful chest rose with the deep breath he took and he slowly crossed the room toward her.

Lightning flashed across the room followed by a low rumble of thunder that pulled at her insides.

Asa slid onto the bench beside her and his eyes drifted over her chest and down. A large warm palm glided over her knee, up her thigh and his Adam's apple bobbed. His gaze came back to hers, heated and dark.

"What are you wearing?" he asked, his voice a low rumble that matched the thunder inside of her.

She licked her lips and noticed her own palm pressed to the center of his chest. She flexed her fingers against his skin, feeling his heartbeat just beneath the surface. He covered her hand with his own.

"Zara," he whispered.

Her gaze tangled with his and she reached up with her other hand to slide her fingers through his thick hair at the temple. She trailed her touch along his jaw and leaned closer. Wanting, wanting, *wanting*.

The hand covering her own fell away only to catch her behind the neck. And with a groan that would be burned into her memory for the rest of her life, his mouth met hers.

Chapter Twenty-One
Love Me Back to Life

ZARA

The thunder that rumbled through the house matched the pounding of her heart. Lightning flashed through the room and the rain on the window played a tune just for them.

Did he pick her up and move her to straddle his lap or did she do that on her own? Her knees met the cool bench and his hands tightened around her waist as her center met the hard length under his thin lounge pants.

Her fingers threaded through his thick hair as their tongues tangled and slid against one another.

He felt so good against her. All hard muscles and warm skin. His hands everywhere, pushing up the hem of her nightie, gliding along her spine, twisting in her hair.

This wasn't like their first few kisses. This was something else. Primal and urgent and *right*. Like her body had been made for his hands to explore. Like her mouth was always meant to find that place on his neck that made him groan out curses. His hands clamped down on her hips as she ground against him.

His tongue swirled over her pulse point and she dropped her head back to give him better access. He held her firmly as his mouth worked its way down to her collarbone, then between her breasts. Warmth enveloped a nipple through the thin lace and she moaned, clutching his head to her chest.

He pulled back and their eyes met. Heat and lust ricocheted between them.

There were probably a million reasons to stop.

But she couldn't think of a single one.

Making a decision, he slid to the end of the bench and put her on her feet. Then he took her by her hand and led her up the stairs to her bedroom.

"Gimme a second," she said, letting go of his hand and heading into the bathroom.

She closed the door and took a deep breath. She caught her eyes in the mirror and was stunned by her appearance.

Flushed skin, kissed swollen lips, mussed hair…and a shine in her eyes she'd never seen before. She bit her bottom lip as a soft smile spread across her face. Had she ever looked so happy?

Had she ever *been* this happy?

No.

She could honestly say that she'd never felt a lot of the things she was feeling.

Remembering why she came in there, she opened the vanity and searched for the "emergency kit" Gregor always packed for her wherever she went. She used to think it was silly but at that moment she was incredibly thankful. So thankful that she was going to be giving Gregor a massive raise.

She opened the leather bag—which was really just a dopp kit he'd modified for her filled with condoms, lube, body oil, and other things she would have to check out later. She grabbed the lube and the condoms and went back to Asa.

He was standing in her room, head bent, one hand on the back of his neck, the other on his hip, like he was rethinking this entire situation. His head came up when she stepped closer. His dark eyes traveled over her features, her body, back to her face, taking their time. She hoped he saw what she had seen.

He held out his hands and took the condoms and lube from her. He placed them on the nightstand and then took his glasses off and put them down too.

They met each other in the middle, easily and swiftly resuming their intensity from before. His arms went around her and her hands went to his shoulders and then his hair. His tongue plunged into her mouth, hot and wet. She hopped and he caught her by the backs of her thighs.

He turned, put a knee to the bed and slowly lowered her to the mattress. He dropped his hips and ground against her center. She arched her neck and moaned at the intense pleasure.

She had a feeling she was about to embarrass herself.

She'd only had sex with one person her entire life. And those times had always left her feeling sad and unfulfilled. Logan had said she just wasn't good at sex. Which was why they'd almost never had it. It had been stiff and uncomfortable. Rationally she knew it wasn't her fault. But now that she was close to doing it with someone who she felt more for than she had felt for anyone, she was suddenly really fucking anxious.

"I haven't," she panted as the backs of his fingers grazed a nipple and his mouth moved along her neck. "I might not be good at this," she finally got out. Because she wanted to warn him. In case he had certain expectations that she was about ready to not meet.

He lifted his head and gazed down at her with a soft frown. He rubbed his thumb over her lower lip and then slid his fingers into her hair at the temple. "What do you mean?" he asked, voice low and soft.

She shook her head, regretting saying anything at all. Wishing she could rewind the last thirty seconds and just go with it.

He studied her for a beat. He must've seen something there because his gaze gentled.

"Zara," he said, making sure to have her eyes. "What's happening between us isn't just sex. You know that right?"

She nodded. She did know that. And it felt amazing to have him say it. But... "I don't want to disappoint you." She managed to get the words out and then swallowed hard.

A sly smile spread across his lips and his eyes went liquid. "Impossible." He dipped his head and slid his tongue into her mouth. He worked her mouth, slow and deep, his tongue dragging over hers, his teeth nipping at her lips and then soothing with soft, teasing kisses.

He kept kissing her until her body was languid and hot with need. Only then did he let his hands roam, sliding her panties off, pushing her nighty up and over her head. His fingers hovered over her belly, his eyes raking over her nakedness with a hunger she'd never experienced.

He palmed one breast while licking and tonguing the other, and then switched. She writhed and panted and mewled beneath him. His hand glided down her belly to her center. He watched her face as he gently dipped a finger into the slick folds.

"You let me in there, babe, and there's no going back," he said.

"Is that a warning or a promise," she managed to ask, barely recognizing her own voice. It was so husky and seductive.

He chuckled and the sound was so deliciously dark she almost came right then.

A finger entered her and she whimpered. Another finger joined the first and the noise she made was positively sinful. She didn't even know she could sound like that.

He pumped his fingers into her and her hips lifted, searching for more.

He cursed and then his hand was gone. She barely had time to complain before she heard the ripping of a condom wrapper.

Her eyes fluttered open and met his in a flash of lightning.

He'd gotten rid of his pants and was sliding a condom down over his thick, hard length. She stared at the erection pointed directly at her and she couldn't help it when she said, "yes, please."

He chuckled again and then lowered himself to settle right at her entrance. His dark eyes met hers, checking in. She lifted her hips, encouraging him, wanting to feel him filling her.

Slowly he sank into her.

She tried to relax, to make room for him. He pressed in and then retreated and then pushed in deeper until he was fully seated inside her.

"Oh my god," she breathed, arching her neck and gripping his shoulders.

He started a slow rhythm that was both insistent and clever. Two short thrusts, one long, one short, two long, two short. She clung to his shoulders, their mouths grazing with every thrust.

The neatly trimmed hair around his cock brushed against her clit again and again, taking her higher. Her orgasm built low in her belly and it surprised her. It seemed too soon. To easy.

"Fuckkkk," he hissed. "You feel so good."

His words went right to her center and she clenched around him. He moaned against her neck.

"Asa," she whimpered. "Please…" But she didn't even know what to ask for.

"I got you, baby," he said in her ear as his hand went between them and began circling her clit. He touched it once, twice, circled it, applied just the right amount of pressure while stroking and—

Her orgasm hit her like a freight train filled with fireworks. Her body bowed and convulsed as wave after wave coursed through her. Light exploded behind her vision and she cried out in sounds of pure ecstasy.

His hand left her clit and moved to her hip, slid down her thigh and brought her leg up high against his side. His thrusts increased in tempo, drawing out her pleasure. Then he planted deep inside her and groaned his own release. She felt him pulse inside her and she held him tight in both arms.

Hot, slow kisses covered her neck and face as she came back down to earth. Her eyes fluttered open and Asa carefully slid out of her. She moaned again, still sensitive and enjoying it.

He collapsed on the bed beside her and pressed his lips to her neck, his arms going around her middle.

She stared at the light still flashing across the ceiling, trying to catch her breath. Trying to understand what had just happened.

Sex had never been like that. Her body was still tingling in various places. Her mind enjoying casual explosions of enlightenment and afterglow.

His lips grazed hers in a leisurely kiss. "I'll be back." He pulled the sheet over her before he climbed off the bed and went into the bathroom.

He was back a moment later and joined her under the covers.

She rolled toward him, tired and satiated. He kissed her shoulder, then her neck, pulling her naked body against his.

"You should go to the bathroom before you fall asleep, *tesoro,*" he murmured against her skin.

"Yeah," she agreed sleepily, not opening her eyes. She let herself enjoy the warmth for another minute before rolling away and getting out of bed.

When she finished in the bathroom, she didn't bother to put her nightie back on. She just walked back into the bedroom, naked. Asa flicked the covers over both of them and pulled her against his body. Their legs and arms tangled and overlapped and she settled her face right between his pecs.

"I don't think I've ever felt so…" She searched for the word.

"Tired?" he guessed.

"Peaceful."

He hummed and she felt pressure on the top of her head like he'd kissed her.

Sleep was threatening to pull her into blissful oblivion but she'd been wondering something and so she asked.

"What's that word you sometimes call me?"

"Hm?"

"*Tesoro.* I don't know what it means."

His hand smoothed up her spine and back down, curving over her ass and stayed there. "It means *treasure* in Italian."

"Oh." Well.

She wasn't going to overthink it. Not the word he called her or what it meant in her mind. She also wasn't going to wonder about how easy it had been for him to touch her and find her and make her feel sexy and alive.

She pressed closer to his warmth and he tightened his arms around her. And somewhere between not thinking about it and making it a core memory, she fell asleep.

Chapter Twenty-Two
Wanted Man

ASA

He woke up with Zara's naked body sprawled on top of him. Her hair spread out on the pillow behind her, her cheek on his shoulder, one arm slung across his chest, one leg hitched up and across his hips, her breasts pressed to his side. He had one arm beneath her and wrapped around her body, his hand resting on her ass.

For a minute he blinked at the ceiling trying to figure out if he was stuck in a dream or if what had happened last night really happened. Because he'd had this exact dream numerous times. She stirred against him and his dick twitched.

Last night had been completely unexpected.

Writing with her, creating with her, being so near in such an open and vulnerable place for both of them had seemed to weaken whatever flimsy walls they'd tried to keep up between each other.

He'd heard the thunder and knew she'd be awake. Everything in him chose to seek her out. To be near her. To never be away from her again.

When he'd found her at the piano everything inside him relaxed.

She was it for him.

He'd never been so sure of anything in his life.

And then the kissing…her body and her sounds and her taste. If he hadn't been gone for her before that, he certainly was now.

He'd meant what he'd told her. Once he knew what it was like to be inside her, there was no going back.

He tipped his chin down and found her citrine eyes on him.

A shy smile tugged at her lips and his dick twitched again.

Last night had been a major step in their relationship. But he had a feeling that how he handled the next few moments was even more crucial.

He brushed the back of his fingers along her cheek. "You're so beautiful," he whispered.

Her eyebrows twitched like she wanted to frown but held back. He was reminded of something she'd said last night, about not disappointing him. He examined her expression carefully and realized he didn't know this one.

It was guarded and curious with just a hint of hope.

Hmm.

"Do you regret what we did last night?" she asked, voice soft.

"No," he replied immediately. "Do you?"

Her lips tugged up a little more at the corners. "No."

He wanted to go to the bathroom and use her mouthwash. His worry about his morning breath was distracting. But he didn't want to move from where he was and change the vibe.

"Did you…" She stopped and her eyes dropped to his chin as she swallowed. "Did you enjoy it?"

Okay, what?

He shifted their bodies, moving her off him and propping his elbow in the bed and his head in his hand. He ran his other hand over her cheek and through her thick hair.

"Tell me what's going on in there," he said gently.

Her eyes shuttered immediately, telling him there was *definitely* something she was holding back.

Her hand rested on the bed between them. He picked it up and brought it to his lips. "I don't want to be crude but I think you need to hear it very plainly. That was the best sex of my life, babe. And I'm not exaggerating."

Her smile and the blush that barely showed below her tan skin told him she liked hearing that. He rubbed his thumb over the tops of her knuckles. "Please talk to me," he said.

She sighed and made a face, scrunching up her nose. "I don't want to."

He chuckled. "Okay, fair. But what if I told you there's nothing you could say to me that will change how I feel about you?"

She grew so still he wondered if he'd hit a pain point without realizing it.

"I haven't had a lot of sex…" she started slowly, her gaze on his chin again. "And last night was—" she swallowed "the first time I've enjoyed it."

What.

The.

Fuck.

But she wasn't done. "You know I've only been with the one guy." He noticed she didn't say Logan's name. And he really should have braced but he didn't. "And my orgasm was always my responsibility. Sex with him was…mostly uncomfortable."

"Did he hurt you?" Asa asked more forcefully than he meant to.

She shook her head but the shadows in her eyes hinted at something she didn't want to share.

"Zara," he said seriously.

"No," she said, her eyes avoiding his. "He didn't hurt me. Not like that. But he would tell me that I wasn't good at it." Her eyebrows tipped up. "Though, after last night, I'm pretty sure it was him who wasn't good."

Asa slowly lowered himself onto his back and scrubbed a hand over his face. "Oh, I'm gonna go to jail."

Zara huffed a surprised laugh. "What?"

He twisted his head to look at her extraordinary beauty and his chest got tight. Logan fucking Black was the biggest piece of shit in the world. Never in his life had Asa felt such acute hatred for a specific person.

"That guy is a fucking idiot," he said, not using Logan's name either. If she didn't want to hear it, then he'd honor that. Then something else occurred to him. "So you had sex with me without knowing if you'd enjoy it or not?" he asked.

She gave a small shrug. "I mean…"

He put a fist to his forehead and closed his eyes. Fuck. "I handled that wrong." He should have taken his time.

"I did enjoy it though," she said, putting a hand on his arm. "A lot."

Dammit. Now she was trying to comfort him? Bianca had it right, the next time he saw Logan Black it was on sight.

"Look," Zara said, still reading his reaction wrong and trying to placate him. "I've been working full-time since I was sixteen. I was busy when everyone learned about sex. I trusted the wrong person with it and by the time I figured out he didn't have my best interests in mind, I had decided that sex just wasn't going to be my thing. And he enforced that by saying things like, 'good girls don't really like sex' and half the time he didn't get off anyway, so…"

Asa closed his eyes and visualized punching Logan in the face over and over again. He was also pissed at himself. She'd hinted at things like this, how kissing was her favorite and how little experience she had.

Logan Black wasn't the only idiot.

"When you handed me the lube last night…" He shook his head. "Lube is great and sometimes it's needed and there's absolutely nothing wrong with that," he said, his frustration rising. Because he *knew.* "That fuckwad never got you wet, did he?"

Zara cleared her throat. It told him everything. Logan Black was a selfish piece of shit.

"This is the kind of conversation we should have had before we had sex," he muttered.

"I'm sorry," she said softly.

His eyes flew open and he rolled toward her. "Do not apologize. You didn't do anything wrong." Her eyes widened at his intensity and he cupped her cheek. "You really let me in there without knowing how it would go. Baby, that's not something you ever have to wonder about again. Okay?"

Heat flashed in her eyes and he wrote that promise on his ribcage. Her pleasure would be his priority. She deserved nothing less.

"I'm guessing he also never went down on you," Asa said, watching her reaction carefully.

Her chin jerked slightly and she blinked in surprise. "I…uh…" She took a breath and let it out.

He flashed her a wicked smile. "Good. Because you deserve to have it done right." She deserved to be worshipped and adored and to have endless orgasms every single day. Starting now, he'd spend the rest of his life wiping away every horrible experience she'd ever had with that jackass.

He slid a hand over her waist and dropped soft kisses on her collarbone. She released a small sigh and arched her neck so he could reach her easier. He moved his mouth down her chest toward her breasts, tugging the sheet down as he went.

Her body opened up to him, her trust so easily earned. He would never take it for granted.

Her phone rang from the nightstand, interrupting his intentions. He raised his head and shot her a smile so she knew he wasn't upset. This was life. Her life. And he wasn't going to be a little bitch about it.

"Hello?" she answered. She looked at the phone screen again and then put it back to her ear. "I didn't realize it was so late. I was sleeping. Gimme a few and we'll be right down." She hung up the phone and gave him a sad smile. "Nikki's set up and ready for us."

He kissed the top swell of a breast, letting his lips linger for a moment on her soft skin. "Then we better get going."

She reached for him, running her hands over his shoulders and up his neck. "Thank you," she said, her voice this tender thing that he wanted to wrap up in his heart for safe keeping.

* * *

They didn't shower together even though she offered. He knew it would be incredibly hard to leave the house if they did that. Emphasis on hard.

Cas picked them up and took them to the studio since Asa had left his bike there the day before.

They hadn't discussed what, if anything, they would tell anyone else about "them." It was another thing they should probably talk about. But the moment they walked into the studio, that craving to make music overtook both of them again.

Words and music had never come so easy to him. And every note was drenched with life. His life up until Zara had just been existing.

But now he was breathing, and chasing, and fighting. He was wildly alive and he was desperately in love with that life. Almost as much as he was in love with her.

The realization was so acute that he felt it grab hold of his heart and squeeze.

"I need a minute," he said in the middle of something Nikki was explaining. He snagged the notebook they'd been working out of and a pen and headed for the upstairs lounge.

He'd barely taken a seat at the table before he was scribbling in the notebook. Words poured from him and he scratched them down as fast as he could. He put his phone on the table and opened the voice memos app and started recording. He hummed and mouthed the melody coursing through his brain as more words came to him.

When the words slowed down and he went back up the page and read through what he had. The song began to take shape and he moved pieces around.

That went there. This word should actually be here. This fits better in the bridge.

His heart thundered, his veins pulsing with adrenaline.

He sat back and read through it again. But he could *hear* it in his mind.

Grinning, he snatched up his phone and his notes and jogged back to the control room.

Nikki stopped talking and both she and Zara turned to him in surprise.

"You got something?" Zara asked.

He nodded and picked up the guitar, sat down on the leather sofa and started to play. Zara picked up the notebook and sat beside him, holding the lyrics up for them both.

She automatically began to add harmony and chills raced down his spine. The good kind. The kind that told him something magical was happening.

"Yeah, yeah, yeah," Zara said excitedly when they'd reached the end. "And then we do like a nah, nah, nah thing here but subtle, right?" she made a mark on the page.

"And maybe pick up the tempo on the second chorus," Asa said, making the adjustment to what he was already playing.

"Yes," she said in the same way she said it when he was kissing her neck last night. It flooded his mind with images of her naked beneath him and he shook his head, trying not to blush.

Later.

He would make love to her later.

Nikki started flipping switches on the console and Zara got to her feet.

"Oh my god, I have the perfect riff for this." She went out the door and down into the live room where she picked up a Fender Stratocaster.

He thought of the night they'd kissed for the first time and the things she'd played for him. She was right, she already had the perfect riff written.

"What is happening?" Asa muttered around a chuckle.

"I told you," Nikki said, keying up the necessary settings. "This place is magic."

"That you did."

She glanced at him and smiled. Did she know what had happened, what was still happening between him and Zara? Probably.

But then she said the last thing he expected.

"Welcome back to the land of the living, Ace. I've sure missed you."

Chapter Twenty-Three
Dress

ZARA

"Good day?" Cas asked.

She glanced up and caught his eyes in the rearview mirror. Smiling, she nodded. "Very good," she confirmed. Settling back in the middle seat she glanced out the window as Cas steered them out of the studio's parking lot and headed for home.

The rumble of a motorcycle sounded from behind them and she twisted in her seat to see Asa following.

Her skin got hot and her stomach trembled as images from the night before flashed through her mind. She crossed one leg over the other as the heat spread lower.

Between all the writing and recording they'd done that day, she hadn't stopped thinking about his hands and how they'd felt on her body. Or the weight of him pressing…in.

She inhaled a shaky breath as electricity tripped her heart.

It was beautiful and scary and new and confusing. And she finally understood why people acted like sex was such a big deal. Because it was a really big fucking deal. No pun intended.

And the songwriting!

The things they'd tracked that day were some of her best work ever. It felt like everything she'd learned so far about music and creativity and art had finally coalesced into this massive glittering haze of perfection.

As if her heart's purpose had been unlocked and it all made sense now.

The SUV pulled into the garage and Devan got out first. She went into the house for the initial check. Cas followed, Zara brought up the rear, lost in a daydream of words and music and late-night kisses.

She made her way up to the kitchen and got a bottle of wine out of the fridge. She poured herself a glass.

"Are you guys hungry?" she asked Cas when he came back to the kitchen after they finished checking the house for security risks.

He shook his head.

"Are you sure? I have tamales…" she tried to tempt him, opening the freezer. She had so many tamales.

"Will you need a ride to the studio tomorrow?" Cas asked.

Zara sighed and closed the freezer. She clicked her nails on the quartz countertop. "Yes?" she said.

Cas's lips twitched. "What time?"

Asa entered the kitchen and Zara's eyes went to him immediately only to find his attention already on her.

Oh why did that do things to her insides?

The way he looked at her made her feel like he saw more than others. But instead of feeling exposed or vulnerable, she just felt safe.

"What time should Cas be by to take us to the studio and also, do you want tamales?" she asked both questions at once.

Asa hummed. "Yes, to the tamales," he replied. "I don't know about the other one. Are you gonna want to sleep in?" he asked, with a slight twitch of his cheek.

Yes, please. With you. Naked.

She swallowed as her heart took off like it had been loaded into a slingshot. She wanted two things in equal amounts. She never wanted to leave his bed, and she also wanted to keep making music because she'd entered a new level of intensity.

Or was it insanity? It was hard to tell.

Slowly, she faced Cas. "Can I text you after breakfast?"

Cas nodded and headed for the exit. Devan appeared out of the shadows and joined him.

And then they were alone again for the first time since that morning.

"Are you hungry?" she asked because she didn't know how to bridge one moment to the next. What she wanted was to throw herself at him and start taking off their clothes.

Which was such a different feeling for her that she didn't know if that was okay or not. They'd crossed into a new realm of their relationship and she didn't want to ruin it by being too eager.

Asa was older; his experience was vastly different than hers. She didn't want to come across as chaotically naïve. And the thing was, she trusted him to tell her. To be honest, to teach her what she didn't know about how it could be without making her feel stupid.

He came around the island, his dark eyes holding her in place. When he reached her, he slipped a hand in between the opening of her black silk blouse. It was easy for him to glide his warm palm across her belly up to her ribs because she'd only fastened one button at the center of her chest.

Her lips parted and she had to tilt her head back to continue meeting his eyes. Her hands landed on his biceps and she slid her fingers under the hem of his short sleeves.

Touching him, being touched by him…nothing else felt so natural but also filled her with tiny explosions of awareness.

"Are *you* hungry?" he asked, voice low. Gentle. His other hand swept her hair off her neck before settling on her hip.

"Not for food," she said, her voice a strained whisper.

His eyes danced over her face, lingering on her mouth in a way that shot heat straight to her lower regions.

"Let's eat later," she suggested.

His answering smile was all kinds of hot. He dipped his head and she closed her eyes. But instead of kissing her, he nuzzled the side of her neck and spoke low in her ear. "Will you let me show you how much I want you?"

She inhaled a shaky breath as heat flooded her body. His hand on her ribs moved higher and his thumb grazed her nipple through the thin lace of her bra.

"I've wanted to kiss you all day," he murmured, his lips pressing light kisses to the shell of her ear and the side of her neck. "To touch you," he whispered, his thumb making another pass over her nipple. "To taste you." His hand on her hip pulled her against him.

She moved her hands from his biceps to his face, forcing him to look at her.

Her eyes searched his, looking for something. Something that was also screaming inside of her.

"Is this okay?" she asked. "Is it okay for me to want you this much?"

She knew what she was asking, but did he? Was it okay to be in this with him? Was she safe? Was she ruining everything by wanting not just more, but all of it?

His blink was slow, careful. His expression open and honest. "Only if you understand that I probably want this—want *you*—even more than that," he said seriously.

Her apprehension and hope must've shown on her face because his eyes gentled even more.

"It's okay if you don't believe me yet," he said. "I'm going to enjoy proving it to you." His mouth claimed hers in a slow searing kiss that ignited her skin and set her insides on fire.

She let out a small gasp as he scooped her into his arms and headed for the stairs.

Asa's strength was something that she rarely noticed in the abstract. It just…was. Not his physical strength (which she'd actually thought about a lot since that day in the backyard with the hose), but his emotional depth and strength of character. And so, him carrying her up two flights of stairs didn't seem unmanageable.

Logan would have dropped her. Who was she kidding? Logan wouldn't have even tried.

She shoved thoughts of Logan out of her mind. She didn't want him here. Not now. Not ever again.

They reached her bedroom and Asa carefully set her on her feet. He caught her mouth with his and she pushed up on her toes, trying to get closer. Hands, arms, bodies, all angled to increase the contact between them.

He moved his mouth to her cheek and then her ear where his tongue swirled over the sensitive skin just below her earlobe. "Your skin is so soft," he whisper-growled in her ear, unbuttoning her shirt.

He slid the black silk down over her shoulders while his mouth trailed hot kisses down her neck, to her chest, to her stomach.

Her back hit the wall and her hands tangled in his thick hair. He looked up at her from his knees, a devilish smirk on his gorgeous face.

"Put my glasses on the table, baby," he instructed, his hands kneading her hips.

She slid his glasses off his face and went to set them on the nearby night-stand but lost focus when his tongue swirled along the top hem of her jeans. The glasses clattered onto the nightstand and her hands went right back to his hair.

He undid her jeans and pushed them down her hips. He helped her step out of them before sliding her black panties down next. Moving his hands over her thighs and around her hips and back again, he lifted his eyes to hers.

The raw hunger she saw there made her knees weak.

"You're so gorgeous," he said before kissing below her bellybutton while maintaining eye contact.

She let out a little whimper and he moved his mouth lower, placing hot, wet kisses along her upper thighs and across her bikini line. One hand hooked behind her knee and he positioned her leg over his shoulder, opening her to him.

She'd never been affected like this. With every hot caress she knew she would be altered forever. Never again would she be able to feign ignorance of what she was capable of experiencing. And the way he touched her, with reverence and care, convinced her that she should only experience this type of adulation in her life.

He used his mouth and his hands to hold her open and dismantle her one breathless pant at a time. Her head tipped back against the wall as she moaned and whimpered, the pleasure so new and rewarding.

And overwhelming.

"Asa," she whimpered. "I can't!"

It felt too good. She was unraveling in a way she knew she'd never fully put herself back together.

"You can," he replied with conviction. "Let go, baby," he encouraged. "Let me give this to you."

So many sensations bombarded her, his beard on her inner thighs, his tongue dancing and flicking over her clit, his lips sucking and kissing, his hands stroking and entering, his words coaxing and encouraging.

Her orgasm built quickly, spiraling toward her center in a reckless, unex-pected pressure.

"Ace!" she cried, feeling her entire world about to come apart. "I'm…

I'm," she panted, unsure what she needed to say. It was all too much. Way too much. So much more than she'd ever experienced or deserved.

He groaned his praise, sending vibrations through her sex. It sent her over the edge, flying into an oblivion of ecstasy.

He held her hips in a firm grasp as his mouth lapped up the result of his determination. Both of her hands were in his hair and she knew she was holding him too tight but she couldn't stop rocking herself against his mouth, as wave after wave crashed through her.

Her body shook and trembled as she came down from the most intense orgasm of her life. He slowed his ministrations, reading her body language like he was born to it.

"That's my girl," he growled against her inner thigh, his hands stroking and kneading the muscles of her hips and ass. "That's my fucking girl," he said again, kissing his way up to her belly and slowly getting to his feet.

Her body sagged against him and he caught her. He brushed her wild hair out of her face, his eyes taking in the aftermath of his handywork.

She gripped his wrists and tried to blink her way back to coherency.

He'd ruined her. He'd dismantled her body on a molecular level and reassembled it so that he would only ever be the one who knew how to touch it.

A sideways smile slowly spread across his face like he knew exactly what she'd just been thinking. And maybe he did. Maybe he was an actual wizard because what had just happened was definitely magical.

"That was—" she started to say but his mouth was on her neck and her eyes rolled to the back of her head.

He hummed against her skin as he went to work on the hooks of her bra. It released and he slipped the straps down her arms, only pulling away far enough to let the clothing drop to the floor. He tugged his t-shirt over his head and tossed it aside.

Her breasts pressed against his warm chest and he held her to him. She was all supple limbs and satisfied sighs as he brought her to the bed and laid her down in the center.

He discarded his jeans and boxers before joining her.

She reached for him, needing more. To touch him, to hold him, to make sure he was real and not a very powerful fever dream.

"Your skin," he murmured between indulgent kisses. "Is impossibly soft." He skimmed his mouth over her neck like he was memorizing the texture of it. His hands roamed like they were on their own exploratory mission so she allowed hers to do the same.

She was jealous of the ink that graced his arms, wishing she too could wrap herself around him and stay forever.

His round shoulders were solid and warm like a stone left in the sun. His chest firm, with dark hair sprinkled across the expanse and trailing down his flat abs.

He was so hot and he smelled so good. How did he smell this good? She couldn't remember a man ever smelling amazing to the point of actually turning her on. It was some combination of his soap and shampoo and deodorant and whatever he used on his beard. She grabbed his face and pressed her mouth to his and he groaned when her tongue slipped into his mouth. She tasted him and her mixed together and if anyone had asked her if that was something she'd enjoy she'd have said no.

But she'd have been lying.

His large, capable hands caressed her breasts, fingers circling her nipples before lightly pinching and tugging on them.

Zara arched her back, pressing herself into his touch, feeling that lazy spiral of arousal begin to quicken.

He left her mouth to make-out with her breasts and she sighed and squirmed beneath him. Electricity shot from her nipple to her navel when he sucked her into his mouth. Her moans and sighs grew louder, encouraging, desperate, as he did the same thing to the other breast.

"You're so fucking perfect," he murmured, lifting his head and raking his eyes over her. He smoothed his hand over her belly, up her breast, back down, curving around her hip. "Gorgeous doesn't even cover it."

She reached between them and took hold of his erection. His eyes rolled back and he cursed under his breath as she pumped his length once. She watched his reaction as she slid her thumb over the tip, smearing the small amount of liquid over the end.

The tendons in his neck grew thick and he closed his eyes, dropping his head forward. "Oh, fuck, Zara."

His tone, his words, his face, all caused wetness to rush to her center.

She made a soft noise of desperation and his eyes opened to hers. Heat flashed between them and he kneed her legs apart, settling in between them. He grabbed a condom from the nightstand and sat back on his heels.

She couldn't take her eyes off him, sitting up in the moonlight. His dark hair, damp with exertion, messy from her fingers, his hardpacked muscles curving and straining in all the right places. His tall, thick erection standing proud between them.

He rolled the condom on and braced himself over her.

Holding eye contact, he took her hand and brought it down between them.

"Are you wet enough?" he asked, putting her fingers at her entrance.

Her slickness surprised her and she nodded. He moved her hand to his shaft. She encircled his length and he let go, catching her leg behind the knee and pulling it high along his ribs.

He was telling her to guide him in. To put him where she wanted him.

Putting her in control by teaching her how she should be fucked. How she should be loved.

She'd never experienced this kind of intimacy. Sure, they were having sex which was as physically intimate as you could get. But it was all the eye contact. The pauses in between. The gentle check-ins. Like he wanted to make sure she knew it was him who was drawing out her pleasure. That it was Asa who touched her like his life depended on it. That he was the one fully committed to her in this moment.

She lined his cock up with her entrance and lifted her hips. He slowly pushed inside her, pressing in inch by inch until she was full of him. They both moaned.

He started a slow rhythm meant to torture her and she loved every stroke. His breath mingled with hers, their pants in tandem.

"Oh, fuck," he growled, a light sheen of sweat breaking out along his forehead. "You feel so fucking good. Like you were made for me."

Maybe she was. Because it felt the same for her.

Like he'd unlocked parts of her body and soul that had been hidden all this time. She'd never been vocal during sex, never saw the point. But she could hear herself now. Didn't understand it, wasn't in control of it. The whimpers and moans and cries of a woman awakened.

Asa leaned down and touched his forehead to hers. "Fucking hell, Zara," he panted. "Nothing has ever felt this good."

She pulled his face to hers and kissed him hard, her tongue sliding along his. He groaned into her mouth and she clenched around his cock. He slipped a hand between them and started to circle her clit.

"Come with me," he said, his voice an urgent rasp that did things to her.

She said his name, or tried to, as the delicious tension in her body found its outlet and her sex exploded in a shower of sparks. Her body bowed and bucked and the movement of his hips turned jerky until they were both spent and clinging to one another.

He tried to hold his weight off her body but she wrapped her legs around him, not wanting him to go anywhere yet. An aftershock clenched her core and he groaned in response.

He placed slow, tender kisses all around her face and hairline. Her spent and blissful body relaxed beneath him and she dropped her legs to the side. He slid out of her and pulled her into his arms.

"How does it get better every time?" she asked, breathless and delighted.

"That's all you, gorgeous." He kissed her temple, her cheek, her lips.

"Pretty sure it was you," she said with a side eye.

He chuckled a deep, sexy rumble. "I think it's both of us." He smiled down at her and tucked a strand of hair behind her ear.

"I guess I'll accept that answer," she acquiesced and his smile grew lazy.

"Are you hungry?" he asked.

She actually *was* kind of hungry. They hadn't eaten when they'd gotten home, had they? They'd just gotten right to business.

"I'm going to use the bathroom and then I'll make some food for you," he suggested, his dark eyes liquid pools of endless warmth.

"You're going to make me food?" she asked, blinking up at him as tears stung the back of her eyes.

He smiled at her like she was being silly, pressed a kiss to her lips, and got out of the bed.

She rolled over and watched him walk to the bathroom and close the door.

After all that and it was the fact that he was going to make food for her that hit that tender spot in between her ribs.

The tear that leaked out was wiped away almost immediately. But not before she understood what it meant.

She was stupid in love with this man. And she'd never be the same again.

* * *

ASA

. . .

"Oh my God, that smells amazing," Zara said, entering the kitchen.

He glanced over his shoulder from where he was whisking the eggs and cream together. She was in his t-shirt and nothing else, her hair a wild mess that he'd helped create.

Fuck, she was gorgeous.

She slid her arms around his waist from behind and peeked around his arm at the cast iron skillet on the stovetop. "What are you making?"

"A frittata." With spinach, peppers, cheese, potatoes, and garlic. He put the bowl of eggs down and turned in her arms. She beamed up at him and he dipped lower to kiss her forehead. He wrapped his arms around her and she rested her cheek against his bare chest.

After a moment there, she let go and opened the fridge. "Do you want some juice?" she asked, taking the container of orange-pineapple juice out.

He murmured an affirmative and watched her from the corner of his eye as she moved around the kitchen getting glasses and plates out.

She sat down on one of the stools on the opposite side of the island and propped her elbow on the counter, her chin in her palm.

"I like this," she said, a dreamy smile on her lips.

"What? Me making you food?" he asked, shooting her a grin over his shoulder.

"Well, that too. But I meant you walking around in your boxers." She whistled softly. "Look at that ass."

His neck heated and he chuckled while stirring the veggies. "You're ridiculous."

"I just think you underestimate how hot you are. Remember that day I hosed you off in Nikki's backyard?"

"How could I forget?" The day she'd come crashing back into his life. Why had he resisted her pull so much? All of his reasons seemed so trivial now.

"I've never gotten that booty out of my mind. It's been a massive distraction."

He wiggled said booty in her direction and smiled when she giggled.

He poured the eggs into the pan and let them set before sticking the frittata in the oven to finish.

When he served her the finished food on a plate, her amber eyes sparkled at him and she tried to hide her shy smile.

"What?" he asked, taking a seat beside her at the island.

"Nothing." She shook her head once and smiled down at her plate. "I'm just happy is all."

He pulled his stool closer to hers and sat sideways so his bent knees caged her in. He tucked a strand of hair behind her ear and kissed her neck below her earlobe. "I'm happy too," he murmured.

She tilted her head his direction. "Yeah?"

He slowly inhaled and then released it, his heart settling like a content kitten in the sun. "Yeah."

She swallowed and rolled her lips inward, like she was trying to talk herself into saying something. He waited.

"After this will you stay with me? Upstairs?" She turned those gold eyes on him and he got a little lost in her unguarded sincerity. "From now on?"

"If that's what the lady wants," he said, voice rough. His hand on her knee flexed and he had to purposely hold still and not take her into his arms.

"I want that," she answered in a soft, tentative breath.

This was big for her. He could feel it. To ask. To express her wishes.

In her business and in her art she knew exactly what she wanted and wasn't afraid to demand it. She didn't let anyone push her around.

But when it came to things that were only for her—intimate, vulnerable, relationship things, the places where trusting someone had left scars and taught hesitancy—she kept quiet.

So, yeah, he knew the enormity of her request. And it filled him with determination. He would never be one of those people who left her with scars. In fact, she'd have to be the one to leave him. Because he knew he'd never willingly leave her.

"Okay, killer," he said, touching her arm. "I got you."

Chapter Twenty-Four
Times Like These

ASA

He woke up that morning to a very naked Zara pressing soft kisses to his chest and neck. What followed could only be described as fantasy levels of perfection.

She'd never had shower sex before—which frankly was almost a crime —and he was happy to introduce that to her life.

They'd had coffee and breakfast and forced themselves to get dressed before Cas arrived.

But it wasn't easy.

When they arrived at the studio it was as if they had the same mind about work. While the desire to touch her and kiss her and hold her was still very powerful, he had the self-control and wherewithal to know they'd have time later. And the waiting added an intoxicating layer to how much he craved her.

In his mind they were very careful about how close they stood, how much they touched, how long his gaze lingered. They hadn't discussed what, if anything, they would tell the people around them.

He was fine with taking their time during this transition.

And he wasn't exaggerating when he thought the music they made in the studio was the best of his life.

It was like discovering everything he loved about music and songwriting for the first time. Like the dream he had long ago wasn't lost. It had just taken a detour and *this* was where he was always supposed to end up.

Making music with her.

Making love to her.

He felt alive and on fire and he hoped it never stopped.

Apparently he wasn't the only one who thought what they were making was amazing. At one point he glanced up to say something to Zara in the vocal booth and realized the control room was full of people. Nikki, Johnny, Hannah, Shawn, Justin, and Sunshine were all silently watching and listening to the magic being made.

Also, he finally understood Nikki's warning. Because it couldn't be explained. It didn't make sense. But there was definitely something special about that studio. He was so glad he'd decided to do his bestie a favor all those months ago.

A couple hours later he came out of the bathroom and nearly jumped out of his skin.

Hannah Lee was standing around the corner, her arms crossed, back to the wall, eyes on him.

"Whoa. Hey, Hannah," he said, hesitating before moving past her. He had a weird feeling—

"We need to talk," she said, hooking his elbow with a hand and tugging him across the hall.

Yep. That checked out.

He went into the small storage room and turned around just as she closed the door.

The closet was packed floor to ceiling with boxes and gear and smelled like rubber and old electronics. A single light bulb hung from the center of the ceiling and Hannah yanked the string, casting the small space in a yellow glow.

She blinked the slowest blink ever over her icy blue eyes and Asa fought the urge to freak out.

"Anything you want to tell me, rock star?" she asked.

He grimaced. "Is it that obvious?"

Hannah glanced to the side. It wasn't an eye roll but it also wasn't *not* an eye roll. "To me? Or to normal people?"

Asa took a deep breath. "It's not a fling," he said.

"No shit," she deadpanned.

He frowned. Maybe he didn't know what this was about then.

"Do you know what you're getting into?" she asked. Not in a snarky, smartass way, but in all sincerity.

"What do you mean?"

Hannah sighed and looked past him for a second. She came back and her expression shifted to something softer, more compassionate.

"She's not just Zara," Hannah said. She held her hands up, curved like they were holding a ball. "There's a whole world of crazy that surrounds her. Fans, record executives, media, touring, travel, lack of privacy. She's at the center. But you don't get her without all the rest. You know what I'm saying?"

The tension in Asa's stomach loosened and he nodded. "I know that."

Hannah's eyes narrowed. "Those things aren't optional. Just because you guys have had this little bubble all to yourselves doesn't mean it's going to stay that way—what?"

As she'd continued her very valid warning, Asa started to smile. Because he wasn't afraid of any of that. And wasn't that what he'd told Zara months ago in that hotel room in LA?

"I know the job," Asa said, nodding.

Hannah pressed her lips together and eyed him critically.

She had every right to be skeptical. She'd been there, on the side of fame where it got intense and unmanageable. Having an authentic relationship was a rarity.

"What's in it for you?" Hannah asked, her blue eyes glowing in the dark room like she was peering into his soul.

"I get to be hers."

* * *

The next week was a blur of creativity, music, bliss, and the best sex of his life.

He fucking loved that he'd been the one to ignite her sexual awakening. It made him feel like he had superpowers. And he planned on only ever using those powers for good.

Her good, specifically.

After his conversation with Hannah, he was more confident than ever in what they shared. It wasn't normal. It was better than that. And he wasn't worried about his anxiety. He'd figure it out. He'd go to therapy, get medication, do yoga. Whatever it fucking took. Never again would he let his internal fears take away something he loved. He was done being anxiety's bitch.

Those were the thoughts on his mind as he slipped from the bed to make her coffee. He slid on his boxers and headed for the stairs.

He hit the kitchen and stopped short.

Cas sat at the island, coffee in hand.

Asa pressed his mouth into a firm line and met the bodyguard's gaze head on.

So far, they'd successfully hidden their intimate relationship from everyone else. Or so they thought.

No reason to pretend like nothing had happened. They were all adults after all.

Cas's cool gray eyes scanned Asa's almost naked appearance and narrowed slightly.

Shit.

Asa swallowed down his brief apprehension and went to the coffee maker. He got two cups down and the half and half out of the fridge.

"We have to talk," Cas said, voice stern.

Asa nodded, figuring as much. Everyone who cared about Zara was going to want to have a conversation with him. It was a testament to how much she was loved. And for good reason.

He turned around and met Cas's glare. "What do you need from me?"

Cas was silent for so long that Asa was able to start the second cup of coffee.

When the bodyguard still didn't say anything, Asa spoke again. "This isn't casual for me. I care about her." He almost said he loved her but he didn't want to say that for the first time to anyone else but her.

"I know that," Cas replied, slightly offended.

Asa's eyebrows dipped. He did?

Cas rolled his eyes at Asa's expression. "That's not what we have to talk about."

It wasn't?

Cas glanced toward the stairs and then huffed an exasperated sigh. "I've been protecting her since she was sixteen. You think I don't know the difference between someone who wants to use her and someone who's in love with her? If I thought you were the former, I'd have made up something about your background check to keep you away. It wouldn't have been difficult."

Asa's eyebrows climbed higher the longer Cas spoke. In all the months he'd been around the big man, he'd never used so many words at once outside of orientation.

"Then what do we have to talk about?" Asa croaked.

Cas sighed and took out his phone. He tapped on the screen a few times and slid it across the island. Asa picked it up and read the opened article.

BREAKING NEWS—The man arrested early last week after being found by staff in Zara Lorna's NoHo penthouse was a no-show to his hearing yesterday morning.

Authorities were called to the pop star's residence just before dawn last Monday. The man had broken in some time in the night and had fallen asleep in her bed. Zara Lorna was not home at the time of the break-in. The intruder's possessions included zip ties, duct tape, several pairs of latex gloves, and prescription tranquilizers.

He was charged with trespassing and posted bond after three days in jail.

The man, identified as Lyle Kramer, spoke to news outlets outside the jail after his release.

"I just want to know she's okay," Kramer said. "I haven't been able to get in touch with her and we usually speak every week. I need to know she's safe."

Sources say that Kramer has been on the watch list of Zara's security team for two years. Kramer's social media reveals several lengthy posts and videos of how he believes he's in a romantic relationship with the singer and has been for years. He claims she's being held against her will by her management team and he has a plan that will free both of them forever.

His trespassing hearing for yesterday morning was rescheduled after he didn't show and a bench warrant was issued. Later that day, security footage was released of Kramer allegedly breaking into Zara Lorna's management's office. Police were called but he had already fled the scene by the time authorities arrived.

Sources say no one knows Kramer's whereabouts. Authorities have asked that if you see Lyle Kramer to please contact your local police and do not approach.

"What the fuck is this?" Asa asked, reading the article again, his stomach twisting in on itself.

"She's not going to want to talk about it," Cas said. "But we need to make some changes to her current arrangements."

The hair on the back of Asa's neck stood up and he rubbed at it reflexively. "Why? Is she in danger?"

Cas took in a careful breath, his gray eyes unflinching as he studied Asa's reaction. "It's not immediate—"

"But it could be pretty fucking immediate in a minute," Asa finished for him.

Cas nodded once.

This was part of it, he tried to remind himself. He'd been so proud of himself for accepting all the extra stuff that came with loving Zara like the paparazzi and the super fans, but for some stupid reason, he'd blacked out on the dangerous stuff. Hadn't she mentioned a stalker in LA when she'd first come to Chicago? Why did he have a feeling it wasn't the same one?

Zara hit the room with her customary radiance wearing only his Black Flag t-shirt, big hair and bare legs. She felt the tension immediately and her smile faded. "What's going on?" she asked slowly.

Cas took his phone back and put it away. Asa wondered why he hadn't shown the article to Zara but he had mentioned she didn't want to know any of it. How often did shit like this happen? So often that she couldn't stand to see the details anymore?

"There was an incident this week with a trespasser," Cas said.

"You mean stalker," Asa corrected him.

Cas's big shoulders rose with his deep breath.

Zara's expression darkened. "Which one?"

She knew them by name? Was there a list he should know about? Did they have a newsletter with their mugshots and stats that got sent out once a month?

"Kramer."

The shudder that rolled through Zara was subtle but he noticed it. He went to her and she melted into his chest as he wrapped his arms around her shoulders. He pressed his mouth to the top of her head.

It would be okay.

It had to be okay.

He would make it okay.

Somehow.

"We need to talk about moving you to a place with better security," Cas said after a beat.

Zara stiffened in his arms. He was pretty sure he knew what she was thinking because he'd had the same thought. Their privacy was getting ready to evaporate.

But it didn't matter. She needed to be kept safe.

She tipped her head back and looked at him. A thousand emotions swam through those amber gold eyes. All at once they stilled, settling on one he wasn't too familiar with. "I'm going to go shower." She squeezed him and let go, grabbing her coffee on her way to the stairs. "Will you take us to the studio in a few?" she asked Cas on her way by.

Cas nodded.

She left and Asa stared at where she'd disappeared. What the hell had just happened?

He shook his head once, trying to clear it. "Uh," he started, not sure where to go.

Cas sighed and rolled his eyes. "She doesn't like to talk about it."

Who would? But that wasn't the point.

Asa scrubbed a hand over his face. "What do you want to do? Maybe I can talk to her."

Cas tapped on the island with his fingers as he worked his jaw back and forth with thought. "I'd like her to be in a place that was more secure. I have a couple calls out to some colleagues for suggestions."

Asa's mind immediately went to where Hannah Lee James and Sunshine Capone lived. Maybe he could ask them about that.

"I don't want to increase the detail surrounding her until we have more of a cause. We tend to draw attention without meaning to. If she's still flying under the radar here, I want to keep it that way." He measured his next words before saying them. "She can't be alone right now. Not with Kramer in the wind."

Ice settled in the pit of Asa's stomach. "He's that much of a threat?"

Cas's cheek twitched. "He's persistent and slippery. I don't like that he broke into Sonja's office. It doesn't sit well with me."

Asa laced his fingers together behind his head and stared up at the ceiling.

They dealt with this all the time. This was just another regular part of her life, wasn't it? This was why she didn't want to stay long term with her family, because it put them in this kind of risk. It wasn't just the media frenzy. It was the deranged fan that followed the trail the media left.

"Go shower. She's going to want to leave soon and you'll want to be ready," Cas said, interrupting Asa's internal freakout. "And you're going to want to brace yourself."

Asa righted his head and frowned at Cas. "What do you mean?"

Cas's head ticked to the side as he lifted his cup of coffee to his lips. "She has a stubborn streak you haven't met yet."

Instantly, Asa was irritated at the implication that Zara was going to be unreasonable. She wasn't unreasonable. She had a reason for everything. They just didn't always agree with it.

He shook his head and headed for the stairs going up.

Cas made a noise of warning but didn't stop him.

He reached her bedroom, his eyes darting to the French doors on the opposite side. Sure, Cas had installed extra sensors on the terrace outside and the door itself, but it wasn't a moat. Anyone with a brick and a screw loose could just walk right in here.

"Babe?" he called, stepping into the bathroom.

"In here," she replied over the running water of the shower.

"Can we talk?" he asked, leaning a shoulder against the wall. He could see the fogged-up shower window in the mirror from where he stood, the shadow of her body moving beyond it.

"You don't want to join me?" she asked.

He did want to join her. Obviously.

Instead of answering her, he got right into it. "Maybe we should think about leaving Lincoln Park."

She didn't say anything and he chewed on his lower lip.

The timing for this was shit.

Not that there was ever a good time to have a stalker.

But they were in the middle of writing and recording…something. They still hadn't discussed the endgame for their project. And moving houses could very well stop the creative flow they'd been on.

The water turned off and he realized she still hadn't replied.

She stepped out of the shower, a towel wrapped around her hair and another around her body. Walking past him, she let her fingers trail over his abs and he automatically flexed them.

"Are you going to shower before we go?" she asked, moving into the bedroom and then the closet.

"Can we talk about this?" he asked, following her.

"What's there to talk about?" she asked. "I'm not going to turn my life upside down just because some guy somewhere is unstable." She took something off a hanger and started rummaging through a drawer.

"He's dangerous," Asa said, his frown deepening and his heart getting heavy in his chest.

She snorted. "They're always dangerous."

Asa blinked, taken aback by her casual remark. How many times had she been in this position? How many stalkers were never addressed in the media? How many were smart enough not to have been noticed yet?

The idea of her being in danger was a thick fog that cloaked all his previous confidence. No amount of anxiety medication and therapy would make her safe from a *fucking stalker*.

His mind raced with horrible possibilities. Selena, John Lennon, Dimebag Darrell, Christina Grimmie…all killed by fans.

Suddenly their little bubble seemed more fragile than ever.

She set a pair of black panties and a matching bra on top of the first piece of clothing. Then she took a pair of jeans out of a different drawer and set those aside as well.

Not waiting for him to turn around, she dropped the towel. He beheld her glorious naked body for a moment before averting his gaze and turning around. Was she trying to distract him? If so, well played. His mind scrambled to remember what it was he'd been about to say.

"Maybe just temporarily," he suggested. "Until they find the guy."

"Then they'll be another threat. It never ends." She hummed a melody they had been working on yesterday. "Do you think you could distort a tornado siren? Like make it kind of sad sounding and slowed down? I was thinking about how to open 'Runaway Soul' and I keep coming back to like a whiny, ominous like…" She made the noise best she could.

Adorable as usual.

He squeezed his hands into fists in response to the swift subject change. "Zara—"

"Then fade it out and back in at the end? I think that might be cool. Can we try it when we get to the studio?" She moved past him, fully dressed, and went back to the bathroom.

He followed.

She hung up her towel and then removed the one around her hair. Her eyes met his in the mirror.

There was something there… something she wasn't saying.

"Can we please talk about it?" he asked, trying again. Because he'd always try again. As many times as he had to. For her. Forever.

She sighed and turned around. "Okay," she relented. "Let's talk about it."

He breathed a short sigh of relief. "Is there a reason you won't consider moving? Even if it's temporary?"

Her lips twisted to the side. "Because I like it here. I like living here with you. No one knows I'm in Chicago so there's no reason to start panicking just because the police are looking for someone a thousand miles away."

"But what if someone finds out you're here?" he asked.

She shrugged. "There's always a what-if. I don't want you to think I'm not taking it seriously. I am. I do." She blinked rapidly as her eyes glossed over. "Shit." She swiped at her eyes.

He stepped toward her and grabbed her gently by her shoulders. "What's going on?" he asked softly.

She closed her eyes and took a breath. When she opened them he could finally see all the turmoil, the hesitation, the doubt and worry and responsibility she felt.

"I hate this part," she said. "I don't talk about it because I know it comes with the life and there's nothing anyone can do to change it. It's just one more reason that being with me is an impossible ask."

He wanted to correct her but waited because it felt like she wasn't done.

"I just don't want to talk about all the ways I've prepared for the worst possible thing to happen." She shrugged. "It's not fun or sexy to go into detail about all the med kits I have in nearly every room of every place I stay. And I really hate talking about how I've taken Tactical Emergency Casualty Care Training *multiple* times so I can be prepared for a variety of horrible scenarios such as gunshots or stabbings to myself or the people around me. In fact, all of the people who work for me are required to take it." Her eyes drifted to the side.

"I don't like to talk about how many times I've participated in an active shooter simulation. Or how I've never made it through one without crying even though I know it's not real. It *could* be real someday and that terrifies me. And all of it might not even matter. None of it is guaranteed to save my life if someone is that determined to hurt me."

While she spoke his entire world view crumbled at his feet.

"You shouldn't have to do all that," he said just above a whisper. "I'm so sorry."

Her gaze dropped to the center of his chest and her shoulders slumped under his hands. "I'm afraid that it's going to be those things, the things I *can't* control that will make you…"

She didn't finish. She didn't need to.

"Hey," he said, catching her chin with a finger and thumb. "I'm not stupid." He cracked a smile. "I know who you are. I'm all in this with you. Both eyes open."

He pressed a kiss to her forehead, trying to ignore the injustice of it all. She shouldn't have to know how to do those things. She was a pop star, not a field medic.

"Whatever you want to do, I've got your back," he said.

She glanced up at him, eyes round and curious with just enough hope to make his knees weak.

"This is your life. I trust you to make the right call."

"Yeah?" she asked. "If we left, you'd come with me?"

He knew the answer before she'd even asked the question. Of course he'd go with her. He'd follow her to hell and back if she asked him to.

Maybe that was crazy.

But he didn't think so.

He was pretty sure it was just what you did for someone you loved.

* * *

CELEBX

Don't forget to send in your "celebrity sighting" every week! CelebX will post your pics online and tag your account. We couldn't do our jobs without you!

One celeb to be on the lookout for is Zara Lorna. She hasn't shown up in our inbox since last April. No one seems to know where she is these days. If you see her, let us know!

Chapter Twenty-Five
I Know Places

ZARA

She could feel Cas and Devan's worry like another member of her security team. They tried to hide it but they'd been with her too long. The whispers they thought she couldn't hear. The way they gave her space but really created a wall of protection around her like a human prison.

Addressing it would only cause them to get defensive and ultimately feel helpless.

She understood it, on a fundamental level. They had a job they took very seriously. And it was good for her that they did.

But it was a constant reminder that her life wasn't normal.

And sure, maybe "normal" was subjective. Like a goldfish in a bathtub, her life had grown to fit its container. The container being Earth. Which made her little goldfish career enormous.

It had gotten to a point that it was difficult to feel normal anymore.

Except for these few stolen months she'd had in Chicago with Asa.

For the first time in her life, she didn't feel entirely alone at the center of the hurricane that was her life. She had someone with her. A partner who was both a best friend and a lover who really *saw* her.

Asa was this incredible anchor, keeping her tethered to reality. But he was also a source of freedom that existed so far outside the limitations she'd been trying to survive in.

How could a person be both?

She didn't know. But he was.

It made her simultaneously thankful and apprehensive.

Because while she was mostly used to her life being insane and gargantuan, he had only seen glimpses of it. Small flashes of crazy and massive.

And that was probably her driving principle in wanting to keep things from being upended.

She wasn't ready to be without him. But in the back of her mind, she knew it was unreasonable to ask him to stick around when this wasn't a life he wanted. He'd expressed that many times. The anxiety that being in the public eye brought out in him wasn't a joke. And it wasn't something she could fix or pretend not to see. She wasn't going to stop being *Zara Lorna, Pop Star*, and he wasn't going to magically become comfortable being judged and analyzed by strangers.

Which meant the worst heartbreak of her life was just on the horizon.

So she was going to grab his hand and run in the opposite direction for as long as she could.

And that direction was to her happy place—the studio.

Because at the absolute very least, she'd have the best music she'd ever made to look back on and say, "That was real. That really happened. I loved and I was loved and this is what it felt like."

The door to the control room opened and she lifted her head to see who it was. She'd been lying on the couch, her head in Asa's lap, as they ran through different lyrical shifts for the song they were working on.

Nikki entered the room and eyed their physical proximity to one another. It wasn't just that they were on the couch together. It was also how Asa was touching her. One hand was tucked into her hair while the other lazily traced a line from her neck down the center of her chest, stopping just between her breasts and then back up again. It was both soothing and sensual. She absolutely loved it.

But it was more intimate than they had been in front of others. Something about that morning's unfortunate discourse had shifted them. They'd left their secret bubble and had walked casually into the open, hand in hand.

"You ready to do the bass track?" Nikki asked, her eyes skating over them. She sat down at the control board, her expression neutral.

Asa nodded and Zara sat up so he could go. But he didn't leave right away. Instead he curved a hand around her jaw and held her eyes for a beat, not saying anything. His gaze moved over her face in a slow perusal, like he was memorizing it.

She leaned into his touch and he brushed a thumb over her lips. His eyelids dropped halfway and a lazy smile tugged at the corner of his mouth.

"Be right back," he promised needlessly.

He let her go and left the control room. She sank back into the sofa and wrapped her arms around her middle, trying to hold all of her feelings inside.

She loved him like she loved breathing. The same way she loved music. Like he was a part of her soul, both innocent and imperative. The rest in her sleep, the sweet in her dreams.

"So you and Asa, huh?" Nikki asked too casually, flipping switches and twisting dials.

Zara chewed on her bottom lip and waited. What was she supposed to say? Nikki and Asa had been friends for years. Maybe they should have told her first?

Nikki laughed softly to herself. "I guess I'm not surprised."

"You're not?" Zara asked.

Nikki shrugged and glanced at Zara over her shoulder. "Not really. I fully expected him to fall in love with you. You're almost impossible not to love."

Zara rolled her eyes even as she smiled at her friend. She knew she'd been pushy with Nikki. Basically forcing her to be her friend and then to produce her record (which won them all the awards so she wasn't even a little sorry).

"But Asa…?" Nikki continued. She looked out the control window at him. "He's a little more difficult to fall in love with. It takes a minute. He keeps his heart well hidden under that grumpy old man exterior. But once you've had him in your corner, there's really no going back. You can't buy loyalty and devotion like that. He'd fight a bear in a typhoon with one hand tied behind his back for someone he loves."

Zara didn't correct Nikki's assertion that they were in love. She did love Asa. Even if she hadn't told him yet. He hadn't said it in so many words but she could feel it, see it, touch it, every time she was with him.

"I don't know," Zara said thoughtfully. "I think I started falling in love with him the moment he grabbed my hand at that afterparty. It wasn't difficult at all. Staying away from him, pretending not to have feelings? *That* was difficult. But loving him is easy."

Nikki's smile was like pure sunshine and Zara rolled her eyes.

"Stop it."

"Nope." Nikki shook her head. "I'm happy and I'm not about to hide it."

* * *

ASA

The soft launch of their relationship seemed to be going well.

After they'd finished recording the bass track, Nikki cornered him in the supply closet where she hugged him and then threatened him. And then hugged him again.

Honestly, it was on the subdued side of what he'd expected from Nikki.

It was early evening when they decided to call it a day. Mostly because they'd already accomplished so much. They had enough songs recorded for an album. Two actually. All that was left was mixing and mastering.

But also, Zara had waylaid him in the hallway with a kiss so scandalous he was surprised he didn't burst into flames on the spot.

Getting home and getting her naked became priority one.

Nikki wanted to go home anyway. Baby Amber had developed a bit of a fever after her shots that morning and Nikki wanted to snuggle her baby.

They headed for the exit, talking and laughing about something banal and forgettable. Nikki walked backwards in front of them, Asa had his arm around Zara, Devan brought up the rear, Cas had gone to get the SUV and pull it around back.

It was the familiarity of being at the studio where he worked, of being surrounded by people he knew and trusted, of being so blissfully distracted by Zara's hand in his back pocket as they walked out the backdoor that made him so incredibly stupid.

Nikki laughed as she crossed the threshold outside. She turned around and stopped suddenly, a choked gasp coming out of her. "Demon!"

Asa and Zara kept walking, bumping into her. Asa hadn't even processed what was happening before Nikki was using both hands to push him and Zara back towards the door.

"Nikki, what on earth—?"

"Gogogogogogo," Nikki hissed.

"Oh wow. I've missed you too, Nikki."

Asa's blood ran cold. He knew that voice. He hadn't heard it in a long time and not without it spewing drunken curses at him. But he knew that voice. His arm tightened around Zara and his eyes darted around Nikki, finding the last person he wanted to see.

Shelby stood with her back to the passenger side door of a car he didn't recognize. Casually posed with one arm crossed over her middle, the other holding up her phone like she was taking pictures or video.

Asa moved Zara behind him and backed toward the door. He glanced over his shoulder to see Devan who had assessed the situation correctly and already had hold of Zara and she was speaking into her wrist. She pulled Zara back into the studio and Nikki followed, shutting the door.

Leaving Asa alone with his sister.

She was in skintight black jeans and a black tank top. Her hair was the color of old rust because she'd bleached and colored it so many times, the ends brittle and broken off. She was only two years older than him but she appeared to be so much more. Her skin was lined by her life choices and a thousand too many cigarettes.

He'd feel pity for her if she wasn't such an asshole.

"I didn't realize they moved the location to the gates of hell," Asa said by way of greeting.

"Hello, little brother. Miss me?"

"Almost as much as I miss having the stomach flu," he replied.

She narrowed her eyes at him and ran her tongue over her teeth. He glanced at her phone again.

"What are you doing here?" he asked, though he had a pretty good idea. "Is there a used port-a-potty support group in town?"

She curled an unamused lip at him. "I had a hunch and I followed it." Her expression turned devious. "I was right. You're fucking the pop star." She waved her phone at him and arched her eyebrows. "And guess who caught it all on video?"

Squealing tires announced Cas's arrival and Asa could have kissed the man if he thought he wouldn't get punched.

Cas brought the SUV to a lurching stop and came around the vehicle, angry gray eyes leveled at Shelby.

Shelby didn't even flinch.

Cas grabbed her phone out of her hand and threw it on the ground, smashing it.

"Ooh," Shelby said, dripping with sarcasm. "Scary. C'mon, beefcake," she said, addressing Cas. "Like they're not already in the cloud." She rolled her eyes.

"What do you want, Shelby?" Asa asked taking a step toward her, his hands clenched into fists at his side.

"Money." She spit out a number that was so astronomical and ludicrous he almost laughed out loud.

"Shelby, I don't have that kind of money."

"Ask your little princess for it."

Asa stared at her, his mouth opening and closing in disbelief. She was the living *worst*.

Shelby looked around the parking lot and back at the studio. They'd recorded Winking Pete's first and only album behind those doors.

He wondered if she regretted any of it. If she was sorry for anything she'd done.

Probably not.

But he still wondered.

"Must be fucking nice to get everything you want and nothing you deserve," she said with a sneer. "You have an hour to let me know. And then they get sent."

She winked at Cas and got into her car and drove away.

Asa stood in the parking lot trying to breathe through the urge to throw up.

His fucking, shithead sister.

"We have to tell Zara," Cas said, as if he didn't already know.

The big man followed him back into the studio.

The photos hit the internet ten minutes later.

Chapter Twenty-Six
Fire and the Flood

S POTTED! *Fans saw Zara Lorna exiting a recording studio in Chicago with her beau Asa Young. CelebX was first to report the two dating back in October. Even though both sides denied the relationship it looks as though they're still going strong.*

XY Records is where she recorded her last major album. Does this mean another one is on the way? Also spotted in the photos is NMA's Producer of the Year, Nikki Harry, leading fans to speculate new music is imminent.

Zara broke up with longtime boyfriend Logan Black last October. They met when they were sixteen and have always referred to the other as "the love of their life." Logan more than hinted that Zara had been less than faithful in their relationship, even talking on a podcast last month about how he's healing and moving on from "the biggest betrayal of his life."

Diehard fans of Zara (Zaranators) have defended her online saying they hope she's finally in a relationship with someone who makes her happy and casting doubt on Logan's allegations.

CELEBX has reached out to Zara's people for a comment but haven't heard back.

Click here for a timeline of Logan and Zara's relationship.

* * *

ZARA

The moments following Asa's horrible sister posting her location online were kind of a blur.

Devan and Cas put her in the SUV along with Asa and just started driving.

Devan drove and Cas made phone calls. Zara didn't know where they were going. She also didn't ask. She didn't anything.

She just stared out the window as they drove through the streets of Chicago, lights and cars and people, flying by.

Asa's phone started to go off nonstop and he shut it down.

"Gregor will be here in a couple hours. Kenna and Sonja will fly in tomorrow morning," Cas said.

Zara nodded.

All hands on deck.

Her house of cards falling in slow motion.

She'd known this day would come. She'd foolishly hoped she had more time.

They pulled into an underground garage of some kind. "Where are we?" she asked, sitting up straight and looking around.

"East Randolph Residence. It's a secure complex. We already have a condo ready for you," Cas answered.

She frowned and glanced over at Asa who averted his eyes.

Wait.

"Did you know about this?" she asked him.

He swallowed and finally met her eyes. "It was my idea."

"What?" she breathed. When? How? *What?*

They parked and Cas got out of the SUV. He greeted someone in a suit and then waved at Devan.

Asa, for his part, looked guiltier than she'd ever seen him. "I called Sunshine and he told me to call Cipher Security. Cas knew someone there and we got you a safe house. Just in case."

With every word he spoke, more of the floor fell out beneath her.

"You went behind my back, knowing how I felt, while promising to be on my side—"

"I *am* on your side, Zara. It was just a precaution. Peace of mind. And now I'm really glad—"

"You're really glad you did it?" she asked, her insides starting to tremble.

His dark eyes pleaded with her in the back of the SUV. "I just want you to be safe," he whispered.

Part of her knew he was right. He hadn't done anything wrong. Not really. But in her mind Asa had always been *hers*. He wasn't a part of the system that surrounded her. The one she paid to manage her life.

But he'd worked with Cas, despite her wishes, and had gotten her a new place to live. All without her knowing. She hadn't suspected and he hadn't felt it necessary to mention it.

She hadn't even suspected…

Yanking the door open, she left the vehicle, slamming the door behind her.

Cas eyed her but didn't say anything. This was something she expected from him. His job was to protect her, it's what she paid him to do. It annoyed her sometimes when his priorities were different from hers. But he didn't take it personally and neither did she.

She didn't want to be annoyed with Asa.

She wanted to trust him. That had always been one of his most appealing character traits, his honesty.

This move didn't feel honest.

It felt manipulative.

Which made her insides curl in on themselves.

She wrapped her arms around her middle and followed Cas, Devan right behind her, Asa somewhere behind her. After an elevator ride and a walk down a hallway, they stopped at a door. The man Cas had met in the garage opened the door and she went inside.

It was larger than she expected and fully furnished. But it wasn't the house she'd grown accustomed to in East Lincoln Park. It wasn't home.

"So what makes this better than where I was?" she asked Cas, ignoring Asa entirely.

"It's the most secure residence building in the city. On site security guards, cameras, and it's un-hackable," Cas explained.

"What does that mean?"

Cas shrugged. "Not even the government can get to you."

Well.

That sounded pretty secure. Still. She wasn't happy about how this had happened.

Devan lifted her eyebrows at Cas and gestured toward the door.

Cas took a breath. "Right." He faced Zara. "We have to go check out the Lincoln Park house. On our way over here, the alarm was tripped and then disabled."

Zara's breathing stopped. "What?" she breathed. "The house alarm?"

Cas held her eyes for a beat, face hard as stone. "The alarms on the terrace. Do not leave here. Promise me."

Zara's gaze flicked to Asa who had a hand on the back of his neck but was watching her closely. She swallowed but her throat felt tight. "Okay."

"Promise," Cas repeated.

"I promise." She sucked in a breath. "Do you have to go? Can't you send the police?"

A muscle jumped in Cas's cheek. "I'll be right back," he said, sounding more confident than she felt.

She nodded and her stomach churned as she watched him and Devan walk out the door. She caught a glimpse of a man in black standing guard outside the door right before it closed.

The silence in the apartment filled her head until her ears rang.

What if it was Kramer? Or someone else? How had they found where she was living so fast? The photos had only gone public an hour ago. Maybe it was nothing. Maybe it was a blip in the electricity. Or the property owner checking in on things.

What if Cas and Devan got hurt?

Because of her.

She pressed a hand to her stomach and started to pace.

"Are you okay?" Asa asked.

She ignored him and kept pacing. Her stomach roiled and she squeezed her eyes shut.

No, no, no, no, no. I'm not going to be sick. No. Not now.

But then she thought about Cas and Devan walking into an unknown situation *because of her* and she was bolting down the hall, hoping the bathroom was nearby.

It was.

* * *

"Hey." Asa knocked on the door of the bathroom. "Are you okay?"

Zara turned off the faucet and looked at herself in the mirror. Mascara pooled in black smears under her eyes, above flushed cheeks. She grabbed a towel and dried her face.

She didn't even have a toothbrush here. Tears welled in her eyes again and she sank back to her knees on the floor.

"Zara?" Asa asked.

She buried her face in the towel and tried to cry as quietly as possible. She didn't want him to know. She didn't want to talk to him. She didn't want to be worried about Cas and Devan. And she didn't want to be in this place that didn't feel like hers.

She wanted to go home.

She sucked in a shuddering breath and sat down, pushing her back against the wall.

I want to go home.

A therapist she once went to told her that the desire to go home came from a place of anxiety. An intense longing for safety and familiarity.

It didn't happen all the time, but when it did, it hurt deep in her chest. A hollow burning like she couldn't breathe.

I want to go home.

"Zara?" came his voice again, this time softer, and closer to the ground like he knew she was sitting down.

She sniffled and he sighed.

"Why did you do that?" she asked.

He shifted and she heard a soft thud on the door like he was dropping his head there.

"I get so tired of explaining myself over and over and everyone else is so busy talking over me and telling me what I need that they never actually hear me." She rolled the towel into a ball in her lap, unrolled it and then re-rolled it again.

"Would you have ever told me?" she asked, her voice cracking. "Or was it just going to be this secret thing you did behind my back?" She pitched her voice deeper. *"What she doesn't know won't hurt her."*

Fresh tears filled her eyes. "What else would you end up hiding from me?" she whispered. "You're just like the rest of them."

"Please let me in," he begged softly, voice strained.

"No. I'm mad at you," she said. She didn't sound mad though and she hated that.

"You can be mad at me. I just don't want you to be alone. Please…"

She didn't want to be alone either. She wanted to be held by him. But not the him right now. The him she thought he was before. The man she trusted and loved and adored and who would *never* deceive her. For any reason. Not even to protect her.

He had been hers. He hadn't been part of the system around her. He wasn't part of the brand or the industry, he'd been…hers.

And now…now she didn't know what he was.

She knew her life came with a certain amount of threat. She wasn't completely naïve to how the world worked. That's why she had the best protecting her.

Oh, God. Cas. Devan.

What if something happened to them?

It was all her fault. They wouldn't be in danger if it wasn't for her. If she'd just listened to them instead of thinking she knew everything.

"What if something happens—" Her voice cut off, choked with terrifying possibilities.

Panic compressed her chest and cramped her stomach.

She reached up and unlocked the door.

He slowly pushed it open and she was right, he *was* lying on the floor.

He crawled into the bathroom and sat beside her, his shoulder brushing hers, their hips aligned, their legs stretched out in front of them.

Exactly how they'd sat beside each other that October night. Except she was the one freaking out this time.

Her breaths came in heavy pants as she tried to get them under control. Hot tears ran unchecked down her face and she pressed her hands to her stomach. A mournful sob echoed from her chest and she curled in on herself.

Strong arms came around her as he pulled her into his lap. She buried her face in his neck, clutching at his t-shirt. He caged her in with his legs on either side and his arms around her shoulders.

"I'm so stupid," she cried against him, her lungs laboring to get a whole breath. "This is all my fault!"

His chest rumbled with soft words she couldn't understand. A hand rubbed up and down her spine and made slow circles at the top and bottom of each pass.

She wanted to crawl inside his warmth and never come out.

His rumbled words turned into something familiar. It wasn't until her breathing had steadied and her tears had slowed that she began to hear the song he was singing to her.

Maybe because she was from Jersey so he chose another Jersey native to bring her comfort. Maybe because he'd caught her listening to this band more than once. Maybe because they were connected in places no one else could begin to grasp.

But his calm and careful rendition of Bleachers' "Isimo" sliced through her anxiety and soothed some primal part of her soul.

And she wanted, wanted, *wanted* to believe him.

* * *

ASA

He didn't know how long he held her. A while.

Eventually her body relaxed against his and her breathing evened out. She was awake but somewhere else mentally. He kept singing and smoothing his hand up and down her spine.

She let go of his shirt and wrapped her arms around his middle.

The door to the apartment opened and he turned his head to the bathroom doorway in time to see a man with a military style haircut dressed like he was trying too hard to look like a civilian.

"They're in here," he said, stepping aside for another man to join them.

Zara didn't move. Her body gave no indication that she knew anyone else had arrived.

The second man took in Asa and Zara's position, the proximity to the toilet, and the towels she'd thrown on the floor.

He licked his lips and nodded once. "I have something that will ease her stomach," he said.

Asa didn't want to move her though. She'd finally stopped crying.

The man, who Asa had deduced was Gregor, left and came back with some pills and a glass of water. He sat down beside Asa and nudged Zara's shoulder gently.

"You want some water?" he asked.

Zara gradually straightened a bit and looked over at Gregor. Her eyebrows lifted slowly like she just realized he was there. She nodded.

He handed her the pills and the glass. She took them and handed the water back when she was done.

"What if we go sit in the living room?" Gregor asked gently.

Asa held perfectly still. If she didn't want to move, he wasn't making her. He wasn't ever making that mistake again.

The look in her eyes when she'd found out he'd gotten her this apartment… She'd never looked at him like that. Like he'd just surprised her in the worst way.

He still maintained that having a backup plan was a good idea. But he shouldn't have done it secretly.

It had become painfully clear within seconds that he'd overstepped. Protective wasn't a valid excuse for disrespecting her autonomy.

He'd experienced regret in his life more times than he could count. But the regret he felt in that moment was like a knife to his soul.

Her broken questions through the door had driven the knife deeper. When she'd opened the door he knew it wasn't for his benefit. It was because she was hurting and scared and she didn't want to be alone.

Zara nodded in answer to Gregor's question but she didn't move. Asa couldn't get up without her participation so he didn't move either.

After a few minutes, she let him go and started to unfold her body.

His muscles tightened as they fought against pulling her back into his arms. Cold air swirled in the gap between their bodies and he helped her get to her feet.

Gregor took her hand and led her out of the bathroom.

Asa followed, though he felt less needed than he had a minute ago.

She sat down on the couch, her tan complexion paler than he'd ever seen it, her golden eyes downturned and flat. She wrapped her arms around her middle and shivered.

Asa shed his flannel and handed it to her. She put her arms in the holes and pulled it tight around her even though she didn't look at him once.

Gregor's eyes bounced between the two of them but he didn't say anything.

Asa had heard all about Gregor, the world's greatest assistant. But this was their first time meeting. Which sucked for a lot of reasons.

"Have you heard from…?" Asa asked, not wanting to say the names in case it made her start crying again.

Gregor shook his head once and the door to the apartment opened.

All of them looked that direction as Cas and Devan entered.

Zara made a noise that was half-shout half-sob and threw herself at the enormous bodyguard.

Cas caught her, one big palm on the back of her head. He smiled the smallest, sweetest smile as he returned the embrace.

"We're okay," he said.

"What happened?" Gregor asked immediately.

Cas took a big breath and waited for Zara to let him go. "We should sit."

Zara returned to the couch next to Gregor. Asa stayed standing near the opposite wall, unsure he be welcomed on the couch.

Cas took a seat in a chair that creaked under his size. Devan slid onto a stool at the breakfast bar and Asa noticed she was wearing different clothes than she had been earlier. His eyes flicked back to Cas. So was he.

"Lyle Kramer is in police custody," Cas said.

Zara sucked in a short breath. "Was he—?"

Cas nodded. "He was at Lincoln Park when we arrived." He cast a glance toward Devan whose expression was more impassive than usual. "We easily overpowered him and waited for the police."

Asa heard something in his voice and he wondered…

"Tell me all of it," Zara said, voice stony. She'd heard it too.

Cas swallowed. "He'd gotten in through the French doors in the upstairs bedroom. We found him in the closet. We believe his plan was to hide until you'd fallen asleep. He…fought us and was injured in the process. His wounds weren't fatal."

Zara touched her lips with her fingertips.

"There's more." Cas took another breath. "His clothes had been soaked in kerosene. He had brought enough accelerant to burn down the house. We think that was his backup plan. We searched through his personal items and found the Lincoln Park address in a text two days ago from a number we're still tracking down."

Cas's gray eyes flicked to Asa's for a beat and he knew exactly why. It wasn't Shelby that had led him to her.

"If those pictures hadn't gotten leaked…" Zara said, her expression clearly working out the math of the day. Her gaze landed on Asa. "Then we would have been home when he broke in."

"We would have found him with our sweep," Cas reassured her.

But that would have put her there, with Kramer, even if only for a moment. And if he had fought Cas and Devan to the point of getting wounded, there was no telling how he would have behaved if Zara had been present.

If they all would have gone up in flames.

Zara seemed to be thinking that as well because a shiver racked her body.

Everything inside him reached for her. From bones to blood, it brought him to her side, whether she wanted him there or not.

He'd barely taken a seat when she pushed herself onto his lap. His arms went around her and he tried to absorb the tiny tremors running through her frame.

Discussion continued around them in murmured tones. Gregor and Cas moved into the kitchen with Devan. Asa didn't care what they said or what plans they needed to make. His priority, the one thing that mattered and would only ever matter to him, was the woman in his arms.

Her delicate heart and tender soul. She put on this brave, unflappable face because her job required her to be invincible. But she wasn't.

All those qualities that her fans adored about her, the honesty and the vulnerability. The way she bared her emotions in her music and songwriting, the reason so many could relate to her, was because of the way she carried her heart out into the world like an offering.

Sacrificing its safety for the benefit of people she didn't even know.

She was the bravest person he'd ever known.

He'd follow her forever.

Her soft breath puffed against his neck and he tightened his hold on her.

"You were right," she said. Another tremor rippled through her.

He closed his eyes and pressed his lips to the top of her head. A chasm of agony opened up through his middle. He wasn't right. Not in the thing that mattered.

Shelby had given him enough experience with crazy that he'd been able to predict a logical outcome to the Lyle Kramer shit. But he wasn't right in how he'd handled it.

And he didn't know if there was anything he could do to fix the damage he'd done to her. To them.

Because what was love without trust?

The worst part was knowing she'd never have done that to him. She'd have kept talking to him, appealed to his sensibilities, continued communication instead of what he'd done.

In one well-intentioned move, he'd placed himself in the court of people who cared about her, surrounded her, but didn't stand with her.

Leaving her alone in the center of a storm.

"Please don't leave me," she said.

Her words ripped his soul in two.

This was what he'd done. He'd introduced doubt into something that had been balanced and beautiful. And now she felt she didn't know him enough to know there was no way he'd leave her.

"Never," he promised, his voice cracking with the weight of his regret.

Nothing about her life—the crowds, the media, the stalkers, the constant attention—scared him the way the thought of losing her did.

Because being with her was the only thing that made sense.

In a world filled with fakery and fear, she was the truest thing he'd ever known. His heart would never belong to anyone else. It was hers forever.

Chapter Twenty-Seven
I'm On Your Side

ZARA

She'd cried herself to sleep last night.

Not because she'd wanted to but because her body needed to release the amount of stress it had endured that day.

So when she woke up, her eyes were overly dry and puffy, but her body and mind were clear and calm.

Such was the benefit of a good cry.

A heavy arm encircled her waist and heat at her back let her know Asa hadn't left even after she'd fallen asleep. Not that she'd given him much reason to stay.

Carefully, she slid out from under the covers and out of his embrace, still fully clothed in the bodysuit and jeans she'd put on yesterday and the flannel that he'd given her at some point.

She went to the bathroom just off the bedroom, not the one in the hall where she'd spent so much time breaking down yesterday. The sight of her ridiculous hair brought her a small amount of peace. Some things were just always going to be consistent. Even if they weren't the most helpful.

Someone had left toiletries in the bathroom for her and a change of clothes. Probably Gregor. She brushed her teeth and changed into the clean undergarments and fresh jeans. After she washed her face and failed to tame her hair, she put Asa's blue and white flannel back on and buttoned it halfway. It was her flannel now. She wasn't ever giving it back.

Back in the bedroom, she paused to watch Asa sleeping.

His handsome face frowning even in his dreams, his dark hair messy, his tattooed arm still outstretched to where she had been.

Her heart gave a small lurch, demanding she return to the bed, to wake him up and tell him all was forgiven. But she'd learned the hard way that her heart was stupid and did stupid things.

She needed a minute to think.

It wasn't even so much what he'd done. It was how what he'd done had ricocheted through her belief in him, tearing it to shreds. One bullet breaking into a thousand tiny fragments that imbedded themselves in all the tenderest parts of her. The spaces she'd willingly let him into because she thought it had been safe. Which wasn't even his fault.

It wasn't anyone's fault.

It was just a consequence.

The culmination of a lifetime of being let down and deceived and the loneliness that came with all of it.

She'd made the tragic mistake of putting all her faith in someone who was wholly human. He hadn't done anything wrong. Not really. She even understood it.

But all the rationality in the world didn't magically make the turmoil go away. It still felt uneven. Unsteady. Basically, the opposite of how she'd always felt with him.

And she didn't know what to do with it.

Carefully, so she didn't wake him, she left the bedroom, closing the door behind her.

And entered a war room.

"Whoa," she said, stopping short.

Gregor put a cup of coffee in her hand. "How you feeling?"

"Fine." She nodded and took a sip.

"Are you ready for an update or do you want breakfast first?" he asked, eyeing her clothing choice but making no comment.

"Both is good," she said, walking further into the living room that was now full.

Sonja was on the phone standing near the balcony door, Kenna sat on the couch typing furiously on her tablet.

Devan and Cas were chatting with a handful of similarly dressed men and women—no doubt extra security. She was pretty sure she recognized some of them.

Gregor pointed her to the breakfast bar and she took a seat. She watched her team work around her and each other like a well-oiled machine.

With the Kramer issue solved, that just left the fallout from Shelby's actions to deal with.

She took out her phone and despite her better judgement, she searched her name.

Holy fuck.

The first thing that came up was a photo of XY Records with a small crowd of people loitering outside. She clicked on it to find it had been taken a just a couple hours before.

Johnny and Hannah were going to be pissed.

God, her life was always ruining things for everyone she cared about.

Gregor placed an egg white omelet in front of her and she put down the phone. She started to eat while Gregor filled her in.

"The Lincoln Park house will need to be cleaned up a little before you can go back," he started. Because of the mess created when Kramer did whatever it was he did. "*If* you want to go back." He didn't wait for her to decide. "It's safe to say you're no longer living here in secret. The internet is having a shit hemorrhage about you being in Chicago. Several media outlets have asked for a statement. I'm pretty sure Kenna just keeps putting them on hold."

Zara snickered.

She hadn't realized it, but she'd missed her team. They were good people. Not that she regretted her time in Chicago, far from it. But going back to her version of "normal" wasn't going to be a hardship. As long as she didn't think about what that meant for her and Asa.

"Which reminds me, does he have people?" Gregor asked.

"Hm?" Zara lifted her eyebrows in question.

Gregor jerked his chin toward the back bedroom. "The tattooed hunk of handsome who may or may not be part Belgian Malinois."

Zara smiled down at her now empty plate and picked up her coffee. "He doesn't have people."

Gregor watched her carefully and nodded. She wondered how much he knew. It had to be quite a bit because Cas kept the team updated on the different people in her life. And she'd mentioned Asa to him in their weekly calls but had never detailed the extent of their relationship.

"He wouldn't let any of us do anything last night," Gregor said.

"What do you mean?" she asked, setting down her coffee mug. "What the hell were you trying to do?"

"We were going to start moving your stuff to the house in London and get you out of here in the morning. We thought it'd be best to get you as far away from this mess as possible. He pretty much told us all to fuck off and wait until you woke up. Cas and Devan backed him up."

Huh.

He did that? Stood up to her team when she couldn't?

Something about Cas and Devan having his back, as if he was just as much a part of her as anyone could be…

Some of those achy spots inside hurt a little less.

"I don't want to go to London. I'm not done here yet," she said, picking her coffee back up and ignoring all the tremors of warmth threatening to take over her thoughts.

"What *are* you doing here?" Gregor asked.

"Making something important," she replied. Her gaze lost focus as she thought about all the things they'd created and all the things she still wanted to make with him.

She met Gregor's gaze and he asked without asking. But she didn't have an answer for herself let alone him. So she changed the subject.

"Is the label still pissed I ghosted them?" she asked.

When she'd left New York, she'd stopped returning their calls. Over and over again they'd violated her boundaries and ignored her requests. So she'd stopped giving them access to her. Sonja handled the legal parts of it, but Zara had decided that if they wouldn't start treating her like an equal, she was out. She could get another contract easily. Or hell, even start her own label. Maybe she could partner with Johnny and Hannah.

Gregor smirked. "About that."

She lifted her eyebrows, interested.

"They've…" Gregor twisted his lips to the side like he was searching for the right word. "*Reconsidered* the structure of the board."

"Oh?"

"Let's just say, you can do whatever you want. They've offered a new contract that you should probably read with Sonja, but they're not going to risk losing you. It's everything you've ever wanted."

"Huh." She blinked and contemplated the implications of such an offer. "I wouldn't have to release on such a strict schedule."

"Nope. The Beastie Boys would disappear for like five years between releases and no one freaked out. Their fandom didn't dimmish and they made the music they wanted to make. You have that same magnetism."

Zara smiled. "The Beastie Boys, huh? You think I'm good enough to compare to them?"

Gregor rolled his eyes. "My love, you compare to no one. But you've worked incredibly hard to be this successful. You've earned the trust of your fans. Do what you want. Follow your inspiration and we'll follow you."

She could make the music she wanted *when* she wanted. With whom she wanted.

The idea opened up the door to possibilities which filled her with a rush of excitement.

"You came here to get away from everything," Gregor continued. "To put space between you and the world. To give them less to talk about. And the moment you're spotted, it's like a tidal wave. You're trending on every site. Your being seen is the top five stories of every publication. The fanboards have exploded with theories and speculation and rumors. It's almost as if your being away amplified their obsession with you."

Her excitement fizzled a bit. He was right.

She thought about that photo of XY Records.

Asa's life was about to be split right open. Again. The scrutiny and violations of privacy would never stop. If anything, they'd get a whole lot worse the longer his name was attached to hers.

Could she ask him to stand in the middle of her hurricane with her? Bigger question, could she truly trust him to be in it *with* her? As her partner? As her safe place? For the right reasons?

It was ironic in a way. All the things she could offer to someone to make them stay; money, security, travel, excitement. They were all the things Asa didn't want or need. If he stayed, it could only be for one reason.

And that scared her more than anything.

If only she had someone who had been there. Someone she could talk to about balance and life and what happens when the person you've fallen in love with doesn't do well with crowds. And how to trust that it's real.

Beyond Gregor's shoulder Cas caught her eye. He lifted his chin, a subtle way of asking her to come talk to him.

She eased off the stool and patted Gregor's shoulder.

When she reached Cas and Devan her body flooded with relief mixed with guilt again. Last night could have gone so differently. Impulsively, she hugged both of them.

Devan chuckled and Cas patted her head. They probably thought she was silly but that was because they didn't know how much they meant to her. An error she would rectify moving forward.

"We found Shelby," Cas said, almost imperceptibly.

Zara's whole body tightened and her heart took off at a gallop.

She'd assumed they'd look for Asa's sister of course. But she had no idea they'd find her that quickly.

"Do you want to speak to her?" Cas asked, watching her carefully.

Zara nodded once. Slowly.

She had a few things to say.

* * *

Cas and Devan took her back to the parking garage, to a different vehicle than the one they'd been using, with blackout windows. They drove to a huge building and into the underground garage, where someone met them and led them to a secure, private elevator. Down a few corridors, up another elevator and to a floor marked Cipher Security.

Through all this Zara didn't ask any questions. She'd assumed they were going to the police station or something. This wasn't what she'd expected but she didn't mind. The fewer people who saw her, the better.

At least until after she'd spoken with Kenna on the next steps for PR.

Cas led her to an empty conference room with a long table, chairs around it, and different coffee makers and accoutrements against one wall. She looked to her security for the next steps when someone she didn't know entered the room.

She took in his black suit, shaved head, and the glimpse of neck tattoos that peeked out of the top of his buttoned-up collar.

"Oh good. You're here," he greeted Cas in a thick Boston accent. "That woman is a real fucking piece of work. What a mouth on her. And that's coming from me." His gaze flicked to Zara and he blinked. "Whoa. You're right there."

Zara's face grew hot. What did he mean by that?

"Sorry," he went on with a short shake of his head. "I'm usually in Boston. There's a huge billboard with your face on it. I drive past it every day. Seeing you in real life is…different." He cleared his throat and shrugged. "Do you want me to bring her in here now? Or wait for Quinn and Alex?"

Was he talking about Shelby? And who were Quinn and Alex?

"Let's wait," Cas said. "Zara, this is Dan O'Malley. He's head of Cipher Security and helped us track down Shelby."

Dan nodded and rock back on his heels. "She wasn't hard to find. She's got a loud mouth. Getting her here was like wrestling a feral cat into a bath though." He made a face. "She's mean."

Zara snorted at his delivery. "Thank you for your help," she said.

He shrugged like it was no big deal and she wondered how Cas knew him. He'd brought her Gregor, had taken care of Kramer and now there was this Dan O'Malley guy with the neck tattoos. He was this never-ending cornucopia of interesting revelations.

Needing to busy herself, she wandered over to the coffee station and started making coffee for everyone in the room.

She checked her phone and wondered if Asa was awake yet.

Her stomach threatened to cramp at the thought of him not being there when she got back. She wasn't as upset with him as she'd been last night. But they definitely needed to talk. And it needed to be the kind of talk where big decisions were made.

The bubble was gone and it was time to find out if this thing was as real and scary as she hoped it was.

"Hey, Dan, big guy, Devan, right?"

Zara slowly turned towards the doorway to see Hannah Lee James entering the conference room and greeting the bodyguards.

What was she doing here?

Zara's brain paused.

Of course. *Of course!* Why hadn't she thought about Hannah until then? Hannah had left the industry, had found peace and love and happiness. If anyone could give Zara any kind of helpful advice or hard-earned wisdom, it would be her.

"I need to talk to you," Zara blurted as the former reigning queen of pop approached her.

Hannah arched an eyebrow, her mouth tilting into a small smile. "I know you do." She gestured to the table. "Let's have a chat."

Zara grabbed her coffee and took a seat. Hannah made herself a coffee and joined her. They turned their chairs to face one another.

Several years ago, Zara had won Best New Artist at the NMAs. Hannah had presented her with the award. It was the same night Hannah got arrested for assaulting a producer backstage and then subsequently disappeared from the industry. It wasn't until Zara had started recording at XY Records with Sunshine Capone that she'd "re-met" Hannah in her new life.

She was settled. Happy. Still living mostly off-grid and adamant on keeping it that way.

Zara thought of the people outside XY Records that day and sighed. "I'm sorry about what's happened."

Hannah chuckled. "Babe. I saw this coming months ago. It's fine. It's all been prepared for."

"How?"

Hannah hummed as she drummed her nails lightly on the table. "I'm so intensely paranoid when it comes to protecting the people I love that I make plans I hope never have to be used. And I happen to have…people that are even more paranoid than I am. The first time you showed up in the studio I knew this was a possibility. We started building contingencies at that time. And then after you and Asa made headlines last October, we had a direction."

"You didn't say anything," Zara replied, throat dry.

"We spoke to Asa about it. Created a false business address in Miami where we listed him as an employee just to throw off anyone snooping too closely." Hannah's gaze lost focus and her lips tilted up on one side. "But when we asked him about his relationship with you, he lied."

Zara swallowed. "What did he say?"

"He said there wasn't anything happening between you two." Hannah took a sip of coffee, her ice blue eyes on Zara.

"In October there wasn't anything. He wouldn't even return my texts." Zara chewed on her lower lip. She should have just left him alone. None of this would have happened.

"And now?" Hannah asked.

Now?

She didn't know. She loved him. But… She shook her head. "How did you balance it? The music and the fame and relationships?"

"Oh. My sweet summer child," Hannah said with a small laugh. "I didn't. I self-medicated with anything I could get my hands on."

"But not now."

"No. Not now. Now? I have more than I deserve. And I work really hard at protecting it." Her smile turned soft as her expression turned reflective. "We protect our peace for as long as we can. But this is an imperfect world with imperfect people. All we can expect from them, and from ourselves, is to do our best with what we have. I'm fond of reminding myself that all we can do is all we can do."

Those words were filled with more hope than Zara was ready to absorb in the moment.

Hannah was right. Asa did a human thing. Thinking he was doing the right thing. How often did she do that too? A little more of the hurt slipped away.

But what about the rest? Being in love in the public eye would ask so much from the both of them.

"I can see your mind is working up the urge to freak out," Hannah interrupted her thoughts. "I spoke to Asa again. Just a few days ago."

Zara was afraid to move. Afraid to breathe. Did she want to know the rest of what Hannah knew?

"He's not stupid, Zara," Hannah said softly. "He knows what the job is. He's in this with you as much as you'll let him be."

Her mind raced back to that night in LA. Suddenly her hope was a large stone, pushing her anxiety and doubt out of the way and taking up her entire chest.

"Job is probably the wrong word for it. But if someone wants to be in a relationship with you, they're gonna have to check their ego at the door. They have to be secure enough to step back and let you shine. They should be your biggest fan. I feel like that goes without saying."

Was that—? Was this—? Did he—?

Zara blinked back the sudden moisture in her eyes. Hannah was right. Asa wasn't stupid. He knew exactly who she was and what being with her meant. He'd known it the whole time.

Why did that make everything in her body feel like it was flying?

Hannah smiled a small smile like she knew what was happening in Zara's head and heart. She checked her watch. "I have to get going. I don't want to be here when…you'll see." She finished her coffee and stood. "And trust me, Quinn's services are well worth it. Oh! And maybe have Sabine talk to Ace. She might have some pointers on being the not-so-famous partner."

That was a really good idea, Zara realized. Sabine had been thrust into the spotlight the first time she'd been seen with her rock star husband. Plus she was a kickass teacher. She probably had great advice.

Zara stood as well and watched Hannah leave.

She must've only been there to talk to her. That was super sweet. It made Zara feel less alone in all this. And Hannah hadn't seemed pissed about the media attention either.

She finished her coffee and decided to make another one.

"Ms. Lorna, I hope we didn't keep you waiting for too long."

She turned to see a tall man in an expensive suit with chiseled features and icy eyes pull a chair out at the conference table. He didn't sit down.

"I'm just Zara," she said.

He nodded and another man, also tall, dark, and handsome but with glasses, took a seat next to the one the first man had pulled out.

"I am Quinn Sullivan," the first man introduced. "And this is my associate, Alex Green."

Okay, now she knew Quinn and Alex.

"We've set this up at the request of your head of security and Hannah Lee James."

All right. Some things were starting to make sense.

Cas pulled out a seat at the head of the table and directed her to it.

"So you all know each other?" Zara asked, taking a seat.

"Some of my people have worked with Cas and Devan before," Dan explained.

Alex opened a laptop and started clicking and typing, a bored look on his face.

"Let's get the worst part out of the way, shall we?" Quinn nodded at Dan.

Dan made a face and left the room.

"I'm still not sure what's going on," Zara said propping her chin in her hand her elbow on the table. "In case anyone wants to fill me in."

Alex's lips twitched with the hint of a smile.

"I'm the one responsible for Ms. James' continued privacy and long-term protection."

"Just you?" Alex muttered.

Quinn sighed. "*We* are responsible."

Alex nodded in agreement.

"Shit," Zara said. "Does this mean I'm in trouble? For bringing the paps to XY?"

"Not at all." Quinn shook his head. "We'll go over everything my services cover in a minute."

"In here?"

All eyes turned to the doorway as Asa's sister, Shelby entered.

She was in the same clothes Zara had seen her in the day before; black jeans and a black tank top. Her burnt orange colored hair pulled back into a short ponytail. She crossed her arms over her chest as her eyes roamed over the faces in the room.

"What's going on, guys?" Shelby asked as she carefully made her way into the conference room. Her gaze continued to flick from person to person, but lingered on Zara the longest. She walked all the way around the table and chose a seat across from Quinn but close to Zara.

It was so weird. Her dark brown eyes and the shape of her nose were so similar to Asa. But vastly different. Where Asa's eyes were warm and honest, Shelby's were small and mean. Hard.

Shelby made a show of looking around the room. "I don't see my brother here."

Zara swallowed and sat back in her chair.

Shelby shifted, getting comfortable. She leaned forward, putting her hands on the table. "I still have the video and I'll take what CELEBX paid me for the photos. For an extra 10k I'll throw in Asa's demos that he…left behind at my dad's house."

She couldn't be serious.

Zara's left eye twitched.

"You misunderstand," Quinn said coolly. "You're not here to be paid off."

Shelby turned her attention on him and seemed to take a second look.

"People like you," Quinn said, letting the "you" hang in the air for a beat to make his point. "Come back again, and again. You're blackholes of greed and self-interest. No amount of money can make you go away. No, I've found the most effective way of handling your impulses is to threaten you."

Shelby's eyes flared and her mouth grew tight. She sat back in her chair and crossed her arms over her chest. "Is that so?"

Quinn's eyes slid toward Alex.

"You're currently unemployed and living with your mother in southeast Iowa," Alex said with a hint of smugness. "You're under investigation for embezzlement and fraud in three different counties. There's a bench warrant out for your arrest for failure to appear for a drunk driving charge. And you're married to two different people in two different states making one of those marriages unlawful. Does the poor bastard even know?"

Shelby curled her lip at Alex. "You gonna turn me in or something?" she asked, unimpressed.

"I was thinking about adding more to it," Quinn said.

"What do you mean?" Shelby asked.

Quinn shrugged. "You're not a productive member of society. You seem to take pleasure in hurting others and being irresponsible. So what's a few more charges? How about some felonies?"

Alex nodded and started typing.

"Trespassing, vandalism," Quinn continued. "What does someone get for felony extortion these days?"

"Up to thirty," Dan said, rubbing his chin thoughtfully.

Shelby's confidence began to dissolve. "Extortion?" She puffed a laugh. "Yeah, okay."

"Oh, I get it," Quinn said, his voice glacial. "Because you've had mediocre success manipulating people in your life—people who care about you, no doubt—that's given you a false sense of security. You think you can game your way out of anything."

Quinn's expression took on a wolfish quality.

"But you see, I don't care about you. I think you'll find it difficult to manipulate me. We have you on video threatening to release the photos if payment wasn't provided. Further, a man was arrested later that night with intent to harm Ms. Lorna."

Zara wished he'd stop with the Ms. Lorna. Also, Kramer didn't find her place because of Shelby. She darted a glance to Cas who shook his head once.

"I didn't mean—"

"What did you mean?" Quinn asked, his voice a sharp crack that made Shelby flinch.

Shelby's face flushed a deep maroon and her eyes glossed over. She looked down at her lap and back up, her gaze connecting with Zara's.

"It was Asa's idea," Shelby said softly. "I told him I didn't want to do it but he insisted."

What was this fresh hell?

"He said that if I leaked the pictures, you'd be more willing to pay for the video. I was supposed to get half."

Zara covered her mouth with a hand to keep from laughing. Not because it was funny, but because it was so absolutely tragic. Shelby sat there, unflinching eye contact, and lied.

Not a small lie either. But the kind meant to destroy. To ruin. All for what?

"I never learn," Shelby continued, sounding appropriately contrite as she self-flagellated. "He's always been like this. And I get caught up in it because he's my brother and I care about him. I mean, you must know how he can be."

Damn. She was so convincing. But Zara knew the truth. She knew Asa the way she knew her own mind. Not only would he never conceive of this kind of scheme, but he'd also never do anything to trick her or hurt her. Even his actions the day before had been an attempt to protect her.

For a moment, she was able to put herself in his shoes. See the maneuvering happening in front of her, recognize it for what it was, and know that she'd do anything to protect him as well.

Zara's gaze slid to Cas. To Devan. To Dan. To Alex. To Quinn.

Quinn rolled his eyes and turned his body toward Zara. "What do you want me to do?" he asked.

Shelby fell silent, a hopeful breath paused in her lungs.

Zara stared at her. This familiar but unremarkable human who had brought so much chaos to the mind of the man she loved. Made him doubt his talent. Punished him when he dared to find happiness.

Part of her recognized that Shelby would never stop. Every time she was reminded that Asa had anything she didn't think he deserved, she'd find ways of reminding him.

So threats it had to be.

"I like your ideas," she said to Quinn.

Shelby's eyes widened a fraction. She hadn't been expecting that. "But it was Asa's idea!" she repeated.

"No, it wasn't." Zara tilted her neck from side to side, stretching out the tired and tight muscles.

"Yes, it was. I can prove it," Shelby started to pat her thighs and she lasered in on Dan. "Where's my phone?"

Dan took a phone out of his pocket and handed it over with a small, unamused smirk on his face.

Shelby snatched up the device and started tapping frantically on the screen. "He called me three days ago. It's in my call log. Wait. Where is it?" She shot angry daggers at Dan. "You tampered with my phone," she accused.

"Nope." Dan shook his head, unworried.

She was a quick thinker, Zara decided. Too bad she didn't use those skills for something more beneficial.

"He did. He called me." Shelby put both hands on the table and opened her eyes wide, pleading with Zara. "You've gotta believe me."

Zara pressed her mouth together to keep from smiling, because she recognized that look. It was the same thing Logan would do to her. His, "please believe me, I'm lying my ass off" look. If she hadn't had the kind of history she did, she might have been inclined to believe the woman across from her.

"I don't believe you," Zara replied. Further, she wasn't going to waste her time explaining why.

She rotated slightly in her chair to face Quinn, a man she barely knew but still trusted more than Shelby. "This is what I want." She held up a hand and ticked off her points on her fingers. "I don't care about the photos or video. What's done is done. Destroy them, sell them, print them and hang them on your wall. I really don't care. I don't want her to have contact with me or Asa ever again. Or Nikki. Actually, anyone in my life. All of them are off limits. I want her to get whatever she's earned on her own, good or bad. I don't want to know what that ends up being. And I don't want her to hurt anyone ever again." She faced Shelby as she said the last part. "No more schemes, scams, or manipulations. I want her life to be boring and unbothered."

Quinn nodded. Alex looked slightly disappointed.

Shelby inhaled, her eyes getting small and hard. "And what's to keep me from telling this to the press?"

"Try it," Quinn said, unconcerned.

Shelby swallowed and sat back in her chair.

"Time to go," Dan said, gesturing for Shelby to get up.

Shelby's eyes swung around the room, looking for someone she could latch onto. "That's it?" she asked.

"For now," Quinn replied, waving a hand in dismissal.

Dan took Shelby's arm and helped her out the door.

After their voices faded away down the hall, Quinn smoothed a nonexistent wrinkle from his suit. "On to the matter of my services and how much they cost."

"You're hired," Zara said. She didn't care about the details.

Quinn chuckled. "You may want to have a lawyer go over the contract with you. My fees are not…inexpensive."

"That's fine. I like it when my money goes to a good cause." She glanced at Cas. "And I get to keep my security."

"Of course," Quinn nodded in agreement.

He went on to explain what he did and what Alex did. Most of it, she didn't understand. Quinn owned, like, everything. Including the East Randolph Residence where she'd stayed last night. He also owned Cipher Security which was the company Cas had been working with.

Alex was a hacker. Okay, they didn't say that in so many words, but Zara wasn't an idiot.

"I've taken the liberty of familiarizing myself with your situation," Quinn said, getting to the point. "If I'm assuming correctly, you want a permanent place in Chicago. I have a few options that might interest you. I've looked at the place you're renting in Lincoln Park. They'd sell."

"How would buying that house help?" Zara asked. "If anything it would make it easier for people to find me. It would draw more attention to XY." But the thought of owning the house where she and Asa had fallen in love sent a ripple of excitement through her.

Quinn shrugged. "Maybe. But the houses next door would sell. And so would the ones across the street. In fact, the entire block is a reasonable investment and you'd get a good price."

"Buy a city block?" she scoffed, crossing her arms. But then the idea took hold in her head.

Buy a city block.

"What's the point in having all the money in the world if you can't use it to make your life what you want it to be? And you can live in one of my apartments while you make the needed updates to Lincoln Park. Such as reinforced windows and camera installation. Things of that nature. We can help set all that up of course."

Zara's gaze lost focus as she considered what he suggested. She rubbed a hand along her forehead, thinking.

But Quinn wasn't finished. "You don't have what you want? Then build it. Just like you've done with everything else. Make it happen."

"That easy, huh?" she said with more than a little sarcasm.

"Yes," he replied evenly. "Exactly that easy. Your rise to stardom wasn't a fluke. Your peace of mind and happiness won't be one either."

She chewed on her lower lip as his words sank in.

He was right. She had never given up on something she wanted before, why would this be any different? And she knew without knowing how, she wouldn't have to build it alone. She'd have Asa.

Her heart lit up like a Christmas tree at the thought of building something with him.

She didn't have to go back to how it had been before him. He didn't have to fit in her world because they could create a new one that fit both of them.

And they were really good at creating things together.

Chapter Twenty-Eight
Hardliners

He let out a slow breath. "Okay," he muttered under his breath.

He knew the place would be full of people. But it was still jarring to walk into the living room and have so many eyes turn his way.

And none of them were Zara.

"She and Cas had a meeting," Gregor informed him, handing him a cup of coffee. "They'll be back later."

Asa took a sip. It had half and half already stirred into it. That wasn't weird.

"Kenna has some questions for you when you're ready," Gregor said, indicating the blonde on the phone who held up a finger in their direction. "But I can make you some food first if you're hungry."

Asa took a deep breath, his head spinning. It wasn't like he didn't know that her professional life would completely steamroll him the moment it returned. But he didn't know if he could adapt that quickly. Especially since he didn't know how she was doing.

Last night had been intense. Actually, intense wasn't a strong enough word.

He wanted to check in with her, make sure she was okay. And he wanted to do that before he did anything else.

Though if she was with Cas, she was probably doing fine.

It wasn't like she'd waited around for him to follow her. She had a whole team of people looking out for her. He was just…the guy she slept with.

Who was also hopelessly, uselessly, in love with her.

"I know it's a lot," Gregor said, dropping his voice. "I will try to make the transition as easy on you as possible."

Asa's frown deepened as he narrowed his eyes at the assistant. Why? Had he been instructed to do so? And transition into what? Or where? Back to his regular life? Or maybe…

Gregor opened his mouth to say more when they were interrupted by a knock at the door.

The energy in the room shifted as all focus turned that direction.

The door opened and Asa blinked in surprise when Logan Black stood there. Before he could even acknowledge what was happening, his legs were already carrying him toward Zara's ex.

The security at the door moved aside and he tried not to notice.

Logan looked through most of the people in the room. He paused on Gregor and his cheek twitched. Finally his eyes landed on Asa.

"She's still got you around, huh?" Logan said.

"What are you doing here?" Asa asked.

Logan rolled his eyes and took a step further into the apartment. "I just want to check on her. See if she's okay."

Like hell he did. He saw an opportunity to reinsert himself. That's the only reason he was there.

"She's fine. You can leave now." Asa positioned his body to block more of Logan's view into the apartment. How the hell did this guy even find out where she was at? Though maybe it was an unspoken rule that all celebrities were allowed to know more than the general public.

"Listen, I get it, okay? You think you're her hero, you want to protect her. But I know her. You can't just erase the kind of history we have." Logan shrugged like he was apologizing for having to deliver the truth. "You're not the first guy she's fucked to get back at me."

Asa took a slow, deep breath, relaxing his hands at his side. Wow, this guy. He really thought he had something to say, didn't he? His lips twitched with annoyed amusement.

Logan's gaze narrowed on Asa's face. "What's that look for?"

"Nothing," Asa said, shaking his head. "Just get out of here."

"She's still in a snit? She's such a fuckin' brat." Logan snickered and rolled his eyes.

Asa knew he shouldn't. He knew there were better ways to handle himself. But he didn't care about any of that. Logan Black had it coming.

It happened so fast, the moment between thought and action. Asa's balled up fist connected with the singer's nose in one single pop. A quick as lightning punch to the center of Logan's face.

He didn't think he'd hit him that hard but Logan cried out and dropped to his knees, covering his nose. Logan's security surrounded him and pulled him to his feet.

"What the fuck?" Logan yelled, blood starting to seep from his nose. He pulled his hand back and looked at the red there, his eyes going round and wild. "I'm gonna sue the ever-loving shit out of you!"

Asa expected as much.

Still worth it.

Someone grabbed him by the arm and tugged him aside. Gregor put himself between Asa and Logan.

"That's crazy how you tried to push your way into a room—uninvited—directly after an attempted attack on Zara. And her security accidentally bumped your nose because they didn't know who you were. What an insane set of circumstances. Wouldn't you agree, Kenna?" Gregor said, his voice one of over emphasized shock and wonder.

Kenna slipped past Asa to stand by Gregor's shoulder. "So crazy, who would even believe it? Good thing we have an entire room of witnesses."

Logan's angry expression slowly melted to incredulity as his gaze bounced from person to person in the room and he found no allies.

"Fuck you all in your fucking faces you fucking fucks," he said.

"He's such an orator," Gregor said with a solemn nod.

"Best of our time," Kenna agreed.

Logan sputtered, squealed a bit, and then left in a huff.

"He'll be fine," Gregor said, turning around after the door closed. "His mom has a plastic surgeon on retainer. No one will even know."

Asa didn't know what to think. On one hand, he's been fully ready to go to jail for punching that asshole in the face. On the other, he was confused and grateful for Gregor and Kenna's intervention.

"How about some food?" Gregor asked, patting him on the shoulder once.

"I could eat," Asa replied. He slid onto a stool at the breakfast bar.

"Do you need ice for your hand?" Gregor asked, moving around the kitchen like he'd been there for ages and not just a few hours.

Asa flexed his hand a few times. "It doesn't hurt. His nose crumbled like a sandcastle."

Gregor chuckled and Asa watched him work in the kitchen.

He didn't look the way Asa had assumed he would. Not that he knew a lot of personal assistants. Gregor looked a lot like Cas. Not in the face so much, but the build, the size, the mannerisms.

"Why did you guys do that?" Asa asked, not specifying.

Gregor smiled to himself and kept working. "She hasn't had any stomach issues since she's been here." He put a sandwich on a plate in front of Asa. "She's never not had stomach issues."

"Until last night," Asa pointed out.

Gregor nodded in agreement. "A lot happened last night. I didn't say she was cured."

Asa thought about the last night and wondered what would happen next with them. Sure, she'd asked him to stay but like Gregor had said, a lot had happened last night.

"Asa Young," a woman with dark brown hair and a meticulous pantsuit sidled up to him at the island. "I'm Sonja, Zara's manager."

He shook her hand and braced. Was this where he got his walking papers? It was one thing for everyone to be happy he'd punched Logan. It was another to let him stick around when he wasn't wanted.

"Do you have management?" Sonja asked curiously.

Asa recognized something in Sonja's tone and the shrewdness of her gaze. This woman was a shark.

"No, ma'am," he replied.

Her lips twitched with the "ma'am" comment but she let it slide.

"I've been over your career—"

Asa held back his laugh. Career. Hilarious.

"And Zara has told me of your invaluable talent. I trust her judgement. She has yet to make me anything other than insidiously rich. Let's have a meeting, the three of us, and chat about the future."

It wasn't a question. She slid her card across the counter and held Asa's gaze for a beat before smiling and turning to Gregor.

"I am going to the hotel now for a rest. Will you tell our darling girl that she may call me at any time?"

Gregor nodded once and Sonja left, taking three of the bodyguards with her.

"She's scary, right?" Asa asked after Sonja was gone.

"Terrifying," Gregor replied. "I heard heads rolled before she left Boston last night. Kramer bribed someone in her office to find out where Zara was. I guess it wasn't pretty when Sonja figured it out."

The knot in Asa's stomach started to loosen. These people were good, kind people. They adored Zara. Probably loved her more than she knew. She was in good hands. It started to make sense now. How she'd been able to hold onto her sunny outlook on life through all of the shit the industry threw at her; she was surrounded by people who encouraged her, cared about her.

She didn't need him. Not really.

Huh.

Instead of feeling terrible about that fact, it eased his conscience.

She didn't need him.

She didn't need him to protect her, or take care of her, or validate her. She was wonderfully and completely whole. She had a team that took care of those things.

But out of all the people in the world, she'd chosen him. Trusted him. Asked nothing of him except to love her.

And he could do that.

He could do that better than anyone.

* * *

ZARA

They left Quinn's office and headed back to the apartment.

"How do you feel about your options?" Cas asked from the front passenger seat as Devan drove.

Zara smiled and it felt like her first genuine smile since the day before. "Really good," she answered honestly. "Thank you."

Cas shrugged like it wasn't a big deal. Maybe to him it wasn't. But she knew what it meant to her. His phone chimed and he glanced at the screen and snorted.

"Logan Black stopped by while we were gone," Cas said.

Devan growled low in her throat.

"Why?" Zara asked, instantly annoyed.

Cas, still reading the message on his phone, started to smile. "Asa punched him in the nose."

Devan barked a laugh and Cas chuckled. Zara sat there, stunned. She wanted to laugh. She also wanted to cry.

Because they were the same.

She'd just dealt with Asa's sister in order to protect him while at the same time he'd dealt with her ex.

She loved him so much. She needed to tell him as soon as possible.

They made it back to the apartment and it wasn't as full of people as when she'd left.

Her eyes found Asa immediately.

Her heart lurched his direction and she obliged its request.

He was standing near the balcony door with Kenna and Gregor who looked like they were prepping him for some kind of PR stunt.

He spotted her on the way over and the deep lines in his face relaxed. His brown eyes got lazy and a crooked smile curved his mouth. "Hey, killer," he said when she was near enough. "Nice shirt."

She wrapped her arms across her middle, pulling the flannel closer. "Thanks. It's new."

He looked her up and down, taking his time in both directions. Like he was verifying she was all in one piece.

He'd showered and changed his clothes; his shirt was plain black and probably not one of his own.

"What's going on here?" she asked Kenna and Gregor who were openly watching their interaction.

Kenna clucked her tongue. "How much do you trust me?"

Zara blinked at her publicist.

"Don't scare her." Gregor chuckled. "We just want the both of you to step out onto the balcony." He tilted his head toward the door.

"And do what?" she asked.

Kenna pursed her lips and looked away.

"Do whatever you want. Chat or say nothing. Do a dance if you're so inclined," Gregor encouraged. "Whatever it is you kids do."

"I have a photographer positioned below. It's someone we've worked with before and we can get some tasteful, candid shots of you two being relaxed and happy," Kenna explained.

"Ah, yes. The staged candid. My favorite," Zara said dryly.

"It's the best idea to counter the stories out there right now. We verify you're in Chicago but not in Lincoln Park, and that yes, you're with Asa, but that it's not necessarily romantic." Kenna eyed Zara's shirt. "If you're not together, you need to change your shirt."

Zara's gaze darted to Asa. She'd wanted to have a conversation with him, privately, before having to make any kind of public declaration.

"Unless you're ready to go public with a relationship," Gregor suggested. "If that's the case, may I recommend a snog with an ass grab."

"Gregor!" Zara chastised.

Kenna rolled her eyes and held up a hand. "Honestly, you don't have to do that. If being out there together makes you uncomfortable then we can just have one of you do it. Either is fine, but Devan doesn't want Zara out there alone. We need you to be out there for at least thirty minutes so Lacie —the photographer—can get several shots from different locations."

Zara sighed. She had to do this in Rome once. When she'd been spotted having dinner with an actor well-known for his superhero movie franchise. It hadn't been a date. It had been business. But a picture had been taken of both of them laughing while they were leaning in towards each other. The internet fed off that for weeks.

She'd had to stand on a balcony for an hour so they could prove she was alone in Italy, not a romantic vacation. He had to be seen in a farmer's market on another continent having cider with his costar.

That had been a weird month.

Light pressure on her lower lip had her sucking in a startled breath and her eyes snapping to Asa.

"Please stop chewing on that lip," he said, his thumb lingering on her mouth.

Her skin caught fire where he touched her and she found herself leaning toward him. His lips tipped up on one side and his gaze softened.

He dropped his hand only to take hers and back toward the balcony door. She followed him outside; Gregor closed the door behind them. She looked back over her shoulder at her assistant who gave her a thumbs up.

For fuck's sake.

It was weird to have Gregor and Kenna be so…encouraging with Asa. The only experience she had with them and her relationships was with Logan. And they openly hated Logan.

But that's because they had come along later. After Logan had already transitioned into his final form. They didn't know him when he was sixteen the way she had. They weren't there to see him struggle through auditions and bad reviews and disappointment.

But she remembered all of it.

That's probably the main reason she'd stuck around for so long. Because she still remembered the kid in him. She still didn't hate that kid. But he was so far away from who he used to be, it was like he'd become a different person.

"What are you thinking about?" Asa asked.

He'd let go of her hand and they stood together, side by side, looking out over the city, elbows resting on the railing.

"I was thinking about what it means to grow up," she answered honestly. She took a breath and focused on the clouds in the distance. "Growing up is so much more than getting older. It's choosing to learn about yourself; learning to let go of certain ideas; learning to explore new ones. It's scary. Sometimes the person we used to be is better. Growing up doesn't necessarily mean positive things. We hope it does. We hope that we get to a certain point in our lives that we're proud of." She smiled a sad smile as a multitude of past regrets sprang to mind.

He bumped her shoulder with her own but didn't move away. Instead their arms stayed pressed together, sharing warmth and stability.

"I punched Logan," he said.

She nodded. "I turned Shelby over to her own consequences."

He looked at her for a beat and then back out over the city.

"I'm sorry," Asa said into the silence. "About last night. I shouldn't have gone behind your back like that."

"But if you hadn't—"

"Doesn't matter," he cut her off. He turned his body to face her. His dark eyes searching and sincere. "I won't ever do anything like that again." His

Adam's apple bobbed with a hard swallow and a muscle jumped in his jaw. "I keep thinking about how you looked at me when you found out." He shook his head and blinked like he was seeing it even now. "I never want to be the cause of that. I'm sorry I hurt you."

She didn't know how much she needed to hear him say it. To hear him acknowledge what he'd done. She didn't have to walk him through and tell him the right things to say. He'd gotten there all on his own.

And the tattered edges of her belief stopped flapping in the wind and started to stick together.

"I can work on being more sensitive to your concerns," she admitted. "If I'd listened to you, we probably would have come to the same solution anyway." She smiled apologetically. "We usually do."

He brushed her arm with careful fingertips, his gaze asking something he was afraid to ask.

"It won't be the last time my life is in danger," she admitted, hating every word even though it was true. "Is that something you can live with?"

His eyebrows lifted and he huffed a humorless laugh. "I don't think I have a choice."

She licked her lips and blinked away the sting in her eyes. She didn't like the next part. The part that felt like stepping onto the edge of a cliff. "But you do. You don't have to do any of this. You don't have to…stay."

His gaze turned soft and he curved a hand around her jaw. She leaned into his touch. God, she'd missed him. She missed his warmth and the connection they'd shared since the beginning. It had grown and taken deep roots inside her.

She'd be okay if he decided this was all too much. She'd cry and parts of her would be changed forever. But she'd be okay.

"It's like you're trying to convince me I don't need air to breathe," Asa said, his voice warm and thoughtful.

She put a hand over his on her face because she didn't want him to move away.

Asa's eyes drifted over her face. Slow, calm, earnest. "Don't you know what you mean to me?" he asked.

She inhaled, trying to fill her lungs and flood her brain with oxygen so she could think clearly. Her heart pounded like a demigod's hammer on her sternum.

"Zara," he said, the sound of her name on his lips soothing and exciting at the same time. "I love you."

Her entire world stopped. He curved his other hand around her neck and jaw, cradling her face in both hands. His long fingers threaded through her hair and wrapped around the base of her skull.

"I love you," he repeated. His eyes were like dark hot springs, full of healing and warmth. He held her gaze, making his meaning clear.

"But…"

He cut her off with a headshake. "No. Wherever you are is where I want to be. I don't care what happens or where, I'll choose you every time."

"Really?" she asked, the disbelief in her voice betraying more honesty than she'd wanted. Not because she didn't believe him; she just didn't believe someone would choose her. After seeing what would happen, knowing the chaos and the drama and the lack of privacy. Who would choose that? Who would love her enough to put up with all the extra stuff she brought to the table?

He studied her, his eyes dropped to her mouth for a beat. "I love you so much," he said, voice rough. "I love your mind and your laugh and your heart. The way you feel and create and dream. Everything that comes with you is worth it. You're worth it."

Maybe he had more to say, she didn't know. Her arms had encircled his neck and she pulled him down while simultaneously pushing up on her toes as high as she could go. When their lips met a small sound of relief echoed through her chest and throat.

His hands moved, one across her back and the other to the back of her head.

And he kissed her.

He kissed her and kissed her and kissed her. Sweet relief and tender tastes mingled between them. Their bodies pressed together, as close as they could get and everything inside her came to rest.

All of her doubt and fear and apprehension ceased their chattering and she was left with a peaceful knowing.

This was it.

She was kissing the rest of her life.

* * *

ASA

How could a kiss feel like redemption? He didn't know, but there it was anyway. Such was the power she had over him.

He pulled back just enough to look into her beautiful eyes. "I am yours. I will always be yours," he promised.

"I love you." She inhaled swiftly as if those words were terrifying to admit. But he already knew it. He'd known it for a while. He wasn't sure when it had become clear. Just that one day he'd looked at her and he could see it. Love shining out of her eyes directly at him.

"I have so many things to tell you," she whispered.

He kissed the corner of her mouth. "Tell me."

Her amber gold eyes wandered over his face like she couldn't quite believe he was there. She touched his bearded cheek with her fingertips.

"It might take a minute but I'm going to change some things about how my life is managed and organized. To insulate us from…all of that."

"I told you, I'm with you in all of it," he said. "You don't have to change anything."

A smile fluttered on her lips and she pressed her palm flat to the center of his chest. "This," she emphasized with pressure on his sternum. "This is worth protecting."

His heart pulsed against her hand, deciding it would be better off with her than him. He couldn't argue.

"There will always be cameras and opinions and liars who don't want us to be okay," she went on. "Love and happiness are a threat to the status quo. We will always be surrounded, photographed. Watched." She swallowed, observing his reaction. For him to realize he didn't know what he'd promised.

But he knew all of it.

And he wasn't afraid.

Not when he was with her.

"It'll be us at the center then," he said. "Together."

Her eyes glossed over and a soft smile graced the most beautiful lips in the world. "I am so in love with you," she said.

Just before his mouth descended on hers again, intent on stealing her breath, he hovered over her lips. "I love you," he said once more before sealing it with a kiss that was also a promise.

In the face of what he felt for her, all of that other stuff didn't even register anymore. Maybe it was because he'd returned to music so life couldn't overwhelm him the way it used to. Maybe it was because what he felt for her was so enormous, it made everything else small by comparison.

He'd been dead. Lost in the darkness for way too long. And she'd slowly and tenderly loved him back to life. He'd spend the rest of that life trying to make her as happy as she made him.

They were different. Together they could get through anything. And when one of them needed to be carried, the other would be right there. He knew it as surely as he knew the sun was going to rise again tomorrow.

Their lives wouldn't look like anyone else's. That's because their love wasn't like anyone else's either.

CONFIRMED!

Even though both parties denied it months ago, Zara Lorna and Asa Young were spotted on a balcony in Chicago. And if the pictures are anything to go by, they aren't "just friends."

The two were photographed sharing an intimate moment just hours after news broke that Lyle Kramer had been apprehended.

Fans pointed out that Zara was wearing the shirt Asa had been photographed in the day before. It's safe to say the two have a very close relationship.

CELEBX received a statement from Lorna's publicist seemingly confirming the relationship. "Zara and Asa have asked for privacy as they step into this new chapter of their lives."

Friends say Asa Young, musician and former bass player for Winking Pete was only in town to visit family when he ran into Zara at XY Records.

The award-winning songstress has been in hiding for months after a very public breakup with Logan Black.

Sources say she and Asa are taking things slow. What do you think? Drop your comments below on what you think of the new couple.

COMMENTS

He's so hot.

They look really good together.

Get you somebody that looks at you the way Asa Young looks at Zara Lorna.

She deserves to be happy.

Logan Black really fumbled the ball.

OMG, their babies are going to be so cute!

This makes me believe in love.

Chapter Twenty-Nine
Fall Into Me

EIGHTEEN-ISH MONTHS LATER

ASA

He checked his phone again. Not even a whole minute had passed since the last time he'd looked.

Butterflies filled his stomach and he couldn't quite get rid of the grin that had been on his face all day.

It wasn't his day. Not really.

But he was so damn proud of her he could burst.

A heavy hand patted his shoulder and he smiled over at Zara's dad.

"Ready?" the older man asked.

Asa nodded as the lights dropped and a heavy buzz thrummed through the floors of the arena.

The past eighteen months had flown by.

She'd released the album they'd recorded to monstrous acclaim. The response to "A Fool's Hope" was everything he knew it would be, and nothing she'd expected.

It was as if the whole world took another look at Zara Lorna and realized they'd been sleeping on a legend.

They planned and plotted a tour called "A Hopeful Tour." The dates had sold out in a matter of days.

She'd worked damn hard during rehearsal and only a handful of people knew the presentation she'd planned.

It was two years to the day she'd hosed him off in Nikki's backyard.

Smoke filled the stage and a bass line that he'd written popped out a driving beat.

Zara, on a platform, rose from the center of the stage, already purring the opening lines to the song.

The arena exploded in screams and thunderous applause.

Asa laughed but couldn't hear himself over the noise of the crowd which just made him laugh harder. It was unreal how adored she was.

Zara stepped down the risers to the rhythm and was joined by her dancers.

And Asa felt that overwhelming rush of pure excitement and pride and love take over his entire body.

She strutted down the length of the stage, wearing a black, lace body suit, with strategic cutouts. Her body was insane in its strength and beauty. Her long, black hair hung wild and free over her shoulders and down her back.

And that voice.

That voice would forever be the sound of freedom to him.

Amazing didn't cover it. So far, he hadn't been able to find the right words to describe her or how fun she made their life. But he'd keep trying.

Because writing had come back to him and it had stayed. He could write by himself, or with others, or with her. He'd been nominated for an award at the upcoming NMAs for a song he'd written with Shawn Torres. He was currently working on a song with Nash Ellis that was going to make people feel their feelings.

And he was happy.

Life with Zara wasn't a normal life.

It was better.

Because it was theirs.

And there she was, night one of a tour that was sure to catapult her further into the stratosphere.

And he was *so* there for every second of it.

Epilogue

ZARA LORNA HAS SECRET WEDDING IN CHICAGO

*Z*ara Lorna is married!

The singer, 26, wed Asa Young during a ceremony at a private estate in Chicago, Ill., on Saturday, a source tells CELEBX. Several entertainment outlets reported the news over the weekend but without any details.

Many of the couple's famous friends were spotted in the Windy City for the wedding, including Lorna's frequent collaborator Sunshine Capone and his wife Sabine, as well as Nash Ellis and Abram Fletcher.

Phones were confiscated at the door and few details have leaked. The guest list was small, with only close friends and family. One source who has asked to remain anonymous said security was tight but the guests didn't seem to mind. Everyone was laughing and dancing well into the night. Rumors have circulated that the bride and groom wrote their own vows and there was an impromptu performance from Shawn Torres and Ashton James.

Representatives for both Lorna and Young did not immediately respond to CelebX's request for comment.

Playlist/Chapter Titles

1. Absolution Calling…Incubus
2. State of the Art…Incubus
3. Ultraviolet…Misterwives
4. Bastards…Kesha
5. Landmine…Post Malone
6. Nice to Know You…Incubus
7. Stop Making This Hurt…Bleachers
8. gold rush…Taylor Swift
9. Paper Fish…Jim Ward
10. Overdrive…Post Malone
11. February Stars…Foo Fighters
12. Wake Me…Bleachers
13. Drive all night…NEEDTOBREATHE
14. Broken Songs…Jim Ward
15. Crack the Code…311
16. Finally // beautiful stranger…Halsey
17. Glitch…Taylor Swift
18. Chinatown…Bleachers
19. Echo…Incubus
20. India Ink…311
21. Love Me Back to Life…Bon Jovi

22. Wanted Man…NEEDTOBREATHE
23. Dress…Taylor Swift
24. Times Like These…Foo Fighters
25. I Know Places…Taylor Swift
26. Don't Go Dark…Bleachers
27. I'm on your side…NEEDTOBREATH
28. Hardliners…Holcombe Waller
29. Fall into Me …Forest Blakk

About the Author

Heidi writes stories that she hopes will inspire her readers to take their hearts on one more adventure.

She still lives in the Black Hills with her alarmingly handsome husband, their fearless child, and a rather large and spoiled dog.

She is fueled by her unwavering and perfectly normal devotion to Dave Grohl and coffee.

And a whole lotta love.

heidih.net
Email: heidih.writer@gmail.com

Find Smartypants Romance online:
Website: www.smartypantsromance.com
Facebook: www.facebook.com/smartypantsromance/
Goodreads: www.goodreads.com/smartypantsromance
Twitter: @smartypantsrom
Instagram: @smartypantsromance

Also by Heidi Hutchinson

Double Blind Study Rock Star Series:

(Interconnected standalones, Adult Contemporary, Romantic Comedy)

Learn to Fly

In Your Honor

Deepest Blues

The Hope That Starts

Brand New Sky

Into the Night We Shine

Matter of Fact (holiday novella)

Things That Shine (crossover with Bria Quinlan)

Soaring Bird Surf Series:

(Interconnected standalones, Adult Contemporary, Sports Romance, DBS spinoff)

Tectonic (#0.5)

Like the Back of My Halo

Sushi and Sun Salutations

Puppy Love and Peanut Butter

Rope a Dope

Caught a Vibe

Smartypants Romance XY Records Series:

(Rock Star Romance)

Key Change

Lost Track

All Mixed Up

Write or Wrong

In Between Series:

<u>The Green Valley Library Series</u>

Prose Before Bros by Cathy Yardley (#1)

Shelf Awareness by Katie Ashley (#2)

Dewey Belong Together by Ann Whynot (#3)

Checking You Out by Ann Whynot (#4)

<u>Scorned Women's Society Series</u>

My Bare Lady by Piper Sheldon (#1)

The Treble with Men by Piper Sheldon (#2)

The One That I Want by Piper Sheldon (#3)

Hopelessly Devoted by Piper Sheldon (#3.5)

It Takes a Woman by Piper Sheldon (#4)

<u>Park Ranger Series</u>

Happy Trail by Daisy Prescott (#1)

Stranger Ranger by Daisy Prescott (#2)

<u>The Leffersbee Series</u>

Been There Done That by Hope Ellis (#1)

Before and After You by Hope Ellis (#2)

<u>The Higher Learning Series</u>

Upsy Daisy by Chelsie Edwards (#1)

<u>Green Valley Heroes Series</u>

Forrest for the Trees by Kilby Blades (#1)

Parks and Provocation by Juliette Cross (#2)

Letter Late Than Never by Lauren Connolly (#3)

Peaches and Dreams by Juliette Cross (#4)

Young Buck by Kilby Blades (#5)

Package Makes Perfect by Lauren Connolly (#6)

All Fired Up by Allie Winters (#7)

Wild Goose Chase by Kilby Blades (#8)

The Teachers' Lounge Series

Passing Notes by Nora Everly (#1)

Band Together by Piper Sheldon (#2)

Ex Marks the Spot by Hazel James (#3)

Past Tents by Stacy Travis (#4)

Story of Us Collection

My Story of Us: Zach by Chris Brinkley (#1)

My Story of Us: Thomas by Chris Brinkley (#2)

My Story of Us: Grayson by Chris Brinkley (#3)

Seduction in the City

Cipher Security Series

Code of Conduct by April White (#1)

Code of Honor by April White (#2)

Code of Matrimony by April White (#2.5)

Code of Ethics by April White (#3)

Cipher Office Series

Weight Expectations by M.E. Carter (#1)

Sticking to the Script by Stella Weaver (#2)

Cutie and the Beast by M.E. Carter (#3)

Weights of Wrath by M.E. Carter (#4)

Common Threads Series

Mad About Ewe by Susannah Nix (#1)

Give Love a Chai by Nanxi Wen (#2)

Not Since Ewe by Susannah Nix (#3)

Ewe Complete Me by Susannah Nix (#4)

Meet Your Matcha by Nanxi Wen (#5)

XY Records Series

Key Change by Heidi Hutchinson (#1)

Lost Track by Heidi Hutchinson (#2)

All Mixed Up by Heidi Hutchinson (#3)

Write or Wrong by Heidi Hutchinson (#4)

Bad Habit Book Club Series

Nun Too Soon by Lissa Sharpe (#1)

Nun the Wiser by Lissa Sharpe (#2)

Second to Nun by Lissa Sharpe (#3)

Educated Romance

Work For It Series

Street Smart by Aly Stiles (#1)

Heart Smart by Emma Lee Jayne (#2)

Book Smart by Amanda Pennington (#3)

Smart Mouth by Emma Lee Jayne (#4)

Play Smart by Aly Stiles (#5)

Look Smart by Aly Stiles (#6)

Smart Move by Amanda Pennington (#7)

Stage Smart by Aly Stiles (#8)

Lessons Learned Series

Under Pressure by Allie Winters (#1)

Not Fooling Anyone by Allie Winters (#2)

Can't Fight It by Allie Winters (#3)

The Vinyl Frontier by Lola West (#4)

Out of this World

London Ladies Embroidery Series

Neanderthal Seeks Duchess by Laney Hatcher (#1)

Well Acquainted by Laney Hatcher (#2)

Love Matched by Laney Hatcher (#3)

www.ingramcontent.com/pod-product-compliance
Lightning Source LLC
Chambersburg PA
CBHW030116010826
48973CB00002B/293

9781959097860